THESE THIN LINES

MILENA MCKAY

PRAISE FOR A WHISPER OF SOLACE

When I think of McKay's writing style, I think of 19th century grand opera. She conveys big, bold emotions within fantastic plots that challenge the reader to come along for the ride.

— VICTORIA THOMAS, THE LESBIAN REVIEW

Damn, this book... Seriously. So. Many. Feelings

— JUDE SILBERFELD, WWW.JUDEINTHESTARS.COM

Every 'rule' broken, yet it leaves me breathlessly anticipating what McKay will do with the Lesfic genre next.

— THE READING ROOM

To those who struggled with learning and to those who held their hand along the way...

When you light a candle, you also cast a shadow.

— URSULA K. LE GUIN

PART I

CANDLE

CANDLE

PART 1

1

ONCE UPON A FAIRYTALE

Genevieve Courtenay's life was a fairytale. That is, if fairytales had a distant and withholding father. And a disinterested and occasionally cruel stepmother. As well as two ignorant and dismissive stepsisters.

So, a fairytale... Except unlike most main characters of every such story, Genevieve wasn't perfect. In fact, she was pretty terrible at, you know, those fabled things that endeared heroines to the readers.

You name it, and it was fairly guaranteed that she'd been told she was bad at it. Daughter? Yep, her dad stated every day how completely useless she was. So perhaps he had reasons to be so distant with her.

Stepdaughter? Her stepmother reminded her of her ungratefulness on a regular basis. That is, when she could be bothered to notice her at all and wasn't slugging down expensive wine at other people's fancy parties. And why would she notice Genevieve anyway? There was nothing remarkable about her.

Sister? Well, Gigi and Kylie probably would have agreed with all of the statements above, but they mostly ignored her.

Unless she could do something for them. Then her stepsisters snapped their fingers at her.

Still, Vi, as she was known to her very few friends, did something very well. So well in fact, that she, on occasion, wished she wasn't quite as good at it. Because if she were bad at this one thing, maybe she would have shown her stuck-up, blue-blooded, touch-of-royalty relatives the finger and walked away.

Vi loved deeply and very well indeed. She was loyal and headstrong in the intensity of her love. Her love for her ungrateful, demanding family, for those few friends she'd collected and lost over the years and now, seemingly, for the one woman she had no business having any kind of feelings for.

Because that woman was somebody's wife and therefore so off limits, she might as well not be on planet Earth.

Vi's heart, however, hadn't gotten the memo. Not only was its desire out of bounds, the woman was also out of Vi's league. Hell, Vi's heart's desire was out of pretty much everyone's league. Including her own wife's. Vi always felt particularly bitter when her mind wandered in that direction, but there was no helping these notions.

And no, her thoughts weren't particularly covetous either. Vi did not want the woman for herself. She was too... everything. Vi's heart would simply explode in that absolutely impossible scenario. But while she yearned and pined like any of the Brontë sisters' characters, she also resented the fact that the object of all her longing was living in a complete—in Vi's opinion—marital mismatch.

Simply put, Chiara Conti-Lilienfeld was too good for the likes of Franziska "Frankie" Lilienfeld.

It didn't matter that Frankie was one of the greatest couturiers of her generation. It didn't matter that the *Lilien Haus of Fashion* was one of the most progressive and famous brands in the whole world. It didn't even matter that Frankie was suave and smooth and charming, and very handsome. In Vi's naïve, twenty-five-year-old eyes, nobody was good enough for Chiara.

The fact that Frankie was also Vi's boss somehow hadn't registered until after Vi had realized she had fallen smack-in, first lust, then gradually in love with the former supermodel. And once Vi had cottoned on to it, honestly, it was by far the least of her worries. Vi Courtenay was raised to keep bigger secrets, after all. And keep those secrets she did.

TO HER CREDIT, Vi had realized she was in trouble the moment said trouble was upon her. Even years later, when asked when she'd known Chiara Conti was the one, she'd say it happened on a day that was rather momentous to begin with.

To her overwhelming astonishment, after denying her the chance to actually work for a living her entire life—"we are the Courtenays, other people work, we live!"—her father had not only found her this shiny new opportunity but also encouraged her, in his own laconic way, that it was, "high time you made something of yourself, all that studying does a woman no good."

She remembered how, last night, he'd placed a delicate china tea cup on its saucer, gave her a passing look before unfolding Le Figaro with a throwaway, "Please, try to do well. And maybe don't screw it up. For once, Genevieve. Just this one time."

She could still hear his scornful words ringing in her ears, although she chose to believe it was the croissant he'd been too busy chewing that had stopped him from properly wishing her luck.

~

VI DECIDED to overlook the previous day's derision as she stood motionless in front of the classic Parisian four-story townhouse on Rue Saint-Honoré. The early morning light played off the gleaming windows, winking at her, promising something, luring her in, like the beam of a lighthouse.

She shook her head at her vision and her own silliness. Hadn't her father repeatedly told her to quit daydreaming and stop making things up?

It was time to focus on the task at hand and on the place in front of her. A place that looked very much like the facades of all the other buildings in the vicinity. After all, she was surrounded by Lucci, Dior and Longchamps and YSL. There were other fashion houses whose names Vi could not remember to save her life. Fashion was not her thing. Not even a little.

And neither were the massive luxury hotels this part of town was so famous for. On her way to Lilien Haus, she passed by the Crillon, and the doorman gave her the 'move along, you don't belong here' look. Which, to be fair, was kind of true. Vi *didn't* belong at the most luxurious hotel in the world. Not anymore.

The majestic Crillon and the stately Ritz a bit farther down the street and the Mandarin Oriental, also nestled along her walk to Rue Saint-Honoré captured Vi's imagination with their masonry and the play of glass and light on their facades.

Her hands itched for her beat-up camera, before she shook herself. She had nothing to offer any of these stone giants, and they were not establishments that Vi Courtenay could afford to even set foot in. Sure, her father and Gwyneth and Gigi and Kylie frequented the parties thrown at these places, playing at being rich and famous and trading on their name, but they couldn't afford to stay here either.

Nobody knew that, of course, but Vi was aware the other shoe could drop any minute, and the bursting of their fake bubble of veneered wealth with ugly debts, unpaid favors, and bounced checks was imminent.

The hotels, beyond their majestic beauty, didn't interest her anyway. Neither did the other fashion houses and their luxurious stores. No, this particular building was why she'd made the long trek to the 1st arrondissement. This one had a certain *je ne sais quoi...*

Her breathing shallowed. There was a stirring in her chest that made her slightly lightheaded. And with it, a premonition arose of something coming, an event, an occurrence that would change everything. A line was about to be crossed. She felt like the second she stepped over the threshold, magic would happen.

And happen it did. Magic. Or something like it. And much more of that *something* than Vi had ever intended. But that also was par for the course for her. Vi's family didn't call her 'clumsy' on a daily basis for nothing. She had come by that adjective honestly.

In her awe of the place she was finding herself in, Vi knocked, the beautiful lily-shaped knocker heavy and cold in her fingers. And as the door opened, she did what was so in character for her that she didn't even find it ironic.

She stumbled over her own feet and landed face first on a plush, ivory carpet, which probably saved her from a broken nose. And then Vi just sighed. Or maybe she groaned. Whatever it was, she hoped that unlike her fall—since there was *no hope* for that—whatever sound she'd made had been somewhat graceful at least.

As she stood up and tried to catch her breath, she looked around, then simply closed her eyes. In her relief over her unbroken face, Vi realized she had lost her shoe, the too-big-for-her good-as-new Converse from the secondhand store down the street from her apartment sliding easily off her socked foot and landing somewhere in front of her in the vast expanse of the foyer.

She said a silent prayer to whichever guardian angel of hers was on duty that day. Vi needed her wits about her. She touched her face. Her glasses seemed intact. But as she squinted and tried to fix them from their crooked position, her last cogent thought was that it must have been the wrong angel —a very amorous one and not the sanguine one she desperately needed.

All her proper musings evaporated, and only the improper ones remained. She was looking at the most beautiful woman in the world. Universe. What was bigger than a universe? Something, surely, because the woman was... Ethereal. And she was looking straight at Vi with the ghost of a smile on her incredible face.

The early morning light landed on the chiseled sharp features, caressing those planes and angles of cheekbone and jaw, and Vi was mesmerized by the play of shadows, hiding the familiarity of the face. But even in her flustered and embarrassed state, Vi knew this woman.

"*Che cortese...* You certainly know how to make an entrance, Cinderella."

Vi had enough Italian to understand the remark. Courteous. Yes, it was quite the courtesy to fall flat on your face in front of the lady of the house. And she probably should have fixed her clothes, or her face, or put her shoe back on. Really, done something other than stare. But the voice... silk over steel with a note of... melancholy, was it? The voice had her enraptured. It had her imagining slaying whatever dragons were making this princess sad.

Then the massive amber eyes crinkled at the corners, the beautiful crow's feet deepening, and an eyebrow rose up regally.

Not a Princess then, a Queen. Would genuflecting be too much?

"Take a picture, darling. It will last longer. Though judging by the suspenders, you probably had several of mine on your wall growing up."

The words were sarcastic, but the smile curving the wide mouth grew warmer. Vi stupidly found herself smiling back. Of course she'd be pegged as a lesbian. She'd long ago stopped pretending to be something she wasn't. But this was impressive gaydar, nonetheless. And of course it would be this woman who'd be in possession of it. Chiara. *The Chiara.*

Still, Vi didn't think she was necessarily telegraphing anything. She'd pulled back her long, auburn curls and covered her freckles with makeup. Her outfit was straight enough that her father hadn't rolled his eyes at her when she'd stopped by his house earlier. She did sneak the suspenders under the blazer, so maybe...

Then she remembered that she was in the presence of lesbian royalty, and figured being seen and being known was nothing unusual within these walls. Which made her both terrified and brave—never a good combination for Vi, because it led to her saying inane things.

"I might have. This surely proves my good taste."

Silence reigned, and the smiling mouth opened just a touch in obvious shock at the brazenness—or stupidity—of the remark. Vi wanted to sink through the carpet. She was desperate enough to disappear that she'd dig her way through the marble underneath.

But then the smile bloomed fully, and the silence was broken by gorgeous, deep laughter, sincere and contagious.

Vi stared before averting her eyes. Of all the times to so boldly exhibit her innate clumsiness and foot-in-mouth disease, today was not the day to do it. Today was important, her one chance to make something of herself, a chance so rare she hadn't even been sure her father would ever allow it, yet he had, and the gravity of her situation weighed heavily on her. Still, as she peeked from under her lashes, the object of her befuddlement winked at her. Vi felt the tips of her ears go pink.

And then, as she sat awkwardly on the soft carpet, sinking deeper into the woolen luxury, the woman from her posters knelt down beside her, and long fingers gently encircled her ankle, sliding her foot into the runaway sneaker.

Vi hyperventilated and was fairly certain Chiara could feel the pulse hammering under her skin where the cool fingers touched her. The smug lift of the lips told her as much, and as the graceful hand offered to pull her up, Vi felt her color turn ruddy.

"My god, she's delicious. And ridiculous. Aren't you, love? Who might you be?"

Belatedly, Vi realized there were other people in the room. Two, in fact. The one speaking with a pronounced Irish accent was much shorter, with wild hair and wilder clothes. *Was she really wearing an elaborate wife-beater?* But her eyes were kind, even if Vi could tell they were laughing at her. Little devils played in them, twinkling and teasing, and Vi found herself grinning.

"I think this is our new summer intern, Aoife. Consider acting professionally. We don't need lawsuits. Of any kind..." The words sounded ominous, and this woman was taller, statelier, and older. The severe, no-nonsense face was devoid of the mischief so easily found in the other two women who were looking at Vi.

"Oh, oh, the Courtenay!" Aoife made a gesture that Vi could only assume was some kind of elaborate curtsey. Vi felt like sinking through the floor from a different kind of embarrassment.

"Sully..." Now Chiara's velvety voice had a tone of warning

in it, and Vi's eyes followed the staying, long-fingered hand laid on Aoife's forearm. Vi licked her lips. Such a simple gesture, it made her envious. Not of Aoife and not of Chiara, but of the ease to touch and be touched by another person.

"Ms. Courtenay, welcome to Lilien Haus of Fashion. This is Renate Lilienfeld, the company's financial director."

Renate inclined her head, but didn't offer her hand, and Vi was silently glad she hadn't stuck hers out like an overeager kid.

Perfectly comfortable with the other woman's brusque manner, Chiara went on.

"This is Aoife Sullivan, head of production. She's in charge, so be afraid." After an awkward beat, all three women laughed. Aoife had no misgivings about pumping Vi's hand several times, the shake strong and warm. Vi unclenched her jaw.

"Yeah, not so much. But you're gonna be with me, kiddo. So stick close." The Irish accent was strong, musical to Vi's ear.

"Regardless of what she says, Ms. Courtenay, I'd listen. Though perhaps, only believe half of her stories." As she spoke, Chiara's wide, amber eyes looked at her with so much playfulness, Vi swallowed nervously and wanted to tug on her nonexistent tie. Was it really this hot in the foyer?

"And I'm Chiara Conti-Lilienfeld. But you already know that. It's a..." She seemed to be searching for a word, but when she finally spoke, Vi had gotten her confirmation that, not only was the space hot, it was also small and devoid of oxygen. "... Pleasure to meet you."

Mercy, oh mercy.

"Who's playing dirty now? Stop messing with my intern's head and take your amazing ass to the studio, love. I will see you at lunch." Before she knew it, Aoife grabbed Vi's forearm with little ceremony and dragged her towards the massive awning at the end of the hallway. Vi glimpsed Renate shaking her head at their antics as Chiara's laughter followed them all the way to the door.

～

AS THEY MADE their way through a series of doors, Vi barely kept up with Aoife.

"Um—"

"Not now, Cinderella. Let me show you around first, and then you can bombard me with all the questions you undoubtedly have."

"I assume the Cinderella bit will not be going away any time soon?"

Aoife spared her a sideways glance.

"You make that kind of entrance, you get a nickname, and there are only so many times I can call you 'kiddo' before I start to feel old, kiddo."

Finally, Aoife dragged her up two flights of stairs into what looked like a gallery that occupied the entire floor. She pushed Vi inside and turned in a circle.

"Welcome to my humble abode." She twirled once more, and Vi smiled.

"Not much humble about it—"

"Ha, mouthy. I like you." Aoife gave her a slap on the shoulder and Vi almost lost her footing. "Puny though. We'll have to toughen you up some, Courtenay."

Vi rubbed her shoulder and grimaced.

"It's Genevieve. Well, Vi."

"You do realize that I was given power here, kid. Which means I will now proceed to get drunk on it, and so it's nicknames from here on in, each one more demeaning than the next, all under the guise of not showing my soft and cuddly side." Aoife's eyes danced merrily, and Vi knew she was being messed with. Strangely, it felt good, like a warm hug of acceptance.

"Yes, because you are a mean and domineering kind of person." Voice dripping with sarcasm, she looked down at her new supervisor.

"I definitely like you. You speak my language. Sarcasm is underrated, Cinderella, *so* underrated. So is clumsiness. You got brownie points from me the moment you swan-dived across the threshold. Not Renate, she believes things such as humanity are entirely passe and everyone should be functioning like her beloved Swiss watches. But fortunately, Chiara has many a soft spot for an underdog and a spectacular fall will always endear you to her."

Vi rubbed the nape of her neck exposed by the messy bun her hair was pulled into.

"I suppose asking if it was at least a graceful swan dive is pointless?"

Aoife laughed and Vi found herself smiling, the sting of embarrassment dissipating.

"I've seen bears do smoother pirouettes. But, I was wondering what kind of stuck-up, rich, asshole intern was being sent over to ruin my summer, and that single event dispelled that notion."

"What, rich, stuck-up assholes don't fall on their faces?"

"They do. But something tells me you're not one of those? Fancy-ass 'niece of the King of Savoy' lineage aside."

Vi rolled her eyes and shook her head.

"Well, disregarding my *fancy-ass* family tree, I try not to be either of those things."

"Either rich or an asshole?" Aoife's eyes narrowed for a second as she spoke, but she waved her hand at Vi not to answer and the conversation moved on. Vi tried not to exhale her relief too loudly.

"Well, enough small talk. Take a look around. You like?"

There was so much pride and pleasure in the voice that Vi didn't have the heart to tell her she had no idea where she was and what was supposed to be happening. Aoife's brow was already furrowing.

"From the vacant expression on your face, am I to understand you have no clue what any of this is?"

Vi just nodded and wrapped her arms around herself. She didn't even care how defensive she looked. Her fall and her lack of knowledge about anything that might remotely pertain to fashion aside, Vi still had no idea what she was doing here. Working for Frankie Lilienfeld was not exactly a dream, but an amazing opportunity for someone trying to establish a path for herself outside of the crushing thumb of her family. Observing some of the photoshoots alone would be invaluable for her.

"You're gonna tell me you have no idea how to use a sewing machine, right, kid?"

Oh, swell, they were back to 'kid'. She'd managed to disappoint people on her very first day. So what else was new? Except, Aoife didn't look upset. She gave Vi one last considering look before moving farther into the massive open space flanked by columns and floor-to-ceiling windows.

"This is where the magic happens. Don't let anyone, especially Our Lady of Conti upstairs, tell you differently."

Before Vi could ask anything, Aoife was in motion again. "C'mon. I guess I will have to take pity on you and really show you around and explain things. Too bad, I hate talking..." Aoife gave her a long look at the end of which both of them laughed.

Vi's shoulders relaxed again, despite still feeling like a total fish out of water.

"So this is the in-house production studio. This is what I do. I get the designs they send from upstairs and turn them into actual things. Clothes. At times, accessories." She ran her fingers over the silvery curves and what looked like thousands of levers and buttons of the Singer sewing machine and it emitted a little purr. Vi jumped at the unexpected noise and Aoife laughed.

"I've got twenty years on you, gotta keep you on your toes."

They moved farther, to a row of work benches— material and clothes strewn all over them in a state of creative chaos. Vi could respect that.

"I prefer to work alone. So this whole space is mine. But we occasionally have people from the main production building here. Yeah, you might have guessed right, here on Saint-Honoré we have the sort of business-facing side of the house. The flagship store is here. You saw it on your way in. I don't go in there. Once the clothes are finished, they're outside my purview." Aoife turned on her heel and pointed up the stairs. "The financial and legal offices are on the third floor. Renate reigns supreme there. She's the money whiz."

Vi nodded, though most of what Aoife was telling her sounded only vaguely intelligible. Her anxiety was getting the best of her. She could feel her hands grow numb and colder with every second. Her mentor seemed to understand she was struggling. Aoife gestured upstairs and motioned with her head for Vi to follow her.

"You'll catch on. Despite that deer-in-the-headlights expression on your face right now. You really gotta do something about that."

"I guess my being totally ignorant might upset Ms. Lilienfeld—" Vi finally voiced her biggest anxiety.

"I assume you mean Frankie?" Both eyebrows raised, Aoife looked at Vi, who nodded before lowering her face. "Pfft kiddo, Frankie won't care. Frankie won't even care that you are here, to be honest. Now, Chiara might. About both. She's thoughtful like that."

Vi lifted her face so quickly at the name that Aoife looked blurry for a second before coming back into focus. And the eyes that fixed on Vi were knowing. But all she said was, "Frankie is of no concern to you. C'mon, I'll show you."

Vi nodded again, deciding that silent agreement was the safest way to go since Aoife was already moving on and walking back towards the staircase leading them to the floor above. This one was divided into glass cubicles, with several people working diligently on their computers or talking on the phone, snippets of their conversation in French, English, and what sounded like Chinese, reaching Vi's ears as she and Aoife passed through.

Vi recognized Renate in the corner office, gesticulating gracefully as she spoke to a swankily dressed man with a luxurious mane of blond hair seated in front of her desk. He winked at Vi from behind the glass wall as she and Aoife passed by, prompting Vi to stumble again. Aoife proceeded to flip him off and Vi gawked at her. In response, Renate threw a stern glare at Aoife and pressed a button on her desk, the glass instantly frosting over.

"Kiddo, what kind of lesbian are you? Don't pay Lance any attention. He's only teasing you, anyway. He's Renate's right-hand man. Great with numbers, can't dress himself to save his or his wife's life. Good thing Véronique, who is also our in-house attorney, does have a brilliant eye for clothes." Aoife's mouth twisted like she had bitten into a lemon, and Vi wisely chose to school her features and not ask questions about whatever conflict there was between her supervisor and the fashion-forward lawyer.

They walked the entire floor, with Aoife pointing at various people. Chief accountant. Chief something or other. Véronique, she-of-the-good-taste and even better legs. Marketing.

Vi valiantly tried to remember names and positions, but it appeared that Aoife had only two speeds—fast and faster—and Vi quickly figured out that the people she liked least, got the shortest amount of her time, with her basically sprinting past their offices. So Vi chose to focus instead on the ones that got a minimum of five seconds of Aoife's attention.

"And that's the executive floor. May we never come here again this month." She giggled as Vi stared back in confusion, absolutely certain she would never catch on to the myriad of details, names, and tasks being thrown at her. "You'll get the hang of it. Since you're with me, you really won't have much business here. Steer clear of Véronique, shysters are slippery. Renate is strict but fair, so no funny business. And that's all the wisdom I have to impart regarding the third floor. Now onward, *mon petit.*"

Both the grammar and the accent were pretty bad, and Vi bit her lip. However, it seemed Aoife had eyes in the back of her head where Vi was concerned.

"Yes, yes, I see you cringing. Lived in this country for ten years now and haven't learned any kind of passable French. I wish I had, but that ship sailed. Lilien Haus is so cosmopolitan, English is the default here. Don't like the croissants here though. When they all learn to make decent scones, then we'll talk."

"I'm partial to Belgian croissants myself." Vi raised her eyebrow in challenge when Aoife turned to her on the stairs. The stare-down lasted for a few heartbeats.

"The Belgian ones are okay, I guess. But nothing compares to scones with raspberry jam. Nothing. Cream first, then jam. I said what I said. Now, come on, Ms. Posh. Let's go meet Frankie."

Vi barely had time to take a deep breath as Aoife pushed open a wooden door leading into a large space that seemingly occupied the whole floor, save for a sectioned-off area in the corner, which looked like a replica of Renate's office with its glass walls. Except, unlike Renate's, these walls were already frosted.

"Yo, Frankie! The royal newbie is here!" Aoife's voice rose, and a few seconds later the door opened and a cross between a fifty-year-old Brandi Carlile and k.d. lang stepped out, shutting it firmly behind herself.

Her attire was somewhat debonair, torn jeans and an even more massacred t-shirt adorned by a band logo that was indecipherable due to its numerous holes. Her handshake was rushed and her smile—a touch vague—was seemingly permanent.

"Hey, you're the Courtenay kid. Princess Allegra's cousin? Welcome. Welcome. How are you? How are you finding everything?"

Unlike her older sister, Frankie's low voice had only a slight accent that Vi guessed was a remnant of her native Switzerland. The stream of questions was continuous, and Vi found that perhaps she didn't need to reply at all. Frankie was very content to speak.

"Aoife here been showing you around? Good, good. I hope you see a lot, learn a lot, but don't touch anything. Or anyone!" She laughed suddenly, loud and brash, and Vi almost cringed. It wasn't all that funny, or maybe she'd missed the joke.

Aoife coughed and intervened.

"Yeah, okay, Lilienfeld. I'm just showing Vi the ropes. You busy later? We have to discuss some of the spring trends. Chiara said—"

"Later, Sully, later. And just run it by Chiara. She'll know. She always knows better. You think so, anyway." The smile didn't waver. Instead it turned sharp, and Aoife's eyes narrowed in what Vi was beginning to understand was a characteristic gesture. But Aoife said nothing, and Vi felt like she was intruding on an old and particularly unpleasant argument.

For a second, silence reigned, and Vi could have sworn she could hear something moving behind the frosted walls of the office. Frankie followed her line of sight, and her shoulders stiffened before she smiled again, this time fake and mocking.

She positioned herself in front of the door and pointed her thumb at her own chest.

"Genius at work here! Sully, you know how it is. I need my creative peace and quiet. We'll definitely catch up, kid. I'll see you around, talk you through my process." She winked at Vi, but in comparison to Chiara's earlier wink, it lacked in seductiveness, and the way she said 'kid' was indeed demeaning. Aoife had made it sound kind and familiar. Frankie's 'kid' held no warmth and no sincerity.

They exited the fourth floor and Aoife stopped, watching her re-enter her private office. The walls did not turn transparent. For a second, Aoife looked like she might go back. Her hand on the door handle clenched once before relaxing. Her shoulders drooped.

"Okay. Did I not tell you that you won't have to worry about Frankie? *Genius at work.*" She rolled her eyes. "Let's go. I will show you where the genius actually resides."

Like scaling the fairytale ivory tower, they climbed one more flight, and the stairs turned oaken instead of the marble downstairs, becoming narrower, the space more intimate, as if leading to a kingdom entwined in ivy vines, guarding secrets and, perhaps, a sleeping princess.

When they reached their destination, Vi's breath was taken away for the second time this morning. Their path opened directly onto another open floor, massive floor-to-ceiling windows bringing in the early June sun, making the immense room look even bigger and so full of light, it felt as if Paris had stepped inside this space and taken up residence. The air was full of the earlier rain, petrichor seeping into Vi's every inhalation.

The long desks strewn around the dark wooden floors with colorful materials draped over them made the place look inviting and gave it a fascinating, fantasy-like quality. Vi felt like she'd entered a magical realm where every single thing held meaning and purpose.

Everywhere she looked, there was beauty, a piece in progress, a mannequin wearing something amazing... The room was a rich and enticing canvas of colors and various focal points. And there, in the middle of it all, was the centerpiece herself.

Something stirred in Vi. Like a long dormant desire. To belong. To be part. To walk these floors with purpose and a sense of fitting in as seamlessly as Aoife did. She'd never thought herself ambitious. Certainly her family believed she had no drive. But the idea of being good enough, competent enough, suddenly filled her with hope. If she fit here, if she'd find her place in this world, among these people, she would perhaps be free of the confines that stifled her back home.

Chiara was bent over a designer's workstation, her long dark hair on top of her head, with flyaways escaping the haphazard bun held together by a pencil. Vi's hands itched to pull it out, let those tresses fall down the narrow shoulders, and capture this vision on paper, even though she knew her meager drawing skills would never do Chiara justice.

Though she was facing them, Chiara had not raised her head from whatever was holding her attention. Vi's eyes traced the long, graceful lines of the neck and collarbones, marveling at the divine precision of their creation. Surely, whomever had breathed life into that skin and those muscles and those bones deserved all the reverence.

Next to Vi, Aoife seemed to be holding her breath too, and she thought that this woman had that effect on people. You wanted to look at her. To just be allowed to share a space. The moment felt intimate. But with Aoife there, Vi didn't believe she was intruding, more like she was allowed the privilege.

Finally, after what could have been minutes or hours, sad eyes lifted and Vi forgot how to breathe.

"Ms. Courtenay."

Yes, keeping up with the newness of her internship was the least of Vi's troubles. Literally tiny in comparison. And as far as Vi's secrets went, she felt the weight of this one might be the proverbial last straw.

2

ONCE UPON A VISION

Genevieve Courtenay was tongue-tied and suddenly weak in the knees. If asked how she felt under the scrutiny of those amber eyes, that would be how Vi would respond. If she could even say anything. How did one function in the proximity of this woman?

Even Aoife was affected, though after the initial awed reaction, she recovered quickly and sauntered farther into the studio, leaving Vi behind, and made herself comfortable, jumping to sit on the worktable.

Chiara made an expressive gesture with her graceful hands, shooing her away, accompanied by a few chosen words in Italian which Vi assumed were profanities, but Aoife was not to be thwarted.

"This looks amazing." She twisted the arm of the mannequin wearing some kind of toga. "You really nailed it this time. I see you've had an inspired morning!"

"You break it, you buy it, Sully." Chiara barely spared Aoife or the mannequin a glance, engrossed in whatever she had been working on at the design station. Then she sighed, lifted her head, and ran a hand over her neck, stretching it as if working out the kinks.

As she stepped away from the desk, she smoothly removed the pencil from her hair, causing it to cascade down in disarrayed waves. The few silver strands added depth to the silk, and Vi imagined how its softness met the gorgeous satin of the flowing blouse open wide at the neck, how it caressed the sharp collarbones, how it would feel to follow that caress with her own fingertips.

Vi's mouth went dry. This was getting ridiculous. She had to work here. She had to be able to function, had to exhibit some level of coherence and intelligence. At twenty-five, she wasn't a teenager anymore, for crying out loud. The fact that, once upon a time, she'd had a massive crush on the world-renowned supermodel was neither here nor there.

And speaking of this fashion business, one thing took Vi, who had made certain assumptions about Lilien Haus, entirely by surprise... Chiara, *the Chiara,* was actually a couturier these days?

Emboldened by the earlier pep talk, Vi took a few steps into the room and tried to discern what lay on the workstation. As she approached, she could see a sketch.

Though perhaps thinking of it in that simplistic way was not doing it justice. It was a detailed drawing of a dress. The exquisite composition, the details transposed to every single line, so simple yet so delicate.

No, to call it a dress was not doing it justice either. It was a gown. And one that looked like it had been created for a special occasion. One made for memories. One that spoke of intimacy and agelessness. The word "wedding" fell from her mouth before she realized she'd spoken out loud.

Chiara's sharp exhalation right by her side startled Vi. Enchanted by the gown, Vi had edged closer to the desk and thus was standing right by the woman whose hands had created this vision. In fact, the long, slim fingers with their tapered nails were stained with charcoal, and Vi suddenly had the urge to put her own hands in her slacks' pockets. Maybe then they'd stop reaching out to touch, to brush the smudges from those beautiful hands.

"Why?"

Vi blinked. The voice was no more than a whisper as she turned slightly to see Chiara drawing even nearer. She stared down at the sketch, and Vi couldn't help but indulge just a bit and mentally catalog the smallest minutiae about this woman. She had met her just a couple of hours ago, and yet she'd been admiring her all her life, albeit from afar. And now she was allowed the privilege of taking a closer look.

Chiara's trademark, her big, expressive eyes seemed to dominate her face. It was what journalists, photographers, and editors had underscored her entire—short as it was—modeling career. And those eyes were absolutely gorgeous. Crow's feet ran under them and to the side, making them even more dramatic.

The rest of the face was just as arresting. The sharp line of the jaw, the sculpted nose, the wide, unsmiling mouth. It drew Vi's attention as Chiara was lost in thought, her lips pursing slightly. To her surprise, it made Vi sad that the laugh lines around the serious mouth were almost nonexistent.

She sighed and Chiara turned to her fully, eyes alight with curiosity, and Vi tried to not stare anymore. What the hell was she doing? One embarrassing gawking session down in the foyer wasn't enough? Why did she act like a fool around this woman?

Chiara seemed to be amused by Vi's lack of social graces, the corners of her lips lifting slightly, the mouth parting, before the lower lip was suddenly sucked in and chewed on slowly as it was Chiara's turn to peruse Vi's face.

"Tell me, Ms. Courtenay, why did you say 'wedding' just now?"

"Ah…" God, how was she supposed to speak? And how was she supposed to explain her own silly outburst? "It's not… I don't know. The dress—" She could have smacked herself on the forehead. "Gown, sorry, it looks like it's waiting for a moment. I can't explain it exactly. Like it's made for an occasion and I am not sure there's anything more momentous than a wedding?"

Aoife's laughter cut through their tête-à-tête.

"What kind of feminist are ya, kid? Wedding? The *most momentous?* Pfft!"

"Shush, Sully. No, a wedding isn't the most important moment in a woman's life, but it is a moment. Go on, Ms. Courtenay."

The voice was gentle, and a graceful hand gesture encouraged her to go on. Vi felt slightly lightheaded under the focus of those eyes. Had anyone ever really wanted her opinion with this level of interest?

"I'm sorry for not having the words. But it's a vision, a feeling it gives off. It's a love story. One with a happy ending."

They looked at each other in silence, amber on gray, and in the background, Vi could sense Aoife holding her breath. She held hers as well, wondering if she had said something stupid yet again, as the face in front of her was pensive before the corners of the sensuous mouth tipped up once more.

"Maybe, Ms. Courtenay. Maybe." The sadness had lifted from the curious eyes and Chiara stepped away, her fingertips tracing the rough edges of the sketch, smudging the charcoal a little, making what looked like a check mark on the bottom of the paper.

"So that's it?" Aoife jumped off the worktable. "You've found your theme?"

"Ah, I'm sorry, but what's happening here?" Vi looked from one woman to the other.

Chiara took a few steps away from the sketch, walking slowly towards the bank of tall windows. For the first time since entering, Vi noticed small colorful squares that filled one of the panes at eye level.

The sun played with the shadows on Chiara's beautiful features, casting colorful reflections through a myriad of post-it notes that formed a strange mosaic on the glass.

Despite the writing being entirely illegible to Vi, the scroll messy and too sharp, the bright pinks and screaming yellows managed to look both out of place yet remarkably serene, and so did the woman when she turned back to face her companions.

"For the past several months, I've been stuck on this one design. No matter what I drew, nothing else came to me. And even when I did draw this very gown, or variations of it, I just couldn't find that *something* to describe it. Ivory or white, even crimson and cerulean, no matter what color I gave it, I still didn't know what to make of it. I guess I know now."

Chiara reached out and plucked a dark green post-it from the glass, balled it up, and unerringly three-pointed it into the garbage can. The slim shoulders seemed to relax, as if a weight had lifted.

Chiara smiled again, the gesture reaching her eyes, and as she spoke, the characteristic hand gestures she'd been quite famous for back in the days of regular interviews and appearances, were once again on display. Such an Italian stereotype.

But Vi found the movements elegant, refined. Like a dancer. Vi supposed Chiara could have been one. Tall, very slim still, even after twenty years off the catwalks, long-limbed, she had a fluidity to her gait and movements that reminded Vi of the grand ballet mistresses of old. Maya Plisetskaya came to mind, both in statute and coloring. Vi was fascinated all over again.

An elbow to her ribs rather rudely interrupted said fascination.

"Honestly, kiddo. Stop with the staring. We get it. You actually did have her posters on your wall." Aoife's smile cushioned the sting of the words somewhat.

"Don't let her bully you, Ms. Courtenay." Chiara came back to them and laid her chin on Aoife's head, affectionately hugging her from behind. Vi felt the envy at the ease of their touch in her bones. And then the anger at her own need for affection singed her stomach even as she tried not to turn away.

"Hey, hey, I may be a short-arse, but there's no need for such a public display of superiority, Conti!" Aoife bristled and half-heartedly tried to extricate herself from the embrace.

"There's no 'may be' about you being short, Sully." Chiara's laughter was bright and unrestrained, peels of it echoing across the studio's tall ceiling, and to Vi's surprise, Aoife stopped struggling and allowed herself to be held, turning around and burying her face in Chiara's shoulder.

Chiara just tsked and pulled her closer. The poison of envy dissipated, and Vi soaked in the happiness and genuine affection. She just wished she could bask in the sunshine that radiated off Chiara a little bit, her locks catching the glint of the beams of light trickling through the small forest of post-its and her eyes alight with humor and mischief.

"You have an eye, Ms. Courtenay. For what I don't yet know. And given that I've read your CV and found no visual artistic pursuits of any kind in there, I am intrigued by it. Do you draw?"

Chiara's amusement remained evident in her tone, but the eyes had turned shrewd on a dime, assessing, as if looking right through Vi, who really wanted to explain her nascent attempts at photography mostly hidden from her family who'd deride them for their amateurism, but the words did not come. She wasn't any good at any of that, anyway.

And when she shrugged, unable to really voice how much that eye for things and drawing had gotten her into trouble and ridiculed as a child, the shrewdness was replaced with understanding. The soft, warm expression of a person meeting one of their own. Like knowing, like recognition. Of what, Vi had no idea, but the gaze made her want to confess all her sins and some that weren't her own at all.

She shook her head and took a deep breath. This was getting absurd. How would Chiara know? How could she see? Chiara's sketch showed so much skill and talent, there was no way... Distracted by her own musings and worries, Vi missed Chiara moving closer to her.

And then, just because it seemed to be Vi's lucky day—her falling flat on her face already forgotten—she was suddenly enveloped in those gentle, willowy arms herself, Aoife cackling next to them, and Chiara's voice, low and so warm, murmured in her ear.

"We will have to explore this penchant of yours. It's quite ingenious that you've given me direction with one word. That, with one glance, you saw and understood that *something* that was inside of me yet eluded me." And there was that word again. *Understanding.*

Her brain wanted to latch on to it, except all her senses were overwhelmed. That hunger, that starvation-like longing for a touch, was currently being sated with soft skin gliding over hers as Chiara's fingertips cheerfully ran along the nape of her neck, making her want to sob. How long had it been?

Vi stood very still in Chiara's embrace, afraid to move. Afraid to breathe. Afraid to make a sound, because this surely had to be a dream and she would wake up at any moment alone in her bed.

Chiara's voice had her by the throat.

"You've given me something precious today, so you deserve a hug as well."

"Aww, this is so sweet. The newbie gets a very warm welcome indeed, as I see. Are we celebrating something?" And just like that, the dreamlike state was broken like glass into jagged, painful slivers, as a loud, abrasive voice she'd heard just half an hour earlier interrupted.

Frankie swaggered in, her boots loud on the polished, oaken floors. Vi stilled, apprehensive about whatever would come next, but Frankie made no other comment about Chiara still holding her in her arms and instead zeroed in on the sketch.

"Not this again!" The unpleasant voice rose, scratchy and rough. "I thought you were hugging it out because you finally managed to figure things out for the next spring concept. And you're still stuck on *this* crap? Is this you being hyper-focused again? Just take something and stop this, Chiara!"

Hyper-focus?

As she was trying to form cogent thoughts among the confusion and the cotton clouding her mind, Vi could swear she heard Aoife actually growl. Before anyone could say anything, Chiara let go of Vi and moved towards Frankie, who raised her hands in surrender and leaned in to give her wife a rather long, sloppy, and thoroughly inappropriate kiss, considering Vi's proximity and Aoife's presence in the room.

"I'm sorry, I'm sorry. Just a lot of stress. Nothing came to me either, even if I did lock myself in the office, and we're getting rather close to the start of the campaign for the spring collection. Poise and the rest of those scavengers will be knocking on our door any moment now, and I'm not telling them that the best fashion house in Europe doesn't even have a concept to draw from."

If Chiara had been serene and radiant before, all open smiles and joyful laughter, then Vi thought the light had been turned off the moment Frankie metaphorically stomped all over the sketch. Her eyes were shadowed as she slowly and carefully took the paper out of Frankie's hands.

"We will figure things out." Chiara's tone was resigned, conciliatory even, as her eyes returned to their earlier sadness. "We always do. How was your day?"

And now Vi did feel like she was indeed intruding. On something she not only had no business being privy to but also had no wish to see. As if reading her thoughts, Aoife tugged on her arm and unceremoniously dragged her out of the room.

The last thing Vi saw was Frankie enveloping Chiara in an awkward embrace, to which Chiara reluctantly submitted, before relaxing into her wife's arms and wrapping her own around Frankie's shoulders.

～

"... THAT BLOODY..." All the way down to the second floor production studio, Vi was catching snippets of mumblings coming from Aoife who was now several steps ahead of her, despite Vi's much longer legs.

"... had I not sworn to shut up... disrespectful bitch..."

As they finally entered Aoife's space, Vi decided to take matters into her own hands. "Hey, that seems to be a fascinating subject you're discussing there, Ms. Sullivan. Do you want to share with the class?"

Aoife barked out a loud laugh before settling into an ergonomic chair by one of the shiny sewing machines.

"You're a funny one, kid." She lifted her legs onto the corner of the desk and gave Vi a long once-over. "Thought you're one of those pompous royals. Then, after your amazingly executed belly flop, I thought you're some talentless klutz who nobody wanted and who's been hoisted on us—"

Because this supposition was so damn close to the truth, Vi felt her breathing go shallow. She touched her sternum and tried to look anywhere but at Aoife, who was still watching her closely.

"—but after seeing you with Chiara..." She trailed off, and Vi all but hyperventilated. *Did she have to be this transparent?*

"Look, I confess. It's true. She was right. I did have posters..." Vi rubbed the back of her neck, absolutely certain her complexion was giving away how embarrassed she really was. The curse of the redheads. "What's not to worship? C'mon, the first openly lesbian supermodel? The first openly lesbian supermodel to marry the first openly lesbian fashion designer and actually do it legally by eloping to the Netherlands?

"So I had a poster of her on my wall in college. So what? I take pride in being who I am, and I take pride in admiring the people who came before me..." She trailed off as Aoife was now staring at her owlishly, blinking eyes almost glazing over.

"Well, this is way more than I ever wanted to know, and I have nobody but myself to blame. How about we never, ever mention your puerile fantasies or whatever it is you were trying to tell me here under the guise of 'respecting your queer elders', because she's only forty and I'm three years older than her, and I am nobody's 'elder.'" Aoife got up slowly, cracking her spine with gusto, and made her way to the small fridge secreted away behind a panel in the corner of the studio and pulled out two beers.

Deciding that she'd already said more than she ever wished for another human being to know, Vi accepted the bottle, took a big gulp, and kept her mouth shut after that. It was five o'clock somewhere, and she chose to follow Aoife's lead.

"What I meant to say, before you shared all your teenage angst with me, Courtenay, is that we have been trying to figure out what she's been drawing for months." Aoife took a long pull and went on, still giving Vi a closed-off look.

"She has a process, you see. One that is very involved. It's post-its and reminders and apps and journals and all the other small and big details that make her function and create the way only she can. And we have all pitched in, to help, to facilitate, to somehow streamline this process that had seemingly stalled, because she just couldn't move on from that one design. And you waltzed in, took one look and said bloody 'wedding.' I wanted to hug you. I would, but you're tall and that would just serve as a reminder of how short I am, so no. Chiara already gave you enough material to feature in your dreams. In tech-nicolor."

Vi wanted to grit her teeth and say something that would perhaps cost her the only friend she had made here so far. Something along the lines of, 'maybe you all should just accept a person the way she is and not give her grief about how her talent manifests itself...' Instead she shut her mouth, shoved the thought farther into her already overthinking brain and chose to move on. It had been an amazing hug.

She gave Aoife a cheeky grin and received a giggle in response.

"Okay, okay, I'll lay off. But listen. You're a smart kid. Frankie really thinks you will give her an *in* with the Kingdom of Savoy monarchs, which is none of my business. But she also assigned you to me. And since we already established you're bright but pretty much useless, sewing and pattern-cutting wise, you will spend a lot of time among these walls doing all the crap I don't want to do. Running errands. *Gopher*. Get it?"

Vi nodded, stoically choosing to keep her silence. She took another swig of beer, which she might have enjoyed on a good day, but today it slid down her throat like lead.

"My point is, you'll realize very quickly who is who and what is what around here. And you'll learn that, when Chiara gets her creative juices flowing, Lilien Haus makes great fashion."

Vi filed all that information away, her previous assumptions confirmed, and put the half-finished bottle in the trash, mindful not to tip it, before finally getting her courage up to speak again.

"I honestly didn't do anything. About the sketch. It's something that just popped into my head."

"I dunno, kid. I dunno. But we've all been trying, and for the life of me, I didn't see that dress as a wedding gown until you said it. And I've seen it in all the colors Chiara tried. Now that she knows what direction this is going, I think she'll try ivory once again. Though something might be missing. She'll figure it out now, and maybe it will free up her mind and her creativity enough to move on to the new spring collection. Though, perhaps Frankie should be doing a better job of nurturing her wife's muse."

The last comment was mumbled more than said out loud, with Aoife walking to the far corner of the studio, affecting an air of extreme involvement with a piece of ivory silk. Vi decided that some things were better left alone. She had poked the bear a bit too much today as it was. She liked Aoife, who was jovial and funny and so far kind to her.

Vi didn't have many friends, and with the summer and fall months of this internship looming ahead, she wanted to do well. For her father, for herself, and maybe a little bit for the woman upstairs, who was somebody's wife and whom Vi had no business thinking about.

IN THE END, her first errand turned out to be getting lunch. Vi almost raised an eyebrow at the list of dishes being rattled off to her from the top of her supervisor's head, and decided not to ask why they didn't simply order delivery. *Gopher*. She'd known what she was agreeing to when she'd signed on. It was time to go and do her job now.

She was relieved she hadn't mouthed off to Aoife about the delivery situation, because the bistro a block away did not, in fact, actually deliver. That alone was strange, but once she stepped into the small space—that looked more like a hole-in-the-wall truck stop in the middle of Nowhere, Indiana, than off the Rue de Rivoli—many other things seemed even more peculiar.

The man behind the counter had a scraggly mustache and an air of invincibility that made him appear like a direct descendant of Napoleon himself. He raised his head from a badly battered copy of what looked like The Catcher in the Rye and gave his facial hair a rather theatrical spin.

He did not bother with French.

"Are you Madame Chiara's new raccoon?"

Vi decided that she wouldn't bother to speak French either. Though she immediately wanted to rub that air of Gallic superiority off his face. Her English noble half—direct descendents of William The Conqueror—wanted to remind him of the Battle of Agincourt.

"It's *gopher*."

He very demonstratively puffed his lips at her, and she wondered if the bistro wasn't on candid camera, because surely he had to be playing to an invisible crowd.

"Same thing. The lunch order is ready. Since you are new and English, I can't trust your taste to be of any quality, so I made the house special for you. The rest have their usual orders packed."

Vi raised her eyebrow at the needless memorization Aoife had subjected her to, then decided that there were more important matters at hand.

"I'm only half English." She straightened to her last inch,

throwing back her shoulders, and looked down on him from her almost six feet. "My Savoy side has not offended the French, to my knowledge."

He paused the twirling of his mustache and cracked a small smile. "We would've beaten them into submission if they'd dared."

"That's what you said about the Russians in 1812 and the Brits at Waterloo in 1815, and how did that turn out for you?"

He stared at her and then began puffing out again with patriotic pride. But before he could argue that the Russians didn't actually defeat the French in 1812, and it was in fact the cold weather and hunger that had caused so many of them to perish on the march back from Moscow, Vi shook her head at him and lifted her hands palms up.

"Never mind, just... Why did Aoife make me memorize the order if you had already completed it?"

Vi looked at the two bags on the counter in front of her, noticing that the man was giving her an appraising, lecherous look now. That raised her hackles immediately.

"The food smells good, I'll give you that. But if you've been dealing with the Lilien Haus crowd long enough to know their specific order without me having to rattle it off and still can't recognize a lesbian when she walks in, I got nothing for you, brother."

To his credit, he didn't startle this time nor fluster. He shrugged, and then his face took on a blissful, faraway look.

"Lesbian, schmesbian..." He actually sighed loudly. "Chiara Conti is a goddess. You foreigners don't appreciate beauty if you think we French can't deify a woman who looks like that. She doesn't have to be straight. She just has to *be*. I'm a beauty connoisseur."

Then he leaned in and offered Vi his rather large—for such a scrawny man—hand. She responded on instinct and found his handshake to be strong, firm, and warm. His eyes looked directly into hers and he simply said, "Zizou. Like the greatest football player that ever played for France."

"Vi. Genevieve. Like my great-grandmother who slept with the future king of England, and as she got older, retold the story of that night at every party to the profound embarrassment of the entire family."

As they both dissolved into laughter, Vi grabbed the bags and exited the bistro, thinking she might have just made another friend.

~

HER DAY WAS a blur after lunch. For a person who proclaimed herself to be a 'one-woman-show', Aoife had a very well thought-out task list for Vi that made Vi feel productive, despite most of those tasks being menial. Still, it was good to be doing something and be appreciated for it.

As the evening descended on the warm and slightly suffocating Paris June, Vi hurried down Rue Saint-Honoré, trying to outrun the rain that would surely split the tumultuous sky at any moment. She stumbled, almost going head over heels on her own shoelaces, and as she crouched down to tie them, juggling her messenger bag and the papers she was delivering for Aoife, she heard something right as the clouds finally opened to release the first rivulets of a summer shower.

A meow. A tiny, pitiful—yet all things considered rather demanding—meow. She turned around, still crouching, and that's when she saw it. Him? Her? A rather dirty, small thing of undetermined color that could have been anything between gray and black.

The animal looked back at her and meowed again, the sound even more obnoxious than the first time. Vi, who was getting soggier by the second, just managed to stuff the paperwork into her bag, certainly mangling it in the process, and as she extended a hand towards the creature who was lounging on the wet sidewalk as if it was a throne, it swiped at her hand, fortunately missing it entirely.

Vi yelped at the unexpected attack but still made a grab for the cat who struggled in her hold and tried to bite her, meowing even louder and, to Vi's ears, even more demandingly. That's when Vi noticed the rather mangled back paw. Shit. What should she do?

And then, amidst rain and thunder and water running all over her Chucks, a window opened across the street and Chiara's shout shook her out of her indecisive stupor.

"Ms. Courtenay, bring her here!"

"How did you even know she was a *her*?"

Vi ran a towel over her wet hair and said a small prayer that her blazer had kept most of the rain away from her white shirt. As it was, only her shoes, her hair, and her dignity had suffered any lasting damage.

Chiara was running the towel over the no-longer-mewling or struggling cat, who was drying quickly and revealing a very interesting chocolate color to its fur.

"She has been creating a ruckus under my window for half an hour. It sounded all sorts of disdainful. Arrogant even. But also quite majestic. Only a woman would do that." Gentle hands examined the cat's back paw and the crease on Chiara's forehead deepened. "I'd have gone to her sooner had I known she was in trouble. Judging by the meows, I just assumed she was spoiled. Now I'll have to call the vet."

Vi raised her eyebrows.

"You're keeping her?"

"Well, I can't exactly throw her out. She needs help. Afterwards, we shall see, right, *piccola*?" Chiara leaned down, and her nose touched the cat's who allowed Chiara to nuzzle her. Vi goggled. The cat who'd wanted to strip several layers off Vi's skin was rather docile with Chiara. *Well, of course.*

"I don't actually think 'piccola' suits her, though. She looks to be fully grown despite her diminutive size. And the tiny legs."

"I've never seen this breed. Or the color." Vi extended her hand again to try to pet the now-dry cat, only to have it swipe a paw at her once again.

"Ah, ah, ah, play nice... Binoche, that's your savior right there." The cat struggled out of Chiara's hands and sat down on the towel to wash herself.

"Binoche?" Vi was pretty sure she'd misheard. "That's a strange name for a cat. And it rhymes with brioche." As soon as the words left her mouth, Vi wanted to take them back, to sink through the floor. Why did things just escape her lips like that?

The cat gave Vi the dirtiest look possible and turned away from both women, continuing her task. Chiara's expression mirrored the cat's.

"You philistine! Juliette Binoche is *the* national treasure of French cinema. And she happens to have starred in—"

"Chocolat!" Vi smiled widely, pleased with herself for remembering and following Chiara's thought process behind naming the cat, who clearly didn't want anything to do with them, despite her injury.

"Well, maybe not all is lost with you." Chiara's lower lip actually turned down in a pout, the beautiful mouth arranging itself into an irresistible expression. Vi, for the second time in as many minutes, gawked.

Chiara reached for the cat, and Binoche allowed herself to be picked up. For a minute, the woman and the cat just looked at each other, and Chiara sighed.

"An end of my half-year-long creative block, a concept for

the new collection, and a cat. All in one day. You're an over-achiever, Ms. Courtenay. What am I to do with you?"

Despite not looking at her, Vi felt the words seep into every fiber of her being, their warmth, their slight *hauteur*. When Chiara finally did turn away from the purring cat, her pouting lips twitched with exasperation, then turned upwards in a smile, and Vi figured Chiara could do absolutely anything with her. Anything at all.

3

ONCE UPON A LATE NIGHT

Genevieve Courtenay was tired, out of breath, and run ragged. Her plans for showing up for the family dinner at the penthouse were evaporating before her eyes. Not that she really wanted to go. But she knew that, just this once—because he had been this weirdly insistent she take the job—her father would be curious about how her first week had gone.

And while Vi might have, at one time, had some delusions that he'd be interested for her sake, she'd abandoned that fantasy long ago.

No, Charles Courtenay would want to know if she'd embarrassed him with any of the important people. Or whether she had done the family name proud. Or if they'd asked about her connections to the royal family of Savoy. All of which felt like lead in her stomach.

It wasn't like her being the niece of King Aleric or cousin to Princess Allegra was a secret. The Courtenay's line and the Savoy line had intersected when Charles had married King Aleric's younger sister. But since her mother's death at Vi's birth, the Savoys hadn't exactly been close or in any way present in her life. That her father still traded on their name—including in this particular case—had Vi mystified.

It also made her apprehensive that, at any moment, Aoife or Frankie or Chiara might ask her about them. So far, no one had. Aoife teased her about her royal connections, calling her jokingly *Lady Rae*, but clearly couldn't care less. Frankie might as well have been nonexistent for all the time she spent at the *Haus* and had never mentioned them. And Chiara... Well, Chiara... Vi tried very hard not to think about her. Out of self-preservation, if nothing else.

Somebody's wife, somebody's wife.

She rounded the corner of the Rue Saint-Honoré opposite the immense Longchamps store and paid no mind to the sparkling displays of beautiful watches. Her mind returned to her father, who had an impressive collection of timepieces. And kept acquiring new ones. Vi didn't know how. Or why, for that matter.

Well, the *why* probably had a lot to do with the Savoys, who no longer received the Courtenays. And the Courtenays—who held the English Earldom of Rae—still played at being *some-ones*. Vi rolled her eyes at the shallowness.

Living so far beyond their means that it should be criminal was the Courtenay's forte. If anyone knew how to get into every ballroom and party and be invited to all the major events of the year in New York, London or Paris, it was her family.

Vi really couldn't quite complain, since her current employment situation was entirely due to her last name. Yet, she still went home to her shoebox attic of an apartment in Montmartre, whereas the rest of her family lived large on the Place Dauphine, a stone's throw away from Lilien Haus.

Vi sped up her tired steps and decided that pondering their irresponsible behavior was really not her problem. If her father wanted to take on more debt than was perhaps legal, and if he kept lying to all those people latching on to him for his name and titles, they deserved what they got.

None of her business...

She took the stairs up to Aoife's floor two at a time. The call from the production house had come just as she'd been debating how to start her lunch—with the fries or the sandwich—and thus she'd had to forgo both as she spent her afternoon running around the 3rd arrondissement, tracking down various pieces for Aoife's crew of seamstresses.

"I heard you moved mountains, kid!" Her supervisor was sewing cheerfully, and her voice was muffled by her face being almost level with the needle going in and out of what looked like Mulberry Silk.

The things one learned on this job.

"I think it's all straightened out now, boss." Vi longingly looked around the various surfaces to locate the food she'd left behind earlier. None was to be seen.

"Well then, Courtenay, you're not just a good gopher, but also a magician. Because almost half of those women are lesbians, and I have no idea how you managed to straighten them out, but kudos to you." The cheerful cackling that followed was already so endearing and familiar, although Vi had only been there a week.

"Also, I may joke about these magical powers of yours, but let me tell you, in my years of working with that crew, I am yet to resolve matters in the speedy and efficient way you have today. And really all week. Are you after my job, kid?"

It had been a running joke ever since Vi had managed to get into the seamstresses' good graces. Every day, she returned buoyed by successfully fulfilling her assignments, even if she was tired after hours of herding cats over at the atelier.

Still, she was nice to everyone there, and they did what she needed them to do. Everyone was happy and, judging by the grin on Aoife's face, so was she. Vi returned a smile and dug around the little fridge, but came up empty-handed.

"Yes, yes, love, the locusts from the upper floor raided it earlier. I have some of my fries left, though." Aoife pushed the little paper bag her way, and Vi decided that beggars couldn't be choosers.

"Thanks Aoife, you're the best. I saw another container in there, though. Did Chiara not eat?" Vi wanted to add 'again' to her question but stopped herself. Nobody needed to know that she paid close attention to how many meals Chiara missed.

"I think she spent her morning at the vet with that chocolate spawn of the devil. And you know nobody touches Chiara's food."

"Well, that's swell. What am I supposed to tell Zizou tomorrow? He always asks how the food was, and especially how Madame C enjoyed her..." She searched her mind for whatever it was Zizou had packed for Chiara earlier that day. Was it falafel or tuna?

Vi dipped a fry into the mayo and grimaced in disgust. Who chose to have mayo with their fries? "...falafel." She finished the sentence with a forced conviction despite not being at all certain. Then she grinned around a full mouth and raised a hopeful eyebrow, and Aoife just shook her head.

"You can't have Chiara's sandwich. It's sacrosanct and you know it." Vi's head drooped. She didn't want all of it. And the thought of Chiara going hungry again did not sit well with her at all.

However, the few fries she'd gobbled down hadn't even come close to filling the hole in her stomach. "I'll do you one better though, Cinderella. Why don't you deliver that takeout box to Madame C yourself and beg her for scraps?" Aoife shooed Vi, already burying her head back in the ivory fabric, and Vi didn't get a chance to ask her about the re-emergence of the nickname.

On the other hand, every day people around this place called her something new. *Kid, Courtenay, gopher, you there.*

The last appellation—if you could call it that—was from Frankie. She had yet to use Vi's first name. Or her last name, for that matter.

In fact, every time Vi saw her—which was preciously rare—Frankie was either busy doing something completely fashion-unrelated or talking to some model. Hence, the face of Lilien Haus had very little time for the intern who supposedly had been hired to learn from her, if Vi was to believe her father.

WITH CHIARA'S lunch in hand, Vi climbed to the fifth floor, then simply stood at the entrance. Just for one moment. She told herself it was to catch her breath after the three flights of stairs, but she knew she was lying.

The open floor plan allowed her a second or two to bask in the glory that was a barefoot Chiara Conti bent over a workbench with scissors, singing something vaguely resembling an aria, one Vi couldn't pinpoint. Her foot was tapping to her own, completely out-of-tune rhythm, and the pencil stuck in her bun was on the verge of falling out and spilling all those masses of dark, wavy hair onto the sun-kissed shoulders.

A decidedly disgruntled—which, with an ordinary cat, could be explained by a vet visit, but wasn't unusual with this one—Binoche was lounging on a cushion on the windowsill. She looked directly at Vi, probably judging her for the interruption as well as for creepily staring at her mistress.

In the week since Vi had rescued the chocolate feline from the rainstorm and the gutters of Saint-Honoré, Binoche had become a fixture at Lilien Haus. Well, mostly on the fifth floor. Since, it turned out, Frankie was allergic to cats, and Binoche was somehow even more disdainful of Frankie than of other, lesser mortals.

The vet had set Binoche up with a splint on her broken paw and she limped around the place as if she owned it.

Vi had assumed Chiara would find another home for the feline after she healed up—after all, Frankie's allergies were rather severe—but the cat would be staying, despite Vi's assumptions and despite Frankie's cursing.

Binoche tolerated Chiara, ignored Aoife, and had silent contempt for Vi.

Vi could, however, understand all of the above. Everyone adored Chiara, most enjoyed Aoife, and even more people would be annoyed with someone who called them names. Which Vi did with a perverse kind of regularity. Every time she crossed paths with the little chocolate ball of fluff, in fact.

She mouthed 'Brioche' and grinned at the cat, who demonstratively turned away from her. Yes, Vi almost took pleasure in teasing the feline. Mostly because it got an equal rise out of both the cat and her mistress.

Said mistress, who was still singing—if one could call it that because carrying a tune was not one of Chiara's many talents—and was an absolute sight for sore eyes. Since she'd started at Lilien Haus, Vi had only really seen Chiara twice. Maybe three times, but who was counting? Okay, who was she kidding? She'd spoken to her four times and was on constant lookout for more.

The most cherished instance was the night when Chiara had hugged Vi. She still didn't know how to begin to process what had happened, from the sketch of the gown she couldn't stop thinking about, to the slender arms gently encircling her shoulders, how that skin had felt on hers, and how long it had been since Vi had another human's warmth seep into her. Those faint scents of verbena and patchouli had worked themselves into her dreams.

She couldn't stop thinking about that either. How Lilien Haus—which was all about lilies, since they were its symbol, and the flowers were everywhere—still smelled faintly of the earthy notes of those other two plants, so distinct from the sweet, cloying scent of lilies. How one woman, whose presence was largely unseen—except for the occasional seemingly random, bright pink post-it note that was simultaneously perfect in its placement—had imprinted herself so much on everything that Vi could always tell when she was present, up high in her ivory tower, in the studio on the top floor.

And with that, Vi was back to her fairytales. She almost shook her head at herself for being fanciful and romantic and for walking a perilous line. The ring on this princess' finger was very much a reminder of her marital status.

On her second work day she'd seen Chiara's long, slim fingers twisting and twirling that too-large ring in what Vi now, days later, realized was a nervous tell.

Well, there'd been plenty to be anxious about in that particular moment, when Frankie had stalked from one end of the studio to the next like a caged animal, her hands flying, tugging at her own hair, picking up and slamming down various objects. The loud noises sent Binoche running down to Aoife's floor—never having done that before—which was what had attracted Vi up to the fifth floor to begin with.

"...I don't have time for this, Chiara! Lilien doesn't have time for this! We talked about whatever it is you think this will turn into, but for fuck's sake... Son of a bitch. Ow." A pair of scissors had slipped Frankie's grip and, with a heavy thud, landed on her rather grotesquely militarized boot, but not before nicking her hand.

She yelped and brought the wound to her mouth, with several droplets of blood falling to the floor. And as Vi watched, Frankie plucked up the offending scissors and flung them across the room. Chiara flinched but otherwise didn't move, and Frankie stormed away past Vi and down the stairs, still sucking on her bleeding hand.

As the sound of those heavy boots running down the stairs quieted, Chiara seemed to shake herself out of whatever stupor she was in and took several steps towards where the floor was marred with crimson drops. A remarkably steady hand—in such contrast with Vi's own shaking ones that were also holding the trembling cat—reached for a napkin, and Vi held her breath as Chiara knelt down and wiped away the stain.

Vi must have made a sound, because the amber eyes snapped up and for a second, held her paralyzed. Vi couldn't move to save her life. So freezing it was, since there was no fighting that gaze, and there was no fleeing it either. Not without permission, without an absolution for breaking some house rule. *Thou shall not covet your boss' wife, thou shall not..., thou shall not...*

And then Chiara closed her eyes and swallowed, her gulp painfully loud in the silence of the large space, and Vi wanted to run to her, to hold her, to do something. But the eyes did not open, and before Vi could act, Chiara quietly murmured, "don't," and Vi's breath whooshed out of her as if she'd been struck in the solar plexus.

So she'd set down Binoche, turned around and had run as if her life depended on it, trying not to think of blood on those elegant, long-fingered hands and the too thin platinum band that felt too insubstantial to contain all the emotions a marriage was supposed to.

∽

Now, Vi could see the band from her vantage point in the entryway, catching the light off the many lamps that were on in the studio despite the evening light still holding strong in the

Parisian June evening. She coughed to make her presence known and was pleased that Chiara didn't startle.

"I heard you coming up the stairs, Ms. Courtenay. I also know you were mocking my cat just now." She had admired the hands earlier, but the voice...

Vi was no writer, and she didn't consider herself particularly eloquent on her best days.

Still, she'd be hard-pressed not to use cliches like 'smoky whiskey over hand-chiseled granite stones' when describing that sound. The gravel was there, but so was the softness, like a silk ribbon that wrapped itself around you and didn't let go. Vi was so enraptured by the sound of it, she almost missed Chiara's follow-up. "...you aren't particularly stealthy about it either."

"How did you know I was mocking the cat?" Vi stepped into the bright lights and poked out her tongue at Binoche, who stuck her injured leg demonstratively in the air and started washing herself.

"I guessed, Ms. Courtenay."

"Well, I don't think Brioche here minds that much." As if to contradict her, the cat meowed. Vi could swear it sounded like a profanity.

"What are you? Five?" Chiara's mouth twitched in a valiant attempt to hide the smile that was creeping up.

"Six. And you'll see, she'll answer to her name yet."

"Her name is Binoche. A proper, regal name. You calling her a baked good is just beneath her!"

"Well, she *is* kinda small, so being beneath her is difficult."

They looked at each other for a long moment before bursting into laughter as the cat ungracefully plopped down on her bed and proceeded to ignore them.

Vi took a second to relish in the gorgeous smile that was still on Chiara's lips as their laughter subsided. Warm and teasing and a little mischievous.

What was air? What was sanity?

Heaven help her, she was just a poor lesbian. Was peace too much to ask for? But there would be no peace for the moment, and so Vi went for the second best thing.

"So someone from the third floor raided Aoife's fridge and ate my food while I was running around corralling the seamstresses and their wayward orders." Vi was ridiculously pleased with herself when Chiara's smile widened into a grin, except it revealed a set of the most ridiculously attractive dimples, and Vi almost genuflected.

Why me? I am not your strongest soldier...

"Anyway, she sent me up with your food, and I was wondering if you would maybe, perhaps, pretty please share?" She inflected her most pitiful tone into the words and tried for her best Puss-in-Boots, wide-eyed expression.

It must have worked, because Chiara rolled her eyes, and those rarely seen laugh lines mischievously peeked at Vi even as she motioned her closer. The sketch that Vi had seen a week ago was on prominent display on the workstation, and Vi realized that there were certain things that had changed about it.

"Ivory. You chose the color!"

But it wasn't just the color. Now that Chiara had settled on the theme, the gown positively screamed wedding and threw itself at you like a bridal bouquet. Small details were added here and there, a tuck, a piece of lace, and there was very little doubt left about what was in front of her now.

Vi narrowed her eyes and assessed the drawing, cataloging the brilliant additions, her imagination picturing the dress on a model, the newly acquired ivory flowing down in complete harmony with the moment, the occasion, the sentiment.

She turned to Chiara who was observing her with a curious expression, head tilted as if in contemplation, and Vi's heart stuttered in expectation of whatever it was she would say. Would she think she was weird? An oddity, as her family often referred to her, for these silly spaced-out moments of hers?

But Chiara didn't say anything, her eyes still drawn to Vi's face as she nodded, then bit her lip in what Vi was coming to realize was also a characteristic gesture. Chiara stepped away and the moment was broken.

"I have. You opened the door for me, Ms. Courtenay. So I guess you've earned this. Come, follow me, and I'll open one for you. Despite you mocking and tormenting my cat."

She moved with that dancer's grace toward the set of windows only to unlatch one and climb through it, beckoning Vi to follow her.

Vi's mouth went dry, her palms sweaty and her heart in overdrive. Heights were not her strong suit. In fact, heights were not her suit at all. She meekly followed Chiara, shaking like a leaf all the way. A few turns, a few stairs, and they were on the roof of Lilien Haus with Paris all around them, the Eiffel Tower soaring on the other bank of the Seine, the myriad of roofs rising and falling, making the skyscape unforgettable.

Vi turned around, trying to both not look down and still give the impression of taking in her surroundings, only to run headlong into Chiara's assessing look from earlier, accompanied by the same head tilt.

"It's so strange, Ms. Courtenay. It took you a week to straighten out those hellions from Rue de Bretagne. Quite a feat since nobody has managed until now. To ingratiate yourself to Aoife, who is quite a prickly specimen, if I may say so, as her best friend. And now I find myself compelled to welcome you here, where so very few people ever step foot. What is it about you, Ms. Courtenay?"

Her face didn't show much, eyes hooded and reserved. With her fear momentarily forgotten, Vi didn't know how to answer the question, or even if she should. She'd been allowed into the inner sanctum. It remained to be seen why and for how long.

Chiara didn't seem to require anything from her, though. She'd finished her monologue and was now standing an arm's length from Vi, gazing into the distance where the Tuileries could be seen, her face a picture of ease.

Vi looked in the same direction, staring at the horizon, but whatever was left of her own peace was coming from her unwillingness to question it too deeply. All she wanted to do was lie down and bask in the last rays of sun this warm evening and soak up Chiara's presence. And it made her a little brave. She could perhaps even handle being on the roof. As long as she didn't look down. And why would she need to when Chiara was right here? She handed her the white food box and got her courage up.

"Why do you insist on calling me by my last name?"

Chiara opened the container and pulled out what looked like neither falafel nor a tuna sandwich. Zizou would have a lot to answer for tomorrow, Vi decided, accepting half a chicken wrap.

"Isn't that your name? And isn't that the reason for your presence here?"

Touché.

What others were silent about, what Aoife only hinted at, Chiara suddenly confronted her with. Yes, she wouldn't be here if she wasn't a Courtenay with all the connections that implied.

But before Vi could gather her wits to answer, Chiara reached out, and Vi suddenly felt incapable of moving. The words had hurt, but then the cool fingertips touched her face, gently tracing the corner of her mouth, and Vi belatedly realized Chiara must have wiped away some of the darn mayo that seemed to be following her everywhere this evening.

Still, it felt that the tender thumb lingered on her lower lip a little longer than strictly necessary and like Chiara was wiping away the sting of her words.

"Um..." Vi cleared her throat, desperate to remember what

they were talking about. "Well... it is, and that may be true, though I'm not sure what I am doing here. I think Aoife's need for gophers could have been satisfied more easily."

Chiara let her hand fall when Vi started speaking, but for just a second, Vi had felt her own lips move against that gentle fingertip and her knees went weak.

"Sure, however, Aoife deserves the best. And bar that, royalty." This time Vi knew Chiara was joking, because the dimples were peeking out, and she couldn't help but return the smile.

"You could call me Vi, you know. Since that's my name, too."

"Except it's not. *Genevieve* is." Chiara took a delicate bite of her own wrap and gave Vi an appraising look. Then she shook her head, and they both laughed.

"Yeah, I don't think it suits me either. It's a family name." She shrugged. She hadn't picked it, so she wasn't particularly fussed, but Chiara's reticence was interesting.

"I heard. And not just any ancestor's, but one who slept with kings, it seems." The no-longer-sad eyes danced with merriment as she took another bite of her food.

"Aoife." Vi tsked and Chiara shrugged.

"We are horrible gossipers here. All of us. It's an insulated world we live in, and spending days and days with the same people in and out of the building doesn't particularly lend itself to anything other than recounting each other's secrets."

"I did share it with her freely, though now I know she'd be incapable of keeping it to herself." Vi winked to make sure Chiara didn't have any hard feelings about her friend being disparaged. "And all you ever had to do was ask."

Instead of lightening up, Chiara's eyes darkened though, and Vi was afraid she had, indeed, overstepped. She was about to say something—anything to lift the returning veil of sadness from that beautiful face—when Chiara spoke.

"Yes, it was that simple, wasn't it? And you know that's all you have to do, too. Just ask me. You seem to be curious. It's been a while since I've encountered genuine curiosity..." Chiara looked into the dusk falling on the city lying at her feet, but Vi could tell her eyes were unseeing. "So any question, I'll answer."

And suddenly, Vi knew what this was all about. The roof, the questions. Chiara wanted Vi to ask about the last time they'd seen each other. The time Vi had wanted to ride to the rescue of the princess with the bloodied fingers and too-wide wedding band.

But despite Chiara's wishes, the last thing Vi wanted to do was hear about Frankie, or what the raving and ranting had been about. Because Frankie and the fighting put that awful closed-off, melancholy look into the amber eyes that sparkled so brightly when happy, that Vi wanted to avoid the conversation at all cost.

"What is the one memory you cherish most?"

Chiara's eyes widened.

"Well, that's a question out of left field, Ms. Courtenay." But then the smile bloomed shyly on that wide mouth. "Despite being quite a disappointment to my mom, who was absolutely amazing, I don't remember my childhood as unhappy. We had nothing and my mother, a widow, cleaned rich people's houses. We lived in a little town on Lago di Como. I swear, to this day I can't think of anything more beautiful than the lake's water on a summer evening. So maybe that peace of the early Lombardian dusk and the bluish-green of Como is my favorite memory."

Chiara, who had been casting her sight into the distance as she spoke, uttered the last sentence looking straight into Vi's eyes, and then she leaned in and gave her a perfectly innocent, and thus perfectly acceptable, kiss on the cheek.

"Thank you. I needed a little bit of that peace and a little bit of that color tonight." And Vi forgot about all her earlier misgivings and prayers. She was sinking, and she felt like nothing could stop the undertow from pulling her into the deep.

She blinked slowly, lost in the beauty surrounding her, the imagery once again overriding her thought processes. The way the Paris evening hung in the air like a kite in the soft summer breeze, its colors bleeding into the mood of their conversation, leaving marks of wistfulness on Chiara's face. A face that was now close to hers, eyes watchful yet careful in their pursuit.

An eyebrow raised, and Vi felt the kite soar. What a vision Chiara was, the city at her feet, that indolent brow, demanding and arrogant, but the eyes amused.

"You look... All this... I don't know..." Vi trailed off, words escaping her, so she just gestured at Chiara and beyond her at the City of Lights, confused by what she was seeing, at what she wanted to express.

But Chiara just tipped her head to the side slowly, her gaze pensive, before she carefully tucked a flyaway lock behind Vi's ear, making her shiver.

"I wonder..."

The murmur was so quiet that, for a second, Vi believed she'd imagined it. And then Chiara was gone, gait graceful and unhurried. Vi gulped and deliberated if she should follow, but before she could make up her mind, Chiara was back holding her phone. She flicked it open to the camera app.

"Don't worry about the bells and whistles and all the things that make photography so overwhelming. Aperture, depth of field, dynamic range. I don't care about any of that. I've been watching you. You have a vision. You always seem to. The gown, the views, and the people. Show me what you see."

Slender hands pushed the phone into Vi's, and with a practiced assuredness, Chiara took a step forward, closer to the edge, and Vi's breath caught. Paris and Chiara Conti were made for each other. Moody, tempestuous, untamed, a wild spirit wrapped into a veneer of carefully constructed sophistication.

All the hours spent daydreaming with her camera, all the books she'd read under her covers on photography, came roaring back into Vi's mind. She took a breath, focused, and her fingers captured her vision.

When she finished in what could have been seconds or minutes later, Chiara took the phone from her shaking hands, and Vi heard her exhale raggedly. The amber eyes were large, expressive, holding wonder in them like a wounded bird. She lifted them to Vi, and her smile was radiant.

"Ms. Courtenay, you've been holding out on me. On yourself as well, I bet."

Vi could feel the pleasure in her back teeth, like something overly-sweet, it was so acute, so sharp, it verged on pain.

"It seems I have use for you beyond being Aoife's favorite gopher, after all." Chiara pocketed the phone and turned back to the Parisian roofline as the birds made their last circles in the dusk sky. Vi watched them lightheaded. She suspected it was more from Chiara's words than from her fear of heights.

IN THE DISTANCE, someone was playing music, and the heavy thrum of the bass found an outlet in Vi's chest, her heart beating to the slow rhythm as the notes pulsed and saturated the air. They stood there for another hour, the remainder of the food in the container and Vi's plans to attend the family dinner, all forgotten.

Chiara watched the sunset, and Vi watched Chiara, her heart trembling along with the far-away songs. There was such serenity in the other woman's posture, in her slow, deep breathing, that Vi dared not ask anything else at the moment. She decided that she would in the future, now that she had permission.

But she wouldn't touch the topic of Frankie. Or what had happened the other day. Or all the heavy, meaningful silences at Lilien Haus. Eventually she thought she'd figure them out, but this... This quietude she would not mar with whatever those silences meant.

SHE BASKED in the dreamy thud of her heart inside her chest, and in the way it kept her warm and safe all the way to her tin can of an apartment on top of Montmartre. Nothing fazed her. Not the dirty subway car, nor the man in the back of it throwing her dirtier looks, yet.

She was smiling like a loon despite being drenched by the surprise cold shower that had hit her right before she entered the Palais Royal station. Even the wet sounds her Converses made as she climbed the seven stories up to her apartment didn't bother her. Neither did the climb itself. The elevator never worked right in this building.

She felt invincible, the warmth of Chiara's eyes and the soft words of the shared memory spurring her on.

When she opened the door, backing into the room, her eyes were on the few envelopes she'd picked up from her mail box downstairs. The studio was quiet. Perhaps too quiet. She whirled around.

"Genevieve, your place is disgusting."

4

ONCE UPON A TIMELY SCHEME

Genevieve Courtenay was grateful that she managed to swallow the scream of fear, then succeeded in doing the same with the whimper of pain at catching her fingers on the door handle as she fumbled to close it.

Who else but her father could be waiting for her in the dark? And what else would he say? Derision and disgust were two of the emotions most often expressed by Charles Courtenay upon beholding his first- and only-born.

Vi stepped inside, cradling her injured hand, reaching over and turning on the lamp by the door before carefully placing the mail on the breakfast bar that served to divide the kitchen from the main living space. No, it wasn't particularly dirty or cluttered. A coffee mug sat in the sink. A few of the bananas on the counter were beginning to show spots. A t-shirt was carelessly draped over a chair.

Furtively, she threw a look towards the alcove that served as her bedroom. The bed was made. You could not bounce a coin off it, the way he preferred, but it was made, the comforter clean and colorful even in the dim light.

"Good evening, father." She hunched her shoulders, trying to make herself as small as possible in the face of whatever he'd throw at her next. But he was silent as he got up from the battered armchair with its ragged handles, roughened by time and excessive use by whomever had owned it before Vi found it charming enough to haul it up seven stories from the flea market.

He took a few steps and raised his hand to her face and Vi wanted to disappear into dust, desperately craving his comfort and knowing very well he had none to give. She thought of Chiara and of the warmth, and of Aoife laughing, and of Zizou teasing her, and of anything, anything at all, to stop hoping that he would reconsider at the last second instead of doing what he always did. Withhold his affection, ignore her, say something hurtful.

She shouldn't have been surprised, because the gesture was not affectionate at all. His cold, rough fingers swiped at her cheek and came away with red lipstick. Chiara's lips on her cheek. Vi closed her eyes and lowered her head.

"I sent you to Lilien Haus to work, not for whatever this is." Her father cleaned his hand on the dishrag that was neatly folded on the counter next to Vi and took a step back from her.

Absurdly, Vi was so happy when she noticed only a small trace of color on the cloth, because now she knew that, once he was gone, she'd still be able to see remnants of the imprint Chiara's lips had left on her cheek. To use that as a reminder that she wasn't worthless, that she had done something right today.

Vi wanted to lift her hand to the spot that Chiara's lips had touched. Amidst all the hopelessness, all the hunger for love, for attention, there was tangible proof of affection, of gratitude, as fleeting as it might have been. She schooled her features and, to avoid temptation, put her hands in her pockets, as her father spoke without looking at her.

"You didn't show up for dinner tonight. Your mother was worried." His voice echoed along with the thunder outside. No, her 'mother' wasn't worried for her. Her mother was dead, as he so often liked to remind her.

Gwyneth, her stepmother, his fourth wife, could not give a flying fuck about whether Genevieve joined the family or not. The woman was, more often than not, plastered by the time the meal was served.

Vi had always wondered why she'd married her father and whether or not alcohol actually helped her endure him.

"I apologize, father." She kept her voice low and her head down.

"Genevieve, I do not require your apologies. All I need is for you to do what a Courtenay must. Can you appreciate the effort it took?" Vi nodded silently. "Your family worked very hard to get you the position at Lilien."

She bit her lip to keep herself from telling him that asking Frankie to accommodate an internship was hardly work, but she kept her mouth shut.

"This is very important to our family, Genevieve. Do you understand?"

Vi nodded again and belatedly realized her mistake.

"I can't hear you, Genevieve. You never did learn to be polite, girl." His voice held such contempt that this time, Vi did flinch.

"Yes, father. I understand." She took a deep breath and tried not to sound as dejected as she felt. "I'm not sure what you expect me to achieve at Lilien, though."

He walked towards her again and she held her breath, both wishing he'd do something, anything, and at the same time knowing he didn't care enough.

Still, he surprised her for the second time this evening as he laid his large, heavy hand on her shoulder, her bones feeling small and too fragile under his strong fingers. But his palm was warm now, and she drank in the sensation.

"I trust you to figure it out, Genevieve. Am I wrong to assume you are intelligent enough to accomplish that?"

And then he was gone, his heavy steps echoing in the empty stairwell, until another gust of thunder and wind from the outside dulled them into nothing.

Vi exhaled the air she was sadly very much aware she'd been holding in. Romance novels always had their characters hold their breaths and somehow be totally oblivious they were doing it. So strange.

No, Vi knew everything about not breathing. For as long as she could remember, she never quite could inhale with her whole chest around her father. She loved him, she wanted to please him and make him proud. He was all Vi ever had, and his approval was everything she ever dreamed about.

She was also aware of how unhealthy their relationship was. He was a callous man. And she was permanently looking for scraps from his table—which he withheld most of the time —and used his sporadic affection as the perfect carrot for Genevieve, who was used to the painful stick of being dismissed and ignored by now.

Taking a deep breath, she went to the bathroom and, for the longest time, simply stared at her reflection. Red-rimmed empty eyes, freckled sharp cheekbones and the outline of Chiara's lips on her cheek. The perfection of it tarnished by her father's hand. As metaphors went, this one was as obvious as it was poignant.

Vi had been so happy. And he'd ruined it. She sighed and took out a little cotton ball soaked in makeup remover. Her hand trembled when she finally took it away from her face, the white saturated with the blood-red of Chiara's lipstick. Her reflection in the mirror had the same expression as Chiara's when she'd cleaned blood off the floor after her encounter with Frankie.

Vi was grateful to be alone and thought she understood how Chiara must have felt in that moment to plead for Vi to just leave.

She walked into the kitchen, washed her coffee mug, grabbed the discarded t-shirt from the back of the chair, and folded it on autopilot. Something to do, something to take her mind off the visit.

She opened the window to the storm. Anything to wipe away the scent of pipe smoke and bergamot. And then she simply stood facing the raging nature, framed by the darkness outside, the occasional raindrop landing on her face mingling with her tears.

THE NEXT DAY started off with more gopher chores. Vi had been running around all morning when Aoife finally sat her down and made her eat the lunch Vi had fetched earlier. Vi gulped down her sandwich while her boss messed around with the sewing machine and pontificated about the benefits of a Queen Anne line over all others for certain body types. *Riveting.* At least the sandwich was tasty.

Aoife eventually got up from her chair and straightened, stretching to try to reach for the third highest shelf near her. She failed adorably. Vi, who sat on the workstation next to her, smirked.

"Oh, fuck off. I am well aware that, even when you're sitting down, you're taller. I hate you." Aoife flipped her off before stalking to the other end of the studio and getting a few things off the numerous clothes racks assembled there.

"You don't. I bring you food and I listen to you rambling about fashion history, and I do what you tell me to do." When

Aoife narrowed her eyes at her, Vi shrugged. "Well, mostly."
Aoife tsked and Vi three-pointed her sandwich wrapper into
the bin. "Whatcha need, short boss lady?"

"These need to go to Rue de Bretagne and they will give you
several of the dresses they've already finished. Take all of them.
But specifically ask for the cream bodycon. Chiara wants it
tonight."

"And a bodycon is? Also, Chiara wants it? Shouldn't Frau
Franciszka Lilienfeld be the one requesting things instead?" Vi
would have given just about anything to take those words back
the moment they fell out of her mouth. "I'm sorry. I didn't mean
to say all that out loud. It's really none of my business."

Aoife gave her a sidelong glance, then just shook her head.

"First, you are a philistine, Cinderella. You've been with me
for a week and still have no idea about dress styles. Just ask
them. The women at Rue de Bretagne will give it to you if it's
ready. And second, you are right for once. Chiara is none of
your business. And neither is Frau Lilienfeld. And it would pay
for you to remember that they're both Frau Lilienfelds, kid."

Vi almost choked on the remnants of her shake and scur-
ried to throw the plastic cup in the bin and hide her embarrassment. Aoife thumped her on the back. "Now, don't feel bad.
Some things are what they are. Run along, Cinderella."

EVEN WITH AOIFE'S attempt at wiping the sting off the truth, Vi
moped all the way to Rue de Bretagne, and once she got there,
had no time to focus on anything other than the issues at hand.

The place was its usual uncoordinated mess and not for the
first time, Vi wondered why Aoife didn't work with the seamstresses directly, or at least more closely. They could benefit
from her 'sunny' disposition and firm hand. She was certainly

doing a wonderful job with Vi. But that was the least of Vi's concerns.

She'd almost finished sorting through a pile of half sewn garments, only to have Marie—who acted like she was in charge—announce that they had made changes to the design of the bodycon. They, whoever 'they' were—Vi had no idea why Marie was using the French plural of the pronoun—had decided that an A-line would work better for this particular piece.

Vi couldn't tell a sheath from a tent or a babydoll from a princess, but she knew this wasn't what was supposed to happen, hence there would be consequences. Marie was reluctant to discuss any details after Vi voiced her concerns, and the explosion of Gallic words and gestures—none of which were remotely acceptable in polite company—made Vi reconsider complaining. A different tactic was needed.

After an hour of negotiations, Marie agreed to discuss the issue again and said Vi could come by before the end of the day tomorrow. Vi reasoned that she would live to die another day and get better arguments from Aoife to persuade the Rue de Bretagne cohorts.

Satisfied that not all was lost yet, and that she would simply have to avert whatever would befall her upon her return to Saint-Honoré, Vi gathered the pieces and—with many smiles, niceties, and compliments—scrambled out of the converted warehouse.

∾

"WHAT DO YOU MEAN, it's 'better as an A-line?'" Frankie's incredulous, shrill voice rang painfully in Vi's ears.

She'd had the misfortune of entering the studio with the garment bags just as Frankie was raiding Aoife's fridge. Before she could say that the sushi was for Chiara, Frankie had already opened the package and dug in.

Vi decided to do what Aoife had advised earlier. She shut her mouth and got out of the way of Aoife's already unpacking hands.

Binoche, who was lying sprawled on Aoife's workstation and looked suspiciously close to a food coma, got up and, with a disdainful meow towards Frankie, sat on her back haunches, as if ready to watch the spectacle.

Vi wished she could do the same, simply show her displeasure with the scene unfolding like the cat. Sadly she couldn't, because she was snapped out of her musings when the half-finished, cream dress was taken out of her hands. And as Aoife unfolded the clear garment bag, Vi stuttered to explain.

"Marie mentioned that. I assume the ladies—she didn't say exactly who—made the executive decision to amend the style—"

Frankie growled and actually dropped the remaining sushi on the floor. Binoche, with an agility that belied someone still nursing an injured paw, pounced on the slice of tuna and disappeared up the stairs. As they said, when there was bread, circuses were immediately forgotten. Binoche, smart cat that she was, had her priorities straight.

Vi cringed at Frankie's volume, but mostly at the fact that she was certain that the food throwing was for show, and now Chiara would go hungry.

Vi thought fast. If she had all her ducks in a row she'd not only escape Frankie's temper tantrum, but also maybe manage to get some food to Chiara. The only things close by were luxury stores and the Michelin Star hotel restaurants. She'd have to hike back to Zizou's, who was closing soon, but he would set her up. Or to the Monop on Rue de la Bourse. Give or take thirty minutes, and she bet Aoife could spare her for the time.

She tried to make her way out of the studio slowly when Frankie wheeled around on her.

"Why didn't you tell them we need this exactly as specified?" From the corner of her eye, Vi could see Aoife open her mouth to intervene, and while it made Vi feel slightly better that someone was ready to stand up for her, instinct told her it would only make everything worse. She shook her head slowly, warning Aoife off. Vi was in for it now, and she didn't want anyone else to take any flak.

Frankie, by all accounts and from everything Vi had witnessed and heard, did not appreciate being contradicted. She was already on the fence regarding this particular collection's concept, and on a high one at that. Vi really didn't want to start that whole discussion again.

The bandage on Frankie's hand was a poignant reminder of the length the woman would go to, to show her displeasure. To again dredge up how much Frankie hated Chiara's ideas was something Vi wanted to avert at all costs.

If Vi had had any time to ponder the 'why' of her wishes and actions, maybe she would have course-corrected, because Frankie had that slim band on her hand, too, and really, none of this was any of Vi's business.

Except she couldn't forget the shy smile and the pure happiness on the features that lit up the room every time the Wedding Collection was mentioned. Vi wanted to protect that. The collection, she quickly told herself. Chiara did not need to be saved.

Then Vi had an idea. An amazing idea. It could work, or it could get her killed. But really, what did she have to lose?

"Ah... I didn't think the shape would matter all that much? It's, um, just a dress?" She made herself slouch lazily and look as stupid as possible as she drawled her response, and Aoife's jaw hit the floor. Yes, Vi knew she was deliberately provocative, but there were bigger things at stake.

Predictably, Frankie exploded.

"*Just a dress?* Are you even aware of what's at stake here? My whole spring collection hinges on this gown and some seamstress..." Frankie spat the word, and Vi felt like she needed a shower, spittle flying everywhere. "Some talentless hack, some nobody, thought she could just change the concept? After Lilien Haus poured hours of work and talent into it?"

Funny, Vi thought. *Lilien Haus.*

"This is not just some dress. You've been here a week and you've learned nothing! For crying out loud. *Nothing,*" Frankie ranted on.

Vi ran her thumb over one of her fingernails in a deliberate show of calm. "Well, Aoife said the same thing this morning—"

"At least she did something right, even if she can't control those harpies on Rue de Bretagne." Vi managed to throw Aoife a warning glare before her mentor made filet out of Frankie, but she didn't need to, because Aoife was watching everything with narrowed, speculative eyes.

"You must be a special kind of stupid, Courtenay." This one stung, even if it meant Vi had reached her goal of deflecting Frankie's ire, but it was so reminiscent of her family's insults that the humiliation burned like acid in her throat.

Frankie didn't care or notice. "You go back to them, and you tell them that this collection will be the absolute best thing Lilien Haus has ever produced, and they are messing it up for me! I need this piece by tomorrow. You hear me?"

Vi was about to nod, quite happy with how everything was playing out despite the humiliation, only to have the distant staccato of high heels alert her that the commotion Frankie's outburst was causing had attracted the attention of the one person Vi was trying to keep safe and out of the fray.

Chiara's face was drawn as she stood in the doorway to the studio, but she said nothing, amber eyes taking in the scene. Frankie noticed her too, and was already turning towards her, face red and chest heaving, and Vi's mind just kept coming up with more and more self-destructive ideas.

"Ms. Lilienfeld, I will try, but the ladies on Rue de Bretagne are working on an order from Lucci—"

Everything else forgotten, Frankie whirled back on Vi.

"Lucci? What the hell is wrong with you? Courtenay or not, I can't believe you don't know these things. I don't care about Lucci. You can tell Alberto and Romina and all those other Luccis that I run this town. They can fuck the fuck off to Italy. This is my domain."

"Understood." Vi lowered her head, watching the room from under her lashes.

"Understood, what?" Hands on her hips, eyebrows raised, Frankie was clearly enjoying this entire scene.

"Understood, ma'am." The acid returned as the memories of her father's displeasure from last night invaded. However, Vi's mumble was drowned out by Chiara's raised voice.

"That's enough." The high-heeled steps made their way into the room, and Vi could swear the air sang with electricity. Anger, resentment, fear, all flowing together into a Molotov cocktail of explosive human emotions. And Vi had been lighting matches to it since the conversation had started. "Don't talk to her like that."

Frankie's eyes narrowed.

"I will talk to her any way I want! You all seem to have forgotten that this is *my* house, *my* brand, *my* name on every wall." Frankie grabbed the offending dress from Aoife's hands and ground down her booted foot, snagging it on the cream fabric. Whether she noticed it or not, she worked her heel into the delicate material, and now Vi wanted to cry. Yes, the cut was all wrong, but surely the garment didn't deserve this fate.

Chiara's voice broke slightly as she reached Frankie and gently moved her so that she could pick up the dress. "I will fix it. And the rest is coming along well enough. We will have a collection come August. Don't fret, amore."

Frankie groaned, whether in acquiescence or displeasure, Vi couldn't tell, and allowed her boot to be freed from the silk. With a kiss to Chiara's cheek and a parting glare at Vi, she swaggered out of the room.

For a few seconds, the ticking of the clock on the wall was all that could be heard. Vi was afraid to even breathe. Then a cool hand landed on her forearm.

"I'm sorry, Ms. Courtenay—"

"I swear to god, Chiara, how many times will you apologize for Frankie's behavior?" Aoife seemed to snap out of it, her face pale and shoulders squared.

Chiara shrugged, but Aoife was not to be deterred. "If Vi hadn't gone all *master strategist* here fifteen minutes ago, we wouldn't have a fashion house to work in, just rubble. And we will get back to you being this savvy in a minute, kid. Chiara, honestly—"

"Sully, I don't have time for this. I have work to do, and I'll deal with Frankie. I do apologize though."

Vi watched silently as Chiara, eyes everywhere but on her, carefully folded the mangled dress and walked out of the room.

"Aoife—"

But Aoife just shook her head and handed Vi the rest of the garments.

"Take these to her. She really must be out of sorts since she expressly asked for these and forgot to take them. I don't want to go up there. I'm bound to say things I have been holding onto for far too long, and it's really not fair to her."

∾

THE STAIRS to the fifth floor had become her friends. All the staircases at Lilien Haus were rather spectacular, but every time Vi stepped onto the two flights leading up to Chiara's studio, her heart sped up. She knew she was pretty pathetic and really, now was not the time to have all these inappropriate thoughts, but she couldn't help herself.

Arms full of pastel silk, she made her presence known to Chiara who was arranging the damaged gown on a mannequin. Binoche laid curled on the windowsill on her bed, ignoring Vi's very existence. Chiara lifted her face, eyes tired and the worry lines prominent. They stretched into a grimace of a smile that disappeared as soon as it came on, and only sadness remained.

"Oh, thank you. Would you leave them on the bench by the window?" Binoche gave Vi a baleful glance as she approached and turned on her other side, looking thoroughly disgusted as Vi poked out her tongue at her.

Chiara, for once oblivious to their shenanigans, tsked at her handiwork, re-pinned something, removed the pin and tsked again. Then she took the pencil out of her bun before pulling the hair back up into a tighter one. Suddenly, she turned and gave Vi a speculative look.

"Are the ladies on Rue de Bretagne really busy with Lucci? Or was that another white lie to distract Frankie?"

"Another?" Vi felt the heat creep up her neck and decided that her Converses were amazingly interesting all of a sudden. The red really was a good color on the canvas shoes.

"I heard your remark that this is 'just a dress' as I was coming down the stairs. Aoife didn't call you a master strategist for nothing. It only took you one week to figure out some of the dynamics around here. And with one sentence, you managed to both offend me and the collection, and put Frankie in a position to defend it while frothing at the mouth."

Chiara stepped closer and gently lifted Vi's chin, her fingers cool, the touch reaching somewhere way too deeply into Vi.

Deeper than a simple lifting of the chin ever had the right to reach. No matter how foolishly romantic such a gesture was. "And I know very well that you have a much better understanding of what this dress is or isn't. Your education didn't prepare you for this gig, regardless of whatever it was Frankie hired you for. But you do know better now, Ms. Courtenay."

"My education?" The words came out as a high-pitched squeak, and Chiara smiled and let her fingers drop from Vi's face.

"Frankie may have only needed your last name to recommend you for the position as the new intern, her sights on the Savoy Court being what they are." Vi's brows rose, since Frankie certainly didn't act like she wanted or needed Vi's favor, and Chiara gave her nose a gentle flick with a fingertip. "But I looked at your resume. I do my homework, Ms. Courtenay. The brilliant display of your artistic eye yesterday on the roof aside, and we will get back to that, because I have a lot to say…"

Chiara looked directly at her then, and Vi's treacherous heart sped up again, her mind working in overdrive, trying to anticipate any potential move. But Chiara just tucked a flyaway behind Vi's ear.

"As I was saying, yesterday's adventure with the phone aside, your eye for perspective and concept already told me you are much better than the 'oh shucks, ma'am' act you're trying to pull. So what gives?"

The voice and the gesture were certainly warm, but Chiara's eyes were shrewd as Vi met them, and she felt a shiver run down her spine.

"I didn't want to cause you any trouble. Tomorrow, I'll go back to Rue de Bretagne and try to wheedle some time out of them, so that they can redo it, if you want me to… I just wanted to help."

The truth lay between them like a stone, heavy in the ensuing silence. Then Chiara exhaled sharply and stepped back and away. Vi's shoulders drooped. She had said the wrong thing. She had *done* the wrong thing. She really never could quite do anything right... Her father's words rang in her ears, and she allowed her lids to close to stave them.

"Thank you, Ms. Courtenay." Vi's eyes snapped open just in time to see Chiara take the silk off the mannequin. "I appreciate it. The thoughtfulness and the desire to help. That is very much appreciated indeed. Because the entire debacle, from the new shape, to the dress, to you offering to help... It made me think of one way you actually can."

With her back to Vi, Chiara turned her head and threw a bomb over her shoulder, one word from her setting Vi on fire. "Now, strip."

5

ONCE UPON AN UNRAVELING

Genevieve Courtenay wasn't a blushing teenager, but she would bet the color of her cheeks was so intense, it could paint the entire length of the Champs-Élysées. And there would probably be quite a bit left.

Had she heard Chiara right?

Strip?

What?

Instead of helping center her, a low chuckle from the woman who'd caused this state of utter panic only made her thoughts scatter more. Chiara was looking at her with such amusement, Vi got a bit offended. Binoche was characteristically unperturbed.

"Ms. Courtenay, really, you fluster too easily. A woman of your illustrious lineage should not jump to the puerile this quickly." Chiara laughed again. "You mentioned wanting to help. Is that offer still on the table?"

"Y-yes." Vi tried to hide her stammer behind a cough.

"Well then, strip." Chiara's graceful hand made a sweeping gesture across her body, and Vi almost spontaneously combusted. "The dress isn't entirely ruined, but to change the shape and to see how it moves, I need a live model. And you're about the right size."

When Vi just kept staring at her, mouth agape, Chiara let out an exasperated sigh. "Okay, how about this? If your offer to help still stands, would you mind modeling the dress for me as I start making the necessary changes?"

The lightbulb went on. Binoche meowed, surely in disgust at her slowness, and Vi actually sagged, whether in relief or disappointment, she couldn't immediately comprehend.

Given the course her life had taken, when all else failed, Vi thought the least she could do was to hang on for this unbeliev-able ride she was on. Where it would lead, she had no idea, and if given more time to think, she'd perhaps realize it would take her straight to hell, but Vi did *not, in fact,* want to think about it.

So instead, she decided to hold on, because Chiara was watching her with those expressive eyes from under the few flyaways, and Vi's heart, being the traitor that it was, thudded once and then again. *How screwed was she?*

"No, err, yes! I mean no, I don't mind and yes, I'll help!" Vi registered that she was rambling, so she took a long breath and nodded eagerly. Her hands reached the top button of her shirt almost automatically, and Chiara actually threw her head back, exposing the long line of her slender throat, and let out another peel of laughter.

"You are adorable, Cenerella. There's a rack over there and there are a couple of slips, since I assume you aren't wearing a camisole under the haute couture that is your GAP button down?"

Chiara's adorable giggle accompanied Vi to the corner of the studio where a changing screen was set up.

To avoid feeling self-conscious, Vi latched on to something Chiara had said.

"Cenerella?" She had to raise her voice slightly and

dropped her shirt when Chiara's answer sounded just from beyond the paper thin screen.

"It's one of the ways to say Cinderella in Italian. But it also goes so well with your eyes. It comes from the word *cenere*, meaning *ash*." Vi trembled, unsure if it was from Chiara's proximity while she was almost naked or from the fact that Chiara had noticed the color of her eyes. She decided that she really should stop asking questions that would only lead to more trouble and got busy dressing.

The silk of the slip felt strange and decadent on Vi's skin as she put it on and padded barefoot towards Chiara who was holding the remainder of the dress with such care, Vi's eyes pricked with tears.

As Chiara slipped the garment over Vi's head, her predicament finally hit her. The patchouli and verbena reached her a second before Chiara stepped even closer, and Vi felt her body heat. The earlier prediction of being doomed returned tenfold.

What had she gotten herself into?

"Is this all right?" As if sensing her hesitation, hands particularly gentle, Chiara watched her carefully for any signs of discomfort. How was Vi to tell her that there was none of it, only gay panic?

"Yes, just..." Just what? Just *what*? *C'mon, brain, a little help.* "Cold. A little cold."

"Oh, hang on, I'll turn the AC off." As she stepped back, Vi felt like she could breathe again. *What the* hell *had she gotten herself into?*

"It will warm up quickly now. The upper floors can get really hot in the summer, and I tend to either forget and sweat all day or turn on the AC to cool it down quickly and then forget about that too and be cold all the time."

"But you get the trade-off with the nice view."

Chiara smiled at that, then her face suddenly turned serious.

"Ms. Courtenay, it occurred to me that I jumped over quite a few steps here." Vi held her breath, both dreading and anticipating what was to come.

"Consent, darling. It's paramount. We have way too little of it in our industry." Vi's eyes widened and her throat bobbed as Chiara went on. "I just want to make sure you're comfortable and absolutely okay with this. I am not your boss. You aren't compelled to do this. I could use your assistance, and I would appreciate it, but this involves me touching you, and I cannot do that without you being okay with this."

Vi wanted to marvel at the thoughtfulness of the words, of the gesture, but her mind screeched to a halt at the image of Chiara working so close to her, *on her*, in fact, and so she just stood still waiting for what was to come.

"Before you say anything and before I do anything, please know that I will try my best to work as carefully as possible and to touch you strictly the necessary amount." Vi almost whimpered as the balloon of her daydream was being burst with tact and concern. "So, do we have an understanding?"

Still lost in her disappointment at Chiara's practicality, Vi just nodded.

"Use your words, Ms. Courtenay."

Vi could feel the hairs on the back of her neck stand up. Had she ever been this turned on with just words?

Mercy...

"Yes, Chiara."

"Yes what?"

Oh, mercy...

"I consent." And then, just because, and to try to lighten the tense mood, Vi added, "Do you want it in writing? In duplicate? Notarized? Or should we, you know, get to it already?"

Chiara's mouth opened and that laughter—the one Vi was becoming addicted to and craved to elicit at all times, the open sincere one—sounded brightly, smokily right next to her ear.

"Touché, Cenerella. Cheeky as always. Let's... get to it then, as you so eloquently put it."

Vi decided that, if she was to keep her thoughts at bay about how close Chiara was and about the things her hands were doing, gently brushing against Vi's body, her best bet was to distract herself.

"Why did you choose the fifth floor? I imagine you had your pick when you bought the building?"

Chiara hummed absently, her mind clearly on the task at hand now, and when she spoke, her voice was muffled around a pin in the corner of her mouth.

"You'd imagine correctly. You know about where I grew up. So very rural. So very rustic." Chiara pinned a fold on the shoulder, and Vi looked up a bit to see the face in deep thought, a small furrow between the inky eyebrows.

For the first time, Vi noticed a dusting of silver among the stark black on the temple. She forced herself to stand very still as her fingertips itched to trace the few lines. Chiara's hair looked like satin, shining and so very soft.

"... the idea of a view was very different there than what I have here. I'm grateful for it. Change is... welcome." Chiara put a few more pins in her mouth and stepped to the side, and Vi thought the floor was tilting as breasts brushed her arm. She heard her own breath catch sharply, but the competent hands did not waver. Vi watched in the tall mirror in the back of the room as Chiara diligently continued her task, her eyes focused on the material.

She wanted to shake herself. Of course she was in this alone. The woman was married. Yes, to an asshole who did not appreciate her. But married nonetheless. She sighed and shook her head. Chiara's eyes met hers in the mirror.

"What has gotten you sad, Ms. Courtenay? I don't think I've seen you brood much. Joyful, mischievous, scheming to get

Aoife's food out from under her nose, but not brooding. Not that it doesn't suit you, mind."

Suddenly, Chiara stepped out of her heels with what could only be called a sigh of relief, and Vi kept watching as their eyes were now level. They were of the same height, and for some reason, her stomach clenched.

"Sorry, I am so used to them, I tend to forget that, as much as I love them, they don't love me back." Chiara's pout at her Jimmy Choos was endearing and so very her, Vi wanted to shoo away the hundreds of butterflies that nestled in her chest.

Married... Married.. Married... Not cute, nor adorable, nor as gorgeous in bare feet as she was in those gorgeous high heels that made her already gorgeous legs go for more gorgeous miles than was legal...

God, even her thoughts had gone haywire, unable to stop repeating the same word over and over where Chiara was concerned.

Gorgeous, gorgeous, gorgeous...

Chiara looked at her with a raised eyebrow, and Vi realized that there must have been a question she'd either ignored or left unanswered. *Oh, brooding. Yeah, okay.*

"Ah... No reason? A long day? Family stuff?"

"You want me to pick?" Chiara reached for another set of pins and gently lifted Vi's left arm, her fingers leaving a trail of goosebumps in their wake. "Hold it like this for me for a bit."

Vi gulped as she both felt and saw those hands slowly move up her side from waist to armpit, and as they inched closer to the side of her breast, Vi was afraid she'd break into a sweat and the dress would need to be dry-cleaned. The thin platinum wedding band caught the last of the dusk sunlight, and Vi swallowed around the lump in her throat.

"No, not pick. Just a lot of things going on."

"Tell me about your family." Chiara traced the seam of the bodice before taking Vi's hand and allowing it to come down to her side. But Vi shook her head, and when Chiara looked up suddenly, their faces were inches apart, worried amber eyes on dejected gray ones.

"Family... is hard. So no family talk. Plus, you promised me an answer to a question." Where had that boldness come from? Desperation for her own secrets to not be touched? Vi didn't know, but Chiara's eyes narrowed minutely before she gave a small nod and bent her head to her task again.

"Didn't I already answer the one about the view?"

Vi tsked, and Chiara gave her a mischievous gaze from under those impossibly inky lashes.

"Another one then? Please?" Vi knew she was pouting, and even as she tried to swiftly pull back her lower lip, Chiara bumped her hip.

"If you're allowed to keep your secrets, Ms. Courtenay, and be nosy, the least I can do is tease you, wouldn't you say?"

Vi stuck out her lip again and sighed in mock exasperation.

"Fine. So why did you leave the catwalk?"

Chiara faltered slightly, but that was the only tell that she'd heard the question, because the silence stretched for so long, Vi thought she'd put her foot in it again. She was about to say something, to apologize, when Chiara spoke up.

"To quote this bratty intern of Aoife's, *family is hard*, Ms. Courtenay." The deft hands resumed, making quick work of folding and pinning the fabric across her back. Soon, Chiara turned her around to face the mirror where their eyes met again. The now familiar sadness was back, and Vi cursed herself for putting it there.

"We all do what we must. Am I right?"

What did Chiara know about her family? Vi's eyes widened, burning hot with unshed tears. Chiara observed her in kind silence.

"Yes. We love them, and we want them to love us. Want ourselves to be good enough to be loved." Something hollow darkened Chiara's gaze before she took a step back from Vi and looked her up and down.

Her name fell off those sensual lips in an exhalation, like deliverance, and Vi suddenly wanted to cry. "Vi, when you are loved, you believe yourself eternal. Have you ever felt it?" Chiara's faraway look told Vi that she wasn't really seeking an answer. "And then I imagine it's like being cast out of heaven. Or thrown down from Olympus. The titans had a lot to begrudge the Olympians, didn't they?"

A mirthless laugh and a tilt of the head, and Chiara's eyes turned empty on a dime. "I guess what I'm trying to say via this very circuitous route is that the people in our lives... they should love us already."

Vi didn't know how Chiara knew, but something in her opened up with a twin ache, one of empathy, of understanding, of recognition. They were talking about completely different situations that had nothing and yet everything in common, and Vi wished she could rest her head on the cool glass of the mirror and let her tears fall.

She had long ago resigned herself to not having love in her life, but for this woman, this beautiful soul, to know what having affection withheld felt like? It just seemed like such a tragedy, such a complete injustice.

A hand on her cheek made her flinch, and then they both stood absolutely still before the fingers trailed higher and came away with what Vi realized was a tear. She was crying, after all.

Vi shook her head again and dared not lift her eyes to Chiara's. It didn't matter, as the wet fingers tipped her chin up again in a characteristic gesture that was becoming more and more familiar. Vi's skin was getting accustomed to the touch and to Chiara's eyes on her, and it felt both amazing and like blasphemy to ever get used to any of it.

This time, however, the grip held a touch of ice to it and when she finally looked up, there was no warmth in Chiara's gaze. The steel that Vi always knew was beneath the velvet was on full display. She gasped, but Chiara's grip just tightened.

"If these are for me, I don't want them, Ms. Courtenay. You can change back into your clothes. I will finish on the mannequin."

"I'm sorry—" Regret rang loudly in her voice, and Vi almost reached out to grasp the hand that was already letting go of her.

"I will see you tomorrow. We can talk about your photography assignment. I have some ideas." And with that, Chiara was gone, leaving Vi alone with her regret.

As Vi TRUDGED to work the next day and passed Zizou's bistro, the cover of Le Figaro caught her attention. She picked it up and was reading the headlines screaming from the front page when his grumpy voice interrupted her.

"Catching up on current events? You know, despite the whole 'dad got me a job at the important fashion house' vibe, you don't really look like anyone who'd give a damn about said events, or fashion, for that matter." He waved his scrawny hand at her, and Vi's temper shorted.

"What? You're not even going to say 'no offense?'"

Zizou did not look deterred in the least, but before he could answer, a voice from one of the tables on the sidewalk interrupted their squabble.

"If you think you can shame him into apologizing for being rude, you are mistaken, Ms. Courtenay. He's Parisian. And he's a man."

Vi thought how unfair the assessment was to all Parisians, but to her surprise, Zizou blushed to the roots of his dark hair and looked discombobulated. Vi understood his predicament. She had only interacted with Renate Lilienfeld twice. When they met and when she'd briskly handed her the non-disclo-sure agreement along with her contract and a pen. They must have exchanged all of ten words in the couple of weeks that Vi had been at Lilien Haus.

The matron—as that was how Vi thought of her, mostly due to her age and to being Frankie's older sister—was always ensconced in her glass office, ruling over the administrative side of running a fashion house. Vi was never dispatched to bring her lunch and generally steered clear of her. Not that she wasn't curious about the woman.

"Take a seat, Ms. Courtenay. I see Aoife has not beaten the bad habit of staring out of you yet. And she's had weeks to do it. Her famed powers of intimidation must be waning."

An eyebrow rose in challenge, and Vi found herself smiling. They may be sisters, but Frankie and Renate were nothing alike. For one, Renate possessed a sense of humor. Dry as a slice of Pecorino Romano cheese, but a sense of humor, none-theless.

Her insides quivering, Vi gathered all her wits about herself. She felt that she would need every last one of them.

"Aoife might wish she was intimidating, but she isn't, and she doesn't possess the dubiously effective method of beating her employees. Browbeat maybe?" Vi made a show of getting comfortable on the iron-wrought chair opposite Renate's, despite her hands going numb.

"I'm glad to not be forced to deal with lawsuits from that direction down the line then. I'm not the one looking for more legal trouble, as it were, don't you agree, Ms. Courtenay?"

More legal trouble?

Unreadable eyes held Vi's for a second, and then, before Vi could comprehend what Renate was asking her, her inter-locutor took a sip from her delicate coffee cup.

"Zizou, make yourself useful and bring Ms. Courtenay breakfast." Vi blinked at his raising an eyebrow in her direction then, as if shaking himself, quickly scrambling into action. Renate smirked. "He's spoiled by all of you kowtowing to him. A genius with food, but he needs a shorter leash."

Vi's anxiety conjured an image she really didn't need in that particular moment, despite it being a humorous, if highly pornographic, one. She valiantly chose not to look at him as he brought her a tray with scrambled eggs and, inexplicably, a mug of herbal tea. She stared up at him.

"Ugh..."

Renate lifted her chin to dismiss Zizou before he could answer.

"Like you need more caffeine, Ms. Courtenay."

Vi granted her the point and decided to eat her food. If her mouth was occupied, there was less chance she might say something to offend the formidable woman in front of her. Plus, she had a feeling Renate had flagged her down for a reason.

Silence reigned for a while, with Renate seemingly oblivious to her breakfast companion and Vi biding her time.

Renate placed her hand on the front page of Le Figaro, and Vi felt everything inside her tense up.

Here it comes...

But Renate turned away for a second, as if prolonging the moment, drawing out the expectations, or perhaps considering her next words. Her eyes took in the busy street coming alive around them, with people hurrying about their mornings, dogs being walked, and pigeons overlooking the bustle with disgust and feigning indifference towards the scraps.

Finally, she turned back, and the eyes leisurely observing the street were now honed on Vi with determination.

"Lucci will be foregoing all shows for the next year, both their spring and the fall haute couture collections scrapped. This...," she said, tapping a finger on the cover of the newspaper, "is what attracted your attention earlier."

Something in Renate's tone made Vi take notice. With her heart already in her throat, she struggled to swallow her rather excellent food. Since it had been phrased as a statement and not a question, Vi forced herself to continue to eat and allow Renate to say what she obviously wanted to say.

"Word is that their designs for the spring and fall of next year were stolen."

Vi concentrated on not allowing her hand to shake as she forked up more eggs, while Renate proceeded, never taking her eyes off Vi.

"Fashion espionage is both very common and absolutely uncommon at these levels, Ms. Courtenay." When Vi raised her eyes, Renate's burned with strange fervor.

"What do you mean?" She almost gave herself a high five for keeping her voice steady.

"Concepts get stolen all the time, we just don't call it theft. Fashion is not a precise science and two things can look alike without being a carbon copy of each other. You can be inspired by someone else's design, you can even come up with something that is astonishingly close to what another designer has envisioned."

Renate took a small silver case out of her gigantic purse and lit up a long, black cigarillo.

"However." She took a long drag, and Vi was mesmerized by how Zizou materialized seemingly out of thin air with an ashtray, which Renate accepted with an almost imperceptible nod. "When the whole collection appears as a cheap knockoff with an online outlet, stitch for stitch, a year before it is supposed to go into production? That is corporate espionage and subsequent theft, Ms. Courtenay. And that is why Lucci pulled next year's entire lineup."

Vi gulped and hoped that the street noise covered the sound. Her palms were wet and her stomach was in knots.

"Do the police have any leads?"

Renate made a face. "I have no faith in the French police. But rumor has it that Alberto and Romina hired a very expensive private investigative firm to look into the whole thing."

Before Vi could reply, Renate made a dismissive gesture. "Waste of money, if you ask me. But insurance? That's a different story. They will dig and dig and dig, because if Lucci's theft insurance is anything like ours, the payout will be massive, and the insurance company will be desperate to find the culprit."

Vi gulped again and tried to cover it with a cough, though she suspected Renate could see right through her, and through all of her sudden suspicions regarding the true reasons for her internship. Even so, Renate seemed to choose to ignore it for now, and continued.

"They've shut down the website that sold the designs, but it already made millions overnight. And once this kind of genie is out of the bottle, putting it back will be impossible. Thousands of websites will sprout up in the coming weeks, carrying Lucci knockoff designs that will look and feel like the pulled collection and cost a fraction of what Lucci would have charged for them."

She took another drag of her cigarillo, and Vi could see how much the conversation was affecting Renate, the knuckles of her other hand white against her coffee cup.

"The efforts of a great number of people, the efforts of countless days, millions of dollars, were in vain because someone just wanted their work product. And then took it. Because they had the opportunity to do so."

The look in Renate's eyes made the hair on Vi's neck stand on end, except not in a good way this time. She reached for her tea, and now her hand did tremble. Renate watched her take a sip, then extinguished the cigarillo by stabbing it in the ashtray with considerably more force than necessary.

"I've never heard of anything like this happening." The words left Vi's mouth before she could stop them.

What an inane thing to say.

Who was she to think herself an expert? But Renate didn't mock her, nor did she wave at her dismissively as Vi had expected.

"It's because when it does happen, it is mostly kept quiet. The fact that the Luccis are going to the media with this and are willing to withstand public scrutiny and law enforcement involvement is new and unprecedented. And maybe, just maybe, they will be able to stop this."

"Stop what?" Vi's voice was barely a whisper as she watched Renate's eyes look at her through the cloud of smoke as she lit a new cigarillo.

"Stop this from happening again. Happening elsewhere. Happening at Lilien." The pit in Vi's stomach widened, and the food churned in it unpleasantly.

6

ONCE UPON A SAFE HAVEN

enevieve Courtenay was a very bad liar. It was a
well-documented affliction. God knows she'd paid
for it with nannies, boarding school teachers, and
pupils alike many times, because she was that bad at it. So
often, she had, in fact, dropped the practice altogether.

She'd come out to her parents pretty much as soon as she'd
figured herself out, since there was no use hiding it. Her father,
absent as he often was, would have still seen through whatever
stammering explanation she'd have given to his vague,
perfunctory question whether she was seeing anyone. So Vi
stopped hiding and took his disappointment, as well as her
stepsisters' ridicule. If her stepmother had thoughts about the
matter, Gwyneth did not bother sharing.

She rarely bothered with anything when it came to Vi.
She'd married her father when Vi was a shy, introverted, and
mostly silent teenager hiding in her room, and she never cared
enough to pry her out of it. Gwyneth had her daughters, who
were the apple of her eye, and the rest mattered very little. She
liked her clothes to be couture, her cars to be Mercedes, and

her lodgings at the Ritz. She also liked that Vi was rarely heard or seen.

So it was particularly disconcerting that, during dinner at her parents' penthouse on the Rue de Rivoli, it was Gwyneth who homed in on Vi's skittishness surrounding the subject of her current employment.

"How is Lilien Haus, Genevieve? Rumor has it Franziska is having a difficult time with next year's collection."

That was the other thing. Gwyneth, who was neither gainful nor employed, knew every single rumor that Paris—or London or New York, depending on where the family was at the given moment—had to offer. She attended every party, every event, and every drawing room tea, where such salient details were currency. And Gwyneth knew their value very well.

With all the sisters employed at various fashion houses this summer, it appeared like, for once, the entirety of the Courtenays' world revolved around couture. Vi, who hadn't given it any thought months ago when the arrangements were announced, was now second-guessing many of those decisions.

"Ah...", she took a careful bite of her fish, the cook as excellent as ever, and pretended to chew to allow anyone else to interject.

Inevitably, and blessedly in this instance, Kylie took it upon herself to make that happen.

"I heard she's a raving demon. And that Lilien is a hellscape. That she runs around in those shit-stomping boots of hers, kicking everything and everyone. I actually half expected Vi to come home beaten and bruised. If anyone is going to set that woman off, it's sure to be you. What with you falling and stumbling and stammering and whatever other disaster you manage to get yourself into..."

The old jab didn't even hurt. Kylie wasn't trying too hard. Vi stabbed a piece of glazed carrot and waited for another beat.

True to form, Gigi wasn't far behind. "Mother, I kept telling you it was a bad idea to get Vi this job. Either Kylie or I should have landed Lilien Haus. It's actually a challenge. I'm already bored with my cozy office and attending all these planning meetings." Gigi looked Vi up and down with a smirk on her face, and Vi took a calming breath.

Never let them see you uncomfortable. They will stick their fingers in that wound until it bleeds all over you.

The piece of fortune cookie wisdom came to her unbidden. She didn't need a self-help book to keep her mouth shut. That was the only thing that had saved her these past ten years, anyway.

Gigi sneered, her pretty face turning ugly on a dime. "Still, this one being the walking calamity she is, I bet she's getting a lot of menial tasks there. Are you a good little gopher, Vi?"

The girls laughed, and Gwyneth proceeded to signal for a second helping with a snap of her fingers, already looking bored with the conversation around her.

Vi lowered her eyes to her plate. The joy of being more than that in the past weeks, the nights spent with Chiara practicing photography or being her own personal mannequin—even if she'd opened her big mouth and somehow offended Chiara— was all hers, and she was not going to be sharing any of that with her family.

Still, when she noticed the sudden chill, she lifted her head to see her father's gaze on her. His expression was calculating, eyes cold and aloof. Vi had seen that look before. As if he wasn't looking at her at all, as if she was not important in what he was thinking, a means to an end, a tool, and he was figuring out how to use it more efficiently.

Vi almost shivered, collecting herself at the last moment and reaching for her glass. Charles said nothing, his eyes finally leaving her, and focusing his attention on Kylie who was shifting in her seat, a ball of energy this evening, her voice high-pitched with excitement as she spoke.

"And how did you all like the mess at Lucci? Total disaster. I thought Romina would fling herself off that ridiculous, kitschy balcony of theirs. So much drama!"

Vi gripped the fork tighter as dread pooled in her stomach. Her stepsister was spending her summer working for them. She, of course, wasn't a gopher. Tucked safely into the marketing department, away from any kind of hard labor, Kylie was enjoying a decidedly fun and easy time.

"How did Alberto react?" Charles' voice held all the nonchalance of a summer breeze, yet it set Vi's teeth on edge. He wasn't the family member who'd care about any of this. Gwyneth was the gossipy fashionista. But her stepmother held her tongue.

Kylie—pleased to, for once, attract Charles' precious attention—preened at being center stage at the family table. Vi could practically see Gigi fuming in helpless bitterness at being downgraded to 'of no consequence' again.

"Alberto was turning all kinds of different shades of color. I've never seen a man go from pale to red to purple in the span of minutes. I swear, I thought he'd suffered some kind of heart attack. He's such a handsome man. Dunno what he's doing with that insipid Romina."

"Romina is the heiress to the vast Lucci fortune. The man is a leech. Albeit a handsome one." Gwyneth's remark made both Kylie and Gigi stick their heads together and giggle.

"You mean like Chiara?" Gigi's remark was thrown out there carelessly, yet Vi dropped her fork with enough clatter to suddenly find all eyes on her.

"She isn't a leech." She heard the words drop out of her mouth and, more so than usual, desperately wished to grab them, to swallow them, to have never uttered anything at all.

She so rarely gave her family any ammunition because, without fail, they'd load their viciousness onto those bullets and turn them against her.

"And what is she, Genevieve? Come now, impart your dubious wisdom on us..." Her father's sharp gaze was unwavering. She'd given him an opening, shown a vulnerability, and he'd taken it and made that bullet hole wider.

"She... um... She does designs." She looked anywhere but at Charles as she spoke and could sense the irritation radiating from him.

"Speak up, girl! *Mumble, mumble.* If that is how you speak at Lilien, it's no wonder Frankie walks all over you." His voice dripped with so much disdain, Vi, for the thousandth time, wondered why he hated her so much, and what she could do so her own father would look at her with something at least resembling love for once. She'd probably give her left hand for that. Right hand too. How pathetic was it to wish for love from a parent who had nothing but contempt for you?

Still, he glared at her expectantly, and Kylie and Gigi grinned from ear to ear, enjoying her misery. Gwyneth was scrolling through her phone and predictably could not be bothered.

"Chiara designs most of Lilien's concepts. Frankie is just there. A figurehead, if you will. From everything I've seen, Chiara is solely responsible for all the new collections and has been for much of the past decade." For a second, a pin could have dropped and it would have been as loud as thunder.

If Vi thought imparting this massive bit of information to her family would make her feel accomplished, she was mistaken. Because—despite the whispered 'omg', 'no way', and 'this is huge' from her stepsisters and stepmother—observing the sly smile curve her father's lips, she instantly regretted divulging this tidbit to him.

To them, information did equal currency, after all. If

Charles Courtenay had taught her one thing, it was that. And she had just given him power in some wicked game he was playing in which she knew she was nothing but a pawn. A pawn who seemed to have done her job for the day, because as his lips stretched back into a thin line, he looked at Vi with approval.

Still, something in Vi sensed that the approbation was dangerous. To whom or why, she couldn't say, and so she did the only thing that remained. Misdirection. Call the fire onto herself and make him forget. Strange how she was doing so much of that these days. And all for Chiara. Maybe it was something she needed to think about more, but right now it was imperative he be distracted from whatever sinister plot he was concocting.

"And she is teaching me photography. I think she believes I can be one of the in-house photographers."

That didn't get Charles to even lower his wine glass.

"You? A photographer? Are we back to those useless 'visions' of yours, Genevieve?"

Charles reached for the newspaper again, obviously not impressed with either the conversation around him or his dinner.

"She believes in my abilities."

Well, now she had his full attention.

"Genevieve, once this summer is over, you will go back to being what a Courtenay is, and all this ridiculous idiocy you call ambition and *vision* is just that... *idiocy*. A Courtenay is not a goddamn gopher taking pictures! They serve us. I have been teaching you for years, and you still don't understand the place you occupy in society. You should aspire to marry, have children, continue my line. Bar that, at least make something useful of your life, not hide behind pipe dreams—"

"Charles."

To Vi's surprise, a quiet word from Gwyneth stopped the

customary tirade. Her stepmother touched her temple and closed her eyes. Well, Charles' outbursts were known to give headaches to those unfortunate enough to be nearby.

"Genevieve, that's enough." Vi almost smiled. Gwyneth knew Vi wasn't the one causing the commotion, but chastising her father wasn't something her stepmother ever attempted. Funny how women always played this game of deflection in the name of peace.

Gwyneth's eyes were as disinterested as always when she spoke again.

"Before Chiara realizes that she's wasting her time, the minimum you can do is try to learn something. There's a Nikon in the second parlor. At least have good enough equipment not to embarrass your father further, since I can only imagine what the people at Lilien think of the way you dress and conduct yourself."

Vi mumbled her apologies and her thanks, but inside she was soaring. In spite of her long-term interest in photography, she'd never had money for a good camera. And while Chiara would surely have provided her with the right equipment, she knew she actually brought something to the table now, and there wouldn't be any pity for her in Chiara's eyes this time around.

Charles, clearly having moved on from the subject, leaned over to Gwyneth to ask about some reception or other they were going to after dinner.

Vi had never been more glad not to be invited, but when the housekeeper cleaned the table and brought her father his ever-present after-dinner glass of port, she again found herself alone in his presence as the other women went to get ready.

They were silent for a long moment, him sipping his wine and not paying any attention to her, and her trying to figure out how to unobtrusively get up and ask to be excused—from this exorbitant penthouse, perhaps from this family, if only that were possible.

He beat her to it, though, still not looking at her.

"You can leave, Genevieve." He lit up his cigar, knowing full well she hated the smell, and frowned when she coughed. As she stood and hurried to the door, his quietly murmured, "and don't screw up," followed her out the door.

Screw up what?

The thought raced through her mind even as the smell chased her away.

THE SUMMER EVENING welcomed her with a light drizzle, and she mindlessly followed the crowds meandering in the warmth and in the remarkably fresh scent of the Parisian streets, thankful for her waterproof backpack that shielded her newly acquired camera. She had no destination, so the cafes and bars passed her by, people enjoying their evening under awnings and parasols, sipping Bordeaux or whatever else one sipped while enjoying an evening out, while Vi's shirt was getting heavier on her shoulders.

The coolness of the raindrops provided a welcome distraction from the burning shame that was eating at her.

She understood her father didn't love her, although she didn't know why. She lived with it, was accustomed to it, and had long since stopped questioning the reasons. But on nights like this, the skin she'd grown over old wounds broke open, and the desperation of a child seeking her dad's approval surfaced in all its pitiful meekness for everyone to see. It was never pretty. Yet it was always painful. And as he rejected her again and again, shame always followed in the footsteps of her desperation.

Vi walked on, the drizzle turning into a steady rainfall, her shirt clinging to her skin and her Converses filling with water. She shivered.

The cold Vi could bear. It was the knowledge that she had once again been this hungry for approval and even for a hint of affection from her family, that she'd inadvertently spilled other people's secrets that now burned her throat.

When her angry tears fell, the rain obscured them among the rivulets on her face, and she felt somewhat comforted.

And when Rue Saint-Honoré's pavement greeted her shoes, she felt safer still. She said a silent prayer, even as the bellhop at the Hotel Crillon gave her his usual dirty look as she passed by.

Vi knew she looked awful. She didn't need the overworked man to tell her so. Hair plastered to her scalp and clothes drenched, water sloshing in her shoes, she was sure a drowned rat made for a seemlier picture. It didn't matter. Her legs were taking her to where her heart wanted to be. Guilty as it was. Of so many things.

So what was one more? One more secret. One more betrayal. One more instance of greed. Of coveting something that wasn't hers and would never *be* hers.

Vi bit her lip in an effort to stop the tears, then bit harder when the treacherous emotions overwhelmed her, anyway.

By the time she reached Lilien Haus, she was shaking like a leaf and unable to stop. Clearly, this has not been her best decision. But the lights from the fifth floor shone like a beacon. Chiara was still here, and despite the way they parted the last time they'd seen each other, Vi knew she couldn't turn away.

The lion-headed door knocker felt like it was made of lead, so heavy, her fingers seemed unable to even encircle it.

She sent a prayer that her feeble attempts would be successful, hoping the sounds would echo up the empty hall-ways, then shook her head at the situation where a 'godless heathen' like her—according to her father—who believed in nothing, had suddenly found religion.

Time stretched. Interminable. And among the storm and Vi's turmoil, the door opened and there was the goddess Vi realized she was praying to.

Chiara stood in front of her, illuminated by the light of the bright foyer, her hair held up by the ever-present pencil, signaling she had been working. Her dark eyes widened with honest concern, followed by a semblance of understanding Vi could only wish to ever achieve. Since she herself couldn't explain why she was even here.

But Chiara, in her great wisdom, seemed to comprehend. And in her even greater kindness did not ask any questions. She simply extended her hand, blue veins translucent under the pale skin, and Vi surrendered.

"Come," Chiara took her frigid fingers in her warm ones and instead of heading for the stairs, led Vi to the rarely used elevator in the corner of the foyer. The ride up was slow, but Chiara's hand did not let go of hers, and Vi proceeded to close her eyes and imagined the warmth of that hand slowly spreading through hers, up her arm and into her heart. The thought was so foolish. *She* was such a fool. And Vi was so done for.

When the door slid open, the lights of the studio were like a balm on her aching skin. Despite their brightness, despite their harshness, Vi felt at home. Even Binoche's displeasure at her interrupted sleep was comforting. It was so damn absurd. So...

"...silly." She heard herself say the word and stopped in her tracks, expecting Chiara to ask her, to react in some way. Instead, her hand was gently tugged in the direction of the bathroom. There, Chiara took one of the soft, fluffy towels hanging off the hook in the corner, and to Vi's shock, slowly started to wipe her tear- and rain-stained face.

"It's not absurd. Something happened and it hurt you, and

it's not silly to feel the way you do." Chiara's voice sounded so matter-of-fact, so devoid of pity or any other outward emotion, Vi was mortified.

"The way I feel?" She didn't recognize her own voice, broken and hollow even to her ears.

"Adrift," Chiara murmured, and her hand settled on the nape of Vi's neck, steadying her, terrifying her with how amazing it felt to be touched, to be anchored.

"I guess... I'm sorry, I'm intruding. I don't know why I came here..." Vi stumbled over her own words. But she was embarrassed and also scared.

It was too much. Too good. The towel was heavenly on her skin, so soft it was making her feel sleepy, which was quite a contrast to the strange sensation spreading through her from her neck, still being firmly held in that graceful hand.

"Are you hungry? Have you had anything to eat today, Vi? You're shaking." Chiara's expressive eyes were staring right at her, and Vi felt herself sink deeper, breathless.

What was air?

"You called me Vi. Again." She wanted the ground to swallow her. Why was her brain not connecting with her mouth today of all days? First at her father's dinner and now here, twice already?

"I did, and I will go back to 'Ms. Courtenay' if you don't relax. If I didn't want visitors, I wouldn't have come down, and if I didn't want you, I wouldn't have opened the door when I realized it was you."

Vi almost shook her head when her heart sped up a bit at the double entendre. Or at what she desperately wanted to believe was one.

"You're busy." Vi didn't ask. Chiara was here, in this studio, so she was obviously occupied. That was the default for this woman, whom Vi had seen bent over the drawing board at all hours. Wouldn't she be home otherwise? With Frankie... Vi's stomach plummeted at that thought, and then she felt embarrassed again.

But Chiara just shook her head and tugged on the soggy tails of Vi's shirt, hanging limply at her waist.

"I have some of my clothes here. You need to get out of these. I can't imagine it's all that comfortable, wet as you are." But just as Vi opened her mouth to argue, a fingertip landed on her lips, rendering her absolutely still, certain that a mere breeze could knock her over. The skin against her mouth was soft, the subtle fragrance of patchouli reaching her, no doubt from being applied to that wrist all those hours ago when Chiara had gotten ready for her day.

"Don't fight me on this, darling. I'll bring the clothes, you dry off, and we will see about the weight of the world on your shoulders that brought you here."

And with that, she was gone, leaving Vi with the ghost of her fingers on her lips and a whole heart full of longing.

7

ONCE UPON A FAMILY RECIPE

Genevieve Courtenay was in trouble. There wasn't any other way to describe what was happening to her. Not when it came to Chiara Conti-Lilienfeld.

Thirty minutes ago, she'd basically sleepwalked her way to Rue Saint-Honoré and interrupted Chiara's work, only to be smothered in fluffy towels, given a change of clothes that consisted of a pair of Chiara's own jeans and a white, flowing button-down. It took all her strength of will to not bury her face in the soft, worn cotton that smelled like verbena, patchouli and something that could only be Chiara.

Vi mentally patted herself on the back for acting like a grownup and not a teenager with a crush. A teen she was not. Her feelings, however, were a lot tougher to disprove. She looked at herself in the mirror. Cheeks flaming, eyes alight. Yeah, some things she couldn't deny. Like the crush. Or the sleeves that were way too long.

"I can't help loving manly cuts." Chiara murmured, reading Vi's mind. It seemed this woman was always halfway in her head, and Vi fervently hoped she would be able to at least hide some of her thoughts from her. Some of her emotions. She was starting to recognize there were a lot of them. Hence her earlier realization that she was done for.

Vi rolled her eyes at herself. When you knew who owned a piece of clothing by simply sniffing it, you were indeed absolutely and completely in the deepest of troubles. The kind that was not only bothersome but also painful. Because, as Vi was used to reminding herself on a daily basis by now, *this* particular trouble, carefully rolling up the sleeves for her now—was it hot in here?—was somebody's wife.

If Vi had any issue remembering Chiara's marital status, her phone vibrated right on time, and one glance at the screen confirmed it was Frankie. Chiara's eyes did not waver from her task of arranging the shirt's open collar, and she kept at it until she was finished, giving Vi's cleft chin a tap with her fingertip before she finally picked it up, only to lay it back down carefully. Too carefully.

"How about dinner? You didn't answer me earlier when I asked if you'd had any?" The voice, again, was too careful, too precise, lacking any true emotion, and Vi found herself shaking her head. A few bites of fish and carrots didn't count.

"Settled then. Any preference as to what you'd like to eat? I know Zizou kind of takes our opinions out of the equation, since he decides what we should eat every day, but tonight, we'll feast like queens with our own free will." She laughed, the joy just as forced as her nonchalant tone.

"Are you all right?" Vi's words seemed to surprise Chiara, and maybe she shouldn't have said them, but by now Vi was pretty much resigned to uttering things around this woman that were impossible to explain or contain. She briefly wondered if she'd offended again, and was ready with an apology for butting into what was obviously none of her business.

Yet Chiara didn't look upset or annoyed. As the mask of nonchalance slipped for a moment, that dreaded sad look was back, the worry line between her brows deepening, before smoothing out as she visibly collected herself. She passed by the little bread loaf that Binoche made on the windowsill and gave the cat an absentminded pat, as if drawing strength from the tidy little animal.

"Why?" Vi wasn't entirely certain that Chiara really wanted to know the reason behind her earlier questions.

"It's, well..., late, and you're still here."

Somewhere in the distance, a church bell rang. Chiara's face, half-hidden in shadows, looked angelic, like it was made for towers and damnation, gothic cathedrals and absolution.

"This is the time when I feel most like myself. Nobody calls, nobody needs anything, there are no expectations of me, hence no consequences for not meeting them."

Vi felt her eyebrows rising, it was such a peculiar thing to say. But Chiara just waved her curiosity away.

"Never mind that. Honestly if you're asking me about my time management, you might as well be asking me about dragon herding. I'm equally good at both. Or, well... equally as bad. The post-its only do so much, darling."

As Vi's eyebrows rose even higher so they damn near crawled off her forehead, Chiara simply took her hand.

"Actually, I think I'd manage dragons much better." She winked at Vi, who felt herself smiling back awkwardly, as Chiara went on. "Listen, my mother's recipes always make me feel better, regardless of how shitty my day is. Or how many bad memories are associated with my childhood. Any of those meals still reminds me of being cared for, no matter what. And I didn't have many *no matter whats* back then either. How about I cook you dinner, darling, and you tell me what brought you here?"

Vi actually looked around herself on instinct and immediately felt ashamed of her own gesture. She hunched her shoulders, but Chiara just tsked and then tugged her by the hand to the far corner of the studio. Vi sighed at the continued skin-to-skin contact that felt so good. Too good.

Married... married... married...

The chant in her head, however, was quickly replaced by surprise as a panel in the wall opened into a small but brightly lit kitchen with stainless steel appliances and a marble-topped island in the center. It was cozy, with potted ivy plants arranged to hang off several of the built-ins and a well-used cast-iron skillet peeking at her from one of the assorted hooks.

"Sit, Cinderella, and talk. Start with, are you allergic to anything? Garlic? Oregano? Basil or parsley?"

"What are you making?" Vi made herself comfortable at the island on one of the barstools with soft, brown leather seats.

Chiara opened the large fridge, hidden behind a wood panel that made it seem like it was just another kitchen cabinet, and tsked.

"I'm not yet sure."

Vi smiled. "Then why ask me about garlic or oregano or basil or parsley?"

Chiara turned to her, hands full of produce, and laughed.

"For someone who has lived as cosmopolitan a life as you have, and with your noble blood and royal relations, you're a peasant when it comes to cuisine. This is pretty much you telling me you were raised as an American without telling me you were raised as an American. Philistines, the lot of them. Because they bastardize Italian cooking and still have no idea what it truly is. And yes, I am very much a snob who is a fan of generalization."

Eyes sparkling, hands waving, Chiara was a sight to see. Dropping every pretense, she was clearly on a long-established rant about an issue that was important to her. Vi's smile turned into a full-blown grin, and Chiara's eyes narrowed.

"Laughing at me now? When I'm cooking you a feast?"

"Well, you were so aggrieved just then about Americans and their lack of gastronomic culture, it was kind of funny. But I do understand what you're saying... That Italian cuisine is pretty much made up of all those herbs and vegetables. To which I am not allergic. Except to anything olive-related." Vi shuddered. "I used to call them 'little poison balls' as a kid, cause I'd get so sick every time I had them..."

Chiara turned around and gave her one of those looks that would have been comical in how deeply insulted and offended she seemed to be, except she was clearly trying to be sensitive to Vi's condition.

"Really? Oli—" Chiara stopped midway through the word as Vi shriveled into herself, anticipating it. But she didn't say it. "Of all the things..."

"You asked. And yeah, unfortunately, I had to tell Zizou, and he damn near laughed his skinny, non-existent ass off."

"It's not funny. Health issues are never funny, so you can tell him he can piss off. In fact, tell him Madame C said so. That will teach him."

"That would put the fear of God in him." Vi smiled and almost swallowed her tongue as Chiara turned back to her, eyes alight with mischief.

"You think I'm God, darling? How wonderful."

Vi had to laugh. Chiara was being absolutely adorable in light of this domesticity, and Vi felt comfortable, relaxed, her troubles slipping off her shoulders, and that made her just a touch brave.

"I think you're trouble. And I think you enjoy teasing me." Was it the rain that was making her courageous, or the twilight that made everything seem unreal?

"I confess. But only because you're so puzzled by it. It's

endearing. I hear that you move mountains for Aoife, your vision is unrivaled—in fact, I may need to watch my back—and you have the best eye for perspective I've ever seen. Yet you get so adorably flustered, I can't help it. Never change."

Chiara's eyes still danced with the little devils that seemed to have way too much fun, but it didn't come across like it was at Vi's expense. Instead, it felt like a warm hug. Like the one Chiara had given her all those weeks ago. The one that had brought their bodies flush together and gave Vi fever dreams.

"I'm just all sorts of sad for you about the allergy. But it's not a problem. We will improvise."

Magically, a long, slim bottle of grapeseed oil appeared on the kitchen counter.

Chiara rolled her eyes at Vi's jaw going slack and turned back towards the open refrigerator, cursing under her breath when it beeped rather annoyingly, signaling that the door had been ajar for too long. The unnerving sound seemed to make up her mind for her.

"Meatballs it is then." As soon as the sentence had left Chiara's mouth, Binoche was up and running towards them from her perch on the window. Chiara straightened again, knocking the door shut with her knee, since her hands were now full of various containers. She was carefully balancing her load while also trying to avoid stepping on the cat who was doing her damnedest to get in her way.

Placing everything in haphazard order on the counter, Chiara stepped to the sink and smirked at Binoche, who was now sitting on her haunches by her feet, tail tucked neatly around her paws.

Vi watched, mesmerized by the little dance between woman and cat that seemed to have been performed many a time, despite the two of them only having been acquainted for a few weeks.

Had it really been this short of a time? Vi felt like she had known both Chiara and the little cat for years.

Under Vi's gaze, the woman in question thoroughly washed her hands, like a doctor gearing up for surgery. Then she turned and, for a moment, seemed to be lost in thought, eyebrows raised, as if surprised at what she was doing. Vi's heart stuttered, and she was unsure why.

The post-its, the uncertainty at times like these when the tasks were a set of complex steps...

Chiara caught her staring and scrunched her nose, looking ten years younger and so carefree that all of Vi's thoughts scattered.

Then she absentmindedly reached for the first thing on the counter, and it was like the earlier confusion didn't exist. She was full of purpose now, emptying what looked like two different kinds of minced meat into a bowl, but not before she gave a tiny morsel to the daintily meowing Binoche. Chiara suddenly turned her eyes towards Vi, pinning her with a speculative gaze.

"Now that we have established your dubious understanding of cuisine, Ms. Courtenay, feel free to tell me what brings you to my door at whatever ungodly hour it is. And also, tell me why Aoife was crowing that you beat somebody over at Rue de Bretagne into submission. Oh and, I think I have figured out that Queen Anne issue I had with the cream lace."

As Vi still sat silently, blinking in surprise at the stream of topics thrown her way, Chiara waved her free hand at her and reached for a couple of eggs, which she promptly broke into the bowl. Then, as Vi looked on, she took out a baguette and proceeded to tear it into strips, which she carefully added to the egg and mince mix. When Chiara coughed gently, Vi knew her staring time was up.

As Chiara set the bowl aside, she looked down at her white apron and stared at an egg yolk stain. Under Vi's dumbfounded stare, she smiled a bit sheepishly and took off the apron, pulling another one from the cupboard.

"I can't stand yellow stains."

When she started washing the tomatoes and basil leaves, Vi found her voice. It was easier to let her words fly when she was directing them at Chiara's back.

"I'm twenty-five years old, and although I know it's ludicrous. I still hope one day my father will suddenly love me."

Chiara didn't turn around, but the hands that were slicing the tomatoes stopped for a few seconds before her shoulders dropped slightly, and she went back to her task. Vi exhaled, feeling freer than she had in years, simply from speaking the words out loud.

"In his eyes, I can't seem to do anything right. And yet I keep trying. I know that it won't make any difference to him, no matter what I do. But I can't seem to stop, you know?" She wanted to drop her head on the counter. Why would Chiara know? *How* would Chiara know?

"I do, actually." And now Chiara turned, fingers covered in tomato juice, looking a bit like blood in the bright, strangely distorted light of the kitchen. "Sometimes we go our entire lives trying to persuade the people we love that we are worthy of them."

Was Chiara talking about Vi's father? Or was she talking about Frankie? Vi didn't have the courage to ask. It seemed like such an intimate conversation.

"I don't feel I'm worthy, though—"

"You are!" Chiara's voice rang loud, and the knife sliced through the parsley with enough force to impale itself on the wooden cutting board. Binoche meowed, but it sounded more like a sign of support, especially since she was suddenly circling Vi's feet, rubbing herself against her, a rarity in and of itself. She must seem really pitiful to elicit sympathy from a cat.

Chiara resumed her work, periodically giving Vi sidelong

glances as if making sure she'd heard her words. A tiny drop of tomato juice splattered on the front of the apron and Vi lifted her eyebrows, but Chiara simply waved her on.

"It's different. Red stains are fine, it's the yellow ones that are a problem. Sue me. It's my apron." ˙

Chiara took a deep breath, ignored Vi's look of amusement, and went back to the stove with single-minded focus. Silence reigned once again, before Chiara turned back to face Vi, her eyes tumultuous.

"You should never beg for love. And you should never be made to work for it, Vi. It's that simple. There is no earning it, there is no deserving it. You are a joy. And you are precious. Your family, those who vowed to love and cherish you, should not make you prove your worth over and over again." Chiara looked at her with a particular fervor then, and Vi felt pinned by that gaze, imprisoned by its intensity.

When the amber eyes dropped back to the chopping board, Vi thought that it was a very strange choice of words Chiara had made. 'Those who vowed' didn't necessarily describe family. But she refused to allow herself to drift down that pathway. That way lay madness and a glimmering hope that Vi surely was better off extinguishing. Too bad she wasn't strong enough.

If Chiara was unhappy in her marriage, it was none of Vi's business. If Chiara was unhappy, period, it wasn't Vi's business either.

She has a wife... She has a wife...

Meanwhile, the reason for said flickering hope moved to the stove where the iron skillet now sizzled and the sauce simmered.

"I normally bake the meatballs before I fry them. That was my mother's secret. Never *fry* them to readiness, bake them, then put them in the sauce for a few minutes in the skillet. But sadly I'm too hungry, and our conversation is turning really sad, darling. Still, it's nothing that good meatballs with tomato sauce and freshly-baked bread can't cure."

Chiara smiled as she stirred the sauce, and Vi found herself smiling back, basking in the glory of that joy that looked honest and true and so right amidst the storm outside and the turmoil in her own heart. Something to hold on to. Something to cherish. As Chiara should be, held and cherished.

THEY ATE IN COMPANIONABLE SILENCE, dipping torn pieces of their baguette into the skillet that Chiara had placed between them on the island, Binoche in a food coma at their feet.

The sauce burned Vi's mouth, hot, flavor exploding, and she tried to pretend that her eyes were watering from the spices.

Chiara reached over with her hand, and Vi felt her wipe away a tear, and it only made her want to cry all the harder. She willed herself to swallow both the mouthful of delicious food and her melancholy.

"I'm sorry. Here I am, single-handedly disproving your theory of how meatballs make everything better..." Vi deliberately took a big bite from her plate and dunked another piece of bread into the rich sauce.

"Oh, don't worry, they are still the only balls that make anything better. The fact that you've eaten five by now just proves my point." Vi startled and then laughed, guffawing, trying not to choke. "If you think I didn't count, you are deluding yourself. I know I'm a good cook. And it's obvious you love my food."

God, that confidence. So sexy. So damn attractive.

"I'm not denying anything. I mean, after five meatballs, I have no defense left, ma'am. You're fantastic at this. At a great many other things, I reckon..." Vi trailed off, uncertain how her words would be received. She desperately hoped Chiara wouldn't think she was out of line. Because she really wasn't flirting, she wasn't, she meant—

"Fashion?" Chiara gestured towards the studio's lights with her fork, and to the numerous workstations where her designs lay in various states of readiness. The ivory gown that Vi had modeled for alterations was separated from the rest, now on a mannequin, like a beacon, drawing Vi's gaze. It was just so different from everything else, and she couldn't help but find it the most beautiful thing in the room.

Its creator aside.

"Vision." Vi hadn't known what she was going to say until it was out of her mouth, and she wondered about this affliction she was developing—especially around Chiara—and whether it was her nascent feelings or the calm and kindness of her interlocutor that compelled her to speak her mind.

"That's very kind, Ms. Courtenay." Chiara averted her eyes as she spoke, and before Vi could say anything else, rose and took her plate to the sink.

"I am sorry if I upset you. Again, I must say. I didn't mean to now, and I certainly did not mean to last time."

When Chiara turned to her, hands under the running faucet, her smile was wistful. "You didn't. I think I might have overreacted then, and it's in the past now, anyway. And no, you did nothing wrong just now, either. You know how, when you hear something for the first time in a long time, it usually catches you unawares?"

Vi furrowed her brow. "*Something?*"

Chiara turned back to the sink, her shoulders tense and any trace of humor disappeared from her voice when she spoke.

"Apologies."

Vi almost tumbled off her stool, her bare feet slipping on the small stainless steel support, disturbing the lounging

Binoche, and this time Chiara's smile was a touch indulgent as Vi approached her with her own plate.

"I'm surprised you're not all black and blue, the way you go through life, Vi." She said it quietly, and there was so much kindness in those words, in sharp relief from the earlier taunts of her stepsisters, Vi's eyes filled again. So she just stood there as Chiara rinsed her plate and closed the dishwasher before turning to her fully.

The sob caught in her chest, the full comfort of being seen and understood descending upon her like a weighted blanket, as a graceful hand lifted, and Chiara's fingers smoothed the frown line between her brows.

"You are still so tender. Come. With your clothes in the dryer, you're my prisoner for a bit longer. Would you help me with the gown again? I swear I get some of my best ideas when you're wearing my work." She said the last part as she took Vi's hand, but did not tug, and Vi sighed.

Chiara, despite her words, was still giving her a choice, to say no, to leave. And after her dinner with her family, where she couldn't even leave the table to go to the bathroom without being interrogated by her father, she felt her chest expand.

And so she was the one to tug on Chiara's hand. They reached the mannequin, and Chiara gently removed the gown, handing it to Vi. "Can you manage to put it on yourself? Without rending it, if at all possible?"

"I've been dressing myself since I was about three, I think?"

"Ah, sarcasm, a fool's clutch, Ms. Courtenay. Go get dressed, shout for me if you get stuck."

Not a chance, Vi thought.

∼

Vi jinxed herself. The gown was still held together by pins among the temporary stitches, and she got pierced by one.

Then, as she pulled it over her, the unmistakable sound of something rending followed.

"Uh-oh—" She was tempted to smack herself over the forehead and might have, if her arms weren't stuck inside the fabric that was covering her face. But the second she opened her mouth, Chiara's footsteps could be heard hurrying towards her.

"Ms. Courtenay, don't tell me..." She stopped on the other side of the divider still guarding Vi's modesty, which was honestly dwindling by the second. In her panties and bra, the gown now a tangle, half on, half hanging off her arms, Vi closed her eyes and surrendered to her fate.

"How about I won't tell you, but you come in and see for yourself?" There was a sound of the divider sliding open, and then a deep, exasperated sigh. Maybe Chiara would let her live or even leave? Vi was beyond embarrassed, and for some reason, her sense of self-preservation was taking a back seat to her desire not to go. To not cut her time with this woman short just yet, even if it was at the cost of her own humiliation.

But Chiara didn't humiliate her. The sigh was followed by a few words that sounded suspiciously like "*diamine,*" but despite understanding very little of the murmured curses, Vi felt the warm palm on her shoulder blade through the material of the gown. The touch turned into a careful pull as Chiara delicately guided her back under the studio lights. Through the material over her eyes, Vi could see the bright lights and the outline of her savior standing in front of her.

"I'm sorry. I hope I didn't ruin it? If you could just help me get it off, I'll pay to replace the material—"

"Shhh, Ms. Courtenay." The warm hands were back now, and the gown was tenderly, almost reverently, pulled off her face, then down her body. Finally, as she opened her eyes, she saw Chiara now on her knees, tugging the tangled and certainly mangled gown past her hips—which were only covered by a flimsy, lacy pair of boy shorts—then down her thighs and calves. Vi's brain promptly short-circuited.

Chiara was very careful with Vi's naked skin, despite there being so much of it on display, and she was grateful for that. But even as the skillful fingertips turned and straightened and pulled, Vi could feel their lingering touch.

A loud, slightly disgruntled meow sounded from the now ever-present basket on the wide windowsill. Binoche was probably reading her mind again, because the sound was also decidedly judgmental. Well, Vi was judging herself, too. She was ridiculous.

Worse, her reaction was inappropriate, and any second now Chiara would realize it and send her home.

But Chiara continued on her knees, examining what looked like a torn hemline, and Vi's imagination continued to run wild. Chiara hummed and sighed again, before slowly getting up, sure fingers tracing a seam, from knee to breast, setting Vi's skin on fire through the thin fabric. When Chiara's gaze wandered —surely perusing the gown for any other signs of Vi having been her good-old clumsy, destructive self—Vi felt that gaze in her soul.

"You know, Ms. Courtenay, if I was any other person, I'd be slightly more than pissed that, here I am putting all these hours into these creations, and then you stumble about, tear off and ruin hemlines, only to inspire me."

She finished speaking when they were finally face to face and Vi gulped. Those eyes looked into hers, all-seeing, all-understanding. Vi had nowhere to hide, nowhere to shuffle her uncomfortable emotions that pressed so hard on her shoulders.

Chiara angled her head to the side, as she often did when she was trying to figure out the flaw in a design, and Vi found herself scrambling for words.

"A talent?" She quipped uselessly, but to her relief, Chiara's mouth quirked at the corners, and when the expressive eyes crinkled—displaying those crow's feet that were so dangerous to Vi—she felt like she'd touched the sky.

A real smile.

"Well, don't let it go to your head, and please do not ruin any more of my creations. Do we have a deal?" She smoothed the silk at Vi's shoulder, fixing a pin that was coming loose, her hands gentle as always.

"Only on one condition." Where had this piece of courage even come from? Vi almost groaned. Sometimes she really wished she were just a bit better at controlling herself.

"My, you are cheeky. But given how you've just really inspired a breakthrough on this design by mangling the hemline, I'll bite the bullet and ask. What's your condition?"

Grabbing another handful of pins, Chiara was now standing behind Vi, her hands in the mirror a study of proficiency and skill, working fast, carefully, flying along the deep cut of the back. The déjà vu was immersive. Despite having seen it only once before, Vi thought she'd never tire of beholding their reflections together in the mirror. They should not fit, and yet they did. Of the same height, which was a rarity in itself for Vi, of the same build. They looked good. Vi swallowed convulsively and Chiara's eyes gazed up at her, full of concern.

"Can we go back to me asking you questions?" Vi shivered, and Chiara's hands stopped before a shawl was gently placed over her naked shoulders, leaving the lower back exposed to Chiara's ministrations, yet ensuring Vi was kept warm. How was she to tell this woman that she wasn't cold and her shiver had nothing to do with the temperature?

"I have a feeling I know exactly what you're going to ask me, Vi. And if I'm right, I also have a feeling I will regret ever making that promise. But sure, let's see if I can keep some of my secrets from those eyes of yours that are too smart for your own good."

The words alone might have stung, but the kindness behind them encouraged Vi to continue.

"You think I'm too smart?" Okay, that was not what she planned to say. She cringed, the shawl not at all disguising her gesture of embarrassment.

"That is your question?" Chiara tugged on a piece of material at Vi's waist, making her stand straighter and meeting her eyes in the mirror.

"Ah... No?"

"So is it 'ah' or is it 'no', Ms. Courtenay?" An eyebrow rose majestically, and it was just so unfair. Such a regal gesture, so evocative. And one that turned Vi completely useless.

Chiara let the other eyebrow join the first, and Vi could see a blush creep up her chest, generously exposed by the low cut of the unfinished dress. As she closed her eyes, she heard Chiara's chuckle.

"You are so easy to tease, darling. Too easy. But even if that wasn't your question, *you are smart.* And bright. Shining. You are so utterly new to any of this. Life, fashion..."

Chiara grew silent, and her eyes fell back to the pins she was working into a complicated fold on Vi's hip, but Vi felt as if she'd been taunted again. Was that how Chiara saw her? As naïve? As young and inexperienced and childish?

"I beg to differ." This time, Vi didn't cringe. She didn't even care what she was saying and, more importantly, how. She felt like she'd been misunderstood enough for one evening. And while it was par for the course for her family, Chiara was a different story.

It must have been Vi's intonation. Chiara's head whipped up and her hands on Vi stilled. Again, their eyes met in the mirror, and Vi didn't shy away this time. She let the hurt of the slight wash over her. She was so damn tired of everyone treating her like an ingénue, or worse, just gullible.

To her credit, Chiara didn't mock her. Nor did she wave away the situation as Vi had expected her to. She bit her lip, thoughtfully chewing on it, still closely watching Vi in the mirror.

"I apologize, Ms. Courtenay. Sometimes, you remind me of myself at your age. Eager and wide-eyed. Life stepped in and fixed that pretty quickly, though. But please, do not for one moment assume that I don't see the wounds reality already left on you. I don't know much about you. You keep your cards close to your vest, despite being a seemingly open and friendly person. You have a secret, something mysterious about you, Cenerella. There's a reason that nickname stuck with you, and not because you keep losing your shoes."

She leaned just a touch closer, and Vi's breath caught at the intensity of the gaze. "My words were meant to indicate that I envy you. Just a little. Just a touch. I envy you the joy and the serenity and the sheer kindness you carry everywhere despite those wounds, the deep and the shallow."

Vi sighed, letting the air whoosh out of her lungs and taking another deep breath. The room did not tilt. Nor did she hear an operatic aria or anything equally as cliché, but the lamps did seem to shine just a bit brighter. And now Vi did feel foolish. And exposed. And very, very raw.

"I wish for you to always keep it. To hold on to it. To cherish and enhance it as you live. It's so rare. This light of yours. This newness." Chiara's voice sounded both wistful and regretful, and Vi almost turned around, but strong arms settled on her shoulders, over the material, warming her better than the shawl and grounding her like few things ever had. "Now, before both of us get all weepy here, ask your question. The one you really wanted to ask. I assume it was about something I inadvertently blabbered on about earlier in the evening?"

Vi swallowed around the lump in her throat.

"Yes, I wanted to ask about the lack of apologies in your life. But I'm concerned that might lead to more melancholic moments?" Vi's hand trembled, but she didn't care. Under both their gazes, she lifted it and laid it carefully over the one on her left shoulder.

Chiara gasped, then coughed when their skin made contact, but Vi held on, in spite of being ready to be shaken off at any moment. The touch, intimate as it was, had nothing to do with her feelings for Chiara or her marital status or anything in between. Chiara was sad and Vi was there. In that moment, to Vi, that was the extent of it.

She gently squeezed her fingers over Chiara's and felt the hand underneath hers turn so that they were now palm to palm. A few seconds later, Chiara interlaced their fingers, soft skin gliding over soft skin, the lump in Vi's throat getting larger by the second. She gulped around it as Chiara let go and stepped away from Vi.

"And you doubted that you're astute? Case in point. I shared something I shouldn't have uttered out loud, Ms. Courtenay. My issues with my spouse are mine alone. And as much as I like you and respect you, I would never use you. Even as a shoulder to cry on."

"You'd be welcome to it." Vi squeezed her eyes shut. Chiara didn't need her.

"You are very sweet and very endearing, Ms. Courtenay."

Vi huffed and moved closer to the windowsill where Binoche was lying in a perfect cat loaf again, little feet tucked under her chocolate body.

"Brioche is endearing. Chiara, I can help you..."

As expected, Binoche threw her a decidedly dirty look before turning away and making biscuits on the large cat bed before settling down and presenting Vi with her tail end.

Chiara laughed, and this time, Vi thought, the laughter wasn't sincere.

"We all make our choices, Cenerella. And don't call her Brioche, or the Fairy Godmother might not help you go to the ball."

The dark eyes sparkled with something, and Vi's heart lifted.

"Ball?"

8

ONCE UPON A TENNIS MATCH

Genevieve Courtenay had never been to a ball. Her family had attended plenty. Her royal relatives—whom she never saw but frequently heard about, especially since she'd gotten hired at Lilien Haus—had thrown even more. But Vi herself had never been part of the family dealings.

"Why are you this excited?" Aoife took a big swig from her water bottle and made a decisive cut in the light blue chiffon. "Shit."

"What was that saying? Measure twice, cut once? And what did that design even do to you?" Vi focused the shutter and snapped a few pictures of Aoife's disgruntled face. Say what you want about Gwyneth, but her love for all things top-notch was on display here. The camera was state-of-the art.

"Stop it. The fortune cookie wisdom. I don't understand why she has to have this particular cut. She had some kind of epiphany over hemlines." Aoife got up and walked away from the workstation Vi was sitting on. She wisely kept her mouth shut about anything related to adjustments in the design and why Chiara might have changed her mind. A few presses of a button could be heard, and very soon, the aroma of coffee wafted Vi's way.

She knew Aoife wasn't really upset with her when her mentor carried two mugs back from the little kitchenette. Which had nothing on Chiara's beautiful, wood-toned kitchen with its gorgeous island, tasty food, comfortable silences, and absolutely inappropriate fantasies. Vi glugged her coffee, burned her tongue, and felt like it was karma, punishing her for the prurient thoughts.

"To answer your question, Cinderella, I've worked with Chiara for ages now. And I've never had anything like this happen." Vi opened her mouth to ask, then, with her tongue still smarting, once again thought better of it, closed it again, and they instead sat in silence, both sipping their drinks.

Aoife looked at the swaths of material on her workstation that reminded Vi of the sky and shook her head.

"Kid, I was your age when I met her. She was this absolutely massive star on the catwalk, and I was helping my dad, who was the backstage hand at the London Fashion Week. Much like yourself these past few weeks, she just couldn't seem to stop tearing things. I helped her, again, and again. By the end of that week, I was her personal seamstress. When she married Frankie, who was flying high with Lilien Haus, my fate was sealed."

She took a longer sip, eyelids fluttering in the simple plea-sure of enjoying the brew. Vi couldn't relate, even if her mouth hadn't still been burning.

"All of this is just not like her. She calls me in the middle of the night with the same five words that mostly spell doom for me since they'll lead to a shit ton of work. 'I have an idea, Sully!' For the past fifteen years, Lilien Haus' collections have been planned years in advance. Sure, we'd tweak them here and there. We even scrapped a collection once, because Chiara's red theme didn't jibe with the Tuscany Yellow DeVor put out that year."

Aoife guffawed at the memory, and Vi drew her eyebrows together. She had a vague recollection of hearing the name.

"Cinderella, honestly, if not for your storied bloodline and your genuine, good disposition and skill with that monstrosity..." Aoife nodded towards the camera in Vi's hand with her chin. "I wonder about you sometimes. DeVor runs fashion, kiddo. Actually, scratch that! DeVor is *FASHION* with capital letters. They, whoever *they* may be, are a name behind the artist who has a grip on the industry. If you ask me, it's inconvenient. You make plans, and then someone comes in and their whims change everything. But... do not, under any circumstances, tell Chiara I said so."

Vi made the gesture of zipping her mouth shut and waved for Aoife to go on as she tried to sip her coffee slowly, her burned tongue aching in protest. It still didn't taste like anything she wanted to spend her whole life depending on.

"Anyway, Google is your friend, young lady. Especially working in this industry, you can't escape DeVor. I may kvetch that they make us change our plans sometimes, but they're a genius. Frankie wanted to buy Chiara an original DeVor painting once but was outbid at the auction. If you ask me, she wasn't trying hard enough."

Vi's chest clenched as it always did when Frankie's name came up in the context of not doing more for Chiara, so she was hasty in changing the subject.

"I've heard of DeVor. I think my stepmother worships at their altar."

"Ha, of course she does. I mean, good on her for having great taste, but no one has ever accused Gwyneth Courtenay of not being trendy. There were pictures in the evening paper of her and your dad attending something or another at George V. She looked very chic."

Gwyneth always looked chic, even as Vi's father laid off another maid without paying her for the month she'd been hired for, claiming she, 'had not met the expectations of the probation period.' Vi mentally calculated how much was left in her bank account and fervently prayed she'd be able to score more dinners here at Lilien Haus, because she had to pay that poor woman something. And her parents were already looking for a new patsy.

"In any case, it's not important, kid. What *is* important is that this was the first year ever where Chiara didn't have any ideas. I didn't get any midnight calls to discuss the cut and stitching, to argue halter over blouson and pegged line versus V-line." Aoife sighed, and Vi wanted to go and give her a hug.

After a few seconds of deliberation, she chose not to interrupt. She wanted to hear this out all the way through.

"So now, this particular collection? It gives off these wedding vibes that you homed in on that first night. She is holed up there all day and all night, and it doesn't help that Frankie is never around—"

Aoife stopped mid-sentence, narrowed her eyes, and gave Vi a pointed glare.

"This conversation never happened, kid. I will just say that she has struggled with this concept and hence I'm struggling too, because I don't understand it."

Vi nodded, intent on showing Aoife that she could absolutely be trusted. Plus, she really didn't want to hear about how Frankie, once again, was not there for her wife, leaving Chiara to do all the heavy lifting of conceptualizing and putting together a collection.

"In any case, perhaps it's better this way. At least this year, with the Lucci thing. And now, have you heard? Word is D&B are being blackmailed too. Except, unlike Lucci who stood their ground, D&B are actually willing to pay, so that they don't have to cancel their latest line since they are headlining Paris and plan to do a showing at Cannes before then."

Well, this was news to Vi. She felt a chill run down her spine and unbidden, a piece of conversation at the dinner table came back to her. Her step-sisters boasting about access. Vi shivered. First Lucci and now D&B?

This wasn't happening...

Aoife, oblivious to Vi's internal dread, simply continued.

"So, us not having finalized anything before Paris and New York and London is a good thing this time around. But, as your skinny butt knows—I assume that's why you're bouncing around my workstations and counters—Frankie insisted on doing a soft opening of sorts, a pre-showing if you will, and managed to get the head of Hollywood's number one movie studio, Gannon-McMillan's very own Neve Blackthorne, to throw open her mansion's doors to host a private but massive ball. We will be showcasing the new collection—such as it'll be by then—among canapés and good champagne."

Now, Neve Blackthorne Vi had heard of. Even if she wasn't a movie buff, one knew about Neve Blackthorne. One simply tended to. She was inescapable, ever-present. Sort of eternal, despite only being in her late thirties. She ran Hollywood with an iron fist and her name alone sold magazines and movies and goddamn ice cream at the North Pole, if she were to ever lower herself to promoting anything like that.

Even though her stomach was still in knots, Vi couldn't contain her excitement and bounced even higher on her perch.

"Oh, god, you are such a baby gay! Stop that, the woman is married! Not to mention straight."

"*The woman* is going through a very ugly divorce, Aoife, keep up. And I honestly don't care. She is scary as hell, and I doubt I'll speak one word to her. But, I am just so freaking excited to even be there! To actually be contracted to photograph the ball. A dream, Aoife."

Yes, it was an extremely limited showing in terms of pieces, and yes, Vi was part of a bigger team of photographers, but none of that mattered. Vi wasn't *just* going to a ball. She was one step closer to making that dream of having a career in photography come true.

Vi squealed and then glanced down at the cooling mug in her hand. She set it aside carefully, conscious she was always likely to spill it all over her white cargo pants or her equally white Converses. And with her luck, she'd damage the camera too, and that was one thing she cherished most these days. The camera was her ticket to the ball.

Vi was still unsure how it had happened. Her evenings with Chiara had become a fixture in her workdays and so had the photography lessons. She listened to professional podcasts on the subject all the time, devoured every single issue of Poise magazine she could get her hands on, and poured over all the books Chiara's library held.

And Chiara thought she was good. In fact, Chiara had such a high opinion of her skills, she had asked her to shoot the showing of the collection at the Blackthorne Ball at Lago di Como. Vi squealed again and hugged herself. She was going to Italy. In two weeks!

Her enthusiasm almost made her completely skip over the part of the conversation that suddenly let dread into her chest. She wanted to avoid it, wanted to cling to the camera, and maybe sidestep it entirely in her joy. But the cold held her, the numbness of it making her even more aware.

"Aoife... You said D&B are in trouble?" Her own voice sounded rusty, like she had forgotten how to speak, and Aoife's head shot up from her work. She gave Vi a long stare, eyes narrowing before she returned to the sewing machine.

"Not the Lucci kind of trouble, because they're just a different kind of breed, I think. Lucci just changed hands after whatshisface croaked..."

"You mean Santiago Lucci? The late, great Santi Lucci, inventor of no less than twenty variations of the pleated skirt? Like the one you're stitching together right now?" Vi gestured vaguely in the direction of the gown Aoife had been working on and brought the camera to her eye, happy to hide behind it, taking a precious picture of Aoife's disgruntled face.

"Smartass. Didn't know your Dior from your Chanel, your bootcut from your skinny and now you're giving me fashion history lessons? I know all that. And I also know that no one can sew this better than I can anyway, other than the person who designed this gown to begin with. Speaking of which, she's been making you read up on stuff, hasn't she?"

"She has, plus she just loves to talk about it. And I enjoy listening to her." Vi felt her color rise as she stopped abruptly, wishing she could make herself scarce.

But Aoife just shook her head and let the comment slide without mocking her or warning her, or giving her any kind of lecture about crushing on a married woman.

Vi wondered if Aoife was well aware of how hopeless it was anyway, and wasn't even a little bit concerned about Vi making a fool of herself by trying anything. Not that Vi would. Ever. Try anything. She respected Chiara too much. And she was well aware she had exactly zero chances, even if Chiara were single.

It was time to change the subject back to what was making the hairs on her neck stand up in suspicion and vague premonition. Thinking about it made the lump in her throat grow to the size of a baseball.

"So D&B are gonna fight this thing, whatever it is? Blackmail you said?"

"I'm not exactly sure *what* it is, but they haven't pulled out of any of their planned events. Which might mean they will either pay to have the collection concepts safely returned to them. Or they have contacted the police..."

Vi's heart stilled for a moment before going into overdrive.

Her palms got sweaty, and she had to put the camera down on the desk next to herself for fear that it might slip from her fingers.

Police.

Vi gulped and tried to tamp down her anxiety.

"How do you know, Aoife?"

"Renate brought the news this morning. She didn't tell you?"

"I don't think Renate likes me very much." It had been on her mind ever since Renate intercepted her at Zizou's for that impromptu breakfast. Sitting there, barely tasting her food under the steady unblinking gaze that seemed miles away yet still heavily present, Vi knew Renate had some suspicions. Things Vi didn't even want to consider.

"Renate doesn't particularly like anyone. But she pays our salaries and does so on time and they're very generous, so why would I care? And why would you care, for that matter?"

Aoife sat back and gave Vi a long stare.

"I do though—"

"You shouldn't. Take it from me, kiddo, don't give a flying fuck what people think of you. It's called being free. And always take yours. Always. Nobody will ever give you anything. You have to take it." Aoife coughed, trying to mask the way her voice suddenly went gruff, but Vi heard it.

"You've been doing amazing work. The way you show ambition and cleverness, talent, too. Manage to keep that up, and you'll be fine. Just don't miss your big chance. Watch for it and don't let it slip by. Hasn't Chiara taught you that much? Among all those fashion history lessons and photography classes? Freedom is underrated, Vi."

In spite of her worries, Vi wanted to thank Aoife for the compliment, even if it felt not entirely earned, and tell her that yes, Chiara had strongly encouraged independence and not begging for scraps from anyone, her family included.

Right when she opened her mouth, Frankie staggered into the room smelling of cigarettes and something remarkably like cheap gin. Vi was all too familiar with the scent, since that was her father's drink of choice when money was particularly tight.

Frankie's clothes were rumpled and her boots looked like she'd walked through mud instead of being fresh off the plane. Vi remembered Aoife mentioning some event in London at any rate. Or was it Rome? All Vi knew was that Chiara never talked about her wife *or* her trips. And that she herself tried to never, ever place any significance on that fact.

"And how goes—in your case overrated—freedom, Franziska?" Aoife's acid-dripping tone interrupted Vi's musings.

"Wonderful, Sully. Just wonderful. Milan was a blast, thank you very much for asking."

Frankie leaned over Aoife's desk and made a grab for her coffee. She didn't succeed as, to Vi's astonishment, Aoife moved the mug and slapped Frankie's hand. For some reason, the smack sounded and looked like it was harder than the attempted thievery deserved. But Frankie just flashed that charming grin of hers, and Vi sighed.

How many times had she asked herself what Chiara saw in this woman? She was rude, tactless, and often plain cruel and absolutely untempered in pretty much everything. And yet, there was a certain something about her that Vi couldn't put her finger on.

"Milan now, was it? I thought you went to Rome." Aoife challenged as Frankie just waved at her.

"You thought wrong, Sully." Frankie flung off her jacket, then headed to the corner kitchen and made herself at home, opening then closing the refrigerator. When she produced what looked suspiciously like Vi's lunch and gobbled down half of it in two bites, Aoife looked poised to jump up, but Vi just shook her head. There was no point in saying anything anymore.

"There is food in the kitchen in my studio, Frankie." Chiara's voice from the doorway made all three heads turn. Vi's whirled around so abruptly, she felt the world spinning for a second. Or maybe it was just from how beautiful Chiara looked? Yes, Vi was a total goner.

That fresh, no-makeup face, the vivid lines of dark brows, and the sparkling eyes surrounded by the longest lashes. She was barefoot again, which meant she'd been working on the collection. Had she even gone home these past several days?

When Vi arrived in the morning, Chiara would already be at Lilien Haus, and she'd be there every night to push Vi out the door and on her way home through the dark, winding Paris streets.

The room was eerily silent for a few seconds, and only Vi's stomach rumbling interrupted the tension, reminding everyone of the subject at hand.

"No fun in that, my love." Frankie spoke around a mouthful of food and then bent her head to get another even bigger bite from what looked like an excellent croque-monsieur. Zizou had been particularly magnanimous to her today, Vi thought. Shame she wouldn't get to enjoy the result of his generosity.

The response seemed to only upset Chiara more, as the down-turned lips pursed and her eyes narrowed. Vi watched emotions chase one another on that sculpted face before the mask of calmness slipped back on, and Chiara turned her eyes to her.

"Well, in that case, stop by the studio later, Ms. Courtenay. Lunch will be in the oven. I made lasagna last night. No olive oil."

Chiara stepped further into the room and picked up Frankie's discarded leather jacket from the floor. She folded it neatly, but before she could raise it to her face, seemingly to smell it, Frankie enveloped her in a massive hug and took it out of her hands.

"My wife has come down from her royal throne to lay down the law. Mere mortals, bow down to the Queen of Paris. I saw that article in Poise the other day, speculating how the once-reigning royalty of the catwalk is nowhere to be found these days. They even hypothesized whether you are feeding the hungry and the homeless now, Your Majesty."

Vi could see Aoife ball her fists. The article had come out as part of a 'Where Are They Now?' series about former mega-stars of the fashion industry, be it models or designers, who had vanished from the public eye. Vi thought it hadn't been very well-researched for such a massive publication. Chiara, after all, wasn't even hiding.

It was surreal that nobody knew she was, in fact, the genius behind every Lilien Haus creation, but she wasn't exactly cloistered either. If that wasn't enough to anger Vi, Frankie's ridicule and her mocking words in evident jealousy of the title the magazine had bestowed on Chiara were enough to set her teeth on edge.

But Chiara didn't seem to be affected, merely walking up to Aoife's workstation and tracing a line of stitching on the gown draped over it as she spoke. "Well, Ms. Courtenay deserves to have a meal."

And now both Vi and Aoife watched the ongoing conversation as if they were watching a tennis match.

Serve. Parry.

"*Ms. Courtenay*," Frankie almost sang the name, mocking Chiara's inflection, "is a member of a royal family who can feed herself, surely. Dress herself, too. But I'm told you've been mostly undressing her these days."

Vi flinched. *Backhand across the court.*

She wanted to disappear, her earlier desire to make herself scarce returning tenfold. So Frankie knew about their modeling sessions. And mocked those, too. She felt like the Queen Anne dress, stomped into dirt by Frankie's massive boots. Moments she treasured, moments she cherished, were smeared with mud, with malice on that sneering face.

Chiara, however, seemed unperturbed.

"And her standing in as a model has ensured the collection was finished in record time. I can only thank her for her dedication and largesse with her evenings, for which we are not paying her nearly enough."

Another parry, coming much faster and diagonally, Frankie scrambling to keep up.

"Well, she has my thanks then as well."

An appeasing cut to the net.

"And yet, all you do is eat her food. When my *muse* goes to Rome and comes back from Milan, I'm grateful for any and all assistance the Universe provides. You should be too, my love. It's your name on the facade, after all."

And with that devastating forehand to the back line, Chiara exited the studio, taking set, game and match in one strike.

9

ONCE UPON A SILVER GOWN

Genevieve Courtenay was not very good at sitting still. Especially not when her father was monologuing. Particularly not when he was monologuing about their place in the history of European Kings.

But the Earldom of Rae and hence the entire Courtenay lineage, Vi always wanted to counter, weren't kings of anything. She knew better though. In fact, she had known better since he'd grounded her for saying just that years ago. She'd spent the next two Christmases at the boarding school for being a 'disrespectful brat.'

However, it was still nothing but the truth. Her mother had been the king's sister. Since King Aleric had heirs, there'd been close to zero chances that Vi's mother would ascend to the throne. And then her death at childbirth took care of that particular dream for Charles.

Her father himself, as the current Earl of Rae, was a descendent of William the Conqueror, but then who wasn't? The man had more descendants than Genghis Khan. Okay, that was an exaggeration on her part. But many. The man had many. Most

British nobility deemed themselves to be in some way connected to the ginger menace. And so were the Raes.

She blew her too long, ginger bangs out of her face and couldn't suppress a smile at her own train of thought, then quickly schooled her features, but it was too late.

"And what exactly is so funny, Genevieve?"

Her father was glaring at her, her stepsisters were elbowing each other in expectation of an evisceration, and her step-mother just turned the page of the issue of Poise Magazine she was perusing and read on.

"Ah... Nothing, father?"

"And yet you were acting foolishly. Care to explain yourself?"

Vi scrambled for something, *anything* useful to throw her family, who were out for their pound of flesh, and came up short. Her father stood, and she closed her eyes.

Here it comes.

Just then, the trill of her phone sounded from her messenger bag and interrupted the tension. She all but flew to the sofa, pulling out the ringing device.

"Hi Chiara."

The room froze and fell silent. Vi wanted to laugh again at how these people, who claimed blue blood in their veins, were so easily impressed by a famous name.

"I apologize for interrupting what I'm sure is an exciting evening, Ms. Courtenay—" Vi wanted to wrap herself in the low notes of that velvety voice.

"No, no, please, how can I help you?" Her father's face lost some of its rigidity, and he sat back down, his eyes gleaming with a light Vi did not like at all. In fact, this avariciousness where Vi's employment was concerned gave her a decidedly ominous feeling.

On the other hand, Gwyneth was watching her with a curious expression of something very close to actual approval.

"I was wondering if you have a gown to wear for the Blackthorne Ball." The voice sounded far away, like Vi was on speaker while Chiara was doing something at a distance from the phone. Which she probably was. The woman was always working.

"A gown for the Blackthorne Ball? I am sure I will find something?" She felt ridiculous repeating, but Gwyneth's expression grew even warmer, and she nodded slightly. It seemed like, for the first time in a long time, she had done something right.

"All right, then, Ms. Courtenay. But if you'd like my help to alter it, since I imagine it won't be yours..."

Gwyneth must have guessed what was going on, because she smiled wanly and nodded again as Vi hurried to answer. "Yes, yes, that's very generous... I will stop by tom—" Gwyneth's frown had Vi coughing and correcting course, "Tonight! If you're still at Lilien Haus?" Gwyneth had gotten up and motioned for Vi to follow her. Chiara chuckled in her ear, and it sent shivers down Vi's spine. As if intuiting her predicament, Gwyneth just shook her head.

"I will see you soon then, Ms. Courtenay." The line went dead, and Vi found herself in the inner sanctum. Gwyneth's closet. It was probably larger than Vi's shoebox apartment. Granted, the closet did also house several hundred shoeboxes.

She stood gawking, since the abundance of riches filling every cubbyhole, every shelf, never ceased to amaze her. Gwyneth returned with a long garment bag, the logo unmistakable on the front.

Vi's eyes went wide, but Gwyneth simply handed it to her and turned off the light in the magnificent space.

"As your father is prone to say—though god knows why, since you never listen to him anyway—don't screw up, Genevieve."

Vɪ sᴋɪᴘᴘᴇᴅ ᴍᴏʀᴇ than walked the few blocks to Rue Saint-Honoré, the gown in the garment bag giving her wings better than any energy drink ever could.

"I'm going to the ball!" She yelled as she passed Zizou who was quietly smoking on his corner and just shrugged, extinguishing his cigarette before motioning for her to wait. He went inside and returned a few minutes later with a small basket that resembled the traditional picnic variety. Indeed, a corner of a baguette was sticking out of it, and a checkered red and white cloth covered the rest.

"Leftovers. No olives. Now run along," he grouched at her after practically shoving the basket in her hands.

"Zou..."

"Monsieur Zizou to you." He tsked and lit another cigarette, waving her away. "And make sure Madame Conti eats something. She's wasting away."

Ah, Vi almost smiled. Almost. But who'd understand Zizou, who had the most obvious case of pining for Madame Conti, better than she did? The fact that he flat-out refused to call her anything other than "Madame Conti" warmed Vi's heart.

Take that, Frankie!

And she would make sure his request, worded more like an order, would be fulfilled. *Madame Conti* would eat tonight, because despite her always taking care of others, she never looked after herself. Must be all the herding-of-dragons skills she mentioned. Vi smiled at that. Only Chiara could make something challenging endearing.

Wʜɪᴄʜ ᴡᴀs ᴀ ᴛʀᴀᴠᴇsᴛʏ, really, Vi thought as Chiara unpacked the basket and her eyes danced with merriment and delight.

Someone should imprint those emotions on this beautiful face, because Chiara, above all, deserved to be happy. It suited her so well.

Binoche made herself a nuisance around their ankles, despite her bowl being full to the brim with wet food. Vi gave her a meaningful look, but the cat studiously ignored her by loudly demanding her due from her mistress. Chiara, in turn, chose not to pay attention to the little chocolate ball in favor of discovering the treasures Zizou had bestowed upon them.

"He's a good man, Zizou. Surly, but good. And for whatever else, he is an amazing cook." Chiara took out several carefully wrapped items. Vi preferred to look at the beautiful hands rather than at the food. Then what Chiara said caught up with her.

"*Whatever else?*"

Chiara stopped halfway into inventorying the basket, but the smile that followed didn't reach her eyes.

"He's a man of mystery and a Jack of many trades, Ms. Courtenay. Just... don't cross him."

That previous sense of foreboding returned, and Vi made herself appear busy unwrapping the sandwiches while her heart hammered.

Returning her gaze to her host who, with an indulgent smile, watched the cat saunter out of the kitchen with a prized piece of salami in her mouth, Vi racked her brain to try to recall the train of thought their conversation, so rudely interrupted by whatever cryptic warning Chiara had imparted on her earlier, had been on.

When the topic came back to her, Vi wanted to mention that, lately, she'd had no way to appreciate Zizou's great cooking, since her lunches always tended to disappear, but remembering how the last incident had gone, she chose to let it go and lighten the mood instead.

"He is surly, all right. And he's aware you haven't been

eating. Which isn't surprising, I guess. Maybe he isn't just a chef but also a spy and that's why you don't tell me more. Doesn't matter, I don't want to know anyway. La-la-la."

Chiara's smile brightened, and this time it reached her eyes as she bit into a large pear, juice coating her lips. Vi's hands twitched, wanting to reach out, to touch, to lean in and taste those lips that were undoubtedly sweet, even without the fruit making them look more luscious and delicious.

She swallowed hard. God, 'hopeless' wasn't even close to how bad she had it. The dictionary didn't have the words to describe how deeply and terribly Vi was gone for this woman. A woman who was now lifting fruit-stained fingers to her mouth, savoring the taste, making those absolutely illegal sounds of contentment, of satiation. If these sounds emanating from Chiara weren't outlawed yet, they damn sure better be, and soon.

"*Whatever else he is*, Zizou has been on his corner in his bistro for quite some time. He saw us move Lilien Haus from the other part of town to Saint-Honoré a few years ago. And I appreciate his friendship. He has been very good to us from the beginning, feeding us, catering our events, and doing all those other super-secret things that you don't want to know about. No, don't look like that. The man caters like an angel."

Vi faked a grin, happy for the banter and the distraction from all the nefariousness that may or may not be happening, and was about to launch into another litany of 'la-la-las', when Chiara reached across and covered Vi's insolent mouth with her hand.

And suddenly both of them stopped, standing very still, skin on skin, their eyes full of each other. Vi's, she knew, were all longing, and Chiara's held something she couldn't discern. Something hot was burning in those amber depths.

Chiara had touched her before. She'd had to, since she'd pretty much transformed Vi into her personal mannequin, and she had once silenced her in exactly the same fashion. But this was different.

As Vi inhaled the scent of the remnants of the pear, her lips moved ever so slightly over the warm, soft skin of Chiara's palm. She felt like she would never sate this hunger, this need to feel, to taste, like she could do this forever...

Except the moment Vi's lips moved, Chiara gasped, still unable to look away. And now Vi saw the regret and the gossamer apology staring unblinkingly back at her. So she was the one to turn her face, slowly dragging her mouth across the silky skin before breaking contact altogether, already missing the warmth and the connection.

Say something.

For once, Vi's thoughts arranged themselves into somewhat coherent, if faltering, words.

"I'm... uh... I'm kind of sad that we won't get to experience his catering at the Blackthorne Ball then..." She sounded foreign to herself, her voice infused with so much fake cheerfulness. Still, it seemed to work, since Chiara finally snapped out of whatever stupor had come over her when she'd touched Vi.

She moved away to examine the gown in the garment bag, and Vi wanted to weep, to shake her hands at whomever was up there in the clouds for putting her in this situation, where she was so hopelessly, helplessly attracted to someone who froze the moment she touched her skin. God, what must Chiara think of her?

"I don't think you will miss Zizou and his, granted, excellent cooking. Neve Blackthorne is known for her hospitality." Chiara seemed to have moved on from their awkward moment.

She unzipped the garment bag and was carefully extracting the chiffon and gauze. It hadn't occurred to Vi that she herself hadn't even peeked at the dress Gwyneth had handed her. The gown was less important than rushing over to see Chiara, to be with her, to bask in the time they spent together.

Now, seeing the material spilling out, Vi chewed her lip. Silver wasn't really her color. It clashed with her auburn curls and put even more focus on her much detested freckles. She bit her lip harder to avoid saying something that would sound like she was ungrateful or complaining.

Silver it was.

She was going to the ball, where she would enjoy herself and take the best pictures of the Lilien collection she possibly could and do it all in an ill-suited gown. Nobody cared about the photographer anyway. She wasn't in the foreground.

Moving on, then.

"I would have never put Neve Blackthorne and hospitality in the same sentence. She always seems so... I want to say 'aloof,' but it's probably more like 'majestic'. She's just so... everything. A touch scary, I guess." Vi shivered a little, and Chiara smiled.

"Neve is an interesting individual. And power can be scary. But it can also be sexy..." Chiara looked directly at Vi then, and Vi almost gulped, because now there was a mystery lurking behind those eyes, alight with a sort of mischief that Vi was entirely powerless to face. Aoife had been right. She *was* a rather useless baby gay.

"Yes, it can. But she is also very imposing. I mean, people say she rules over the whole of Hollywood." Vi's thoughts were scrambling in her head, jumping from one realization to the next, to the next, and she had no time to catalog them all.

And with Chiara's gaze on her, one eyebrow raised in the kind of expression one has when they read a book that is both amusing and puzzling, all Vi could hope for was that some of her pages would remain off limits, or that Chiara would get bored before she got to the salient parts, the ones that held all those secrets. Secrets that all, bar one, weren't even hers.

And despite Vi's fear that Chiara would be able to read her and unravel everything, the fact that she was falling for this woman was the secret Vi held closest. Tightest. Safest.

Oh, please, don't look!

Still, Chiara seemed content to stick to the surface and not examine things too deeply.

"You'll meet her and then you'll draw your own conclusions. I've stopped listening to what people say, Ms. Courtenay. They're cruel. Sometimes just for sport. And sometimes, they can't help themselves."

Chiara's tone was tinged with sadness again as she finally pulled all of the shimmering silver gown out of the garment bag. *Yep, still silver.* Still not Vi's color. "Will you put this on for me?"

The melancholy eyes narrowed as long fingers ran over the material of the gown.

"Um.." Vi's whole body froze at the way the words 'for me' caressed her skin like velvet. "I mean... Ah... It fits, I'm sure... Gwyneth gave it to me..."

"Gwyneth is your stepmother?" At Vi's nod, Chiara sucked on her lower lip thoughtfully. "This is from her personal wardrobe, I take it?" Something in the way Chiara spoke the word 'personal', the tone of it, had Vi shrinking into herself.

"Yes, again, I'm sorry if this is not fancy enough for the ball —" At the intense stare, Vi closed her mouth with a snap, and her hands automatically reached for the top button of her shirt. Chiara's lips pursed, and she just shook her head and handed Vi the gown. She could feel herself turn crimson. God, please, just once, could she stop falling over herself in front of this woman?

She hurried towards the small alcove where the divider would keep her modesty intact, only to stumble on her way, foot catching on absolutely nothing.

With her hands full of silver chiffon and as good as tied, the smooth floorboards loomed closer, and Vi closed her eyes in anticipation of a very nasty collision with the hard surface. The thought that a bruised black-and-blue face might match the accursed silver gown better than freckles and auburn flitted across her mind.

But before she hit the ground, a strong hand clenched around her upper arm, moments later the second one joined and despite her feet still being tangled around themselves hopelessly, Vi felt suspended for a second before Chiara's strength gave out, and both of them tumbled to the floor in a heap of limbs and chiffon.

Instead of hard wood, Vi found herself face down in the warm skin and soft silk of Chiara's shoulder. The subtleness of verbena, along with that unique glorious scent that was all Chiara, enveloped her. She took a gulp, filling her lungs with it, praying she'd never forget how it felt, and then the shoulder underneath her started to shake.

Vi lifted her head immediately, scrambling for purchase, to sit up, to lift herself off a prone Chiara who must be hurt, who must be having some kind of... fit of giggles?

Chiara was lying on the floor, surrounded by silver, and laughing, one shoulder exposed where her silk blouse had slipped down, and her hair now gloriously loose.

The sound of it filled the room with unabashed happiness. Vi's breath caught. She felt as if the world tilted, and the muted tones of the hot and sweltering Paris suddenly burst with color and vivacity. Chiara's laughter turned into a warm smile, and Vi's weak, already tender heart rolled in her chest. Laughter made Chiara come alive, and that smile made her shine with a different light. One that spoke of intimacy, of promises Vi had no business wanting to hear.

But want them she did. All of them. Even if, in that moment, Vi wondered—and not for the first time—what secrets this woman kept, because her eyes were filled with truth and honesty, with such openness it was painful to behold. Especially for Vi, who held so many.

She smiled, then hiccuped, trying to reign in her own reaction, which only made Chiara laugh harder. When Vi, in an attempt to hide her embarrassment, turned away and tugged her sneaker back on, Chiara sat up and placed a cool hand on Vi's cheek.

"Never ever change, Cinderella. Never. God, you're adorable." She let out another peel of laughter, watching Vi hastily tie the errant shoe.

After a while, Chiara's face settled into an indulgent smile. "I really want to see how the dress fits, since it's not yours. You're going to the ball, Ms. Courtenay. We can't have it look like you're wearing your stepmother's hand-me-down. Generous as it seems."

"You like the dress?" Vi carefully held out her hand, but Chiara was already standing up in one swift, graceful movement that Vi was certain shouldn't be possible for any regular human and was probably taught by yoga masters. It involved no hands and Chiara made it appear like the easiest thing in the world.

"I am not a fan of that brand, darling." Chiara wrinkled her nose, and the cuteness of it had Vi shaking her head. Mostly at herself. Because this infatuation was getting ridiculous. Who was she kidding? It *was* ridiculous.

"Why?"

"My, you'd think I would be used to your questions by now, Ms. Courtenay. I don't make a habit of badmouthing fellow professionals, and many great designers worked for this particular fashion house, but I've never walked for them, nor did I accept their ambassadorship when they offered."

Vi's eyes watched avidly as Chiara tugged on the cottontails of her blouse and popped the collar to give her that wonderful debonair appearance. She opened her mouth to ask for more, for details, but Chiara's raised hand stopped her in her tracks.

"Before you ask, Ms. Courtenay, I've never made any political statements in my life. Models, 'super' or otherwise, aren't hired for their intellect or to take a social stand, but I've always felt that we glossed over the fact that the founder of this brand openly associated with Nazis right here in the heart of Paris for most of the Second World War rather quickly."

Vi instinctively glanced at the small, classy, very recognizable tag among the many frills of the gown in her hands and gulped.

"Don't worry, Ms. Courtenay, the actual designer of this piece was a darling of a man, and as someone who knew him personally for many years, I can confirm he had a lot of love for that particular gown you'll be wearing. I remember the year it was shown in London. He was very proud. I was simply surprised that your stepmother is the one who owns it now."

The sense of dread, of impending doom returned a hundredfold, hitting Vi square in the chest. Had her father given Gwyneth this gown?

Meanwhile Chiara went on, her voice devoid of any emotion, in such contrast to the disquietude wrecking Vi.

"I'm not one to keep track of these things, you might have guessed I don't keep track of much to begin with..." Her smile of self-deprecation was more a grimace of practiced nonchalance. "But I seem to remember that whole collection meeting a rather strange fate and mostly disappearing from the public eye after a series of, shall we say, *mishaps*? Now run along and change, provided you're still willing to model it for me."

It took Vi every single last ounce of control not to gulp again, or blink, or say something undoubtedly foolish.

Mishaps. Right.

Why were there always 'mishaps' when it came to the Courtenays? She felt herself going pale and hoped against hope that her freckles and the diffuse evening light would not let Chiara see it.

But Chiara *did* see it, Vi was certain of it, because she still read Vi like an open book, and instead of skimming the surface, this time the amber eyes were delving in all the way.

And so Vi took off in the direction of the small alcove again, her outer thigh smarting with whatever bruise was forming from the fall and providing a welcome distraction from all the potential pain she didn't want to think about.

WHEN SHE EMERGED, the night was settling heavily outside the windows and the suspended lights of the studio came on. In a familiar pose, Chiara was bent over the workstation, the line of her neck and shoulders open to the cool air. Vi realized she must have lost a shirt button or two in their collision. It was transfixing, light and shadow playing on those chiseled collarbones, over the smooth blades of bone and sinew under translucent skin.

Chiara raised her eyes to Vi, lips wrapped around a pencil, and suddenly it didn't matter that the gown was absolutely wrong for her, and that despite fitting perfectly, the color still washed her out.

It was the wrong gown, the wrong ball, the absolute wrong time. But this was the right woman. The only woman, and Vi looked away, if only to not allow the tears that were burning her eyes to fall. Love hurt.

10

ONCE UPON AN UNWELCOME REVELATION

Genevieve Courtenay usually could control her reactions very well. Especially on the day of a major event, such as the Blackthorne Ball on Lake Como. And especially when one was raised by Charles Courtenay, whose temper was explosive and often resulted in being grounded or dismissed from his attention for weeks, for those who dared to show any kind of emotion he disapproved of. So Vi knew how to school her features.

Thanks, Dad.

However, even years of humiliating remarks from her father did not prepare her for acting like a Sphinx when certain things were on display right in front of her. Like a half-naked model in an ivory gown Vi herself had worn many times—since she'd been the original mannequin—that was practically sewn on and who was splayed on Neve Blackthorne's Louis XIV dining room table, with three of Frankie Lilienfeld's fingers knuckle-deep, pumping inside of her.

Vi dropped her clutch and was eternally grateful the precious camera was hanging off her neck, because surely she'd have smashed the lens. Her stomach dropped, as usually happened to her in situations of heightened tension.

And there was a lot of tension, judging by the corded muscles and tendons on the long neck of the still-nameless model. She was clearly very close, and in observing said rapture, Frankie was equally distracted. But not distracted enough, because the second the clutch hit the floor, she turned, her handsome face undergoing quite a transformation from ecstasy to shock to fear and then to absolute rage.

Well, rage Vi was very familiar with, as well as screaming. Because a lot of it followed. Both from Frankie and from the model, as her lover wrenched her fingers from her.

"Frankie! For fuck's sake!" The woman wailed, hands immediately clutching her underwear. She would have probably rounded on Frankie, but the latter was already in motion, wiping wet fingers on her purple corduroy trousers and striding towards Vi, who was standing petrified.

She only marginally registered the model, still ivory-clad and wincing in pain, flee through the opposite door. Vi had no time for other observations of any kind. She stood terror-struck, unable to move, like a deer in the headlights, even though Frankie was so very close now.

"I will end you, Courtenay!" and, "here you are, kiddo," sounded at the same time, one from her front and one from behind her, drowning each other out. Vi suddenly found herself sandwiched between the enraged Frankie, who was desperately trying to reel it in, and a concerned and harried Aoife.

"What are you doing here?" and, "what is going on here?" were uttered similarly simultaneously, and now Vi wanted to laugh.

Aoife's arrival had probably interrupted a scene that would have had disastrous results for all involved, because the remnants of Frankie's earlier encounter were smeared all over her pants, and the remains of that insane rage were only now leaving her face. Aoife would have either witnessed the sex or the violence.

What would have happened, Vi couldn't begin to guess, and she peripherally wondered if Frankie had known herself. Her anger was blistering, her fists clenched, and Vi doubted her mind had been fully engaged. Frankie had gone from lust to fury to now trying to hide the results of both.

Aoife, on the other hand, clearly had been rushed and busy and panicking over something or other related to the impending first-ever showing of the Lilien Haus Spring Collection, but now her eyes took on that absolutely focused sheen. They looked from Vi, pale and trembling, to Frankie, face and neck blotched, and back again to Vi, who was desperately attempting not to let her fear show, before finally zeroing back in on Frankie.

She pushed her way into the room, along with the still shaking Vi. With all the doors closed, including the one which the aggrieved model had used to flee, they were now in relative privacy.

In the silence, Frankie's breathing was particularly loud, and Vi refused to look at her crotch to see if the zipper was down. But Aoife gave Frankie, who now hastily retreated to the bar and busied herself with pouring a rather large drink, a long, thorough once-over. Since she didn't immediately tear into her, Vi assumed nothing was out of place. She wanted to sigh in relief.

"Now, Sully—"

"Spare me. Spare this kid, too. From whatever was about to happen here. Or has it already happened then?" Aoife's accent was suddenly a lot more pronounced as her voice rose along with the question.

"No, Aoife—" Frankie took a long gulp of what looked like straight up vodka and Vi almost winced. That had to hurt.

"Shut up. Shut up, because I cannot deal with this now." Aoife tossed her hands up in the air and walked back and forth across the room. She stopped, stomped her foot, gave Frankie a decidedly nasty glare, then looked at Vi. "Chiara needs you, Vi. They are about to start the preparations, and some of the models are already dressed. She said you should be out there since she wants backstage shots." Vi almost collapsed from sheer relief, the weight of the impending confrontation suddenly lifting.

She took the camera strap off her neck and, brandishing it in front of herself, wanted to skip out of the room when a movement next to her caught her eye and she collided with Frankie. Hard. For once, it wasn't her fault. In fact, she was absolutely certain Frankie had put her whole frame into it, into hitting as much of Vi as possible, and since she was sturdier, although also shorter, Vi felt every single one of those collision points.

Shoulder to clavicle, arm to sternum, hip to thigh... She staggered back and only belatedly realized that the whole front of her gown was now wet and so was the one item that was precious beyond all others. The camera was drenched.

"Oh, sorry, Courtenay! You should really watch where you're going, even if you're running to my wife." Frankie laughed, and the sound of that pure, malicious glee, of that cheap shot, hurt more than whatever new bruises would bloom on Vi's skin.

Before Aoife could say anything, Vi turned and fled. She stopped just outside the room and picked up her almost forgotten clutch. Then she quietly closed the door and leaned on it to take a moment to draw a breath and try to calm down. The voices inside the room, however, were not even remotely calm.

"...you did that on purpose, Frankie! You ruined that kid's ball gown, as payback for whatever it is that happened in here!" The corners of Vi's mouth lifted a touch as she splayed her hand across her heart. Her mentor, despite being run ragged and surely anxious about the opening, was as perceptive as ever.

But to her astonishment, Frankie's voice held no trace of remorse.

"Sully, that kid needed to be taken down a peg. Always sticking her nose in other people's business—"

"You know very well that's not true!"

"So loyal, Sully. Remember what loyalty actually is when that blabbering klutz you're so fond and protective of chases after my wife. If you think I haven't noticed, you're getting daft in your old age, my friend."

Vi's breath caught in her throat. Frankie knew. Frankie had known all along.

"Vi's harmless crush has nothing to do with anything, Franziska. And you really shouldn't be speaking to me about protecting your wife. We've had this conversation, and yet here we are."

Something was hurled across the room and smashed into the door Vi was leaning against, startling her almost to death as she heard raining glass on the other side of it. Frankie must have thrown her tumbler. Vi didn't want to stay around and find out. She pressed her clutch and the dripping camera to her chest and ran.

Her surroundings were imprinting themselves in her mind as she rushed through the villa. The high ceilings, the myriad of rooms, the high class of the attendees. Tears pricked the backs of her eyes. There was no way she'd be able to attend the ball now. Even if she could somehow find another camera, with her gown ruined, she'd be forced to abandon her role as one of Lilien Haus' photographers, and she would start processing that as soon as she found the words to tell Chiara.

Frankie had also destroyed her simple joy at the fact that somewhere in this impressive building on the brilliant waters of Lago di Como, Chiara was looking for her, waiting for her. Vi tried to hug that thought to herself despite both her collarbone and her sternum feeling tender and battered.

～

CHIARA WAS INDEED WAITING on the far side of the seemingly endless mansion. Pale, eyes shining with a strange kind of light Vi had never seen before, Chiara was a study of grace in motion. She was flitting from one model to the next, fixing something on each and every one of them. Vi's hand holding the camera lifted of its own accord, and she realized what she was doing only when the sound of her pressing the no-longer-working shutter made Chiara turn around.

"You're he—" She stopped mid-exclamation, and Vi looked at her with trepidation. She hoped that her body didn't show bruises or anything else that would speak of the confrontation, because for the life of her, she had no idea how she would explain it. Belatedly, Vi realized that even if her face was still perfectly made up, her dress showed the carnage from her earlier encounter with Frankie, of her rage and vengefulness.

Chiara moved like a whirlwind then, abandoning a hapless model pretty much holding up her own gown, and Vi's mind played the oldest trick in the book on her.

The speed, the determination, the play of light and shadows on that resolute face, wiped away the beauty and the habitual affection in those eyes, leaving only anger, and Vi shrunk. Simply drew into herself, the hand that wasn't already holding the camera cradling it to her body. Belatedly, she realized what she had done. There was no fixing it. Her breaths were coming out as sobs, chest rising and falling fast, sweat covering her now cold and clammy skin.

Vi staggered into a room that looked like a large closet, away from prying eyes, sinking to the floor, her knees unable to hold her, the panic rising like bile in her throat. Would she throw up and allow that to be the final indignity on this day that was already full of embarrassment?

Then she lifted her unfocused eyes that had been darting from one thing to the next, to the next, only to catch sight of Chiara, who'd followed her in. She watched the color drain from her cheeks and the understanding dawn on her that she must have caused Vi's panic attack to set in.

Chiara's own eyes widened in shock, in pain, filling with tears, and now the heat of shame flushed Vi's entire body, surely evaporating the remnants of vodka on her dress.

She turned away, trying to get up, to run, anywhere as long as it was away from here, because she couldn't stand Chiara knowing, Chiara looking at her with this kind of dejected pity...

"Vi, please... I need to fix your dress."

Was it the 'please', or was it the actual uttering of her name, her real name, the one she claimed, the one she so often hid behind, the one she so rarely heard pass Chiara's lips that stopped her from struggling to get up?

She sensed more than saw Chiara approach, and she wanted to weep all over again, so careful, so gentle. The hands on her shoulders trembled, and Vi trembled with them.

"Vi, Vi, Vi..." Just her name, in that voice and the tears spilled in earnest now, the floodgates opening and only those two tender, strong hands held her together, kept her from breaking at the seams.

"Chiara!" Aoife's arrival broke through the cocoon of safety, and Vi startled anew. "Frankie is drinking again—" Vi's thoughts began to race in anticipation of what was to come, but Aoife waved off any further explanation, and Chiara's expression didn't change, as if Frankie was of no consequence at the moment.

Then Aoife spotted her, and her eyes softened. "Oh, kid, you're here. Yes, good, now don't cry, we will fix this somehow...

Though, honestly, who the hell thought silver was a good color on you?"

The bluntness and the matter-of-fact delivery, so Aoife, so true to who she was, made Vi smile. When she caught the echo of that smile in Chiara's eyes, she hiccuped a giggle, followed by another, until she was laughing. Both Aoife and Chiara watched her with concern, as both mirth and tears mingled on her face.

"Yeah, okay, I don't deal well with waterworks." Aoife's aggrieved expression was so cute, so hilarious, Vi's laughter only raised in pitch, and she hiccuped when she realized that she was probably smearing the remnants of her makeup on the now most certainly wrecked dress. "That other thing..." Aoife hesitated, shooting Chiara a quick look. "We will talk about that later, but now if this is all because of the gown—"

"Sully, stop." As Vi tried to control her ragged breathing, Chiara crouched down next to her and carefully lifted her chin, running cool fingertips over her jaw. "Are you okay to come with me? Aoife will join us, and we will fix this, okay?" Vi watched her speak, but the words didn't register with her as much as the movement of those patient lips forming them.

But then the fingers on her skin firmed a little, making her focus, making her blink away the remaining tears. "Do you understand me, Vi? Use your words, darling. Please."

The tightness of the grip was gone as the second hand joined in, Chiara cradling her face in her cool fingers. Vi began to feel them warm and take away her own angry heat, just like Chiara's voice was taking away the shame, the embarrassment over her panic attack, over her instinctive response to withdraw that she'd been unable to help or hide.

"Yes." This time when her heart stuttered and sped up, it wasn't sheer panic that was driving her. She felt loved, and for once, bathed in Chiara's light, Vi's chest did not hurt.

Before she knew it, Aoife was pulling her up by both hands,

and Chiara was leading the way to a secluded room among the maze of others in this immense mansion. Soon, Aoife was tugging her into another smallish space with a myriad of garment bags and looked at her expectantly.

"All right, kid, strip!" Vi—now very used to commands of all kinds issued by Aoife and gentler ones, but still rather in the same vein, coming from Chiara during their many evenings spent fitting—immediately reached for her side zipper, the smell of alcohol clinging to her hands and chest, even as she peeled back the stained chiffon and lace.

As every other time, Chiara tactfully turned away and pulled on Aoife's forearm. "What? Nothing I've not seen before —" Vi's vision was obscured by material, and she could vaguely hear the subsequent thoroughly disgruntled, "honestly, nothing you haven't seen before either and she's wearing knickers!"

Vi chuckled, and when she was certain her slip, bra, and underwear were more or less in order—the dress having taken the brunt of the impromptu vodka shower—she called for them to turn around. She appreciated their efforts, but there was no fixing this.

"Well, the gown is ruined and the smell... I guess attending the ball is out of the question now. Can't really go out there and take pictures in my jeans and t-shirt. I really am very sorry about this. And I think the camera is beyond repair at this point... I know you counted on me for the photography—"

"Kid," Aoife just waved her protestations away impatiently. "There are like twenty photographers out there, so don't worry yourself—"

"Shhh, Sully." Chiara circled Vi, then leaned in slightly. Vi's knees buckled again when she realized Chiara was smelling her. "And yes, you will need something. Aoife, bring me one of those large washcloths, since she can't take a shower, it will ruin her hair."

For once, Aoife disappeared in a second without any argument, simply sniffing loudly and muttering about how some people really ought to mind their booze consumption. Vi briefly wondered how much Aoife had actually seen or suspected.

"Chiara, I really... listen..." Vi had no idea what she was trying to say, except it seemed like she and Aoife were attempting to somehow salvage the situation. One that was unsalvageable. Vi closed her eyes and focused on her breathing. The words weren't coming to her anyway.

"Do I have to shush you too, Ms. Courtenay?" Chiara still circled her, and her voice sounded from Vi's side. There was a tug on the hem of her slip, then another on the spaghetti strap, followed by a characteristic "tsk" and an even more characteristic "*Santo cielo!*"

Vi shook her head as much in answer to the question as to clear it. Chiara's proximity was wreaking havoc on her already battered system. The silky touch of those fingertips, her scent mingling with the smell of vodka, completely overriding it. Chiara was all Vi could sense.

"I won't ask." Vi opened her eyes and turned her head so quickly towards those words that the room tilted. Chiara stepped even closer, their shoulders touching now, and it was Vi's turn to take her warmth, to absorb as much of it as she could with goosebumps running down her exposed arms.

Vi wondered whether Chiara knew that her reaction had nothing to do with her being cold. She wasn't. She was burning up now. And her earlier shame and embarrassment didn't have anything to do with it either. Because Chiara usually knew. Chiara usually knew everything.

"I won't ask." This time when Chiara repeated the sentence, their eyes were on each other, and Vi understood that she wasn't speaking about the dress, the vodka, or anything related to her now certainly absenting herself from the ball. She was speaking of Vi's panic and Vi's reaction to being seen. She closed her eyes and nodded.

When Aoife blasted through the door a second later, Vi startled and flinched, and the silence was broken even if Chiara's eyes remained all-knowing and all-seeing. There was no hiding from that gaze. So the end of their tête-à-tête was welcome.

For the better, Vi thought, because she'd been on the verge of opening her soul to this perceptive woman, and she knew she simply couldn't let go of her secret. Or her father's. Or Frankie's for that matter. She closed her mouth, and Chiara stepping back reverberated in her bones.

"Here you go. It doesn't smell of anything." Aoife thrust the warm washcloth into Vi's hands and stepped back as Chiara motioned at her.

Vi tried to clean up unobtrusively, but she still didn't want to discard her mangled slip, and there really was no other bra. Her sigh was loud. Why was she even doing this? There was no use in any of it.

Somewhere behind her, Chiara and Aoife were murmuring to each other in hushed tones before Chiara raised her voice slightly to make sure Vi heard her. "Ms. Courtenay, I have to run. The models will not pin themselves, sadly. I will wait for you out there. Please don't take too long, okay?"

Vi wanted to counter that there really wasn't anything or anyone to wait for since she was done for the night, soggy as she was. But as Chiara exited the room, carefully sidestepping her, she turned to Aoife to argue her point and stopped dead.

Or as good as dead. Surely she was having some out-of-body experience, because there was no way... Aoife was holding up one of the most beautiful gowns of vibrant emerald Vi had ever seen.

"You shall go to the ball, Cinderella." Aoife must have been waiting to quote the iconic line for a long time, because her face nearly split in the most joyful grin as she looked exceedingly proud of herself.

"Damn..."

"Yes, that's exactly what I said when Chiara showed it to me." Aoife lovingly caressed the silk in her hands.

"So you didn't...?" Vi made a vague gesture towards the absolute beauty in front of her. She didn't have to worry about being understood though.

"No, kiddo, this was all Chiara herself. Every stitch, every fold. And it's not part of the collection either. I don't know when she worked on this, because both you and I know she had no time to sleep to begin with, considering everything being as late as it was. But, Goddess, if this isn't one of her most amazing works! Ever, Vi. And I've watched her create for nearly twenty years."

They stood motionless, simply looking at the glory in Aoife's hands, and Vi felt her chest expand again. She thought there was no longer any space left there. After all, she loved so many people, but this was different.

This love swept in on the brilliant emerald wings made of silk and lace. It tore through her, through her feeble defenses already weakened by all the moments, big and small, that they'd been having these past months and finally settled down, pushing and pulling until it was sitting comfortably among all the others, resting closest to her heart, enfolding it, keeping it safe.

"No, no, no! You are not going to cry on me again, kiddo! Chiara can't come in here and do that romance movie crap she did before, holding your face or whatever you all swoon over. I don't do that! I will smack you and pull this thing on you and be done with you. No crying! There's no crying in fashion."

But Vi didn't care. She simply moved forward and threw her arms around Aoife, placing her chin on top of her head, obviously making Aoife even more aggrieved with this show of their height difference and the disregard for her earlier instructions of no tears.

Vi let go of her disgruntled mentor and carefully wiped her eyes, and she could swear she heard Aoife sniff.

"Okay, okay, enough mush. Poopy-schmoopy, or whatever the fuck the Fairy Godmother says. Get your skinny ass into this thing, Cinderella. I can't wait to see it on you, and we really need to be going. She can only hold down the fort for so long, and you know Frankie will be half-drunk by now and..."

Aoife trailed off, and her face was no longer sentimental. It was sad, and there was an edge to it, a resolution of sorts that made Vi curious. Aoife just shooed her and thrust the hanger in her hands before demonstratively turning her back to her. But Vi had to ask just this one thing before she could take another step.

"Aoife... About earlier and what you walked into with Frankie and me..."

"Are you gonna tell me what I walked into? Or are you gonna pretend like it was no big deal? Because I have a lot of time for the first scenario and no time at all for the second."

Under the steady glare, Vi simply shook her head and Aoife's shoulders sagged.

"Whatever." There was little inflection in the word, but Vi sensed there was more relief than disappointment and didn't know what to make of that. What would Aoife say if Vi confessed? And what about Chiara?

Vi knew that, despite what she'd seen, nothing had changed, and Aoife's reaction was perhaps proof of that. So she shook her head again. And Aoife seemed to move on. "Put it on, Lady Rae. I'm getting older by the minute here. And while I am like vintage wine and only get better with age, I kinda want to spend some of that time with other people."

This time when Vi laughed, it held no tinge of panic or regret. She was going to the ball.

11

ONCE UPON A WELL-ATTENDED BALL

Genevieve Courtenay was never good at being the center of attention. Maybe that was why she was so comfortable behind the camera. She was an observer by nature. Well, one really had to be, since her life had not facilitated much participation, unless one called cleaning up her family's messes 'participating'. So when she was suddenly thrust into the limelight as unceremoniously as she was now, Vi wanted to disappear.

She really should have known better. Much, much better with the gown she was wearing.

Vi had dressed quickly, with Aoife's help. Though perhaps 'help' was too generous a word, since the assistance mostly revolved around oohing and aahing over every element of the design, exclamations, curses, and alternatively praises and damnations, directed at Chiara's talent.

When she was done, Vi had handed Aoife her soggy slip and bra. The room didn't have any mirrors, but she knew what she looked like, down to the feverish sheen in her eyes. She *looked* the part. As she assessed her image again, her mentor reached behind her and came back with a new camera.

"No mice or pumpkins to finish off your ensemble, but you might need this, Cinderella."

Vi's hands shook when she lifted the camera to her face, tears stinging her eyes. Her dream of shooting the new collection was alive once again.

"Wish me luck, Aoife. This really does feel like a fairytale."

She gave her mentor—still clucking over some tricky fold that Chiara had sewn into the skirt—a brief hug. Though Vi couldn't see anything of the kind since the skirt looked rather simple, flowing down her body in waves of emerald silk, judging by Aoife's reaction, the dress was a work of art.

It certainly felt that way, the bodice hugging her closely, filling her with affection and tenderness. Chiara had taken the time to do this for her. Chiara had noticed that the silver gown didn't suit her. Chiara cared. Vi closed her eyes and took a deep breath. Aoife flicked her on the nose and grinned.

"You won't need luck. You are a whiz with that thing, if any of the thousands of pictures you've taken are any indication. As for all the fairytale bullshit..." Aoife gave her a direct look. It was remarkably steady. "Just remember that your princess is married. For better or for worse—"

"Aoife!" Vi was horrified.

"Frankie is many things, but oblivious is not one of them and neither am I. You're a good kid and hell, half the people down on that beach will be in love with Chiara by the time this evening is over." Aoife bit her lip and focused on Vi's eyes again. "For your own sake, Vi. Just remember that there's no happy ending here. You understand?"

Vi's stomach dropped and her mouth went dry. So she really was transparent. Not that she hadn't suspected, but this warning, this warding her off, away from Chiara, away from the flame she was a moth to...

"Tell me you understand, Vi. And go do good work out there tonight." Aoife had gripped her free hand tightly, too tightly, and Vi took a deep breath. Yes, she understood all too well. She squeezed Aoife's hand back and ran out of the room.

WITHIN MERE HOURS, the collection was successfully shown on the improvised catwalk occupying a private strip of beach on the lake, with yachts and the bluest of waters Vi had ever seen serving as backdrop, and a hundred or so distinguished, hand-selected guests cheering and applauding. All that, coupled with the exquisite evening breeze full of scents of fame and fortune, created an atmosphere of distinct contentment and luxury.

Frankie walked the stage at the end, hugging models, bowing deeply and effusively, her gait relaxed and easy. And Vi took her picture on autopilot, yet craving to capture Chiara, who was inevitably backstage, having touched every swatch of the collection, making sure every single piece was perfect, each model was immaculate, from clothes to makeup, to hair.

Vi craned her neck as Frankie took her umpteenth bow. She bit her lip and couldn't bring herself to take more pictures of this hypocrisy.

"I understand the true star of the show doesn't take the stage at all. What a shame." Vi nearly jumped out of her skin as a low voice, more bourbon than gravel, sounded right next to her ear. She turned and, as was par for the course for her, lost her footing, stumbling in her high heels.

Predictably, the tall, willowy woman caught her by the hand, steadying her. Predictably, because the woman just looked like she would never fail, be it to scare or to save.

"I apologize for startling you."

It took Vi a moment to register what the other woman had said and how strange it was. Did she know? Chiara's involvement in the creation of Lilien Haus' collections wasn't something the public at large was aware of. Except, this wasn't anyone from the mere public. This was—

"You're Neve Blackthorne!" She blurted out the words and immediately wanted to give anything and everything for a do-over.

Oh, great job, Vi. How embarrassing!

But the woman simply shook the inky hair out of eyes that seemed to glow purple in the sunset and raised an eyebrow. Vi had the sensation that this was a characteristic gesture, it came so naturally and fit so perfectly.

"Guilty. And you must be special. Two people have pointed you out to me. And not just because of the gown." Before Vi could answer, or actually ask what the hell was going on because she really wasn't *that*, Neve Blackthorne reached out her majestic hand with its red-tipped fingers and traced the line of emerald fabric along Vi's shoulder.

"If this were part of the collection, I'd have paid Chiara millions for it. But she tells me it's bespoke. Pity. Because it's exquisite. And that makes you special, Ms. Courtenay."

"I would tell you to unhand my cousin, Neve, but I don't think I have any power here."

Vi desperately tried not to stare. First Neve Freaking Blackthorne and now... Vi swallowed hard. Standing in a flawlessly tailored navy pantsuit with her hair flowing freely down her back, was Her Royal Highness, Princess Allegra of Savoy.

Vi curtseyed instinctively, having been taught since early infancy, even if the only time she had to avail herself of the gesture had been decades ago. At their last meeting, Vi was five and her father made a scene at court. That had been the final straw for King Aleric, and the Courtenays were never received in Savoy again.

"Charming, Genevieve. Or is it Vi? I understand from Chiara it's what you've chosen." Vi had the presence of mind to nod. The fact that Chiara spoke about her, and with Princess

Allegra in particular, made Vi's heart flutter. And Allegra, a member of her own family, calling her by her chosen name. It was incredible.

"But no need to be so formal. We're amongst friends here, even if Neve does tend to intimidate people."

Allegra winked at her, and Vi smiled back into gray eyes so like her own. A current of recognition passed between them, and Vi wanted to say something, something smart and important, but Princess Allegra simply shook her head. "We need to talk, cousin. Perhaps it's time the two of us bury the hatchet our fathers so recklessly sharpened. But not now..." She reached into her suit's breast pocket and quickly produced a card before nodding towards the approaching Frankie. With a barely perceptible narrowing of her eyes, she turned in the completely opposite direction and disappeared into the crowd.

"Very special indeed." The low drawl by her side made Vi turn and run straight into the purple gaze of their hostess. Neve Blackthorne gave her a long look before her eyes locked on the graceful back of the retreating Princess as the crowd parted for her, bowing and staring. Vi was once again lost for words.

God, let me think of something...

"You have a beautiful home, ma'am."

Really? This? Thanks for nothing, god...

"I imagine Allegra's is nicer. However, even Her Royal Highness does not look as exquisite as you do tonight, Ms. Courtenay. Quite a feat."

"Careful, Neve, she's already a fan. You don't want her swooning. And hands off." Chiara carefully stepped between them, and Vi suddenly had the sensation that there wasn't enough air on the entire beach. Neve Blackthorne, Chiara Conti-Lilienfeld, Vi thought her sins in a previous life must have been enormous to have been thrown into the deep end like this. The gown that had attracted so much attention didn't have a high collar, or she'd be pulling it up posthaste and hiding behind it.

It didn't even matter that they were squabbling over the gown and not her. She just looked from one to the other and grinned, before she remembered she was still holding the camera and raised her lens, a bit apprehensive to point it at the absolutely gorgeous vista of two of the most beautiful women in the world on the backdrop of Lago di Como.

"Oh, we've got a crafty one, Chiara." Neve's lips curled slightly at the corners as she reached out her hand and angled the lens towards herself, leaning in slightly, suffusing Vi in soft notes of vanilla. Vi finally shook herself out of her stupor, of being allowed to take a picture of the ever-elusive Neve Blackthorne.

When she finally lowered the camera, Neve stepped behind her and gently pressed the *view* button, perusing the last couple of shots. Vi held her breath.

"She is good, just as you said, C. I'll allow this. Give me a call if you need a place for her." And with those last words, she gave Chiara an actual kiss on the cheek, rather than one of those fake air kisses everyone had been engaging in all evening, and departed, leaving a trace of her scent behind.

"Wow..." Vi felt like maybe she'd been given a second lease on life.

"Wow indeed. You survived. Neve almost never allows pictures. She also never touches anyone." Chiara didn't bother to hide her smile. It looked relaxed now, with the showing over and Frankie assumed her usual duties of schmoozing, sucking up to investors, and playing it up for the media.

Chiara was once again left to her own devices, and it seemed that her focus was centered around Vi, those amber eyes honed in on her, perusing every single detail.

"You look beautiful, Ms. Courtenay. Green really is your color."

Whatever breath she'd been holding as Neve had leaned over her, this was on a completely different level. Everything seemed magnified, the water sparkled brighter, her heartbeat was louder in her ears. The aroma of calla lilies was strong in the air, yet it was Chiara she smelled and Chiara she drank in.

"I think you *made* it my color. Thank you." Chiara smiled, and Vi was happy to see that, for once, it touched her eyes that were filled with warmth, the corners crinkling with those faint crow's feet.

"I just designed the dress." Chiara bit her lip and looked into the distance, the gentle waves of the lake seemingly fascinating to her, but Vi could tell she was not seeing them. It was as if she was bracing herself for whatever she was about to say next, hands fiddling with the neckline of her own gown.

"I have to confess, I did not like you in silver. And it wasn't my place to deny you your stepmother's gown, but I've become a bit proprietary and possessive where my favorite model is concerned..." With a cheeky smile, she winked at her, and it took all of Vi's endurance to not melt into a rather embarrassing puddle.

Did the temperature suddenly spike? Vi wanted to fan herself and was grateful when Chiara, again, looked away onto the water. "Not that I was hoping you'd ruin your silver piece of couture history. But knowing you..." She stopped gracefully mid-sentence, and now the warmth in her eyes was distinctly mischievous.

"Yes, knowing me, you could probably place bets not so much on *whether* but on *when* I'd ruin something, right?" Vi gently straightened the skirt of her gown, self-consciously hiding her face.

"Well, in spite of how accident-prone you are, you don't tend to ruin things on your own, as a rule. In fact, you often seem to be... shall we say... *assisted*? I think that would be the right word?"

With a steady hand on Vi's lower back that sent tendrils of both delight and dread up and down her body, Chiara led her down to one of the majestic piers stretching onto the lake.

"Well, I'm sorry?" As they arrived at the railing, the deep azure water shining in the last rays of the setting sun, Vi tried for somewhat honest contrition. It was rather hard, since the gown hadn't actually been ruined by her clumsiness for once, and she was not about to touch the entire subject of Frankie with a ten-foot pole.

"Don't apologize. Especially when you've done nothing wrong." Chiara leaned on her elbows, and for a minute she seemed thousands of miles away. "You stumble over your own feet and tumble out of rooms and generally tend to be adorably uncoordinated, Ms. Courtenay. But, when you're on your game, I have yet to see you damage anything other than your own dignity. I have also yet to see you spill a glass of vodka on yourself, or drink vodka for that matter, period. So, yes, while you believe you're clumsy—and I assume you've had a lifetime of being convinced of it by your illustrious family—I, for one, believe you've routinely had some help in most of your so-called 'accidents.' So who was it this time?"

Vi's hand lifted to her chest of its own accord, because as Chiara turned towards Vi and spoke, her words were like arrows, each one hitting their target, the bullseye being somewhere in the area of Vi's sternum. She rubbed her skin and tried to look anywhere but at the woman beside her.

"Nobody—"

"And then there's the lying." This time, Chiara straightened and turned to face Vi fully. As always, their height allowed their eyes to meet without effort. "Just like you never ruin anything by yourself, you don't lie unless you're covering for people. And while I won't ask about some things, out of respect for your privacy, I will very much ask about this one. Because I know only one person who routinely chugs vodka minutes before a showing." Chiara lifted a graceful eyebrow, and Vi suddenly found the floor to be enormously interesting.

"Chiara... I'm sorry—"

Vi had no idea what to say and why she was even apologizing. In her usual manner, Chiara tsked, and in an even more characteristic gesture, she laid fingertips on Vi's lips.

"*Cenerella*, you may not be a good liar, but you really need to start taking my advice. Stop apologizing. How is it your fault that Frankie is drunk and stupid?"

An inventive Italian curse followed, and Vi stood still, relishing the feel of cool skin on her lips before she forced herself to be the one to break contact.

"She's under a lot of stress, I guess..." She didn't even bother to wince when her own thoughts spilled out of her mouth, despite reasonably expecting some filter to still be in place.

But Chiara was already looking back at the lake, with boats moored not far from the villas on the shore.

"You know, I was born twenty minutes from here." Chiara's voice became unexpectedly low and a touch sad, and Vi waited with bated breath for what would come next.

There'd been a wistful note in Chiara's statement, and with the quiet in front of them contrasted by the brightly lit hum of the afterparty behind them, Vi leaned in and mirrored Chiara's stance, looking out on the darkening expanse, hungry to observe every word.

"I spent my childhood among these villas. Maybe not this one in particular, but that one over there, and the one two piers down from it? I remember that yacht. It was a relic even then. Now it must be a precious antique. I'm surprised these people kept it. Though they probably own a Van Gogh or two and exhibit it on that very boat. Some oil magnate or other."

Vi remained silent, diligently looking where Chiara pointed, observing, listening, wondering.

"My mother cleaned both of these mansions. And several

others, if she could manage." And now there was only coldness in Chiara's tone, all wistfulness gone. "I ran wild among the empty grandeur, dreaming, playing, occasionally helping. Then, less running and more helping as I grew older and she grew sicker."

Vi's hand reached out, seemingly of its own accord, and gently touched Chiara's forearm. If she'd expected to be rebuked or shaken off, it didn't happen, but neither did Chiara acknowledge the silent comfort. Vi soon realized it was entirely possible she didn't even notice it, she was so engrossed in her memories.

"I had a very hard time at school. Funny how it took me years to stop saying I was bad at it and to understand that it wasn't my fault. But the truth of the matter is that I couldn't read till I think, fourth grade?" When Vi nodded tentatively, Chiara's throat worked, but when she spoke again, her voice was steady.

"The reading improved as I grew older and as a professor took pity on me and kept me after class, painstakingly teaching me." She looked onto the water and her voice took on a didactic quality, as if she wasn't talking about herself, as if she was distancing herself from the events.

"You see, apparently people like me are driven by fascination. If a task wasn't interesting, little Chiara could not be bothered. And most everything sounded like boring gibberish early on. Until that one teacher literally took the time to ask me about my interests and bent over backwards to basically create curiosity in me. Get me interested."

Chiara wrapped her arms around herself, even as the corners of her mouth lifted in a dejected smile. "Ironically, she started with books on fashion and vintage dresses. Thus, reading became less of an anxiety-inducing torture tool, but rather opened horizons to lose myself in. Numbers never did make sense though. Math... Let's just say it never added up for me and leave it at that without me blathering on about my dyscalculia. Never ask me to count backwards, Ms. Courtenay."

Chiara smiled, but it was hollow, lips stretching into a sad facsimile of a smile.

"You see, I wasn't hyper. I'd just daydream my way through classes, and since we were so poor and the school not all that progressive, my difficulties either went unnoticed, or were dismissed."

In the distance, an impressive yacht docked to a tiny pier with grace and poise. Chiara shivered in the wind. "All the while my mother dreamt about me being an accountant. That was literally all she wanted in life and all she ever talked about. And every time she did, I—who could not find my way through a multiplication table—shriveled up inside, until there wasn't much left besides this overwhelming guilt."

Vi squeezed Chiara's arm, trying to reassure, to comfort, and Chiara laid her hand over hers, whether in gratitude or to stop her, Vi did not know.

"By the time my mother realized I would never graduate high school, it was too late for me. And she died with that burden. Her one dream, her daughter, a successful professional."

Chiara sighed, her cheeks pale and her gaze fever-bright in contrast.

"And all I could see in those years were my mother's eyes, kind, sad. Filled with so much disillusionment. When she looked at me, until her last day, it was like her dead dream was lying in state in those massive, beautiful eyes of hers. As if she was holding a wake every single time she saw me. I guess I reminded her of what could never be."

Vi breathed in and out, slowly, as quietly as she could, to not disturb Chiara, who seemed a million miles away. Did she realize the sheer horror of what she was telling Vi? The way these moments and these memories shaped her as a person? Vi didn't think so.

She wanted to reach out, to wipe it all away, because Chiara was brilliant, yet here she was, totally unmoored, consumed by guilt and self-loathing.

Vi thought about her own boarding schools, all six of them, and how girls with these types of difficulties were supported from an early age with appropriate interventions, and how they eventually thrived. Some were lawyers, actors, hell, even damn accountants...

Chiara visibly shook herself from her memories and continued.

"In any case, nothing could be done at the time. We didn't have the kind of money a private school and tutors would require, and underneath it all, I simply couldn't. Not until much later, when I was finally diagnosed and pursued the appropriate management for my conditions. I wish I could do my childhood over, knowing what I know now." The smile was self-deprecating. "Still, sticky notes, phone reminders, planners, little marks with a pen on the backs of my hands... Whatever it takes, I do all right, don't you think?"

Vi blinked, not expecting to be asked questions. Chiara did more than all right. Chiara was a genius. Everything she touched turned to gold. Her struggles as a child could have been avoided in a better system and with more support. If only Vi knew how to express all that.

"I drew. I had no attention span for anything else, but drawing was an escape. And then modeling became one, since I was so numb from losing mom, losing her in a way that made me think I was responsible. I still very much feel that way..."

Chiara trailed off, and Vi thought that so many other things in Chiara's life were now more clear. Those shrouds of mystery, of bafflement that Vi often imagined surrounded Chiara, were now less shadowy. Her devotion to lost causes, to Frankie, to

Lilien Haus even when nobody else cared and even when she was never given credit. Chiara was atoning. For her mother? That seemed plausible but also not quite. So what was the woman who carried so much guilt from such an early age doing penance for then?

Chiara's voice reached for her and pulled her out of the gloomy thoughts and into a chillier reality.

"She died when I was seventeen. Just two weeks before I was discovered on the streets of Milano." Chiara lowered her face, and Vi wondered if she even saw the beauty of the lake in front of her. Whether it was beautiful to her at all.

"She never watched me walk the most prestigious catwalks in the world, become an ambassador for the biggest brands. She never got to see that. Her heart gave out, Ms. Courtenay, because she was stressed all her life. Anxious and worried out of her mind about how a widow with no education or major skills would feed the toddler she was left with after her husband died in a boat accident. On this very lake."

Chiara gestured with her free hand, the one holding Vi's never leaving its place. "And you know, I never really knew about any of that stress and that anxiety and that worry until she was so close to the end and I asked her to look at how gorgeous the evening shore was."

Vi saw tears shimmer in Chiara's eyes and felt her own fill.

"She was so tired, she could barely lift her head, but she glanced up and she said something about how it was probably nice, but she couldn't look at it, because this goddamn place had taken my father. She returned to work and I just stood there. My mother hated the damn lake. And despite loathing it as much as she did, she worked on it all her life, to provide for me. So in the end, the lake took my dad and then took her too, in a way."

When Chiara finally faced her, Vi almost flinched away. She

needed all her self-control to remain still as those eyes bored into her, the hand on hers cold and steady.

"Anyway, as you can see, when I am fascinated by a subject, I do tend to go on about it forever, and nothing has made me more of an expert than my ADHD."

Chiara tsked, and Vi lifted her face only to observe her interlocutor shake her head.

"I always shy away from using the term. Even now. I know exactly where the guilt comes from. I have worked for years to extricate myself from its metaphorical embrace. But it's such a deeply ingrained thing, feeling the way I do. My mother, who had nothing and who wanted me to have everything, really built her dreams around my future. And despite knowing that it's not my fault, I feel like I failed her. The fact that I've been diagnosed now doesn't change that. I can't talk to her and explain. It's too late, she's gone, and half my life I didn't even know I function differently."

Chiara smiled crookedly, but her eyes remained sad. "Anyway, my extremely roundabout point—and I really have one with all this droning on about my mother and my neurodivergence—is that I may be doing my penance for sins seen and unseen. But overall, I quite literally don't give a fuck about Frankie being stressed. My mother was stressed. Died from it, in fact. And yet, she never doused anyone in her poison of choice, not that she had one. She never threw temper tantrums about other employees interrupting her. I assume that's what happened since Frankie abhors interruptions..."

Vi knew her eyes grew comically wide, and she sensed the hair stand up on its end at the nape of her neck. Did Chiara know? What should she say? Should she be saying anything at all?

"Ah, and here's my wife! Resplendent in moonlight and fannish worship." Frankie's glistening red lips swooped, and she stood on her tiptoes to plant a wet kiss on Chiara's cheek, giving Vi an exaggerated wink. "I can't escape you, kid! Everywhere I turn, there you are. Quite the little stalker, eh, Courtenay?"

"Stop it!" Chiara's cutting remark coincided with a sudden lull in music, and half a dozen heads turned in their direction, including that of the hostess. Neve gave them a long gaze out of those unreadable violet eyes and lifted an eyebrow at Vi.

What was it with all these older women around her executing the one maneuver that always made Vi totally helpless? All that was left for any of them to do was smirk or purse their lips. Miranda Priestly had a lot to answer for, Vi decided.

After a subtle shake of the head at Neve, she quietly stepped away from Chiara, who stood rigid and taut like a violin string ready to snap at any moment in Frankie's arms. Before Vi could say anything undoubtedly unsuitable, Chiara shook off Frankie's hands and walked in the direction of the mansion without a second look. Vi made to follow, only to have her forearm caught.

"Hey Cinderella, want another drink?" Aoife offered, her face somber, watching Chiara leave and Frankie intercept her. Their hostess, though, smiled at Vi from afar, approval clear on her face. Vi was glad she had done something right. But as she looked at the Lilienfelds walk away, her heart bled all over again.

No, she had no power here, even if she wanted to whisk Chiara far away from all this.

When she turned back, Neve Blackthorne was still looking at her appraisingly. It felt like very little escaped her, especially in her own house. Vi lifted her almost empty glass in the direction of their hostess and turned back to Aoife.

"Hey, Fairy Godmother. No drink, thank you." But she gave Aoife a half hug and laid her cheek on her mentor's head, surely messing up the spiky updo she was sporting. Aoife, for once, didn't complain or give her any grief.

As she straightened and Frankie and Chiara disappeared into the distance, they shared a look, and Vi felt an understanding pass between them. They would not talk about what had happened. At least not now, and she was happy for it. Now was not the time, not among the hordes of gossipmongers and socialites who lived and breathed for these kinds of rumors.

"You know, I'm too young to be your godmother, kid." Aoife poked a finger at her arm.

"I wasn't aware there was a cutoff for these things. Theoretically, we could be the same age and you still could have baptized me... Also, you're forty-three, so if you'd hurried up in your misspent youth, you could have been my mother—"

"Oh piss off, you!" The beloved and delightful Irish accent sprang to life, just as Vi had intended. Aoife nudged her and looked like she was about to stomp away when she suddenly stopped and squeezed Vi's shoulder. "Don't think I don't know what you're doing, missy."

"Aoife, let it rest. Chiara almost got me to spill my guts about her wife attacking me a second before Frankie herself slobbered all over her, so I claim this as a win. Maybe not the whole night, but certain incidents aside, I've had an amazing time. Thanks to Chiara and to you and your poopy-schmoopy, though I'm sure the Fairy Godmother doesn't use those words."

"The words are whatever I say they are, get that straight, Cinderella."

"First of all, if this is my fairytale, it is not ever going to be straight. And second, I did feel like Cinderella, Aoife. Everyone was so nice, from the models to Neve Blackthorne. God, I don't know why people say she's a witch."

"Because she is one. She just took a shine to you, 'cause you are hapless and cute and hopeless. People like clumsy, adorable little things." Vi pushed at Aoife's shoulder, outraged, and Aoife laughed loudly, the pleasure at her own joke so clear, Vi couldn't help but join her.

"I heard Princess Allegra claimed you as one of her own? Frankie damn near broke out in a sweat chasing after her throughout the whole party. Too bad, so sad Her Majesty made herself scarce so early."

"It's Her Highness. She's not queen yet. Aleric is king, she's his heir, and next in line for the throne. So get your titles straight." Vi threw a sideways glance at Aoife, trying to hide her grin.

"Why should I? She's not."

Vi groaned and covered her face with her hands. She didn't want to think about the implications of her cousin being gay. She liked Allegra, and if she was indeed queer, the sheer amount of trouble that would spell for the royal was beyond Vi's comprehension. Savoy was a very conservative kingdom.

"God, Aoife, how should I know...?"

"Nobody looks that good in suspenders and is heterosexual. It's a crime against... well, suspenders."

The mischief, the teasing in Aoife's tone, made Vi peek from between her fingers, then smile and throw her arms around her now squirming and cursing mentor.

"I love you. Please never change."

"If you don't let go of me, and I mean stat, I will take *both* of your shoes and throw them in the goddamn lake. Not sure even your princess will be able to save you then. Now unhand me!"

But Vi did not let go, and a few moments later Aoife's arm folded around her waist, and over her mentor's head, she caught Chiara's smiling eyes watching her with affection. Frankie be damned, this was the best night ever.

12

ONCE UPON A PARISIAN SUNSET

Genevieve Courtenay probably shouldn't have been as dependable and good as she was at her job, if nothing else, then for her own self-preservation.

Sadly, self-preservation had never been in her blood. It must have skipped a generation of Courtenays.

But she was very good and very dependable. Thus she hadn't stopped taking pictures when the door opened and Chiara stepped into the sunlit studio, right into Frankie who was face first in... well, *that* part of Véronique—the Lilien Haus lawyer, who, for someone usually so elegant, had absolutely nothing covering that rather splendid body that Vi always avoided looking at.

After all, Aoife had told her to never mess with Véronique. Frankie had obviously ignored that particular advice, and judging by the state of her face, had made quite a mess of Véronique herself.

If only Vi had averted her eyes in that particular instance as well. If only she had averted her *camera,* too...

Instead, for the next few seconds, she automatically continued to be great at her job and to take those few shots of

Frankie's glistening face and shocked, caught eyes. And of Chiara's shaken, ashen features, her limp hand sliding off the door handle.

Because those pictures... Those pictures ruined Vi's life. And there was nothing she could do about that, even years later, as a mature and established photographer who commanded tens of thousands of dollars per session.

Nothing was ever the same after the moment Vi's hands had directed the camera at that god-awful scene.

YEARS LATER, if you asked her how that ruination started, Vi would probably say it was when everyone at Lilien Haus was signing picture release forms. They were gearing up to present the collection at the first of several more public venues, the whole crew getting ready to fly to New York for a Poise showing. Vi would not be shooting that event, Poise having access to all the biggest photographers in the world.

But that didn't even sting, since, after her Lago di Como work was featured in the promo materials, she was starting to get some calls and offers.

And speaking of Poise, Benedict Stanley, the magazine's esteemed Editor-In-Chief, had offered her an apprenticeship. She suspected his call had a lot to do with a certain Princess, whose card still lay hidden and untouched in her clutch, because she could not fathom contacting her and asking for a favor. It seemed Allegra hadn't waited for Vi to initiate things after all.

So Vi was flying a little aboveground instead of having her feet planted firmly on it, when Renate made her sign a standard release. She had a whole stack of them, all alphabetized on her desk, ready to be scanned. When Vi dared to step into the office and drop off hers, Renate sniffed and looked Vi up and down.

"We need to make sure they are all in order before you take a single picture inside these walls, am I understood? I don't want to miss out on even one solitary good shot for the brochure because you took it prior to the model signing their form."

Renate sat down, put on her reading glasses, and turned away from Vi. The conversation was over.

VI SHOOK off the strange sensation she always had when she ran across Renate and almost skipped all the way up the stairs to Chiara's studio. The idea behind their plans was a simple one. Vi, her newly cleaned and fixed camera, and a videographer would accompany Frankie and Chiara around Lilien Haus for a few days and document their work, showing off interesting bits and pieces of the collections, both new and old. The brochure, along with a short video, would be released as a teaser for the new line. Vi was elated.

Chiara's bright eyes were twinkling with something that Vi couldn't quite identify. She thought she should probably give up trying. Ever since they'd returned from Como two weeks ago, Frankie had become the most attentive of wives.

Predictably, she had also turned into the most impossible of bosses, picking at Vi and harassing her at every step. And she'd become very good at doing it when they were alone and both Chiara and Aoife were out of earshot.

Vi tried not to let it get to her. Her internship would be over in a few weeks. And as soon as they were back from New York, she'd pack up her measly locker, then return to embark on an adventure that any other person would kill to go on.

If only her potentially stellar prospects weren't darkened by this one tiny wrinkle. Well, two. Frankie was still the jerk who did not deserve to kiss the oaken floors her wife's bare feet walked on. And if only Vi weren't very much in love with Frankie's wife.

Actually, make that three. If only Frankie's wife didn't give Vi looks full of mischief and affection. Like she was doing now. Still barefoot, still with a pencil in her hair barely holding up the gorgeous dark curls, and still with a mouthful of pins, Chiara was a vision. Vi's eyes stung for reasons she didn't want to examine too deeply.

"I thought once a collection is shown, you're done working."

"I hear some sort of accusation in your tone, Ms. Courtenay." Chiara's voice was rather comical, as was her indignation, since the corner of her mouth still held on to three pins as she inserted a fourth on the mannequin tucked into the corner of the studio, where a piece of white silk was sure to become something gorgeous and flowing under her skillful hands.

Vi sighed. She knew exactly what those hands felt like on her skin, tucking a fold, or straightening a line. Gentle, careful, beautiful...

"Isn't the workaholic in you ever tired?" Vi raised her camera and took a shot of the very hands she admired so much.

Chiara removed the last pin from her lips and turned to Vi fully, arms crossed over her chest.

"I beg your pardon, Ms. 'I need to finish editing the photos of the collection even if it's four in the morning.'" She probably didn't mean for it to be as cute as it came out, but Vi was enchanted all over.

Yes, she was in too deep and didn't care anymore. There was no salvation here. This woman gave her one of the greatest gifts there could be. Chiara understood her. Her quirks and her idiosyncrasies, and in fact very much displayed them herself.

It warmed Vi all over that Chiara actually paid attention, that she knew and kept track of the things Vi did for Lilien Haus.

But this was not a serious conversation, and since they were needling each other, Vi played along.

"You mean that night of the Como showing when you continued to make adjustments to some of the pieces, even though the media was already smitten?" She leaned slightly closer and managed to capture a raised eyebrow, amused and barely holding back a smile, mouth in a gorgeous closeup.

"Pot, meet kettle, Ms. Courtenay. And you really are very lucky that I've spent a number of years with a camera in my face at all times, or I'd be complaining rather loudly."

"Ha, as if you're not doing just that." Chiara's lips twitched at Vi's comment, and she actually turned away to pick up another pin, seemed to reconsider, then faced Vi again with a more composed expression.

She looked so determined not to let Vi see how much she was enjoying this banter of theirs. But Vi was equally intent. "Also, these aren't just some regular old photos. Come and see for yourself. One day, I will publish them and become filthy rich."

At this, Chiara did snicker, and the sound was glorious to Vi's ears. Chiara came closer, standing slightly behind Vi, leaning over her shoulder as they viewed the latest several shots together. Vi could feel the body heat and the subtle scent of Chiara's unmistakable perfume. It was making her dizzy. This proximity, this shared intimacy. She could turn her head just a touch and she'd be looking directly into Chiara's eyes, their lips a breath apart.

It felt like a flaying, like she was coming out of her shell, inch by agonizing inch, or was the butterfly being pushed back into the cocoon by the more apt metaphor?

The warmth of this woman wrapped itself around Vi,

caressing her touch-starved skin, making her shiver and want. And she never quite knew what to do with that desire. With the longing. With all the *missing of things* she could never have.

And with so many overwhelming feelings, it would not be neat. It would be excruciating when it was over since, unlike all her other dreams, she allowed herself to indulge in this one. To imagine and fantasize and feel.

For weeks now, this overwhelming warmth had permeated every corner of her being, reached the nooks and crannies of her lonely and desperate existence. She had been living off this joy, however hopeless, ever since. Tucking it away without pain was simply not an option. And so she knew she would bleed.

Vi tried to say something, to break the moment that was suddenly becoming too drawn-out for her comfort and perhaps too awkward for Chiara, so she took a step back, only to step into the woman, whose arms lifted as if by reflex to stop her, to prevent them from colliding, only to wrap themselves around Vi.

Suddenly the moment was no longer awkward, it was charged. A lump in Vi's throat the size of a baseball, she took a deep breath, and on the inhale, finally moved.

As if it hadn't been a simple turn of the head but some sort of miracle, they were now face to face, mouths so close, Vi could feel Chiara's startled exhale and realized they were breathing each other's air.

God, how... why...?

Something crashed downstairs, rupturing the silky thread of time, but Chiara didn't bolt, nor did she immediately let go of Vi.

Instead she squeezed her shoulders a little tighter, only then stepping aside. Her face and especially her eyes, usually so expressive, remained blank, their neutrality scraping Vi even more raw.

The bang on the stairs was followed by another and then

another, and very soon Aoife was standing on the landing, cursing under the weight of several boxes that were teetering precariously in her arms.

"I lost several of them on the steps below, but I think I got the best pairs here. Louboutins and Manolos. Your favorite." She placed four shoeboxes on the workstation, then reverentially opened the first and nodded at Vi. "Hey, Cinderella, check out the loot, since shoes seem to be your specialty." Aoife chuckled and Vi stepped closer to the treasure trove.

"Oh..." Vi had no idea she'd actually made a sound, but the shoes were a work of art, and she couldn't contain her awe.

"This is actually quite a compliment to Monsieur Louboutin that, even after months at Lilien Haus, you are still so susceptible to pieces of history." Chiara took out one of the gorgeous, red-soled heels, and Vi wished she could tell her that, yes, the shoes were wonderful, but it was how Chiara's legs would look in these heels that had her by the throat.

Vi remained silent and picked up her camera, diligently documenting Chiara opening the remaining boxes and finally settling on a pair of bright yellow, suede Manolos that would be the absolute icing on the cake with her chosen, all-black outfit. A simple turtleneck with low slung trousers allowed a peek at a strip of her toned stomach every time she raised her arms. The pants hung loosely, after giving her hips one final hug, and ended slightly above her ankles.

The lively heels were perfection, and when Chiara took a few steps towards her instead of Aoife, Vi decided not to read too much into it. She was taking pictures after all, even if the angle was not the best. She didn't want to get out of Chiara's way, she didn't want to say goodbye. And she did not want the assignment to end.

Vi shook her head, trying in vain to dislodge her impossible thoughts about what, and more importantly who, she was leaving behind, causing her heartbeat to pound in her ears.

And when Chiara placed a hand on her shoulder as she passed Vi on her way out of the studio to begin shooting the documentary, she simply closed her eyes.

"Not long now, kid." Aoife's voice and a hand on her back were meant to be steadying, but the prospect of what would come after her stint at Lilien Haus was over, only made Vi nauseous. She took a breath, and then another, and lowered her camera.

"Time to get this show on the road, Fairy Godmother."

Aoife laughed and gave her a good-natured slap on the same shoulder that still carried the sensation of Chiara's fingertips, and Vi was propelled forward.

The rest of her life was about to begin, even if she did not know it yet.

WELL, it didn't take all that long for said rest of her life to materialize. It was a shame Vi hadn't cottoned on to it sooner, because in her desire to shake the malaise of her hopelessly pining heart, she gave the camera her full and undivided attention, foregoing her actual surroundings. Especially those that were not directly relevant to whatever was in front of her lens.

Chiara's excitement at showing them—and thereby their future audiences—around, was contagious. So when Chiara opened the heavy wooden door to Frankie's studio and suddenly stopped in her tracks, Vi continued shooting.

Through her camera, she saw Chiara's face go from joy to visceral shock, and then to complete numbness—a lack of expression even more frightening than the depth of stupor just a second prior.

When Vi's mind finally caught up to what was happening in front of her and why Chiara's gaze was now empty, she almost dropped the Nikon. Her hands shook as she grasped it harder, understanding of what she'd just witnessed, no... *documented* dawning on her.

To Vi it seemed like she was having a déjà vu. A much more graphic, grotesquely explicit one. She blinked slowly, willing the image away from her eyes, but when she opened them again, Frankie was still face-first in a woman's privates.

Without clothes, it took Vi a few seconds to recognize Lilien's lawyer. After all, Véronique usually wore the absolute best things Lilien had to offer. Apparently, Frankie's tongue was the choice of the day.

Belatedly, Vi heard footsteps on the stairs behind her, and Renate, Aoife, the videographer, and Zizou, of all people, stepped into the light of the studio landing one after the other.

"... and then you'll set up somewhere inside Frankie's studio, so that when it's time to eat—Fuck, fuck, fuck!" Aoife stopped mid-sentence and Vi wanted to laugh and probably would have at the coincidence of the direction of the conversation, if only the video weren't still being shot. But with her usual speed, Aoife was already blocking the videographer's access to the studio.

"We won't be needing your services anymore. Shoo, shoo!"

The commotion was getting out of control. Zizou had now joined Aoife in making sure the videographer departed without getting any sort of glimpse at what was happening, the poor man being pushed and shoved down the stairs with both Irish and French expletives hurled his way.

Renate's heels sounded like explosions as she pushed Vi aside and entered the space, completely ignoring a naked Véronique who had been struggling to get any available clothes on herself ever since Frankie's muttered curse a minute prior, when Chiara had opened the door.

The staccato of German, a barrage of outrage and anger, followed Renate's entrance, with Frankie scrambling to get out of her sister's way.

When she nearly succeeded, Renate grabbed the closest thing and hurled it at her. The mug shattered in a shower of porcelain. Vi might have taken the time to ponder how throwing things seemed to be a Lilienfeld family trait, except next to her, Chiara flinched.

Oh, damn...

Even as Aoife and Zizou climbed back up the stairs from dispatching the videographer, Chiara seemed to come alive with each of their steps and then—just as Aoife reached her and extended her arms to hold her, to gather her at her chest— she ran.

Another crash and now howling instead of curses from inside the studio distracted Vi, and she saw Frankie on the floor, her hand holding the side of her head and the arm of a mannequin—presumably hurled by the precise hands of Renate—next to her.

And now Renate finally turned to Véronique, who'd managed to snag a pair of pants but was still very much naked from the waist up.

"I trusted you! I hired you! You ungrateful..." Renate continued in German, her transition from one language to another seamless.

The second arm of the dismembered mannequin flew Véronique's way, but Vi could tell Renate's heart wasn't really in it, because she turned to the door at Aoife's gasp and kicked at a nearby workstation, allowing Véronique to flee.

"Well, this will be quite the walk of shame for our now less-than-esteemed attorney." Aoife stepped into the studio and gave Frankie a dirty look.

"Don't start, Sully—"

"You don't get to call me that anymore!"

Aoife stepped closer to Frankie, and Renate was a ball of fury once again. "You swore on our father's grave two years ago that you stopped! Has this been going on all this time?" A resounding slap rocked Frankie, and Vi jumped a foot in the air when someone simultaneously pulled on her forearm. She turned to see Zizou tug her out of the room and reluctantly followed him.

"You don't need to be part of this." His voice suddenly lost all of his deep accent, and Vi's jaw dropped. "No time to explain, but let's just say this is not what they hired me for when they asked me to look after Lilien Haus, and it looks like Renate's paranoia about corporate espionage was unfounded for once." He wiped his brow and looked into the room where anger and accusations were still raging.

"Zizou? They hired you?"

"Oui, a... what do you call it? A chef, yes, but also a private investigator. Just looking out for Lilien Haus. So that nothing happens to the new collection. Frankie wanted to be introduced to a royal, ignoring the danger... Your father has a reputation for not being honest."

The cold sweat slid down her lower back. So she'd been right to have her suspicions. All her premonitions, all the whispers, all the shadows... Her strategy to keep Chiara, and thus Lilien, safe from her family had proven to be right. Renate had likely hired Zizou as a precaution when she couldn't stop Frankie from agreeing to let Vi intern for them because of their connection to the royal family of Savoy. Well, Charles Courtenay had not held up his end of the bargain.

"You're all right though. You're a good kid. Proved even Renate wrong. Nothing like your family."

He went on, and Vi her body flood with shame.

"Doesn't matter now, Madame Conti is what's important. This will destroy her. You need to go after her. She should not be alone now. Do you know where—"

Before he could finish, Vi, who'd been about to shake her head, suddenly realized that she knew very well where Chiara might be.

"The roof. She'll be on the roof, Zizou!"

He rummaged in his massive overalls' pockets and produced a key for her.

"So she's told you." Zizou's eyes widened comically, and Vi realized that he had not expected Chiara to have shared her secret hiding place. "I think I heard the door slam, so she might have locked it. You can reach her if you climb from my shop—"

"I know all the rooftops from Lilien Haus to your place."

She didn't want to stay longer. Although she had way too many questions for him, questions she wasn't even certain she wanted answers to. But in the end, her priorities were different now. Her concern for Chiara was paramount, so she pocketed the key and, after making sure Chiara had indeed locked the door to her floor, ran outside, shouting at Zizou who was standing rooted to the spot.

"I will meet her halfway."

VI DIDN'T REMEMBER how she'd gotten up the stairs from the cafe. Her hands trembled as she held on tight to the steel rails of the narrow stepladder, the camera still dangling heavy around her neck. Once there, she refused to be distracted by the magnificence of Paris spreading like wings in front of her. She kept her head down and tried not to think about her fear of heights as she jumped from one roof to the next. When she was two buildings away from Lilien Haus, she finally saw her.

Chiara was standing across from Vi, on the very edge of the roofline. It didn't have a railing, and Vi's heart was suddenly in her throat. She didn't know if she should shout, since she might startle Chiara. And with every breath she took, Vi prayed that Chiara's being so close to the edge was by accident. That it meant nothing. That none of this was happening.

Spurred on by the need to do something, Vi took several

careful steps. Then more and more, until she was only a few feet away. Still, her own fear made the lump in her throat insurmountable, choking the life out of her.

Her tears were blinding her. However, none of them were for herself. They were all for the woman who trembled in the wind and seemed a million miles away.

Chiara couldn't jump, Chiara couldn't fall, because Vi would not be able to save her. Vi was too far away, *too far away*...

"I won't, Vi. I'm just... uncentered... Unsteady, I guess."

Had she once again spoken her thoughts out loud? Had Chiara heard her? The low voice, laden with sorrow, was so quiet, Vi could barely hear in spite of being as close as she was now. When she raised her eyes—fear swallowing her whole and tears streaming down her cheeks—and looked at Chiara, she was still near the edge, still motionless, still staring into the distance.

"I heard you cry, darling. Or try not to sob too loudly. I'm sorry they sent you after me. You can go back now. I know you're scared. I knew you were scared the very first time I took you up. But you were so brave, soldiering on."

Vi jerked her head, then realized that Chiara was still not looking at her, but into the beautiful expanse of Paris. She needed to speak, to ask, to deny that she was here on someone else's orders, to find her voice. Yet she felt like everything around her was steeped in molasses. She herself was sluggish, weary, unable to act. Like in one of those dreams where someone is chasing you and you can't move quite fast enough. A dream where her closed-up throat precluded her from uttering a word, from salvation.

Except she didn't need to be saved right now, Chiara did. So Vi gritted her teeth and finally managed to force her mouth to cooperate.

"Nobody sent... Came by myself... Well, not really, Zizou..."
She stopped when she heard Chiara's quiet chuckle.

"Rambling again, Ms. Courtenay?"

The laughter and the words, so familiar, so quintessentially
Chiara, so unlike the cavernous, lifeless 'I won't,' that Vi was
ready to sprint the rest of the way on the warm, gray zinc of the
roof. She chose to temper her zeal and instead take careful
steps towards Chiara.

"You know I ramble when I'm nervous. And no, I didn't
believe you would jump. She doesn't deserve—"

"God, you are so naïve, still!" Chiara finally turned, skew-
ering Vi with a direct look as she stepped away from the edge,
her arm gestures—so rarely employed by her now, yet oh-so-
Italian—underscoring her frustration.

The rare glimpse of temper, so uncharacteristic compared
to her overall calm and collected disposition, was a surprise. A
pleasant one. Anything was better than the prior lifelessness.

Vi knew Chiara's anger and pain over the situation must
have finally taken over, and she didn't mind if it was directed at
her. She didn't care. The ice that had been encasing her chest
ever since she'd seen Chiara teetering on the edge had begun to
thaw. That was all that mattered.

Chiara stalked towards her and grabbed her upper arm, not
so gently taking her farther away from the edge of the roof.

"Naïve and so damn brave I can't even be angry with you.
And I have so much anger now, Vi... So much..." Chiara trailed
off, despite the obvious dark mood, seemingly satisfied now
that Vi couldn't see the street beneath them anymore from
where they stood. She closed her eyes, inhaled deeply, then sat
down, pulling on Vi to join her.

Before she knew what was happening, Vi found herself
shoulder to shoulder with Chiara, engulfed in the remnants of
crackling aggravation still radiating from her companion, who

continued to take deliberate deep breaths to calm herself down.

"I am not sure that strategy has ever helped me." Vi's words took both of them by surprise.

"Are you really criticizing how I cope with my frustration?" Chiara's eyebrow rose indignantly and Vi had to smile.

"I know you want to bite my head off... You could, you know, it's fine. Or you could hold on to me. Because I'm here. Because I'm safe."

And it was Vi's turn to look into the distance, to pretend that the skyline was all she saw when, in fact, she saw nothing at all, her eyes again filling with tears that she couldn't explain or understand.

A gentle touch on her chin made her turn back, then amber eyes perused her face at leisure. And suddenly the air was no longer filled with crackling anger.

The temperature rose each time Chiara lowered her eyes to Vi's mouth. On the last pass, Chiara spoke, and her voice had that low note to it, the one that Vi recognized, because she had been hearing it for months now. And she had never heard it directed at others. She thought she finally knew what it was.

"Whoever is writing my life is perverse." The words were a soft whisper. Chiara's eyes twinkled with gentleness, then she bit her lip, and Vi wanted to whimper.

In the distance, a single bird trilled, flying high in the purpling sky, and Vi's heart wanted to chase it, to fly along.

"You are not safe, darling. Not even close. But you *are* too naïve and too kind, Vi. A gentle soul. Too beautiful. Too... *everything* really, for your own good. You would have tried to save me, wouldn't you?" When Vi tried to shake her head 'no,' she knew what Chiara would say next, because she understood her own eyes had betrayed her.

"Don't lie to me, Vi. You can't pull that off to save your life, anyway. Your face, your eyes will always show me the truth. So don't even try. You never have before. Obviously hidden some things, judging by your lack of surprise at Frankie's choice of mid-afternoon snack..." And now the tone held no warmth, just mocking.

"I—"

"No, Vi, please don't. On some level, I knew. You don't go from a loving, fulfilling sexual partnership to barely touching for years without reason. I should have done something sooner. Confronted her, or even walked away. I carry so much guilt where my mother is concerned, despite years of therapy and knowing full well that her disappointment is not my fault."

Chiara sighed, and the exhalation seeped into Vi's bones. "There were lovers I left with broken dreams and broken promises. Projects, people. And I just wanted to make things work. To try. To do my best and for my best to, for once, be enough."

Chiara's voice trembled on a sob. In the distance, it seemed that Paris stood still, the usual bustle of the capital suddenly quiet. Perhaps the City of Light was giving its queen her due. Oblivious to Vi's thoughts, Chiara went on.

"And I was afraid, Vi. Of failure, yes, of disappointing again, yes. But also of being alone. Unloved, untouched, unwanted. And then you appeared, you and your noble bloodline and your lost shoes. *Cenerella*. You, with your complete understanding of my thoughts and impulses, of my creations, and of my emotions. You, of these gray eyes and that gorgeous auburn hair and adorable freckles, and this face that gives away everything you're thinking and everything you feel."

An unknown and seemingly unknowable emotion of profound happiness washed over Vi. She was full to the brim with something she had never experienced before. The sense of being elated. Everything was magnified, the city suddenly alive around her, vivid colors and sounds enveloping her, as much as Chiara's scent and her warmth.

Vi closed her eyes to hold on to this emotion, only to re-open them swiftly to not miss a thing, a single second of looking into Chiara's, whose mouth was now hiding a smile, as she spoke on.

"You've given me inspiration, you've given up your evenings and your nights to help me, you held back Frankie's secret for me and from me, and even now you're fighting your terror, just to be here, with me..."

Chiara trailed off, still looking at her, and Vi gulped. Because the light of that magical understanding between them, like a silken thread, like one of the many Chiara used in her studio to create masterpieces, had tied itself between their two rib cages, just as Chiara's voice wound itself around Vi, rendering her completely still, incapable of moving, of saying anything.

"I've never once felt like this in my life. Never. Seen, touched, wanted. And I have been somebody's wife for twenty years. You gave me all of this in mere months. Can you blame me then?"

The soft chuckle at the end of the question made Vi shiver. She wasn't yet ready to process that Chiara had known about her feelings, about her desires all along. And she sure as hell wasn't ready to delve into the fact that Chiara perhaps welcomed all of them.

But that one word, *wanted*, washed over her like a consecration. A dream that she scarcely dared to even acknowledge was within reach, as unbelievable and unattainable as it had been to Vi throughout their summer.

The air around her appeared warmer, saturated with her emotion, an emotion that she'd held locked away, a covenant of her own making, to herself, to never ever reveal, yet here it was, out in the open. All she had to do was reach.

She took a few steadying breaths, bracing herself for the

answer to the question she felt compelled to ask. That reach, she was suddenly brave enough to attempt.

"Blame you for what?"

Chiara's face was sober, all traces of amusement gone. She lifted her hands, cool and soft, and cupped Vi's face so gently, her eyes watered at the gesture. She wanted to close them and let herself lean into the cool, beloved hands.

"For being tempted? For wanting this light? This steadiness? This joy that you are? For wanting you all these months?"

And just like that, all the oxygen she'd so diligently inhaled just a moment ago left Vi's lungs in a whoosh. Her heart in her throat and her mind suddenly blank, all she saw were the kind, warm eyes with the fire in them. That same fire she'd never quite been able to explain. Now she knew what it meant.

In the twilight falling like a blanket over them, covering both their bodies and the city that was hurrying along its early evening, busy and beautiful and elegant, Vi felt like the dusk was lulling her into a dream.

Her hand rose of its own accord and she covered Chiara's, turning her face and leaning into their now entwined fingers.

Bravery or foolhardiness overcame her disbelief, her reticence, and she took a chance, kissing the now warm skin of the palm, feeling a shudder pass through Chiara.

And suddenly the city came to life, the birds sang and the cars honked, and the moon's shadow peeked at them, so out of place in this still light sky. Maybe as out of place as Vi herself, on this roof, her lips on the skin of this woman who trembled under her touch.

When she raised her eyes, Chiara's were dark, much darker than the dusk warranted, much hungrier than a single kiss to the palm, and so Vi did the only thing she could. The only thing she, in fact, had been doing for months now. She gave Chiara what she wanted. Vi leaned, closing the distance between their lips halfway, and paused waiting for Chiara to make the final decision.

Chiara's eyes fluttered shut, perhaps at the raw display of her own hunger reflected back at her, or maybe at being allowed to take the final step, at being given a choice. A choice she did not hesitate to make.

She leaned in too, still holding Vi's face in her hands, and their lips touched. Tentatively, gently, brushing once, twice, before Vi found her courage and carefully grasped Chiara's lower lip between hers. A gasp and tiny whimper were her reward, and Vi's heart soared.

She knew there was no way it was still beating in her chest, with the air around them pulsating with something like a rhythm, a rhythm she followed with her mouth. Then, emboldened, she raised her own hand, the one that was not still holding Chiara's, and gently slid it up that sharp edge of the jaw she'd admired so many times, up to the delicate ear, which made Chiara whimper again.

The sound made Vi tremble but she couldn't stop, couldn't get enough of the glorious hair, her fingers delving into the still sun-warmed silk and fisting there, causing Chiara to gasp and open her mouth slightly.

But Vi didn't hurry, didn't use this opportunity to press forward. She simply licked tenderly at Chiara's lower lip and waited, waited patiently until Chiara uttered a sigh of total frustration, let go of Vi's face and slid her arms around her shoulders, finally bringing them chest to chest, pushing the forgotten camera still dangling around her neck to the side, as she herself deepened the kiss.

Overhead, Vi's soaring heart pulsed and trembled, full of love and full of Chiara. And it would stay that way, since the rest of Vi's life had already begun.

13

ONCE UPON A BROKEN FRAME

Genevieve Courtenay was very good at following events unfolding in fast motion. She thought quickly on her feet, she reacted in time, and was proactive. She excelled at being ahead.

Being early, being fast, guaranteed her many things. Safety primarily, but also invisibility and space and peace to be herself. She'd finish her chores, she'd deal with whatever needed to be dealt with after her family came and went, and then she could do as she pleased. Mainly though, it meant she could stay out of the fray.

What she wasn't very good at was slow motion. When time stretched or stopped entirely, and when she was powerlessly watching things happen. One after another after another. As a child, after having been immersed in Greek legends and myths, she always imagined the three Fates and their thread, as it stretched in front of them and as they ruled over it.

Chiara kissed her and Vi felt on top of the world, like she was the one threading time, every single caress of that beautiful mouth making her powerful, giving her strength, breathing light into her. Life bloomed around her, and she was a thief, stealing something that couldn't belong to her, for Vi Courtenay had been taught that she didn't deserve any of this.

So when Chiara pulled back and gazed at her, Vi held her breath. Chiara would wake up from whatever had come over her and tell her—

"I'm sorry..."

Vi closed her eyes. The Fates must have cut the thread, because here she was, hitting the wall at full speed. One really could never outrun those divinities and their spindle and shears.

She shook her head, and Chiara's hands slowly fell away from her cheeks. She made herself card her fingers through Chiara's soft, silky hair one last time as she lowered her own hand.

"Don't say anything. I guess this is that midnight moment. And I know exactly how Cinderella felt. After all, you've been calling me that all summer."

Chiara opened her mouth to speak and caught Vi's arm as she got up, but Vi was having none of it as she shook it off and almost blindly made her way off the roof through the exit towards Zizou's bistro.

When she found herself on the sidewalk, the wind had changed and the sky was becoming more overcast by the minute. A strong gust blew leaves in her direction, and Vi wanted to laugh.

Yes, universe, she got the hint.

Summer was over. It was time to go home. She covered the camera with her hoodie and walked all the way to her apartment in the chilly rain.

VI KNEW her father was in her apartment before she'd closed the door behind herself. Despite the melancholy of being rejected after the absolute best kiss of her life—a kiss so earth-shattering that she would surely divide her life into 'before' and 'after' now—her senses alerted her it was time to be watchful. And Vi sensed him before he stood up from the armchair.

"Hello, father."

She took off her drenched sweatshirt, remarking that, despite its state, the camera was dry as she gently placed it on the kitchen counter next to her open laptop.

Something inside her clicked at seeing it lit, and Zizou's words came back to her. Her suspicions, her premonitions. They'd not been baseless at all. She could see how certain things could have been accomplished despite her vigilance—the method to this entire madness and a way for her father to...

She was afraid to finish her thought. And at this point, there was nothing on the laptop of any importance. The Lilien Haus' collection was out there in the world.

The most he'd find were her pictures of Chiara... Her brain screeched to a halt, the desire to scream in frustration rising in her along with bile, leaving a foul taste in her mouth.

Well, this must be why her stepsisters had mocked her about following Chiara around like a love-sick puppy and for being an embarrassing lesbian pining for a married woman.

Vi was so careful with everything pertaining to Lilien Haus and the collection. It seemed she should have been more cautious about her and Chiara's privacy as well. Her father must have gone through her laptop before and found the numerous pictures she'd taken, and told them. For some reason, it hurt less that he himself had never mentioned it or humiliated her about it in person. Small blessings.

Her shoulders sagged as he finally crossed the room to her. In the dark, that he seemed to prefer when he visited her place unannounced, his face looked strangely animated.

"Genevieve, you're a mess."

Well, maybe calling out her disheveled appearance was

invigorating him. Because she hadn't seen him emote in a really long time.

"Yes, father." The prerequisite words were automatic.

"What happened at Lilien Haus? I heard the police were called?" His voice rose, as if he initially hadn't intended for it to be a question.

He would know if she attempted to lie or evade, and the truth was easier, anyway. Easier, more expedient, and maybe it would save him. Vi bit her cheek until she tasted blood. It washed away the bitterness, but the copper lingered, so familiar, somehow safe.

Blood of his blood.

After everything, she still cared about what happened to him and thought she had an obligation to warn him, even if that left her sullied in ways she did not want to yet contemplate. He was all she had.

"I don't know anything about the police. When I left, Renate and Frankie had a fight. But... The Lilienfelds hired a private investigator. He has been looking into me, into us, really, the whole summer."

Charles' face was stark and still in the darkness of the room. He shrugged, as apathetic and haughty as ever, and looked at her as if she wasn't there, as if she had said nothing of importance.

And for a second, Vi thought that perhaps everyone, her own gut included, had been mistaken where Charles Courtenay was concerned. His reaction wasn't one of a man almost caught. He looked down at his lapel, and with the practiced gesture of an aristocrat, removed a piece of lint from it.

"And your internship?"

"Two more weeks, father." Vi pushed the camera farther from the edge of the counter and stood very still. Something was happening, and she couldn't for the life of her find her footing, her speed and agility, the things that had saved her before, the things that would help her deal with her father.

The moment stretched, painfully so, as he touched a photograph on her wall. Followed by another. And another. When he finally stopped, Vi could see, even in the dim light, that his hand trembled. Her mother smiled easily from the last picture, a large bouquet of yellow tulips in her arms obscuring the bottom half of her face, leaving the shining gray eyes, the happy freckles and all that auburn hair, like the sun, all rays and all warmth.

"No..." Charles didn't turn, but he dropped the hand that was still shaking. The catch in his voice had almost caused Vi to reach out to him, but he suddenly took a step back and faced her, shoving his hands in his pockets. "It ended today. No more of this foolishness. Photography? Please, don't make me laugh. You are exactly like your mother. Creativity skipped two generations."

He spat out the last words, and Vi was afraid for a second that he would turn back and rip the photograph off the wall, there was so much rage emanating from him.

"I have contracts lined up in the States, father. And an apprenticeship. In a few weeks, I have to be in New York." She was pleading, and she was not entirely sure why. Or for what. She was twenty-five years old, and she was begging her father to allow her to do the job she dreamed of.

God, why couldn't she stand up for herself for once?

He came closer, and they looked at each other, her resigned and ashamed of herself, him despondent, angry, and right as he was a breath away from her, her mother's picture fell off the wall.

They both startled, and her father stumbled back to the place where the frame lay in pieces, sharp glass shards strewn across the floor. He jerked away as if he'd cut himself and stepped back as Vi knelt in front of the portrait. Her mother smiled on. Behind her, the front door opened.

Her father's voice was quiet, but Vi refused to turn around, refused to look at him. "You are finished at Lilien Haus, Genevieve. You will come to the penthouse tomorrow evening, and we shall find you something else. I always knew fashion was wasted on all of you. You and Gigi and Kylie, but especially on you. And clean up here."

Surprised by the soundless way the door shut behind him, Vi exhaled. Tears stung her eyes at the thought of surrendering the camera tomorrow, but at least it was her stepmother's and not Chiara's. She wouldn't be keeping it, anyway.

She wasn't going to keep Chiara either. Her evening at the ball had lasted longer than this particular Cinderella had ever dreamt it might. And unlike the real Cinderella, Vi even got a kiss. She looked down at her soggy Converse and laughed. It sounded brittle in the quiet of the room. Nobody, and certainly no princess, was coming to offer her a shoe.

She sat down and checked her laptop—just to make sure she didn't unwillingly expose Lilien, in case her father did snoop around— absentmindedly scrolling through her shots. After months of being around Chiara and the models, around other photographers, after reading her weight in photography books, Vi knew what was there to see. And some of the images were good. Very good, in fact.

That feeling she'd always had, of having a vision, of her mind reeling from so much of it, was now quieted and sated, because here it all was, spilled onto the screen.

Quit? Forget about her future? About America? About Poise or all the other opportunities she had lined up?

Chiara's hands and face were gorgeous on her screen, the shot taken at a strange angle that made it look almost as if Chiara would raise her head any minute, as if her hands would draw that line they were poised to trace at any moment now... There was talent in the composition, in every line.

Her talent.

No, she might quit, because after what happened today, there was no way she could ever go back to the way things were. But she had tasted freedom, she had breathed the air of possibilities. She could not undream her dreams and unhope her hopes, and she could not, *would not*, return to the penthouse.

She glanced at the floor strewn with pieces of glass and at the picture of her mother, smiling at her from where it had fallen. If this wasn't a sign... Vi sighed and stood up to clean when a quiet knock on the door startled her.

Was her father back? Was he here to demand that she go with him right away? And what would she do if he did? She threw one last glance at her mother's portrait and the mess on the floor. Her heart was in overdrive as she slowly opened the door. There would be hell to pay if she did what she wanted to do and told her father she would not acquiesce to his demands.

But it wasn't her father. And even though it wasn't him standing there—the dim bulb of the landing playing on those sharp cheekbones, obscuring the amber eyes and their expression from Vi—she knew there would still be hell. Because where Chiara Conti-Lilienfeld was concerned, Vi would always pay. And the cost would inevitably be more than she could afford. Yet she would do so freely. Eyes opened, heart on her sleeve.

She wrenched the door open wider, and Chiara entered her space for the first time. Vi felt that very same light and shadow that always accompanied Chiara suddenly suffuse her apartment. They wandered around as their mistress did, then settled in the corners, waiting for what would happen next. The same way Vi herself did.

"Hello, Vi."

She could feel the color bloom on her cheeks as hope took

over her heart. Hope for what? She had no idea, but the tone of that voice, the absolutely inadequate words, the oh-so-useless greeting... Perhaps she was not alone in this? They'd always found uncanny ways to understand each other. Maybe this time wouldn't be so different.

Still silent, afraid to break the spell, she gestured to one of the tall chairs at the breakfast bar. It wasn't hospitable to keep the guest in the coldness of the kitchen versus the more inviting chairs of her living space, but Vi thought she couldn't allow Chiara in, not yet. Not without knowing why she was here.

No, she had no defenses where this woman was concerned, and she had to do something, anything, to minimize the damage.

Chiara took a few careful steps towards the bar, stopping as she reached it, and nodded towards the broken glass on the floor in front of her. Vi shrugged, then shook her head when Chiara's eyebrows lifted.

They shared a long look, and after a few moments, Chiara simply motioned for Vi to join her. Well, fair was fair, and so a few seconds later, Vi found herself sitting shoulder to shoulder with Chiara in her kitchen. To say that this was surreal was an understatement.

"I hope you don't mind." Chiara's fingers were on the bar, tracing the marble veins as Vi's eyes did the same with those mirrored on Chiara's hands. She chose silence again and shook her head. Chiara sighed. "Everything changed today. I wanted to believe it's alright that I'm here. And that you will allow me to apologize properly this time."

Even in Chiara's repose, her light and her shadows were tumultuous in the corners, and Vi found herself responding. If only to appease the beasts.

"There isn't anything to apologize for. If anyone should, it's—"

But Chiara interrupted her with a raised hand, and Vi's eyes followed the movement as if mesmerized. *Graceful, commanding.*

Mercy.

Chiara slowly let her hand fall and shook her head.

"No, before you say something undoubtedly self-effacing, it's Frankie who should be apologizing. To many people. Because it seems they knew all along and never told me."

Chiara's hands now lay flat and tense on the counter, and Vi wanted to cover them with her own. She didn't dare, and the absence of courage was like a stab wound.

Before Vi found the voice to speak, to confess that she was also on that list of people who knew about Frankie's affairs, Chiara made a dismissive sound. "I don't care. I don't. It makes me an absolute fool that, apparently this has been going on under my nose for years, and I never saw it. It doesn't matter. So yes, this is on me..."

"You are nobody's fool, Chiara! And none of this is on you." And now Vi gave into her earlier impulse and touched the tense hand that was still gripping the counter. After a moment, she gentled her own fingers and simply traced the blue rivulets of veins running along the translucent skin.

In those shadows that Chiara had brought in with her, their hands looked like a study of contrasts. Chiara's nervous, shaking. Her own relaxed, tender, apologetic. Chiara's nails were painted crimson and Vi caressed them one by one, to assure herself they were real, that Chiara herself was real.

"I seem to be, though. I seem to be a fool for you this time, Vi." The way Chiara said her name took Vi's breath away. Again. How did this woman always do this to her? One syllable. One syllable that she almost never ever used, choosing to call her Ms. Courtenay ad nauseam, only occasionally stooping to a wayward 'darling' or 'Cenerella'.

But when she did call Vi by her chosen name, it was devastating. Maybe that was why she so seldom did, because she knew the power she held?

Finally, the meaning of Chiara's words reached Vi, and she lifted her face from staring at their hands so quickly, it made her dizzy. Unlike the trembling hands, eyes full of calm were watching her with the kind of soft expression one usually gives to someone who cannot, for the life of them, comprehend the most simple of concepts, but one indulges them anyway.

"Wha..."

Her chest was tight, taking a breath was impossible and yet vital. Because somehow tonight her life had taken a turn and everything she had ever dreamed of was here, in front of her, freely offered. Just to her. The tightness did not subside at the realization that her heart hammered a mile a minute in her ears. She tried to shake her head, but dislodging this feeling was impossible, since the one who was responsible for her heart was looking at her, eyes full of affection. She was lost in them, in this emotion, starving for it. There was no shaking it.

"Eloquent, so eloquent." Responding to her earlier half question, Chiara sighed and leaned closer, and now Vi could see mischief along with fondness dancing in those amber depths. "I was having the worst day of my life. The absolute worst. And then, when my world was falling apart, when I was literally standing on the edge, deciding what to do next, and when that one step was so tantalizing... Amidst all that turmoil and pain and grief, I felt as alone as I've ever been—and *alone* and I are on a first name basis. Yet, there you were, ready to save me, even though you were shaking with fear, your teeth chattering and your breath coming out in sobs. I heard you before I saw you. And I was no longer alone. The step was no longer tempting. Because you were there, Vi. You offered that I could hold on to you. And for a precious moment, I held tight."

Chiara turned her hand, palm up, and their fingers tangled sweetly, even as she went on.

"It has been quite a journey, this day. But something kept tugging at my mind, at my heart, really. I wasn't alone. You didn't let me be. In fact, you haven't let me be alone for months now. You've been with me. At first as an adorable peculiarity, but soon you became a steadfast, calming presence, a charming distraction from my crumbling marriage and daily troubles. Except the charming distraction very soon turned into someone I looked forward to seeing and spending time with. Who listened to me. Who inspired me. Vi, surely you know by now that the entire current Lilien Haus collection exists thanks to you. And for you, really. My small gift to you for being there for me."

Vi knew she had tears in her eyes, but she didn't care. The pendulum of the events of the days had swung again, and she was plunged from fear and dread to wonder. Chiara created because of her?

"You understood me, darling. Like nobody before you. You took one look at my vision, as raw as it was, and you saw what I wanted to see, you heard my words before I could utter them. Can you blame me for wanting to hold on to that? To you?"

Vi gripped the fingers holding hers tighter because this was wonderful, but while Chiara was ascribing her all these amazing qualities, she knew her own motives hadn't always been pure. And she had to say so. Something about this woman never quite allowed her to hide the truth.

"I believe you think too highly of me. I'm... I was never... Never selfless..." She stumbled over her own words, and Chiara reached and lifted her chin a little higher, the gesture so familiar. How many times had Chiara raised her face exactly like this, how many times had she looked into her eyes while those cool fingers cradled her jaw, caressing her cheekbone with her thumb?

Vi's eyes suddenly widened. And Chiara's smile bloomed, the sensual lips stretching in mirth.

"I love it when you finally grasp something and it transforms your whole face. So expressive, so gorgeous. What, you were never selfless? My darling, neither was I. Yes, at first I found you interesting, certainly beautiful and too smart for your own good. But nothing more than what romance novels call 'a cinnamon roll.' One that was already so tortured by life. I gave you maybe a passing thought."

Chiara's thumb dropped to caress Vi's lower lip, as her fingers gripped her jaw tighter, and for Vi, the world stilled. Even Paris outside was reverentially silent. Nothing else mattered but this, right here.

"But you are just too bright, too luminous. And even standing in my studio, in wet clothes and dirty shoes, teasing my ridiculous cat... I looked at you and I saw you. And I have kept looking ever since, because I couldn't stop."

The thumb on her mouth was sending ripples of pleasure all over Vi's body and making her brave, braver than she'd ever been. She closed her lips, trapping the fingertip and giving it a slow lick, and it was Chiara's turn to gasp. But she recovered rather quickly, and the now wet finger trailed down Vi's throat and settled on her collarbone.

"And then you do something like this, be it voice an idea, or lick your lips or anything really, that would engage not just my mind or my heart. But parts of me that I pledged to my wife, parts of me that had been asleep for years. And can you fault me when you are always so absolutely alluring?"

Chiara suddenly surged forward and replaced her thumb with her mouth, as if trying to reassure Vi that what had been happening in the past half hour was real.

This *was* happening. And how could she find Vi's steady affection so unbelievable, when Vi was so in love it hurt her chest, because there was simply not enough space in there, between her ribs, to contain all this love, all this devotion?

But Chiara's mouth was real, and whatever it hadn't said out loud, it was doing an amazing job of conveying with gentle caresses and careful little nips to Vi's lower lip. It was glorious. It was magnificent. It was better than their kiss on the roof—

Remembering how that had ended, however, made Vi's mind and her body screech to a halt. She raised her hand, but Chiara had already sensed her hesitation and stopped immediately. A part of Vi wanted to cry all over again.

Instead, she took a deep breath. "On the roof... You said you were sorry." Vi shook her head, her voice quiet. "It made me so unsure. So afraid."

"Darling, of what?" Chiara's brow was furrowed in concern, her eyes searching.

"That you might break me." The words surged from her in a hoarse whisper, and Vi knew she'd spoken nothing but the truth, even if she had never voiced it before, not even to the emptiness of her dark room.

"Oh Vi. I would never. If you believe one thing tonight, let this be it. I was sorry that I kissed you without your permission, without asking for consent." Chiara seemed to struggle for words before soldiering on.

"I am older, certainly I should be wiser... My marriage has been a sinkhole for a while, and despite me trying my best to ignore it, to not disappoint, to be worthy of her, I felt my unhappiness slowly choking me."

Vi wanted to interrupt, to scream and rage at Frankie, at the world that made this miracle of a woman feel unworthy. But Chiara had that look in her eyes, the look of trying to get all the words out before something stopped her, so instead, Vi tucked a stray flyaway behind her ear and nodded for her to continue.

"I was worried that I was using you and you were going along with it. I wanted to stop and ask you." Chiara's hands shook slightly, and she made a move to reach for Vi, but seemed to reconsider at the last moment, gripping the counter, her knuckles white.

Vi's shoulders sagged under the sheer relief. Chiara did not regret anything. Chiara had wanted to kiss her. Chiara wanted her, period. She grinned, even as Chiara's uncertainty turned into exasperation at the sight of her smile, so clear now on her face, eyes wide, brows raised, the wide mouth set in an adorable pout.

"But I didn't know—"

"Well, if only you'd have stopped your self-righteous, woe-is-me march off the roof and listened to me, maybe you would have!" Chiara threw her hands up, then whispered conspiratorially. "It's okay though."

Her expression had all the subtlety of a cat that had eaten a whole bowl of cream. And would probably go back for more any second. Vi trembled for all the right reasons now, and her stomach tightened.

"Is it?" Her voice was quiet even to her own ears, and she bit her lip to hold herself back from blurting out, 'let me get down on my knees in front of you, right here at the breakfast bar.'

When she raised her eyes, Chiara's were knowing, seeing.

"Yes, darling. It showed me that perhaps I was worried for nothing, and that you wanted me as much as I wanted you. But before this goes any further, this time, I'd like you to use your words and tell me. One 'no' from you and I will leave."

Chiara spoke calmly, matter-of-factly almost, but her voice broke a bit at the end of the sentence.

"I will always be grateful for this summer. For you giving me the strength to survive the worst day of my life. And I will always, no matter what happens, cherish you. So if you say 'no,' I'll understand and go. Or you can say 'yes'..."

Chiara stopped, and now it was her turn to bite her lip. Vi shivered at the sensuality of the gesture. Chiara slowly let go of the now plump, red lip and smirked. Vi felt her own smile widen.

"And what happens if I say 'yes?'"

"Whatever it was you were thinking a second ago, whatever had your eyes go dark, hungry... All of that happens. But you have to be sure, darling. I have so much baggage, and I'm in so much trouble, all sorts of trouble, and not just over you—"

It was Vi's turn to press her fingertips to Chiara's lips, and the sensation of that inviting, willing mouth under her skin—despite having kissed it only minutes ago—was addictive. She never wanted to stop touching it, caressing it.

"I know you're trouble, and I know you're troubled. I don't care. I want you." She leaned in, and Chiara actually moaned into her mouth. With that, Vi suddenly remembered that one tiny circumstance that wasn't actually tiny at all.

"Except... Well..."

"What is it, darling?" And the concern, the honesty in those eyes, nearly undid Vi. She lowered her face and mumbled.

Chiara's sigh was teasingly exasperated.

"Darling, you will have to speak up. Communication is key here."

Vi ran her foot over the cold metal rung of the barstool until she felt Chiara's arm touch hers.

"Tell me? Is it about being tested? I was months ago. And I haven't been with Frankie for over a year now..." Vi's eyes widened and Chiara's smile was self-deprecating. "I told you, our issues started long before, and infidelity is honestly not the biggest problem. By far. But let's not go into all that now. What were you trying to say before the floor got so very interesting that you had to talk to it instead of me?"

Vi laced their fingers together, her thumb caressing Chiara's soft skin. She knew what it must've cost Chiara to come here, what it meant for her to be this brave, and that it was Vi's turn to find her own courage once again. So she lifted their joint hands to her mouth, kissing Chiara's fingertips, gently biting one, making both of them tremble. *Into the breach then.*

"I don't have experience."

Chiara's brows lifted and her eyes gentled. But before she could reach the wrong conclusion, Vi hurried on.

"No, no, I've been with women before. Well, one woman and she was older, and it was a long time ago, and... I just don't want you to have any expectations, you know. I might not be very good at this."

"I see." The corners of Chiara's mouth twitched, before giving in to the smile playing there. "Why don't you let me worry about that?" She lowered her gaze a little, seeking eye contact and murmured, "if you're sure?"

Wonderful, amazing words. Vi's heart was full, but it was time to move past talking. Words were no longer enough. She had pined and longed for this woman all summer.

And the moment she had yearned for had finally materialized. Chiara was here, holding her hand, mischief back in her eyes. So Vi nodded and leaned in.

Right before their mouths touched, Chiara's teasing, "an older woman, huh?" made both of them smile, and when their lips collided, so did their joy.

They kissed leisurely, Vi still unsure, exploring, testing and Chiara allowing her to take the lead. From the kitchen to the alcove that held the pristine bed with its fluffy coverlet and soft pillows, by way of the walls and an armchair that they almost fell into, their progress was slow. But oh-so arousing.

Gentle touches and tentative caresses. And kisses. All the kisses. Vi could not stop her mouth from taking more. And Chiara gave everything.

Hands on jaw, a tug on hair to raise the other's face, to angle the chin, to bare the neck to careful nips, then back up for another kiss and another. Vi's mouth kept returning to Chiara's, unwilling to be distracted by the soft skin, by the expanse of it, as she slowly undid the buttons of Chiara's Oxford shirt.

But soon her hands pushed the fabric aside, and her eyes caught sight of the lace underneath and the breasts encased in it, and Vi's mouth actually went slack as her movements halted.

"I should've known you'd be a breast girl." Chiara's chuckle was decidedly dirty. And very self-satisfied. So Vi bit her clavicle, then licked the spot where her teeth had left shallows marks and continued to leave a wet trail downward with her tongue, wiping that smirk off Chiara's face when she reached the top of the bra and sucked there.

Chiara groaned, and her hands in Vi's hair tightened, their grip strong, but never pushing, never hurrying Vi, never rushing her moves—such as they were—because Vi suspected that she really wasn't all that good at this. She tried to make up for her inexperience with enthusiasm, but she was still tentative and awed.

"I don't mind, darling." As if reading her mind, Chiara lowered her face to look at Vi's shy eyes. "Take what you need. Go slow, go fast, take everything. I'm here. I'm with you. *Take what you need.*"

The words enveloped Vi like silk, like satin, like one of Chiara's gowns. She was warmed by them, and if little fires were lighting up everywhere Chiara's hands touched, the words allayed the urgency of desire; gave Vi permission to explore, to try, to please.

And Chiara really did not seem to mind. She didn't rush. Chiara simply let Vi do what she wanted, touch, kiss, caress.

Vi's eyes closed as her lips tasted the notch between the collarbones, salt and sweet and Chiara, full of verbena and patchouli, familiar, beloved. And the scents and the touch were such a déjà vu. Only their places were switched, because they'd been here before, in the gentleness, in the sweetness, in the adoration. Every time Chiara would drape a new piece of satin over Vi, every time her hands would glide over her shoulders, like they did right now, it would be like this. In fact, it would be exactly this. This worship. Chiara had been lifting her onto this altar of love for months, and it was Vi's turn now.

And Chiara, generous and mindful as ever, allowed Vi all the time, all the space, her patience endearing despite Vi's desire at times overwhelming her, like when in the alcove, Vi finally managed to take off the work of art that was the delicate bra, after fumbling with it for what seemed like hours.

Chiara moaned deeply when, after four tries, Vi finally lowered the lace and took a nipple in her mouth, licking, running her tongue over it again and again.

She didn't ask for anything. Vi suspected she was holding back and avoiding putting any pressure on her, but Vi couldn't bear the thought of Chiara inhibiting herself for her sake. So she lifted her face and pressed their foreheads together. Their breaths mingled, and Vi couldn't resist taking a quick bite of that swollen lower lip. When they finally parted, her voice was hoarse from all the want.

"Tell me. Show me. Don't hide from me. I want to see everything, and I want to do everything, everything you need, everything you want."

Chiara's knees bucked at Vi's words, and when she opened her eyes, they were wild and unfocused.

"Everything then, Vi. Give me everything. I won't break. Harder. Love me harder."

Love. Yes, Vi thought. Very much love. And so when she lowered her mouth to Chiara's breasts again and bit and sucked with purpose, that purpose was love.

And it was love when she lowered Chiara onto the soft coverlet, it was love when she finally tugged off the navy linen trousers and feasted her eyes on the long, graceful legs, all sinew and beautiful skin. When she trailed her lips from the ankle to the knee and then higher, up the thigh and higher still into the heat and the wet. When she looked up at Chiara's burning eyes as her tongue took the first taste. And it was love when she watched those eyes close in ecstasy, in abandonment as Vi kept tasting, kept drinking, because she was an addict now.

Nothing and no one had ever meant this much, nothing she ever wanted to achieve, but this pleasure, this woman, this one, *the one.*

Her thoughts chased each other as the taste embedded itself in her mind, in her soul. Nobody would ever compare, she thought, as she felt the slight spasm under her tongue, and Chiara reached for her hand and gripped it right before her back arched and her mouth opened in a soundless cry.

Vi wanted to look at her forever, to remember that perfection, the vision of what it meant to bring Chiara pleasure. It was magnificent. It felt like happiness.

THE MORNING RAYS peeked through the hastily drawn blinds, and Vi's eyes blinked several times before reason caught up with her. She was enveloped in willowy arms, held tight, and her temple was being kissed.

Chiara.

Last night came back to her in full technicolor. Scratch that. In hi-res.

Vi making Chiara come, and right away, before she could recover, taking that still trembling flesh in her mouth again and making Chiara scream. *Vi, Vi, Vi...*

The sweetest sound. The most erotic sound. As enticing as being fully dressed still, while Chiara had lain before her naked and beautiful.

All these memories Vi would relive forever. Like how she'd simply sat and watched that body rise and fall for a moment, and beat and live in front of her, splayed out in all its glory, strong and vulnerable, and so beautiful Vi had to take a deep breath to quiet her racing heart. It beat a staccato against her ribs, spurned by all the tenderness, all the love that filled her in this moment.

Everything had been so amplified it hurt, so Vi had closed her eyes and climbed that exhausted, sated body, kissing every inch of skin she could reach, while Chiara sighed and breathed and moaned, and then as she finally arrived at her destination and kissed that mouth parched from all the exertion of two climaxes, Chiara leaned to bring their lips together only to roll Vi, surprising her, making her laugh. Making her gasp when a gentle hand lowered her zipper and delved in, whispering, "what do you need, tell me? I'll give you anything, anything at all."

Pleasure pierced her, no warning, no regrets. Those skillful fingers had claimed her. Undone her. Once, twice, another thrust and a slow circle of the thumb and Vi, who'd already been on the very edge solely from watching Chiara, had come herself and it had been glorious.

Vi lifted her head and Chiara's wide-awake eyes met hers with so much tenderness, Vi felt tears sting, powerless to contain them. Chiara said nothing, just reached out and kissed them away and tucked Vi's head where it seemed to belong, because it fit like a puzzle piece on Chiara's shoulder. Vi breathed in her scent, mouthing at her neck and murmuring useless, disjointed words of happiness.

Yet Chiara seemed to understand, because she murmured them back, how wonderful it was, how amazing they were, how happy she was, and Vi's poor heart grew more and more, uncontainable, uncontrollable. She hugged Chiara tighter, snuggling in, right before a phone buzzed from the kitchen.

"Nope. Not getting up. Not answering. Not breaking this spell." Vi shook her head, and Chiara, perhaps tickled by the motion of Vi's hair, laughed. Openly, happily. And Vi raised her face again to just look. To take this moment in.

"You don't have to worry, darling. It's probably Aoife. I left rather in an understandable hurry last night, and both she and Renate were embroiled with the police, who'd been called because of all the ruckus. They were torn between the cops and trying to help and figure out what I should do. So Aoife is probably checking on me."

Vi scrunched her nose, not ready for the world to intrude on them. She knew it was out there, full of consequences and responsibilities, but she wanted to put it off, only for a bit, to savor this moment that was theirs alone.

Still, her stomach growled, and Chiara's answered with exactly the same hungry intonation. They looked at each other for a second before dissolving into laughter, and Vi jumped off the bed, taking the covers with her and wrapping them around her body. Chiara stretched fully nude on the bed, and Vi stared, mind blanking, mouth agape.

"God..."

"Well, technically goddess... And you are so cute, it's absolutely fantastic. Completely and totally adorable. A total breast girl."

Vi snickered before stalking to the kitchen counter where Chiara's purse lay. She brought it back to the bed and handed it to its owner, who was now reclining, arms behind her head, unabashed in her nudity, a firm smirk on her lips, observing Vi's total uselessness to the world.

Vi cleared her throat, feeling the blush creep up her neck, and gestured vaguely in Chiara's direction.

"I don't know why you find it in any way surprising. Yours are spectacular."

Chiara laughed, making those spectacular breasts bounce, and Vi thought she might pass out, because suddenly, there was absolutely no oxygen in the entire room.

"Oh, darling, you are smitten, since my size As have nothing on the glory of Sophia Loren and Monica Bellucci. And thank you for this." She dug around for the phone right when it started to buzz again.

"You Italians are so obsessed with your icons."

"They are icons for a reason. And yes, it's Aoife. I'm sorry, darling, I'll take it to tell her I'm fine."

"You are very fine indeed, despite some weird beauty standard you seem focused on. You're perfect." Vi smiled and tugged the sheet around herself tighter as it started to unfold.

"Oh, if this is how you're going to talk, I might not answer Sully. I want to hear more about this perfection that I supposedly am." Chiara smiled as the phone went off yet again, and Vi leaned in and planted a firm kiss on her smiling lips.

"Nothing 'supposed' about your perfection. You simply are. Now talk to Aoife and I will make us breakfast."

Vi walked away and closed the flimsy sliding doors to the alcove to give Chiara some privacy. She rummaged around the fridge, finding enough ingredients for French toast. On a whim, she threw on some clothes and, listening to Chiara's still talking in the bedroom, ran out to the corner shop where her pal Thierry sold flowers.

After one look at the long-stemmed, pristine white roses, Vi dropped the equivalent of a quarter of her salary on a whole bouquet and almost skipped back to her building.

The apartment was quiet when she plated the French toast and arranged the flowers in a vase.

Perfect. Everything was perfect.

AND HOW WAS she to have known that the very rest of the life she was thinking of, the one that had only just begun, was about to turn this way?

Her heart thudded in her chest as Chiara slid the alcove doors open, fully dressed, and Vi knew. Time stopped even as

Chiara moved towards her, languid and graceful and perfect. Except her eyes were closed off and watchful, and when Vi lifted a hand, she was out of reach. In every way possible. Vi sensed she couldn't touch her anymore, even if she were to caress her skin.

"White roses. My favorite. You are such an attentive person, lover. Always were."

Vi recoiled as if she had been slapped. Chiara picked one of the roses from the vase and lifted it to her face, inhaling the fragrant aroma.

"So attentive. Knowing. Seeing. Aren't you, *lover*?"

"Chiara..." What was she even saying? Something had happened while Vi was away, while Chiara was on the phone. Something had happened, and Vi's stomach was a deep well of dread. Surely not, after everything she had done, every step she had taken to protect Lilien and Chiara, whatever her family did, whatever was going on underneath all the veneer, whatever they were not telling her... Surely it had not touched—

"I want to say that it was low of you. That I would have never expected you to do this. Especially not after last night. But then I've been encouraging you to nurture that ambition and stand on your own two feet for months, *lover*."

That word again, mocking. Another slap.

"Stop, Chiara—"

"Stop? There's no stopping this. Look what you've unleashed." She lifted her other hand where her phone was going off in a series of unstoppable vibrations of incoming messages and missed calls. And there, on the screen, was the front page of the Paris Gala... Vi's world tilted. On instinct she darted a glance to the small kitchen table where... the camera no longer lay.

And just like that, the sense of premonition she'd had morphed into a sense of her worst nightmare come to life in the form of the labor of her own hands. Or, well, her father's hands.

But it was a picture she herself had taken. A picture of Chiara watching Frankie cheat on her. The pain etched on that beautiful face. The loss entrenched in those eyes that Vi had made close in ecstasy again and again only a few hours ago.

Those same pained eyes watched her now. A steady hand pocketed the phone and laid the rose on the breakfast bar. Vi opened her mouth to speak and Chiara looked on, daring her. To apologize, to explain. Vi lowered her face instead, tears streaming down her cheeks.

And what could she say? Everything made sense. Why Vi had even been dispatched to Lilien Haus. Why Charles wanted updates and regular visits. He 'd been waiting for something to happen. Something he could use.

And while she had failed with the collection, she had *not* failed with a juicier piece. Everything slid into place. The pieces of the carnage puzzle all fit now. Why her father had been here. Why he'd said she couldn't go back.

And why he took the camera.

He'd gotten what he needed. Charles Courtenay won dirty yet again, as he always did. Underhanded, cheating ,and probably illegal, but her father had been victorious. And Vi lost. Previous times, when he'd grifted and conned his way into money, all Vi had to lose, aside from an occasional payment to staff her family had swindled, was her dignity. This time? Vi lost everything.

She looked at the picture of her mother, still propped up against the wall where it had fallen.

She'd lost everything *again.*

"Why did you do it, Vi? Fame? Money?"

Chiara's voice was barely a whisper.

"I didn't do this," she pleaded. It was the truth, even if it meant nothing at all.

Something shining in Chiara's eyes looked back at her, and

she wanted to wince, to raise her shoulders and shield herself from it, except she didn't think she deserved to.

When Chiara spoke again, the whisper was no more, it was all pained sadness.

"You took the pictures, and even if you didn't sell them yourself, you certainly know who did. So in that case, it might as well have been you. Right?"

Vi shook her head, more out of instinct, then to outright lie. In the silence of the room, she could hear the thread of the breathing, pulsing city outside. Or was it her heart?

Still, it *was* a lie. Because she knew who did all of this. And, in spite of everything, she couldn't betray her father, no matter what it cost her. Her mother kept smiling at her from the picture, as if approving of her choice. Except Vi wasn't so sure she would. This was where Charles had gone too far. Nothing would be as it was ever again. And Vi would pay that price twice over. She was losing Chiara. And she would lose her family too. She would not be able to tolerate it anymore, not after this.

Chiara's voice was sad. A melancholy much worse than the one Vi had gotten used to in that first month at Lilien Haus.

"Oh, Vi. I don't know why I thought you'd be different. Just because you saw me? Simply because I thought you wanted *me* and not *the* Chiara?"

"I did!" Vi's voice broke even as the tears seemed unstoppable now. "I do, Chiara... I love you."

Chiara stood very still, then turned away.

"There's nothing I can do about that, Cinderella."

Closing the door with a soft click that might as well have been a gunshot, Chiara walked out of Vi's life. The sound jolted Vi from her stupor.

She looked around and from her position, she could make out the rumpled bed, the tangled sheets where they'd loved each other. God, she was so stupid, so naïve... Hadn't Chiara called her that only hours ago? It seemed like a lifetime.

She'd really added insult to Chiara's already injured pride. And perhaps not just her pride, because this was a betrayal of the highest order. All of Chiara's pain, all of Chiara's humiliation, out there for the entire world to see. How must she have felt, be feeling?

Vi wiped her face. The tears had somehow stopped. Perhaps she had no more to shed.

Maybe if she explained? Should she confess? Could she risk her father facing repercussions and ostracization? Vi thought that she should run. Should catch up with Chiara. What they had was real. Surely Chiara didn't believe Vi was capable of betraying her like this?

Even as her heart told her that Chiara very much believed her to be this perfidious, and even if the thudding muscle was bleeding with both insult and pain, Vi took two steps towards the front door to go after Chiara, when a sudden pain lanced her foot. Broken glass. Her mother's portrait.

Another step on autopilot and another piece of glass made her stumble and cry out. Blood pooling beneath her feet, Vi just watched the front door, willing it to open. Praying Chiara would hear her, would come back for her.

With a shout, she pulled a glass shard from her skin and, watching blood seep from her foot, slowly closed her eyes and sunk to the floor. Seconds later she slid out of consciousness.

Well, whatever she had thought about the rest of her life back on the rooftop of Rue Saint-Honoré, it was certainly proving to be rather painful.

PART II

SHADOW

SHADOW

PART 2

14

IN A FARAWAY LAND OF THORNY MEMORIES

Chiara Conti's life bore some resemblance to a fairytale. For one, she always tried very hard to be good at a lot of things. And she could honestly say that she thought she was successful. You name it; she was told she was fabulous at that particular thing.

Supermodel? You bet. After all, her name was spoken in the same breath as Claudia Schiffer and Linda Evangelista.

The talent behind a multi-million dollar empire? Well, she had kept Lilien Haus in the top ten of the world's fashion brands for two decades—whether it was public knowledge or not.

And for two, there was that thing she thought she excelled at most—being somebody's wife... Just like in a fairytale, in a crushing blow, it turned out she hadn't been all that good at *that*, after all. If her own, now former, wife was to be believed...

In fact, the déjà vu of trying exceedingly hard to be very good and not succeeding, even by a long shot, was massive. It was both shocking and not at all. After all, it mirrored her childhood all over again. Her mother working herself to the bone to send her to university, only to realize that Chiara would never be graduating. Not from her village school. And not from anywhere else, for that matter.

"I'm not even going to offer any pennies for those thoughts."

Aoife swaggered in, a spring in her step, arms full of ivory satin and lace, and Chiara looked up from the sketch at her workstation. The paper was full of doodles instead of any actual designs, and she had no idea when she'd lost her train of thought and gone down the rabbit hole of her own memories. The light blue sticky note on her desk seemed to frown at her. She had missed her second daily dose of her medication. Again. The morning dose was easy. The afternoon one? Forget it. Or, well, Chiara always did.

Aoife didn't blink as Chiara reached into the small dispenser by the post-it and dry swallowed the pill. For exactly the fifth time this week, Chiara had the distinct thought that she should stop doing that. It was Friday, after all.

"It's been five years. Maybe it's time to let go of some things?" Chiara smiled at her friend's perceptiveness and tact in sidestepping the medication issue. However, Aoife's predilection for dredging up the past wasn't a preferred avenue to go down. At least not now.

"Maybe. And perhaps some things are never meant to be let go of?" She took a step back and gave the cat loaf on the windowsill a gentle ear scratch. Binoche pretended not to notice the caress and then pretended even harder not to enjoy it. Both Chiara and the cat acted as though the chocolate ball of fluff wasn't purring.

"And speaking of letting go of things. In all these years, from Paris, to your year-long hiatus in Milan, and to our relocation to Manhattan, I still don't understand why you took the cat."

Chiara was about to answer when a set of heels clicked on

the dark oaken floors of the atelier and Renate stepped into the light.

"As if the cat is somehow at fault for the fact that a Courtenay ended up being a Courtenay, despite all the signs pointing at her bucking that family trend. But then I told you so from the beginning. I even hired Zizou to keep watch... Too bad he couldn't also look out for some of your softer hearts..."

With a particularly exaggerated roll of her eyes and words that Chiara had heard many times in the past five years during her spats with Aoife, Renate leaned on the doorframe. The overhead skylights bathed her in brightness, and Chiara's fingers twitched with the desire to reach for a pencil. *This was progress.*

No, she had not been terribly creative lately, an uncharacteristic malaise taking over after almost three years of non-stop, intense productivity. So this impetus to draw was a good thing. It wasn't the medication. It was creativity. Or so she told herself.

She reached for the sketchpad, reluctant to deny the impulse, and the severe lines of Renate's face slowly made their way from Chiara's fingers to the page as the surrounding conversation went on.

"I don't know why I'm the voice of reason on this or any issue this afternoon. The time to let go of things has long come and passed. Five years, for Christ's sake. So I was wrong. I have been sorry for it for a long time." Aoife's voice turned grumpy, as it always did when the subject turned to Vi Courtenay and Renate rubbing in the truth.

Chiara could sympathize. After all, wasn't it Aoife who, on so many occasions, had encouraged her protégé to stand on her own two feet and grab any chance with both hands? And then, when she did, Aoife was the one left broken-hearted.

No matter how many times and how vocally she professed not to care, Aoife had fallen for the lanky, clumsy, and perpetually little bit sad redhead. And when all was said and done, Chiara herself had fared no better.

She could only sigh again. Neither Aoife nor Renate were aware that her entanglement with Vi went deeper than a simple breach of trust. The lines both of them had crossed, lines that should have never even been seen, let alone touched...

Vi had fallen for a married woman, and said married woman had reciprocated. Except, Vi had also betrayed her at the very first opportunity, and Chiara... Well, Chiara had known better even then. To have used that infatuation, that adoration to somehow mend her own broken heart after years of a loveless marriage? Some seams should never be exposed, nor rent.

"Haven't we all been sor—" She caught herself, realizing that she had spoken out loud and both pairs of eyes were on her. Chiara ducked back to the sketch on her pad, and Renate's eyes were just as displeased on it as on the person now glaring thunderously. She swallowed, her mouth suddenly parched. "It is what it is, and Aoife is right. Time heals all wounds, and we've all had plenty of time—"

"Does that mean you'll go out with Livia Sabran-McMillan?" Renate's bull in the china shop tactic was spot on, as usual.

"Why would I?" Chiara busied herself with putting the finishing touches on the sketch.

"Because she asked? And because she is one of the most eligible bachelorettes in this entire breadless, tealess country?"

Renate tsked and Aoife snickered. Both she and Chiara knew full well what was to follow. Chiara sat back down on her stool and put the pad down, preparing to enjoy herself.

"The coffee is atrocious, tea is warmed in a microwave, and the bread is like that yellow underwater cartoon character that wears square pants!"

Aoife and Chiara laughed, to Renate's great displeasure.

"And yet here you are with us, among coffee- and tea-heathens. Bestowing high wedding fashion on these very heathens, I might add." Aoife snickered again and peered over Chiara's shoulder to look at the sketch of the disgruntled Renate before giving her a wink.

"I'm here because Chiara chose to be here." And with one sentence, Renate had deflated the balloon of levity that had filled the room.

Yes, Renate Lilienfeld was in New York because, after taking a year off to simply stop her thoughts from bleeding on paper every time she as much as opened her eyes in the morning, Chiara had decided that it was time to move on. From Paris, from her acrimonious divorce, from her painfully loud and inappropriate-in-public wife, who'd refused to facilitate said divorce and had in fact made it as difficult as she possibly could.

～

A YEAR to the day after her attorney filed the paperwork, Chiara had been declared a free woman. As she'd collected her belongings and attempted to place the cat in the carrier—thankful that Frankie was absent from Rue Saint-Honoré, as she'd been through most of the year—she turned around to see Renate watching her from the doorway.

"Milan?" Her now-former sister-in-law's voice was quiet, uncharacteristically so. Or chances were it was simply hoarse from all the shouting, since Frankie had deigned to show her face within the white marbled corridors the day before—even if she no longer climbed up to the fifth floor.

"To begin with. Or perchance to end, too?" Binoche refused to budge from her bed and gave the dreaded carrier a disgusted look. Chiara was about to snap her fingers—the absolute last resort in her exasperated state—when Renate came closer, holding a cat treat. The cat sphinx unfolded with interest.

When she placed the treat into the carrier, Binoche gave both of them a dirty look and reluctantly entered the confines of her temporary prison. She meowed with enough venom, letting the humans know how absolutely unacceptable any of this was. Chiara could sympathize. She looked around the studio. So beloved, so familiar. Twenty years was a very long time to love something. Even if it was a prison.

"I saw the attorney leave. It's done then." It wasn't a question, and so Chiara didn't answer. "What will you do? In Milan. Other than end whatever cycle you need to end? I still remember when the two of you met at Milan Fashion Week."

Suddenly, there was a lump in Chiara's throat, and she lifted her eyes from the cat, now settled in a neat and precise loaf-like position, little paws tucked under her body in the carrier.

She would miss this woman. Severe, cantankerous, and difficult as she was. Renate had been one of her only friends for twenty years, and in the last months, Chiara was hard-pressed to say who was more hurt by Frankie's betrayal.

Her sister-in-law had been on the warpath every time Frankie as much as dropped by. Not that it was all that often. Perhaps afraid of Renate, Frankie preferred to pester Chiara at the hotel she'd moved into, stalking her and accosting her at the entrance every chance she got, to the point where even the paparazzi grew tired of the perpetual outbursts.

Chiara cleared her throat. "I have so many ideas, Renate. They've been crowding my head for a year. And I know exactly where I'm going with them. For better or for worse, Vi's vision of the wedding gown is what seems to be my path. Who'd have thought?" Chiara gave out a quiet chuckle, and Renate's shoulders sagged. "Anyway, stepping away from Lilien and canceling next year's collections has been good for me, Renate."

"Silver linings then?" Renate's smile was sad and somehow

ashamed, though Chiara wondered what she had to be remorseful about. As the silence stretched between them, Renate took a deep breath and Chiara braced herself.

"I resigned from Lilien Haus, effective immediately. And I am selling my fifty percent of the brand." She could have knocked Chiara over with a feather. Renate had been with Lilien for thirty years now. Since day one, in fact. Her steadfast professionalism, her financial acumen, her knowledge of the industry had always guided the fashion house just as much as Frankie's talent initially had, and later Chiara's.

Chiara was sure her sharp inhalation was very much audible. "You are indispensable, Renate. Without you, there is no Lilien. What will Frankie say?"

Renate blew the bangs out of her eyes and her mouth twisted in an unpleasant grimace.

"You are the indispensable one, Chiara Conti." The sound of her name, said in that deep accented voice, so simple, so to the point. Renate was the first to use her maiden name, to give it back to her. Chiara's eyes stung. She swallowed convulsively.

"Renate—"

"I'm guilty. I am. No, don't say anything!" She dismissed Chiara's raised hand and barreled on. "I knew. For years. I knew, and I looked the other way, I covered up, I stood silent."

"I hope you know I don't blame you—"

"*I blame me!*" The outburst, the rage, was so out of character for the usually phlegmatic Swiss. Chiara could count the instances she had ever heard Renate shout on the fingers of one hand. "And not just for the cheating. I blame myself for standing aside while, for twenty years, my sister placed the sole responsibility for our family business on your shoulders. I blame myself for you taking it on and breaking your back while she hawked all the credit and slept with half of Paris and a third of London."

"I think there might have been a quarter of Milan as well?"

Chiara raised an eyebrow and smirked. Her attempt at levity was received with a huff and a twitch of the thin lips.

"I have no idea how you can be so calm about any of this."

"Well, you yelled enough for both of us this past year, and you've thrown more mannequin parts at her than we could spare. I think you single-handedly kept that entire industry in business." Renate's lips twitched again.

Chiara's smile was pensive as she wrapped her arms around herself and she could hear her own voice going hoarse. "The marriage was broken long before she started sleeping around, Renate. And I am no saint, either."

"Oh please..." Renate's dismissive gesture did not soothe.

"I've had an entire year to think about things. I was so desperate to be something she wanted, I forsook myself. Simply dissolved in all of this. And I guess in trying to please her, the Chiara she loved was gone. So I have not been a good wife, Renate. I wasn't, and you know it." Chiara's voice was barely above a whisper. The cat, as if sensing her distress, reached out a paw and patted the mesh of the carrier, trying to get to her.

"When all is said and done, who could fault you? I certainly never would. And honestly, neither did Frankie. She was never easy to be a good *anything* to. Wife, sister. She didn't even use it during the divorce proceedings. This... whatever it is you weren't good at. And god knows, she used every little thing to drag this out."

Renate's tone held a tacit note of disgust, and Chiara smiled mirthlessly.

"Yes, she used it all, and to what end?"

"To the end of you letting her keep absolutely everything!" And now the disgust was loud and clear. "How could you? Why would you? You worked for twenty years! You are solely responsible for Lilien Haus making it onto the haute couture list. Nothing that has been achieved these past two decades could have been done without you."

Renate's chest rose and fell, and she visibly struggled not to raise her voice again. "Yes, she is my sister, and yes, we started this business together, but I was never incognizant of her limitations. She is talented, and her swagger certainly got us very far. But you..." And now the agitated tone broke and Renate's cheek flamed, perhaps embarrassed at her own emotional state.

"You took us beyond anything we ever dreamed of being. Top ten brands in the world. Millions in profit. Biggest, most famous, most innovative and creative... The awards, the accolades. Chiara, *Liebling*, how could you have let her keep it all? After all she has done?"

A tear ran down Renate's cheek, and Chiara uncrossed her arms and wiped it away, then enveloped the older woman in a gentle hug before turning back to the rain-stained windows above Rue Saint-Honoré.

"Are you upset about me not taking half of everything? Or about Frankie not paying?"

She heard Renate shuffle behind her, coming closer until they were side by side, overlooking the gloomy street.

"Honest to goodness, I don't know."

Chiara laughed, and Renate joined her with a smile.

"If I would have demanded anything, so much as a penny, Frankie would have dragged this out even longer. She'd have gotten what she wanted. The attention. My time. My mind, my heart. And I have none of that to spare for her. I've been buried for a year, Renate, and I needed her to tread lightly over my ground. She didn't anyway, but at least I get my peace from now on."

"So you win by letting her keep millions?"

Chiara nodded and looked away. Behind her, Renate's "tsk" was all disgust again.

In the distance, pigeons cooed and cars honked. The familiar and beloved sounds of Paris, soothing her raw, abraded emotions. She would miss this. The view, certainly. But also the safety of this place. The safety that was no longer there.

"I'll go with you." In the quiet of the rainy afternoon, Chiara thought she'd hallucinated the words. She turned to look at Renate, but her companion was focused on the street beneath them, an unlucky pedestrian getting his very nice shoes drenched in the puddles. "I told you I'm selling my half. If she doesn't buy me out, I'll simply sell to the first person who offers me decent money and leave. She can't keep me here, and she can't make me hold on to my share. I don't want it anyway. I love her. And I can't stand her. So that's that."

"Renate..." Chiara felt as if she was submerged in water, too deep to swim, the shock overwhelming.

"*Renate* nothing." Aoife's voice sounded from the doorway with uncharacteristic malice. "She said nothing, did nothing, looked the other way, and you got hurt. And humiliated which, when it comes to you, is even worse with all that pride of yours and all of your history." Chiara wanted to flinch, but Aoife came closer and put her hand on her shoulder, laying her other one on Renate's forearm and looking at Chiara.

"We both did. Her and I. We held on to the damn status quo for so long, we forgot there was a real person in the middle of it all. And when the proverbial chips fell, you were left alone. I didn't know about the cheating. And on top of everything, I let Vi fall head over clumsy tits in love with you and get us into this mess. And for all of that, I'm sorry."

Aoife's brows were furrowed, eyes blinking rapidly, and now Chiara felt like she was swimming in grief. Not of her own making, but grief she deemed imperative she had to end. A year was long enough to wallow.

But before she opened her mouth to speak, Aoife surprised her yet again.

"So, where are we going? Milan, is it? I'm all packed."

Renate smirked, and Aoife's contagious smile soon tugged on her own lips as well.

"I don't know what to say..." she began.

"Nothing *to* say. I left some fish to rot in most of the drawers in my studio downstairs. And in hers. Want me to spread some around here as well?"

With Renate's and Aoife's laughter surrounding her, Chiara had picked up Binoche, her own packed bag, and walked out of the atelier on Rue Saint-Honoré without looking back. They had work to do. And Aoife's fish had needed time to rot and give Frankie a nasty surprise come the Monday that followed.

～

CHIARA WASN'T sure if Aoife's prank had ended up being successful, but the work they had done since then very much had been.

After spending a year in Milan, drawing like she was possessed, Renate's capital and Aoife's drive helped her set the foundation for what today was known as *Chiaroscuro*. A new brand was born. If all she sketched and designed were wedding dresses, she didn't want to delve into her reasons why too deeply.

Just like she didn't want to think about why she took Binoche—not that she'd considered abandoning her even for one second—but after leaving everything in a place where her heart had been broken twice, she ended up with two reminders of the last person to have shattered it.

Even as she drew a Queen Anne bodice on a gown she already knew would be spectacular, Chiara chose not to think about the fact that, after years of trying to find herself, it was Vi's unique vision and perceptiveness that had given her a direction, a breakthrough into what she was meant to do.

Chiara had a little help from her friends. Neve Blackthorne

and Princess Allegra of Savoy had steadfastly stood beside her through her tribulations. And the diamond-encrusted mermaid-line gown worn by the second bride of King Aleric of Savoy—or was it his third?—had landed with the effect of a nuclear detonation, blowing the fashion world's collective minds.

Chiara deliberately shied away from the spotlight, keeping herself in the shadows, creating a sense of mystery about Chiaroscuro. That boon aside, she felt comfortable on the sidelines, having to worry about the creation and not being the face of something she had yet to fully flesh out. Some days, she looked back at her years with Lilien and had a reluctant moment of appreciation of Frankie taking all that attention upon herself. It wasn't easy. And it wasn't all roses, being the public front of a fashion brand.

After the royal wedding, commissions soared, and Renate had put her foot down. No more nomadic lifestyle. No more hotels. No more rental work space. They were going to settle down. They were going to put down roots someplace where they would find their permanence.

Paris was out of the question. With Brexit, London did not appeal. So there was only one sensible destination. The land of the aforementioned subpar coffee, microwave tea and spongy bread. But all that aside, it was and still remained the land of opportunity.

That was how Chiara had found herself in front of the four-story brick, late nineteenth century townhouse in Lower Manhattan, between the Balenciaga and Schiaparelli flagship stores. As she'd taken in her surroundings, the bustling, loud and always busy Mercer Street, she knew that she had found her place again.

Her first thought had been to hide her new endeavor. To keep it amidst coffee shops and less fashion-forward brands. To avoid the limelight. But she was also proud. Of every stitch and every piece of lace. Of every cut and every veil.

Chiaroscuro wedding gowns were taking the world by storm, and the queue for them spanned years in advance. Renate would figure out that aspect of the business, but Chiara liked the exclusivity, the fact that nothing she created was mass-produced, and everything held her touch.

When all was said and done, the three of them were an unbeatable trio.

And so she'd stepped into the Mercer Street townhouse with her head held high and pictured the store on the ground floor and her atelier under the skylights. Then she made the realtor's day, nay year, by taking one sweeping walk around and saying 'yes.'

These days, she found herself saying 'yes' to a lot of things, and as she put the finishing touches on Renate's sketch, she felt that one of those 'yeses' was about to bite her in the ass. Because Renate's eyes were shrewd, and Aoife's arms were holding all that ivory lace after all.

"So are you ready for the Grand Dame?" Aoife didn't hide her awe when she spoke the appellation as if it was sanctified.

The *Grand Dame* in question was none other than the owner of Poise Magazine and dozens of other fashion- and art enterprises and ruler of the New York social scene, the one and only Arabella Archibald Avant.

A week ago, the phone had rung and without preamble, a raspy, no-nonsense voice had stated, "Arabella here. I want you in Poise," and that was that.

Chiara hadn't really had much to say on the matter, because apparently, when Arabella Archibald Avant wanted something, it had to be done. Preferably without delay and any other such nonsense.

And Chiara would have probably acquiesced right away, but the moment she'd opened her mouth, Renate shook her head and in an equally brooking-no-argument tone answered, "Ms. Conti's week is booked. Please get back to us in a few days, and we will see about fitting you in."

Aoife had spilled her coffee and Chiara smiled. Because Renate was right, Chiara should always remember her value. And her position. Five years sadly hadn't cured her of her self-doubt or patched up her self-confidence. Though that, if she ever went into counseling again, would be something her potential therapist would have a field day with.

Lo-and-behold, Arabella's assistant had called Renate a few days later, and the appointment was made. For today, in fact. And so both Renate and Aoife were in her office, where she'd been doodling and drawing portraits instead of focusing on the tasks at hand. So what else was new?

"I'm as ready for her as I will be, Aoife. We don't even know what she really wants."

Chiara tugged on her long sleeve, her gray knit dress hugging her pleasantly, warding off the chill of the early New York fall, offering one more layer of soft armor among the sensory overload that was slowly creeping in.

"Bah, what could that old biddy want?" Uncharacteristically, Renate threw her hands up in the air. Chiara's antennae quivered. Her friend was on edge, and wasn't that curious? Did she know Arabella? Was that the real reason she'd put roadblocks in front of the socialite? Even if they'd also been entirely justifiable.

"I am not really sure, Renate, but do you think I should be worried? After all, I know the Editor-In-Chief fairly well. I don't think Benedict would screw me over. And honestly, even if he and Arabella are up to no good, our outstanding orders are years long. I'm thoroughly uninterested in the glory of it, and you know it."

Chiara almost choked on the lie and wondered at herself. Why deny that she wanted everything? Maybe because it scared her so much. And maybe because the last time she'd put herself out there, had opened herself up, the ensuing betrayal had been witnessed by millions of newspaper readers and internet dwellers. And no, she wasn't thinking about her ex wife's proclivities. Rather, Vi's knife was still sticking out from her back.

Renate scoffed and ran her fingers through her hair, and now Chiara knew she was holding something back. Nobody touched that pristine coif.

"Arabella may have changed some of her fair-weather ways. And Benedict was always upfront and aboveboard in his dealings with Lilien. So no, I don't think either of them will try anything underhanded. But I do want recognition for you. If only to throw a Poise cover in quite a number of people's faces."

"Ah, so it's revenge then." Chiara stood up and handed Renate the finished sketch, making her friend purse her lips and Aoife laugh out loud.

Chiara shook her head. "I can't say that I care all that much about either. I'm..." She wanted to say happy. But the lie didn't roll off her tongue as smoothly as she may have wanted it to in order to convince either Renate or Aoife. So she settled on something closer to the truth.

"I'm content. And I'm busy. Or will be once we get this show on the road and dispense with the prophetic and the fanciful. Arabella will be here soon enough, and then we'll know. And we'll deal with it. As we have the past years. One step at the time. One stitch after the other."

Aoife nodded, and Renate simply held the sketch and shook her head. So much for being convincing then.

As her friends filed out of the studio, something twisted in Chiara's chest, a thin splinter of something long lost, long abandoned. Something that had been keeping her heart sewn together with fragile threads of old yarn was being pulled apart, a stitch at a time, the yarn no match for the sharp edged splinter.

She touched her sternum, absentmindedly, foolishly trying to allay the ache, as the early fall wind played with the red leaves on the street below her.

A stitch gave out, and she sensed that something was coming her way. Arabella was just the harbinger.

15

IN A FARAWAY LAND OF STORMY HARBINGERS

C hiara Conti had never been in the eye of the storm, and thus her contact with tornadoes was rather limited. Finding herself swept up in one named Arabella Archibald Avant was a curious experience. With both Renate and Aoife making themselves scarce, Chiara had to endure the first contact alone.

The woman marched into the studio—there was no other way to describe the way she'd entered Chiaroscuro's atelier— took exactly one cursory look around, inclined her head, and took her phone out of a purse probably big enough to fit the entirety of Chiara's selection that was on display.

"Yes, Bene, scrap whatever you planned for the next issue. We will be doing Chiara Conti. Yes. The entire thing. No, you heard me. I realize we have less than two weeks to shoot and print. I do own a calendar, you know." The voice dripped with so much sarcasm, Chiara tried to hide her smile. She could practically see Benedict Stanley fainting in his tastefully decorated glass office. Arabella's next outburst pulled her attention back to what was happening in her own studio.

"Have I asked who, Benedict Edmund Stanley? I was not

aware I needed permission, you ridiculous man. Now find some smelling salts and get yourself together. Later, dearest."

With enough flourish to break through the soft-looking leather, Arabella threw her phone back into her bag and finally turned around, her shrewd eyes on Chiara.

"So."

And this time Chiara didn't hide her reaction to the tornado making herself at home in her space. She raised an eyebrow and waited. After what seemed like an eternity, the stare down came to an abrupt conclusion when Arabella harrumphed and took a few steps closer to her.

"Oh, for crying out loud, will I have to spell everything out for you as well? Neve swears that you are some kind of genius. And having seen her wedding dresses—both of them—and looking at all this...," the pale hands, weighed down by enough gold hardware to sink a ship, made a sweeping gesture around the atelier, "I tend to agree with the woman. She is so rarely wrong, after all."

"Unless it's men." It really wasn't any of her business whom Neve Blackthorne, of all people, married, but the joke just begged to be told. She braced herself for what would follow, but Arabella threw her head back and her raspy chuckle was contagious.

"Ha, like your spousal track record is stellar, my dear." The words might have stung, but Arabella's eyes were kind, so Chiara smiled.

"Touché."

"But of course, touché, dear. Of course. And I say this with no malice. I've known your ex-wife for twenty years, and I've sat in the front row at her shows many times, and I've worn Lilien's creations with pleasure... But I am quite happy Franziska wasn't the one designing them. Wild that one. And so here we are."

Arabella's eyes looked straight through her and Chiara felt a duality of both a touch of that pride, for the belated recognition of her talent, and a pang of fear of the spotlight.

"I never said—"

Chiara's protest fell on deaf ears.

"Ah, child, lesser mortals may not have made the connection between Lilien Haus' dismal collections over the past four years and your divorce, but I am no lesser mortal. The spark? The genius? The talent? That was all you. Spine too, from what I see. Obstinance. That's fine. A genius has the right to be stubborn."

She touched the bodice of the dress closest to her, rings glinting in tandem with the few strands of gold that ran through the embroidered flowers.

"You can be all these things, including stubborn and temperamental. But you cannot be oblivious. And I don't think you are. Am I right?"

Pale eyes zeroed back in on her, and Chiara felt the power of them.

"I am familiar with you, Ms. Archibald Avant. And I am not a novice to the industry, no matter what my previous venture entailed or how big my exposure was. But I'm still not sure what it is you're asking of me."

"Asking..." Arabella laughed again. "Neve did say you were quite set in your ways. Good on you. As reclusive as your ways are."

Still running her fingers along the bodice with considerable and surprising reverence, Arabella smiled. "I don't blow smoke up people's asses, Chiara Conti. I don't need to. I come in, I look, and things fall in line."

"I am not a *thing*. And I'm not entirely certain what line you're talking about when it comes to Chiaroscuro. But this is personal to me." Insulted, Chiara raised her eyebrow, and Arabella's smile widened.

"That is understandable. If I am right about Franziska—

and I am rarely wrong about people—you've never had much of a say, despite all of your talent and your sacrifices. So of course, in that sense, you are a thing. A commodity. We all are. And we all play our roles in the big scheme of those things. But I will spare you the pretenses and platitudes—"

"Additional ones?" The teasing got Chiara another bark of laughter.

"Oh, I like you. I like you very much, Chiara Conti. And so here is what I want. Spelled out. You probably overheard me earlier anyway. Poise will scrap its entire special holiday issue this October and dedicate one to you. 'Chiara Conti's Big Return.' As a supermodel, you were a star of massive proportions. Unprecedented for your time. An out and proud lesbian walking the biggest catwalks." Arabella's eyes shone with something akin to pride, and Chiara, once again, found herself wondering about the deeper motivation that ran as an undercurrent in this meeting.

With a graceful gesture around herself, Arabella continued. "Right now, you are quietly taking the wedding gown market by storm. And I think all this stealthiness is paying off in some ways. Everyone is curious. Everyone is on the edge of their seats." The pause was as theatrical as it was effective, and Chiara suspected Arabella knew it. "And you and I will blow them all away."

Chiara had to cross her arms over her chest to hide her shaking hands. It was suddenly all so real, so big. "You assume that this kind of fame is something I want, Ms. Archibald Avant."

"You can call me Arabella, Chiara Conti. All those dusty names belong to my husbands, after all. And while I cherish the access and the comfort they provided, Arabella was and is who I actually am."

"And yet, you call me by my full name." Chiara pursed her lips and stared down the older woman.

"That's right. Your full name, child. To remind you that you're no longer a Lilienfeld. To underscore that you already crossed that line. And that it's time to come out from under those murky shadows."

Crafty witch. It was Chiara's turn to concede, and she felt her lips stretch into a grin. *So very cheeky. So very smart.*

Arabella laughed along, presumably at her own astuteness, and the atmosphere in the studio lost its tension.

"An entire special issue?" Chiara narrowed her eyes. She could see the possibilities. On the other hand, Chiaroscuro would be firmly thrust into the spotlight, and she would never be able to get out of it again. It took the control over events away from her, and that sent a shiver down her spine. But it would also bring all that glory Renate and Aoife so wanted for her. Should she risk her privacy, her security in anonymity for the satisfaction of her friends? Oh, who was she kidding? She'd walk to the ends of the earth for either of those two. And then there was her pride.

She met Arabella's gaze head-on.

"I'm not averse to fame."

"Good, because it's already here. You cannot hide Chiaroscuro under a bushel anymore. It's too bright, despite its shadows, too full of light. All the puns intended, dearest. And you deserve more than to just sit here in the safety of those shadows. Nothing is guaranteed, ever, but I have a feeling that there will never be a 'what if I fail?' moment with you. It will be all about 'what if I soar?' from now on. And put quite like that, what's the worst that could happen?"

Unwittingly, Arabella had just uttered the most damaging thing possible. She'd used the exact same words as Frankie when she'd convinced Chiara and Renate to hire a Courtenay.

What's the worst that could happen?

Well, so, so much, really.

The weights of the memories chained to her arms made it

difficult to cross them around her chest, as she turned away from Arabella. It was getting so hard to breathe.

Binoche, as always sensing her distress, let out a disgruntled meow from the windowsill, and Chiara approached her cushion, grateful for the opportunity to put more space between herself and those wretched words.

What's the worst that could happen?

Well, heartbreak for one. And betrayal. And the worst mistake of her life. How to explain this to this coiffed and styled woman, who probably never set a foot wrong in her life unless she intended to, that Chiara had crossed lines that should have never even been seen, not to mention touched?

Under her fingertips, Binoche stretched, and the warmth of her fur soothed, the sensation grounding Chiara. For the millionth time, she wondered why she'd taken the cat who reminded her of nothing else except how she had done things she'd had no business doing, and how those things came back to haunt her.

She could have given Binoche away to a number of people who would have cared for her and loved her and been amazing humans to her. But Chiara held on to the cat, who now purred reluctantly under her caress.

What's the worst that could happen?

Her thoughts tangled. Maybe it was time to move forward, though? Maybe the worst had already happened when she'd crossed a line and gotten burned in a way not even Frankie could have accomplished? And what did it really say about her marriage when a few months of flirtation and one night with a twenty-five-year-old girl had left more scars than her wife cheating on her for years?

Chiara shook her head and her predictable anger at herself, at Vi, at Frankie, reared its ugly head again. Well, perhaps she needed to face some things. And to let go of others. With absolutely no one respecting her wishes and treading lightly and letting her rest, maybe she was due a resurrection?

With one last pet to Binoche's fuzzy belly, she turned to face Arabella, standing surprisingly quietly by the worktable, tactful enough to give her time and space. One look at Chiara's face and Arabella's own shone with triumph.

"Splendid! Benedict will be in touch about the pesky details—"

"Pesky?" Chiara wanted to laugh. The logistics of preparing an entire issue of a magazine in under two weeks? Mind-boggling.

"Dearest, what do I care about any of it? I have people for that. And Benedict Stanley is a shrewd man who has performed greater miracles than this. Plus, I'm not certain this will be a miracle to begin with. He and I were discussing a wedding issue anyway. It's so de rigueur. So very trendy right now. The same trend that you yourself helped usher in. Neve Black-thorne may have kept her wedding dress to herself and her bride, but the new Queen Consort of Savoy? Dearest, that gown alone changed destinies." Arabella took a few steps around the studio, pointing at the various works in progress displayed on assorted mannequins.

"One, two, three... eighteen... You have over what? Twenty? Just here on display? Some may be spoken for, but we will work around that. Between what's already here and what you can deliver, creating an issue of Poise will not be a problem. Plus, you're the true star anyway. A forty-five-year-old who rein-vented herself and rose from the ashes. The public loves a sob story, dearest. Ask anyone."

Chiara wanted to protest at the manipulative narrative she was being fed, but then Arabella winked at her, and she shook her head again instead. No, she had no idea how to act when in the eye of this particular storm.

"So an interview?"

"Oh, dearest, an interview and so much more. A photo-shoot. Several, in fact. You, you and your team, you and this fickle city that is welcoming you twenty-five years after it laid itself down at your feet. My very best photographer—you can call her a project of mine—will make it all perfect. She has that touch. A unique talent. Quite the perfect match to yours, dear-est. Oh, I can already see the copy for this. The story really writes itself."

Apprehension and excitement warred within Chiara. In the end, caution won.

"I will only sign on, on condition of final red pen approval rights."

Arabella's eyes shone with the satisfaction of a cat that got into the cream and found that an entire canary was dunked into it.

"Dearest, I do not give a flying fuck what you say in those interviews and what you want to keep to yourself. You can recite poetry for all I care. Read the damn phone book. Do they even make them anymore? Red pen, blue pen, rainbow pen! Have at it. Just say yes."

Chiara smiled at the boisterousness and extended her hand, which Arabella shook with surprising strength for someone so pampered.

"Wonderful. Wonderful, dearest. Now, where is that exceed-ingly unpleasant receptionist of yours that my secretary had to wear down to get to you?"

Chiara felt the corners of her mouth twitch at the thought of Renate, who ran the show, being mistaken for her secretary, and pressed a button on her intercom, connecting her with the CEO office at the lower floor. At Renate's clipped answer, Chiara smiled into the speaker.

"Yes, hi, would you please come to my studio? I want to introduce you to Arabella."

The line turned silent before it went dead, and Chiara again sensed that something was about to happen, something that had been bubbling under the surface at Chiaroscuro these past few weeks.

The click of high heels announced Renate's arrival, and Chiara realized that it was possible she should have asked more questions about some of that very pointed hostility her former sister-in-law felt towards their new benefactor.

Because Renate walked into the studio, marched up to Arabella, took one sharp breath, and slapped her across the face with a resounding smack.

Chiara gasped and stepped forward—to do what she wasn't quite sure since this was so unprecedented, so entirely out of character and out of anything and everything she herself had witnessed in her life. She was shocked when Arabella raised a hand and cradled her cheek before exhaling loudly.

"Well, I expected this to go slightly better, Rena. But really just slightly."

The unsurprised tone, the lack of any kind of offense or reaction to the slap, was perhaps even more shocking than the action itself.

"Don't you 'Rena' me, Bella. You walked out on me decades ago. Just marched out of there and into the arms of Archibald and told me I should have had zero expectations. After months of promising me the world. And now that you dumped Margo Dresden, you just waltz in here expecting exactly what? Your dance does not change despite the change of tune, *dearest*." Renate's mocking tone was cold as ice. "Of all people, you should know, I do hold a grudge."

Chiara simply stared as Arabella approached Renate carefully, like one would another combatant holding a grenade.

"I do know it. And I had some hope you wouldn't hold this against me, at least professionally speaking."

Renate scoffed and pointed at Chiara.

"This one's talking to you, isn't she? So I have not poisoned that well. Now, you've undoubtedly talked her into whatever cockamamie idea you had. I assume I will have to deal with Benedict? You are free to go now. Or what else could you possibly want?"

Arabella's answer floored everyone. Even Binoche startled, as if she could understand what was happening.

"I know that my past is quite checkered, Rena. So let me start with dinner. And some time to atone. And to start over."

Well, Chiara had seen bold, and she'd seen foolish. But never in a million years would she have thought Arabella Archibald Avant would embody both these qualities under her very own eyes.

16

IN A FARAWAY LAND OF ENTRANCES WELL MADE

Chiara Conti indulged in gossip as much as the next person. With Aoife bouncing off the walls in her studio, she allowed herself some time to do just that.

"I can't believe I missed it!" Aoife seemed inconsolable.

Chiara sat on the windowsill, Binoche curled up next to her, a paw almost touching her thigh, and watched as Aoife wore a stripe into the runner on her studio's floors.

For the past hour, ever since both Arabella and Renate had departed the townhouse—supposedly to go their separate ways in pursuit of whatever errands—Aoife, who'd been eavesdropping and had managed to hear the end of the bombshell revelation, had alternatively been sulking and exclaiming while throwing her hands up in the air.

Chiara sighed. "I have to say, it was quite the spectacle. And certainly a revelation. But, all in all, I would have preferred to avoid it."

Aoife whirled on her. "Well, of course you would have. I've never seen anyone more averse to scandal! You are seriously missing out."

Chiara uncoiled from her position, the chill of the window

glass leaving her slightly uncomfortable, and not even her knitted dress could ward it off. Or perhaps it was the earlier visit and everything it entailed. And not just the revelation of Renate's early-in-life sapphic relationship and the broken heart she'd apparently been nursing ever since. Certainly not the small, sharp sliver in Chiara's chest that felt suspiciously like premonition. Absolutely not that.

"I did not miss *this* one, Aoife. And yes, it was all you'd imagine it to be. The drama, the action, the romance. If you want to call a decades-old betrayal and abandonment, and what appeared like sincere, late-in-life regret 'romance.'"

"Oh, this is grand. And who'd have thought? Renate? Four decades of longing!" Aoife bounced on the balls of her feet.

"If her reception for Arabella is anything to go by, I'm not sure 'longing' is what I'd call it. More like holding a forty-year long grudge—"

"And nobody holds a grudge quite like I do."

Aoife squeaked, while Chiara managed to school her features to not look guilty at being caught gossiping about their friend. Renate seemed unperturbed by either.

"Are you all right?" Chiara searched those austere features for any remaining distress and found nothing but the usual composure.

"Are *you*?" Trust Renate to see through her.

"I shouldn't be?"

Renate tsked. "A question for a question. I should have known. And I should have told you never to meet with that old crone. I knew she'd push you way out of your comfort zone. She has that effect on people. Making them take risks. Often-times unnecessary ones."

"Is that what happened to you?" Aoife piped up, then blinked owlishly and winced at her own audacity.

But Renate didn't snap at her, nor did she dismiss the question. She sat down on the corner of a workstation and wrapped her arms around herself, a faraway look overtaking her eyes.

"She was my first. For the longest time my only. To this day, the only woman. And no, that doesn't speak ill of her in that sense. Perhaps it says more about me? Or about just how much she influenced me, how she pushed and pursued until I relented and let her in. As I said, she has that effect on people." Renate took a long breath, and Chiara could see her eyes slowly clear.

She could sympathize. Letting people in, then being betrayed by them, was also something Chiara was quite intimately familiar with. But then there'd also been the longing in Renate's voice. For what Chiara did not know, but she recognized it. After all, she had five years of feeling the same, even if the object of her yearning was to never darken her doorstep again as Arabella had Renate's.

She was pulled out of her thoughts by Renate's businesslike tone. "In any case, Benedict's assistant has already been in touch, and while some wheels are in motion, we can still back out. Say the word, it will be my pleasure to tell her to go to hell. Again."

And now it was Chiara's turn to take a steadying breath.

"No, she didn't make me do anything. And while I can't say I'm eager to jump into the celebrity aspect of the business, it's past time to be seen. I hid behind Frankie for years. I hid behind the mystery of Chiaroscuro for the last few. Perhaps I should stop hiding from things."

Binoche's meow was quiet, almost pensive, and Chiara smiled.

"See? Even the cat agrees."

"That cat is the devil's spawn." Renate's face showed all the earlier distaste for the cat, who simply rolled into a fuzzball with her back to the room and went back to sleep.

Aoife picked the scissors from the workstation and twirled

them in her fingers, eyes excited. "And seen you shall be, babe! An entire special issue of Poise and all, with your face all over it! Like old times. Goddess, it's been twenty years since your last cover. In fact, wasn't Poise the last one you did before becoming a recluse?" Aoife dropped the scissors and cracked her knuckles as Renate glared at her.

Chiara rolled her eyes, amused by her friend's theatrics. "A bit heavy on the drama, Aoife. I was never a recluse. And while being somebody's wife was not a career ambition, it is what it is. Arabella didn't twist my arm, and a Poise cover is beyond prestigious. God knows, Frankie would have killed to have her face on it years ago and would probably die for it now." Chiara ran her fingers over the silky ear of the sleeping cat, who twitched, but otherwise remained unperturbed.

Renate's phone pinged, and she stood up scrolling through it.

"And speaking of being seen... Well, it looks like the photographer will be here in an hour or so. I guess once Arabella is in, she's all in..."

"I mean, you'd know!" Aoife giggled at her own joke, and Chiara groaned.

Renate raised her eyebrows, her countenance tense. "Is this how it's going to be now?"

"It's what the two of you get since I missed the fireworks. But sure, I'll tone it down for a bit." Aoife danced away from Renate's swiping hand.

"You should do just that, Sully. With only two weeks to fill an entire issue, there really is no time to waste." Renate did manage to pinch Aoife's side before both of them mercifully settled.

Chiara shivered. In the cacophony of her friends teasing and laughing, she felt chilled and even hugging herself didn't help. Surely it was the cold from the open window creeping in.

And premonitions be damned, it was time to get this show on the road.

S<small>HE'D NEVER CONSIDERED</small> herself remotely superstitious despite all the fashion industry's canons. And any and all senses she may have had, clearly left her absolutely unprepared for the major events of her life. Frankie cheating, Vi selling her out to the gossip rags... She'd had no inkling.

Was it a wonder that, when her psyche actually did throw her a bone, she missed it entirely? Because that splinter from earlier in the day, that foreboding chill should have alerted her to something. Although how was she to know that, out of all the photographers in the world—so many of them available to Poise at the snap of fingers—the one Arabella had hired for Chiara's special edition would be... her?

Vi Courtenay did not stumble at the steps of Chiara's townhouse this time around, despite once again not watching her own feet. As déjà vus went, this one was quite momentous. Because just like last time, Cinderella crossed the threshold without taking those gray eyes off Chiara's.

The parallels stopped there, however. This was an older version of Vi, somehow even lankier than she'd been five years ago, the youthful fullness of the face transformed by chiseled cheekbones that were surely able to cut glass.

She didn't walk in as much as she swaggered, taking space and seemingly sucking all the oxygen out of what had been a large and airy room just seconds before.

Chiara steeled herself for those first words, her mind playing tricks on her again and reminding her so clearly of those tremulous, innocent, slightly breathy ones uttered by a twenty-five-year-old girl, shy and embarrassed and maybe a bit awed.

This girl was neither shy, nor embarrassed, nor awed. The glasses Chiara adored so much, were gone. And along with chiseling her face, time had done something to Vi that Chiara thought she'd never get to witness. It had taken away the girl.

In what looked like bespoke Oxford shoes stood a woman. One of means and style, if the rolled-up sleeves of a linen shirt tucked carelessly yet artfully into slightly loose trousers that sat tantalizingly low on sharp hip bones were any indication. Chiara's mouth went dry. Sleeves of tattoos covered both sinewy forearms, and she tried very hard not to stare.

She must have failed, because an eyebrow rose, and the full mouth curved into a knowing smirk. Both of these gestures were so new, Chiara couldn't help but keep cataloging the differences, even as Vi took the last few steps towards her. She licked her parched lips and watched Vi's eyes narrow as they followed the movement with something lurking in those depths.

Chiara was never more thankful for the carefully applied concealer, sure to be hiding her cheeks she could feel paling by the second, when fate in the form of Aoife intervened and saved her from the impending need to speak and to do so now, before Vi had the chance to take her by surprise with anything she might say first.

"Well, well, well, if it isn't Vi Courtenay sneaking in after all these years. You're wearing better shoes this time around, Cinderella."

The smirk turned lethal on a dime, so much so, Chiara could hear Aoife inhaling loudly next to her.

"I did not sneak in, Sully, someone buzzed me in."

Oh, the voice. The voice was the same. The gentle cadence of it, the high and low notes, the caress of the vowels in that slightly British accent. Years. It had been years, and those Paris months came flooding back. Slowly at first, blooming in front of her eyes, then faster, all at once, shaking her to the core.

"Lean on me... I have you, Chiara... I love you."

The same voice. The same eyes. All these words. Poignant, beautiful words. All those lies. *The same voice. The same eyes.*

"Ms. Courtenay."

She was pleased when her own tone did not waver. Neither did her hand when she extended it, feeling her own fingers like ice before they were enfolded in a warm handshake. Had the knuckles grown more prominent with time? Did the hands grow rougher? Their softness seemed to be missing, or it was possible Chiara simply didn't remember them all that well. She clung to that last conclusion with enough force to make Vi give her a strange look.

Chiara extricated her still cold fingers from the handshake and inclined her head for Vi to follow when Renate's cough made them all turn towards the staircase leading to the studio space above the showroom.

"Courtenay."

"Ms. Lilienfeld." If Vi's reply to Aoife held warmth and mischief, the four syllables addressed at Renate held none.

"I counted the silverware. And the gowns." Renate's lips thinned further, but Vi's eyes crinkled at the corners before she spoke.

"I appreciate it. I will try not to commit any acts of commercial espionage while on this assignment. My NDA and contract with Poise are both ironclad to that effect."

Aoife's gasp was quite audible this time around, and the splinter in Chiara's chest twisted harder, rending more stitches, reminding her of that one emotion she'd been suppressing for many years.

Because despite all her guilt and all the self-flagellation she had indulged in quite often on account of this girl—no, woman —her anger at the betrayal was also ever present.

How dare she? How dare Vi, who'd fucked her and then fucked her over, speak of everything that happened with such nonchalance? How could she mock what had been Chiara's torment for years?

"Just reminding you of some things, Courtenay." Oblivious to the storm rocking Chiara—the second one Arabella had unleashed on her—Renate snarked even as Aoife shook her head.

"Look, Renate, maybe now is not the time—"

Vi's cutting reply was only marginally softened by a hand on Aoife's forearm. "No, Sully. There will never really be a time. And there will never really be a place. Because I have an assignment. I assume you have things lined up here, because you agreed to whatever terms Arabella set for this absolutely hare-brained idea of hers." Vi's smile was infused with so much warmth at the name that Chiara had to blink.

"But all her harebrained ideas pay off. The woman doesn't miss. And I have a job to do. We have less than two—four, if I get my way—weeks to do about eight thematic photoshoots and some small, adjacent ones. All that in addition to the interviews, the cover shoot and the personal profile images. If you can't work with me, I respect that. I will walk away now, and no matter what Arabella told you, I will get another photographer assigned—"

Renate looked her up and down. "Such sway you hold with the powers of the world, girl. I see some things have not changed." The derision in her words was downright malicious, and Chiara felt something she'd forgotten had been her primordial emotion for three months that fateful summer: protectiveness.

And maybe the woman didn't deserve any of it, but the girl? That girl, before the world had ended, before all hell broke loose on them, she'd been someone worth protecting. And Chiara couldn't quit now. No matter how much her mind was screaming at her to do just that, her heart was not to be stopped.

"I don't care about any of this." All three other occupants of the foyer observed her with such differing expressions, she actually smiled. "Ms. Courtenay, welcome to Chiaroscuro. I will show you around and we will talk setup and requirements and logistics. We'll bring Aoife and Renate into this, depending on whatever it is you require. Follow me."

She turned on her heel, for once not fearing whether anyone followed. She knew Vi would. If only to finish this wretched assignment Chiara herself, in a roundabout way, had set in motion. And there was some modicum of comfort in that knowledge.

That, despite everything, she could still make this woman follow her.

17

IN A FARAWAY LAND OF PAST HURTS AND NEW PAIN

C hiara Conti had fallen in love with the townhouse on Mercer Street the moment she saw it. The high ceilings, the light, the shelter it offered in plain sight, its dark oaken floors a contrast and a foundation to all that airy space.

As she'd filled it with her creations, her silk and satin, the space had become even more like home. It filled her with pride, with a sense of accomplishment that very few things in her life ever had.

So why, as she climbed the stairs to her studio in front of Vi Courtenay, did everything seem less? Her heart lurched uncomfortably in her chest at the thought of being judged. She wanted to shake her head and her fists.

Not even the presence of Arabella, with all her power and all her influence, had made Chiaroscuro feel small and shabby. And yet this girl, nay this woman, who walked quietly behind her, made Chiara question if all the years that passed since had been for naught.

"I have to say, I was surprised that you landed in New York, of all places." Vi's long fingers glided along the banister, a

contrast of pale skin and dark wood. As they rounded the steps
to the third floor, Chiara stopped and looked at her.

"What's wrong with New York?" Her earlier anger returned,
spurred on by that annoying self-consciousness at Vi being in
her sanctum. And perhaps self-doubt at Vi judging it all
unworthy. Which, in all honesty, was beyond ridiculous.

"Nothing. I suppose it's something that eventually happens
to everyone who works in fashion. I am just surprised that you
did." Vi's tone was neutral, even as her eyes appraised the space
and the objects occupying it. The persistent insouciance got
Chiara's dander up.

"All right, so I will rephrase my question. What is wrong
with me then, if you think New York is somehow too much for
me? Is that what you're saying?"

Vi stopped abruptly, the sharp movement opening her
loose shirt farther, revealing more of those jutting collarbones.

"That wasn't what I was saying, no." The nonchalance was
gone from the achingly familiar voice. Wariness remained. Vi
looked at her as if Chiara was about to lose it at any moment,
and she was trying to figure out what would set her off further.
Chiara instantly hated that measured, appraising gaze. Maybe
even more than the neutral one from before.

"In all honesty, I was making conversation. Small talk, if you
will. And you and I established a long time ago that I'm not
very good at it. When the silence lingered, I figured I had to fill
it. I apologize. I realize now how what I said could be inter-
preted and that I offended you."

Ah, an actual apology. A good one, at that. And the famous
foot-in-mouth? Chiara didn't think the new Vi, the confident,
debonair New Yorker, was still prone to it.

She wanted to smile. It had been such an endearing quality
five years ago, when every other word that would tumble out of
that sensuous mouth was so out of place. Funny or embarrassing or suggestive. Now, despite that very good apology, the

words sounded offensive. Even belittling. And did she just think Vi's mouth was sensuous? *Dio mio...*

She thrust her chin out and raised her eyebrows.

"You didn't offend me, Ms. Courtenay. I'd have to care for your opinion to find you offensive."

Chiara saw that she had scored a direct hit, because something flickered in those deep, calm eyes, and for a second she regretted her words. She felt she'd crossed a line, inflicting that tangible hurt. But then the eyes lost their fire, and the swagger was back, even as a corner of those red lips lifted in a self-deprecating smirk.

"Indeed, Mrs. Conti-Lilienfeld. Miss? Just Conti, these days? I admit, I haven't kept up."

Chiara's answering smirk was sincere. Vi's attempt at parrying her earlier shot had missed entirely. And all because she knew it was a lie on all levels. No, Vi may not have kept up with her endeavors, but she'd known her well enough to realize that Chiara wouldn't have kept the name.

"Oh, you know better than that. And since I never played games with you, maybe you shouldn't either. For old times' sake?" She straightened her shoulders, and from two steps below, Vi gave her the best dismissive glare she could.

She knew she'd scored another direct hit, even as she felt the same shame again. Damn her for being weak. She should be happy, celebrating taking jabs at this woman who'd hurt her so badly. And yet, here she was. Vulnerable and foolish. 'For old times' sake,' indeed.

They entered her atelier and Chiara put as many steps as the space allowed her between them before turning around. "Anyway, Ms. Courtenay, you're here to do a job. What do you need?"

Even as she said the words, she immediately lamented her choice. But this time, it was for an entirely different reason. One that had been dormant in Chiara for five years. Because now the fire in Vi's eyes scorched her with the shared memory of the last time Chiara had uttered them. Whispered them. Moaned them.

Now what little of their respective self-preservation was left seemed to be pulling, tugging at the remnants of control they still possessed over themselves. And if it snapped? If this last line of defense fell? What would she do? And exactly what would she want Vi to do? What did she *fear* she might do?

Too many questions. Too much resentment. And all these words. All these words that said nothing and only filled the time with useless minutiae when the tragedy of them was right here in this room, watching them warily from the corner they both tried their best to steer clear of.

"I need..." Vi's throat worked, a down and up bob of skin and muscle that Chiara followed avidly, then Vi seemed to compose herself. She drew a deep breath, closed her eyes for a moment, and when they opened, there was nothing of Vi in them. Empty. To her horror, Chiara felt the sting of tears. What was happening to her? She hated this woman. Vi had betrayed her. Used her. And now she felt brokenhearted at seeing Vi disappear into herself?

Even as Chiara lowered her head, Vi cleared her throat and that dreadful, empty tone was back.

"I need to look around. Then I need to see what stock you have on hand. How many gowns, accessories. For the logistics and calculations involved in some of the lines you have planned, I'll have to sit down with Aoife and Renate, provided they'll tolerate me long enough..."

Vi trailed off and picked at the hem of her shirt, her expression slightly lost, as if she was sorry for her true but offhand remark. Chiara had to smile. An ugly smile.

Ugly, because they both knew Chiara didn't do the planning and had no say in any of the collections' logistics. That she wasn't any good at it. That she'd get lost in some tiny, useless detail, hyper-fixate and spend days on it, maybe even end up designing a brand new concept instead. And that eventually, Renate would come in and make all the executive decisions. Well, Vi knew her that well. After all, Chiara had shared that much of herself all those years ago.

Chiara set her jaw, venom masking the hurt in her voice. "I'm sure both of them will be accommodating. I would be, but we both know I'd be useless." She stepped away even as Vi made a step towards her.

"Chiara—"

If Chiara detested the nonchalance and the swagger and the newly acquired self-confidence, she had no idea how she'd react to the old misery, the naked sincerity, the shy apology of the old Vi. Well, now she knew. She hated it even more.

Because despite the tattoos, the refined clothes, the air of power and competence projected by this beautiful face, it was still a glimpse of the girl who'd loved her and saved her and then used her. The same girl.

And Chiara had to turn around and look out into the bright and shining light of the Manhattan sun, because the tears that stung the back of her eyes threatened to spill any second now.

God, five years of guilt, of pain, of anger. How she hated herself for using Vi. How she hated Vi for using her.

Behind her, the steps grew closer, and then she was enveloped by the subtle scent of verbena, so like the one she used to wear years ago. Before she could feel the touch on her shoulder, she recoiled, whirling around with enough force to knock the hand away in midair.

"Ms. Courtenay—"

"I'm sorry, I didn't—"

"Stop." The low whisper escaped her, and Vi nodded and lowered her face. "Two weeks. Four, if you have your way, Vi." She swallowed around the name, at once too short, but like a prick of the needle, too painful nonetheless. "We just need to make it through a few weeks. Any insults, any insinuations, all the things you can throw at me can surely wait that long? And when the weeks are up, maybe there will be no need for them, since I probably have more of them—for both myself and you."

Vi raised her head sharply, those cheekbones shadowed by the longer strands of hair escaping the messy bun. Chiara had to dig her nails into her hands as the instinct, so familiar, so much like muscle memory, to tuck those strands behind the small ear almost took over. How was she going to survive this?

Another careful step aside, and the verbena was no longer caressing her senses. She missed the scent and regretted that she had abandoned it after the divorce. Even more so now, when Vi was wearing it, and it felt like she was wearing *her*, still, years later, as a memento of their one night, when Vi had indeed worn Chiara's verbena and so much of Chiara herself. She touched the chilly glass of the window and the cold centered her, gave her a second to collect herself.

"You can look around. I'm not entirely certain how many gowns are finished. Aoife and Renate will be able to give you those numbers." She said it matter-of-factly, but Vi winced nonetheless.

"I really didn't mean it that way, Chiara." The regret hung in the air like a lead balloon about to drop and splash them both with poison.

"It's okay. Really." She knew her voice was warmer than she actually wanted it to sound and couldn't help it. "It's the truth. I don't know how many there are or how many have already been sold. Some might still even be in New York, so perhaps we can bring a few of those back—along with the clients, if they would be willing."

Vi perked up, eyes calculating. "That would be great. I know at least two of them, and one... well, she might be amenable, if she's still speaking to me after our little fling—" She closed her mouth abruptly, ending the oh-so-familiar barrage of words that always seemed to materialize when Vi was nervous or uncomfortable. Some things never changed.

Chiara knew, on some level, that Vi probably didn't live like a nun, but to have it so casually thrown in her face, when she herself had remained untouched since that night, was jarring.

"The details of your exploits don't interest me, Ms. Courtenay." One more step, then another, and Chiara had used the space between them to compose herself again.

"I wasn't about to give you any." Exasperation colored Vi's voice, but she didn't make any attempts to come closer again. Instead, she turned away from Chiara, pulled out a leather notebook and went to work.

Chiara watched her murmur to herself as she walked through the room, counting the gowns and accessories on display in the atelier. She sensed a touch of pride swell inside her when Vi reverently ran her fingers over some of the veils.

More memories of that single-minded focus flooded Chiara. The way those eyes would turn on her, and nothing else existed, how they'd made Chiara feel. Special. Loved.

The sensation of something wet in the palm of her hand made her unclench the fist she was making. Blood. With all her determination to not think about what Vi had done to her all those years ago, she had pierced her own skin.

But she'd spilled that blood for nothing, since it didn't stop her mind from returning there.

A loud, angry meow interrupted her self-recriminations and Binoche swaggered into the workshop, ignoring Vi's presence entirely, which made Chiara smile. The cat that didn't like to be touched walked closer to her mistress and rubbed her compact body on her ankles, twisting and turning, very demonstratively meowing all the way.

Chiara had to laugh, a sound that seemed to surprise Vi, who was watching the cat with some amusement, but suddenly her eyes turned wistful and sad. Chiara refused to analyze why, as she lifted the now loudly and showily purring cat to her face, giving her a nose kiss before setting Binoche on her pillow. As she turned back to Vi, she buried her face back in her notebook.

"I will leave you to it then. And if I were you, I wouldn't disturb Binoche. Though, if you do, just call loudly, and someone will bring you the first aid kit."

With that, she turned away and slowly left the room. As she stood in the doorway, she took one last look. Vi had not raised her eyes from the notebook, but Chiara could see she'd been inching closer to the windowsill. No, Vi still didn't know what was good for her. Or bad, for that matter.

THE PLANS for the magazine turned out to be magnificent, especially in light of the very short amount of time they'd been given.

Chiara's atelier felt crowded, with both Aoife and Renate in her space. "So Benedict, Aoife and I talked Arabella off the ledge. She's pushing the entire October issue back to make room for a special edition. It will be released mid-month, so that gives us another two weeks. Which, all things considered, is a relief, because Courtenay is insane."

Renate voice was a mix of excitement and exasperation as she paced the room, in what was now an all too familiar sight, while Aoife sat perched at Chiara's elbow at the workstation, munching on handfuls of popcorn and watching the scene unfold with avid eyes. At Chiara's glare, she shrugged.

"What? I might as well soothe myself. Had to be Vi Courtenay, of all the photographers in the world? This is a damn mess and I hate it, and I need to get enjoyment where I can." Chiara couldn't fault her. But when offered a handful of the treat, she shook her head.

A thought that she had forgotten to eat breakfast intruded, the next one on its heels being that she hadn't eaten dinner the day before, either. Aoife didn't seem to pay any attention as she reached over and wrote 'order takeout once this goddamn meeting is over' on a pink post-it note.

"Also, I want Renate to tell us more about how her so-called 'work meetings' with Arabella," Aoife dragged the name into twenty suggestive syllables, "are going. 'Cause that is just about as interesting as Chiara here pretending that Vi walking these hallowed halls is not bothering her."

Renate turned, her hand raised and mouth open. Interrupting the impending invective, Chiara simply smacked Aoife on the knee.

"Can we please all act like adults? Nothing can be done about Vi. It's not like we didn't know she had made a huge name for herself as the best fashion photographer in this country of soggy-cardboard-bread." She took a deep, cleansing breath. "Though Aoife is not entirely wrong about everybody wanting to know how you are dealing with Arabella."

She said it with a sly smile and could swear she could see Renate's hair stand on end. How exceedingly interesting.

"And you're the one asking us to act like adults? Never mind Arabella. She is a professional, despite her many terrible qualities. In any case, we all thought that four weeks is much better than two for what Courtenay has in mind. And I have to say I like her proposal. It's fashion at its most influential. It's classic, and both understated and grand. I like it. Damn her."

"But how do you really feel?" Aoife chortled and Chiara simply closed her eyes. So Vi had gotten her way after all. Two weeks were bad enough, but four? How would she cope with that much exposure to Vi? How would she keep tucking the awful tendrils of her guilt and anger away? It was such a dangerous cocktail.

CHIARA DIDN'T KNOW her thoughts were turning prophetic these days, because the entire cocktail turned Molotov on a dime when the interviews started. Ricarda O'Kelly, whose sensuous accent wrapped itself around her subjects like honey, charming and disarming them instantly, was a delight.

Beautiful, funny, with a smile that lit up a room, she joined Chiara and Vi for the cover shoot, observing and making notes.

"Don't mind me, ladies. I just want to get a sense of the person whose name doesn't leave Neve Blackthorne's lips these days." Her eyes crinkled adorably at the corners, and Chiara found herself reciprocating the bright smile. A sharp cough from behind the camera interrupted her, and in her line of vision, Vi frowned.

Ricarda didn't seem to notice Chiara being charmed. "She really is full of so many nice things to say about you—"

Vi's interruption was jarring, even though her voice was measured. "She should be full of nice things to say about her wife instead." Chiara almost lost her footing as she moved from one prop to the next at Vi's words, but Ricarda took everything in stride.

"Oh, she is. Those two are meant to be."

"Good for them." More pouty lips as the shutter clicked away.

"In any case, I was intrigued immediately when she mentioned you. And with all the work you have done these past few years, for the life of me, I cannot understand why your name has not been on more people's lips. You're magnificent."

Ricarda gushed and Vi gnashed her teeth so loudly, Chiara heard the bone-on-bone sound resonate across the studio. Morag, the makeup artist, pretended to be engrossed in her phone.

"Thank you, Ms. O'Kelly." Chiara tried to move as little as

possible as she spoke, but a loud 'tsk' from Vi told her she hadn't succeeded.

"Oh please, it's Ricarda. We're among friends here, aren't we, Vi?" Chiara was certain she could hear Vi almost snap her leash.

However, when she spoke, the voice was steeped in that tone that caused Chiara to feel bile rise up her throat. The complete lack of inflection or emotion. "We are, Ricarda."

"Well then, did I tell you I love this concept? I do! It's gorgeous. I looked through all the previous covers of yours, Chiara, and I have to say, Vi here is going straight for the gold. It'll be amazing. Although, I'm certain nothing with your face on it could be anything but fabulous."

She flittered closer, and Vi moved to the left to get a few side shots, leaving Chiara feeling slightly exposed to the full frontal attack by the reporter.

"You know who else sings your praises? I had lunch with Livia Sabran-McMillan yesterday. My god, the woman is smitten. I'm off the record and am not looking for confirmation, but you'd make a great couple—"

"Ricarda!" Vi's exclamation broke the positively copacetic atmosphere inside the studio. In a totally unnecessary maneuver and with all eyes on her, she stepped in front of Ricarda and called for the makeup artist to touch up Chiara's face. The woman's features as she rolled her eyes before applying a sponge to Chiara's cheekbone spoke volumes about her thoughts on the matter.

As Ricarda stood speechless after Vi's obvious attempt to shut her up, Vi shed her suit jacket, exposing a stylishly ratty t-shirt, those sinewy tattooed forearms, and honest-to-god suspenders, holding up another low slung pair of ankle length trousers. By Chiara's ear, the makeup artist uttered a quiet, "damn girl," before giving out a low whistle.

It was perhaps the whistle that snapped Ricarda out of the insult, and she laughed quietly.

"Well, 'damn girl' is quite right. And for the record Vi, I'd be on the edge too, if two of my exes were married now and minor subjects in a massive special wedding issue, which I was both designing and shooting in its entirety. But with your history, and the swaths you've cut in the lesbian population of this island, I'm not certain that could be avoided." The quiet chuckle was like nails on the board of Chiara's already raw nerves.

Vi's possessiveness and rudeness, Vi acting like Ricarda's flirting was somehow illicit when she herself had... Chiara closed her eyes and mentally counted to ten. When that didn't help, she opened her eyes to the gray ones burning holes in her, both angry and wounded.

Wounded? Chiara felt the short reins of her own temper— stretched tight ever since Vi stepped into Chiaroscuro just days ago and acted like nothing at all had happened between them —finally snap.

"Ricarda, Morag, I think we should all take lunch and reconvene in about an hour and a half." She turned away, effectively dismissing both women.

As she stepped across the studio's threshold, she threw a grenade over her shoulder and kept moving. "Ms. Courtenay, would you mind coming to my office? It seems there are loose ends to our previous conversation that need to be tended to."

18

IN A FARAWAY LAND OF LOANED PLEASURE

Chiara Conti always thought of herself as a calm individual. But it seems there was one person who knew exactly which buttons to push with her.

The sullen look on Vi's face only ignited the embers already alight in Chiara's chest. As she closed the door to the small, rarely used space off the main studio, Chiara turned away from her companion and breathed in deeply, trying to count to ten, to somehow stave off the raw emotion ravaging her, twisting her inside out until she no longer recognized herself.

However, as she turned back, one glimpse at the pouty lips and hooded eyes that looked at her with judgment and dare she say it, matching anger, and Chiara knew she wouldn't be able to hold those runaway reins of hers any longer.

"How dare you?" The insult in her tone rang so clear to her own ears, she didn't even care how transparent she was.

Vi, whose back had been resting on the closed door, pushed off it and took a step closer to her, which, in the close confines of the office, brought her just within reach.

"How dare I? It's been days, and I've been nothing but a beating girl for you, Renate, Aoife..." Vi's mouth twisted into a sneer. "And that's all fine and dandy, but this Ricarda bullshit is a bit too much, even for whatever it is you are doing here, Chiara."

"Whatever it is *I'm* doing? I'm not doing anything!" On pure instinct, Chiara took a step back, bumping against her desk, scattering some of the post-its stuck to it. Vi's eyes followed the falling pieces of paper, and Chiara wanted to slap her. "You have been nothing but insulting since you crossed my threshold."

Vi's throat worked as she visibly tried to contain herself. "I have apologized for the misunderstanding. I thought you knew me better than to think I'd mock you—"

"Well, that is certainly rich coming from you. Because once upon a time I did, in fact, think I knew you better... And that Vi never threw anything in my face. Unlike this version of you, who has done nothing but flaunt your women."

Vi's eyes narrowed speculatively before she took a step closer. When she spoke, her voice had a calculating lilt to it. Too precise, too practiced.

"And would it make you angry, that I've been loved?"

Chiara felt those words hit the mark. Each and every one of them dead center of her heart with vicious intent. Jealousy blacked the corners of her vision. Or was it *greened*?

She couldn't hold in the vitriol. Five years was too long anyway. She'd account for it with herself later, flagellate herself for the truth, for the lies, for everything in between.

"Yes, yes it would."

The words fell out of her mouth like bricks, hard and heavy, clattering to the floor between them. Chiara just stared, realizing how close she and Vi were standing to each other. As her eyes trailed upwards, from the expensive shoes to the fitted trousers hanging on prominent hip bones, to the small gap showing off a toned midriff, then farther up still, she saw how hard Vi was breathing, how fast her heart was hammering with the pulse visible at her long graceful neck, exposed now as her t-shirt slipped down one shoulder.

"Good." Vi's voice was barely discernible in the air of the room that seemed flammable.

Their eyes met. Pain. So much of it, and all of it here, not even under the surface, not even under the skin like the ink of Vi's tattoos. All of it right in this space crackling between them —that was somehow getting smaller—even as Chiara realized Vi was indeed taking one more step and verbena enveloped her senses again. And mixed with all that pain, was the one thing that was neither new, nor good, nor something she'd ever known how to fight. Desire.

A second... A truck passed under the windows, rattling the glass. Another second... Someone yelled an obscenity down the street. Yet one more second, and a ragged breath one of them drew in...

The moment was suspended in the air, stretching like a rubber band until Chiara physically felt it snap and all bets were off. All lines were in the rearview mirror.

She reached for the collar of the t-shirt, even as Vi's hands dove into her hair, tugging and pulling until the pins of the carefully and artfully arranged bun were scattered on the floor.

Their mouths met, lips and tongues and teeth and all that rage, even as Vi lifted her onto the desk, further scattering the notes and the multitude of fountain pens she could never quite decide on.

"Vi..." She didn't recognize her own voice, her own body. So needy. So hot. Her clothes too tight, too suffocating, because only one thing made sense. Everything was wrong. They were wrong. Not good. Not healthy. But so right. Right now.

Vi broke the kiss that was more a devouring than a caress and forced their eyes to meet. And there it was again, that silent *something* in those ash depths, something that hadn't been there five years ago, when Chiara had known every shade, every shadow in them. But it had been here, hanging between them every second since Vi had stepped into Chiaroscuro, like a foreshadowing of things to come.

Their breathing ragged, Vi's thigh between Chiara's pressing just enough to remind her of its presence and not enough to give her anything she really needed, they stared at each other until Chiara could look no more. She was weak. This was wrong. Again.

Wrong.

But she needed this.

Again.

She closed her eyes and nodded, consent given, before reaching for those swollen lips again, licking the bottom one, biting it with just enough force to taste blood.

Whatever tether had been holding Vi back rent, even as copper filled Chiara's mouth, and Vi unceremoniously tore her thong, pieces of ivory satin fluttering to the floor, as strong hands pushed her further onto the desk.

And then Chiara was taken. There was no other way to describe it. Not gentle, not careful. Nothing like their one night. She felt the lack of oxygen and let go of the need to breathe. Vi did not break the kiss as two fingers entered her, rough, forceful, thrusting deep with no preamble.

She came fast. Five years of longing, yearning, missing this very thing.

Maybe under different circumstances, she would have been embarrassed, but Vi was unrelenting, so Chiara let go of the shame as well. She moaned, her own arms limp around Vi's neck, powerless to do anything but weakly hold on as she was taken again.

Another finger joined the first two, and she felt stretched, her own body bearing evidence of years of abstinence, and she whimpered against Vi's lips, still on hers, still ravaging her mouth. As she allowed the sound to escape, Vi slowed her thrusts down with a whispered, "shhh, I'm sorry, baby, I'm sorry...," and the words, as much as the slower, impossibly deeper thrusts, undid her.

The second time, she didn't come as much as she shattered. Vi's mouth swallowed her cry, then full lips kissed away the tears she hadn't realized had fallen.

In the total silence of the dusty space, amidst the disarrayed desk, her breathing sounded almost obscene. Vi held her now that her tears had stopped falling.

When the realization that Vi's fingers were still buried inside her permeated her consciousness, it hit like a runaway train of pure lust. *More.*

She raised her eyes to Vi's and saw her own hunger reflected in them. Before she knew it, Vi was moving, dragging her dress down, exposing her breasts and yanking Chiara to the edge of the desk while kneeling down in front of her.

Her vision grayed as the mouth tasted her, and she may have blacked out, because it seemed like she was coming again within seconds, Vi's ravenous mouth refusing to let up. Chiara needed her unsteady hands to push weakly at that silken hair to make her stop, too sensitive now, too overcome, too overwhelmed, by both her orgasm and the reality suddenly as present as Vi's grip on her thighs.

Rising up, Vi wiped her mouth with the back of her hand, the gesture as irreverent as it was sexy, and Chiara's mouth watered. She wanted to lick herself off those lips. Wanted to push Vi against the wall and take her apart, exactly like she had done for her.

But when she reached out, Vi stepped back. Her eyes were wide, fever-bright, surveying Chiara closely for perhaps a moment too long. Because as Chiara's breathing stilled and she sat up, she became aware of the state Vi had left her in. The dangerous, self-satisfied glint in those eyes began to make sense, even if she wanted to hide.

She was spread on the desk, dress bunched up, leaving her naked from the waist down, exposed and vulnerable, sated and bruised. She knew she looked like she felt, fucked six ways from Sunday and begging for more.

"Vi..." She still did not recognize her own voice, but it was tremulous this time. Like she'd screamed herself hoarse. And maybe she had, since there'd been that rather conspicuous moment when she was almost certain she wasn't entirely conscious. God, the things this woman did to her. After all this time. The power this woman had over her. Vi destroyed her. Sexually and emotionally.

Even now, simply looking at her, eyes feasting on what the mouth had done just moments ago, Chiara felt exposed. Defenseless. Wrung inside out for her own pleasure and on this one woman's whim. Because despite the satisfaction and the haze of her orgasms, Chiara was left completely clueless as to what it meant.

Vi had not allowed her to touch, other than their kisses, and even as Chiara lifted her hand to pull down the hem of her dress, Vi watched her every move speculatively.

"Are you going to fuck me or hit me, Vi?"

Well, that made those eyes finally tear themselves away from the marks on her skin, from her naked breasts and meet hers.

"Is there a difference?" The voice was remarkably steady. Vi lowered her head and came closer again, taking Chiara in her arms with soul shattering gentleness. Like she was broken. Like Vi was the one who broke her.

"I was rough with you. I apologize."

Chiara shook her head, but Vi simply laid a finger on her lips and she quieted.

Yes, Vi was very much aware of her own power these days.

"Shhh..." The sound, the same one Vi had uttered when her fingers were inside her, caused a Pavlovian reflex in Chiara.

Her throat worked, and Vi's lips curved into a smirk. Arrogant. This was new, too. And it was sexy. Chiara opened her mouth and licked at the finger still resting against her lips, finally tasting herself. The smirk widened, and Vi's voice took on that low tone.

"You have such an aversion to apologies. It's an unhealthy habit."

"I seem to have many of them. And most of them where you are concerned." Chiara's hands reached up and tucked a lock behind Vi's ear, letting her fingers trail over the delicate shell, delighting in the shiver her gesture caused.

Vi caught her hand, bringing it to her chest, keeping it there, perhaps thinking Chiara couldn't do much damage that way. Instead, she could feel Vi's heart beating a steady tattoo and Chiara took solace in the rhythm and strength from it. It beat too rapidly, giving Vi away in a way her eyes and her smile did not.

"I was under the impression that you lived a healthy lifestyle, Chiara." Vi squeezed her fingers, and she wondered at the choice of words. Was Vi asking about what she had been up to these past years? Because she'd been so insistent on being totally disinterested only days before.

"I think five years of dieting makes it imperative that I fall off the wagon every once in a while. At least till I get my fill before my next fast. Plus, I can't abstain now. I need to... to you..."

She stumbled over the words, feeling foolish once again. Needy, still aching, and already ready for more. And had she mentioned foolish? She wanted to bolt. She couldn't yet.

They watched each other then. Combatants behind drawn lines, a short armistice to discuss terms. Terms Chiara wished she understood, since she had no idea where her words were coming from or what Vi was really thinking.

The heart under her fingertips kept its elevated beat, and

Chiara felt like it was the only honest thing about them, limbs intertwined, mouths inches apart, Vi's fingers still holding the scent and the essence of Chiara.

Vi's heart was the only true thing? Chiara wanted to laugh at herself. Wasn't this how she had gotten hers *broken* the last time?

Some of her thoughts must have shown on her face, because Vi let go of her hand and gravity did its job, both of them watching it fall limply into her lap.

"You don't need to do anything. And I already apologized for being rough with you earlier. But I won't be your 'cheat meal,' Chiara. I've had the dubious honor of settling for that role once before."

Well, what the girl hadn't been capable of—that cruelty— the woman had become masterful at.

Chiara pushed her away and, with whatever strength her shaking knees could muster, slid off the desk, righting her bodice, tucking away both naked skin and whatever dignity she had left.

"Remember how during that night you said you were afraid that I'd break you?" She straightened her shoulders, pleased when Vi's eyes followed her every move. After a second, the gray orbs lowered, and the nod Chiara received was jerky. "Well, you broke me first."

She heard the exhalation of air Vi let out before she turned away from the hurt expression in those eyes. With that, she gave into that overwhelming wish to get away and swept out of the office and out of the studio and kept walking, the crowds of Mercer Street swallowing her in their soothing bustle.

SHE DIDN'T RETURN that afternoon, choosing to walk away rather than face the scrutiny of a makeup artist and a sharp-eyed interviewer while marked by hands and teeth in quite a few visible places.

Instead, she spent the rest of the day on the streets of Manhattan losing herself in the crowds and the movement of the city that never stopped and didn't care. It felt good to be a speck of lint on the miles of the urban canvas.

Despite the pleasure of being unknown and lost in the crowd, she was aware she would pay for her willfulness and her irresponsible decision to waste the afternoon in light of their restrictive timeframe.

Her predicament became evident as soon as she returned to Chiaroscuro once the dusk was settling behind her on the now much emptier Mercer Street.

"At some point in the last five years you might've mentioned that you and Courtenay did more than solely stare at each other in a haze of longing and unrealized lust, Chiara."

Aoife was on the stairs leading up to the atelier, her voice muffled by what looked like a churro she was chewing.

"There wasn't any point in that." Suddenly, hit by a tiredness that permeated her bones, Chiara sat down, hugging her knees and letting her chin rest on them.

"*Point...*" Aoife repeated the word as if it was foreign to her. Chiara reached over into her friend's flannel shirt's front pocket, trusting she'd find what she needed most in this moment. Faster than Aoife could swat at her, she pulled out the pack.

Aoife still batted her hands away, but offered her the lighter regardless, as Chiara wrapped her lips around a cigarette. The first drag was like a lover's caress. She relished the sensation, the familiar movements, the taste of the smoke on her tongue.

"You quit." Renate's voice, in all its accusatory glory, sounded from behind them, and both of them jumped at the interruption. But Renate just waved them off and opened one of the massive windows overlooking the interior garden, letting in the sounds of the evening city. In the distance, a cacophony of sirens and screeching tires could be heard. Chiara closed her eyes.

"Did I screw up today?"

"If you mean the overall schedule, then no. Courtenay used the afternoon to get some pictures of the atelier itself. Hounded Aoife to pose for some action shots of 'her process.' As if Aoife has a method to her madness—"

"Hey, hey!" Aoife's protest was ignored as Renate went on.

"But if you mean the whole thing about fucking the chief photographer instrumental to the success of your first Poise issue as a designer... A photographer who also *fucked you over* five years ago... One who just happens to be a Courtenay? Well, it seems you crossed that line already, Chiara. Please don't tell me you did it simply because she was there. Then or now."

"I don't know why I did it now." She still remembered the confusion, the anger, the guilt that were all eating her alive, and Vi provided such an outlet to all those emotions she herself was causing.

"And back then?" Aoife's voice was quiet, even as she snatched the cigarette from between Chiara's fingers, took a long drag, and handed it back to her. Before she was able to react, Renate reached for it, and they proceeded to sit in silence as her former sister-in-law polished it off and masterfully flicked it out of the open window.

"Isn't that the million dollar question, Aoife? Because some things make so much sense now, Chiara." Renate's smile was sad. "All that guilt I couldn't understand. With the divorce and with every reference to Courtenay herself. Must have choked you for all those years, didn't it?"

"There was nothing I could do about it anyway." Chiara pushed her guilt aside. She had told the truth. What good was wallowing when she did what she did, using Vi as a catalyst for her new life? Chiara shook her head before slowly unfolding herself from the stairs and took several steps towards the studio. At Aoife's call for her to stop, she looked back down at her friends.

"Although I wasn't able to do anything whatsoever about it then, maybe there is something I can do now. I certainly wasn't expecting her. In fact, if you had told me I'd see her again, I would have been convinced I wouldn't even have recognized her. And yet, it's been years and I still knew those eyes, and they knew me. Not a stranger at all." She ran her hand through her hair, decision made. "I'm sure you could wheedle her address out of Arabella, Renate."

She deliberately did not phrase her request as a question, and the look on both Aoife and Renate's faces told her they disapproved.

As she turned away, Chiara had to smile. If she had been thinking clearly, she too would disapprove. But she didn't have the strength to stay away in those days either.

Five years was a long time to be numb. Vi had awakened her before. And Chiara wanted to be alive again. Plus, she had a debt to pay, and she was never one to renege on her debts.

19

IN A FARAWAY LAND OF ROSES AND DEBTS

C hiara Conti wasn't sure what she'd envisioned when she knocked on the door of the attic apartment just a few blocks from Mercer Street. Her feet hurt, her heart thudded, and her mind reeled.

What was she doing here? What was she doing, period?

Hadn't she done this once before? When she'd first entered the building, she had half expected a man to exit, like five years ago when she had been in a very similar situation.

Except this particular blue door, so much like Vi's Parisian one, stayed closed, and the building sighed heavily around her in a suspended silence. A silence of anticipation, a silence of foreboding. One that spoke of something that was equally horrible and magical.

Chiara knew she was being absurd. *A sighing building.* God, she was losing her mind.

She ran her hand through her hair, tugging on the ends of the longer locks to center herself, to force her scattering thoughts to return to her. She needed all of them with her now. Because she was about to do something so fatuous, she was surprising even herself by how out of character it was. Still, the least she could do was be articulate as she did it.

Her hand shook as she knocked, and the sound came out somehow hollow, wrong. Standing still, her body taut, a bowstring ready for the shot, Chiara listened intently for any signs of life. Except there was no arrow and no target and no life. Just silence. She raised her hand again; her knuckles rapping once, twice on that lovely shade of blue wood with the same result as before. No sound answered her.

Chiara swallowed around the lump in her throat. It was after ten in the evening and Vi was out. Of course she was. Hadn't Ricarda implied that she had the entirety of Manhattan's lesbian population at her fingertips? Fingertips she'd had in Chiara just hours earlier. Her tired knees shook, and she lowered herself to the stairs next to the door.

She closed her eyes for what seemed like a second, the emotions of the day confounding her and ravaging what was left of her composure.

A hand on her shoulder made her start, but the quiet voice soothed even as the hand retreated.

"I had a feeling it wasn't Renate who'd be my late night visitor." Vi had her arms full of white roses of all things and looked remarkably like a prince from all the fairytales Chiara's mother had read to her at bedtime. Tall, slender, a prerequisite tortured expression on those forlorn features.

She didn't offer Chiara a hand to help her up, and they maintained the status quo for a moment longer. One looking up at the other with roses fragrant between them.

Then, just as quietly as she'd appeared, Vi twisted the key in the door and pushed it open. She didn't look back, not even when Chiara followed her through, the door slowly closing behind her.

"I highly doubt Renate would make for a pleasant visitor. At this or any other hour." Chiara moved through the apartment unseeing. What did she care what it all looked like, which paintings and photographs covered its colorful walls?

Vi stood in the center of the space, lit only by the city below filtering in languidly, with street lamps and billboards giving her an otherworldly glow. Reds and blues, a splash of bright yellow... Chiara's fingers twitched, the desire for her pencil almost choking her. *Desire...*

"No, you Lilienfelds are rarely harbingers of good things, late hour or not."

The words, cruel, deliberate, were like a bucket of cold water. What would her pencil draw now? The full lips in a sneer? The eyes blazing with something akin to hatred? Well, Chiara had done enough hating for both of them for five years, and it seemed that it wasn't so potent of an emotion. After all, here she was, about to debase herself in front of the woman whom she had resented so much, and who seemed to despise her right back.

"Do you ever wish we'd never met, Vi?"

Her own voice was barely audible, and Chiara knew she had to push through, to speak, to be heard. But the plump lips, suddenly pale, opened slightly, and she could see her question had come as a surprise. And as a blow. Good, because she had more to say.

"I did, Vi." And now the hurt in the wide eyes was so deep, so vivid, Chiara flinched, yet didn't hurry her words. Some things needed to sink in. "I've had five years of wishing I'd never met you. Because if I never had, I wouldn't have spent those five years wanting to hate you. You know how I detest failing, and in the end, I did anyway. At telling myself you never mattered. At resenting you. Since here we are, with whatever this is between us."

Vi closed her eyes, hiding herself from Chiara's gaze, and Chiara allowed both of them just a moment—to take a breath, to be still before all hell broke loose.

The tearing in her chest was painful, several more stitches coming undone. Chiara briefly wondered if this was her sanity finally giving out, stretched to the limit for years. But she took a step forward, followed by another, and then the pristine white roses were crushed between them as their mouths met again with the same painful intent as just hours ago.

Yes, they did want to hurt. Fuck each other too, but mostly hurt themselves, because Chiara felt the roses' thorns sting her skin and reveled in the pain. Just as much as she reveled in Vi's mouth taking its fill, nipping and biting at hers, no doubt leaving more bruises behind, bruises she'd need to cover for tomorrow's photoshoot.

The roses dropped to the floor as Vi pushed Chiara into the nearest wall and ravaged her throat, sucking greedily on a pulse point, making Chiara forget her purpose, her reason for being here.

Even as she allowed herself to cradle those shadowed cheekbones, Vi was pulling Chiara's hands away, lifting them above her head. She held them firmly against the wall, abrading her skin, already pricked by the roses, and Chiara wanted to allow the lust to wash over her. When Vi's other hand moved under her skirt, sliding up her thigh and caressing her through the decidedly sodden thong, Chiara panted. Wanting and wanton, she felt wild and untethered. When she heard the satin rend yet again, she smiled and knew she looked feral.

"That's two in one day." She rasped. "Keeping the lingerie industry in business single-handedly, Cinderella?" Vi raised her eyes to hers, and Chiara saw something she hadn't expected to find there. Not amidst what was happening here. She would have guessed Vi would look despondent, sullen, arrogant. After all, she was turning Chiara into a quivering mess yet again. But Vi looked... sad.

And Chiara, who could endure many things and had withstood quite a number of them, could not stand this. Her hands still up against the wall, she tugged them out of Vi's grasp and reached for that tormented face, holding it carefully between her palms, never taking her eyes off Vi's.

Then she shifted, turning them around, Vi's back now against the wall, and watched those eyes widen as she knelt. Her hands pulled on the leather belt slowly, allowing Vi to say 'no', to step to the side and away, except the tired eyes just looked on, still wide, still sad. Chiara didn't avert hers as she lowered the zipper, the sound of the brass slider gliding over the metal teeth obscene in this room filled with their breathing.

As her mouth descended on Vi, the last thing she saw were those eyes losing focus and close, but Chiara was aware she hadn't wiped the sadness away, and so when she brought Vi to a shattering climax, it felt like a hollow victory.

IT WAS that lingering sadness that made her get up from her knees and instead of leaving, instead of walking away and not looking back, debts being settled now, she stepped up and into the arms that hung limply at Vi's sides.

It was that slight tremble of the hands that lifted and settled on her shoulders and the tears dancing on the long auburn lashes that made her gather Vi in an embrace and hold her as night settled over Manhattan in earnest.

Against her shoulder, Vi's breathing quieted, and the hands steadied as they dove into her hair.

"Feel better now?" Vi's hoarse voice should have broken the reverie, the suspended state of this dreamlike moment that shouldn't have anything to do with reality because Chiara shouldn't be here, shouldn't still be tasting Vi on her lips. And Vi shouldn't look broken and bruised.

"I don't renege on debts." They were all useless, worthless words, in ragged harsh whispers, yet the moment went on.

Trying to finally break out of it, Chiara leaned back and tipped Vi's face up, her fingers lingering on the angular jaw.

When their eyes met, the dream seemed to only deepen, Chiara finding herself even more powerless to shake it off, as the tears on those long, tangled lashes fell. First one, then another.

She'd cried earlier, when Vi had made her come. Now it was Vi's turn. Was this the true debt they were paying back? And when had she started equating Vi's betrayal with her own sins?

As if reading her thoughts—which had always been the case, and Chiara thought she should perhaps stop being surprised by it—Vi echoed the sentiment.

"*Old* debts, Chiara?"

She tucked Vi's head back against her shoulder, their identical height allowing them to fit like puzzle pieces. Chiara had a fanciful, fleeting thought that she'd heard the shallow click of cardboard slotting into its designated position. How quixotic of her to believe that she could just come over, fuck Vi, waltz back out and return to her life.

The fingers in her hair soothed, the gentle caresses interspersed with an occasional tug, as they'd hit a snag perhaps of Vi's own making, since she'd had her hands in Chiara's hair from the moment Chiara'd knelt in front of her.

As if apologizing, the lips whispered something against her skin and the fingers went back to work, carefully untangling the knot before starting over somewhere else.

It was sweet, Chiara decided, her mind sidestepping the gentleness and the murmurs, choosing not to hear and not to feel.

"I don't have many old debts."

The spell, the dreamlike moment, was instantly broken.

The second the words were out of her mouth, Chiara knew it had been the wrong thing to say. So wrong, yet also the truth. Her guilt being what it was, and considering her feelings five years ago, *Chiara* still wasn't the one holding the thirty pieces of silver. She wasn't the one who'd betrayed.

Nonetheless, it had been the wrong thing to say, because Vi stilled in her arms, then drew back and away, hastily zipping up her trousers and strolling unsteadily towards the bay of windows covering the entire wall overlooking the Village.

Her arms free and her mind reeling, Chiara finally looked around, taking in the cozy, pristine place she found herself in. Black and white photographs adorned the walls, and ivy grew in a myriad of pots scattered around the shelves. Chiara recognized the vision behind the monochrome creations and wanted to smile. Vi had lost nothing of her eye.

There was a comfortable chair and a fuzzy blanket in front of the windows, and Chiara realized instantly that this had to be Vi's favorite spot. The stack of books by its side told her as much. She smiled. Some things never changed.

She must have said it out loud, because Vi turned sharply back to her.

"Would you have actually wanted them to?"

A lump in her throat seemed to have thorns, cutting her to ribbons. This woman always managed to. Chiara wondered whether it was intentional, or if it was some kind of supernatural ability. Because nobody, not her mother, not Frankie, not anyone else, saw her—and slashed through her with the skill and precision Vi did.

"That would imply you reading and being surrounded by all the books was a trait of yours I did not like."

"Bookishness aside, was there actually anything about me that you liked?" Vi spat the last word, her voice rising from quiet to high-pitched, and Chiara felt that same shard twist at the stitches holding her chest together yet again. Or was it just her guilt?

"There were plenty of things I liked about you, Vi. What is it that you want?"

"I'm trying to understand what are you doing here."

Her back against the glass and the booted legs crossed at the ankles, Chiara almost smiled at the oh-so-familiar pose. All Vi needed to do now was wrap her arms around herself, and the image could have belonged on a Parisian rooftop five years ago. Afraid of heights, yet trying not to show it.

When silence stretched, and Vi tsked, then lifted those lanky arms and held herself tight, Chiara did smile at the memory before reaching out on instinct to tuck another lock of hair behind Vi's ear. Except her hand dropped at the last moment, the gravity of their situation weighing heavy.

"I don't know what I'm doing here. Is that so strange? Is that so unusual for me, of all people? I wasn't sure what I was doing here five years ago either—"

"Here?" The question was filled with anxiety, and Chiara could see Vi's shoulders tense up further, her own mirroring them.

"With you. A different room. A roof. A studio. A Parisian street. Anywhere really. Just not where I was supposed to be, because it was with you. Of all the people, I wasn't supposed to be with you. And yet I couldn't help myself. I can't seem to."

"So I'm a mistake?" Vi's voice was quiet as her teary eyes turned cold.

"A vice." Chiara sighed. "One I have paid for, and for some reason, the price hasn't been too high. Or time made it more palatable in dulling its steepness."

"I told you that I didn't do it—"

"In a manner of speaking." She wanted to sound exasperated, but she knew all she pulled off was tired. "It doesn't matter. I asked you a question years ago, when my life was in ruins at your feet. I asked you and you... Well, you had no answer. You shook your head. You had tears in your eyes and roses in your hands. We've come full circle here, Vi. Tears and roses."

Vi flinched, and Chiara regretted the words almost instantly. When had *she* developed a cruel streak? When she'd put her heart in the hands of a twenty-five-year-old girl with a crush that Chiara should have avoided like the plague? Nobody was afraid of plagues these days anyway.

But Chiara still should have known better. Even if the betrayal was one of enormous proportions and the hurt all the more, because unbeknownst to Vi, Chiara's heart had been on the line.

Frankie had destroyed her sense of self. Humiliated her as a woman. Insulted her as a spouse. And in the past five years, Chiara had painstakingly rebuilt most of those intangibles. Time. Distance. Friends. Work and success. All of those helped, and she felt whole again.

But Vi had broken her heart. And it was the one thing Chiara did not know how to repair. How to begin to trust the wretched piece of muscle pumping crimson into her chest with decisions, since it had taken her so long to wrap it in burlap and stitch it together with tattered yarn. Chiara felt that was one skill she did not possess.

"And so we're back to square one. Aside from making me come and repaying a debt you really didn't acquire, why are you here, Chiara?"

As always, the most random thought surfaced, and Chiara simply went with it, her shoulders suddenly heavy and fingers numb.

"To hear you say my name."

Vi let out an exhalation and Chiara finally gave in and her smile bloomed fully. Years had polished this woman, added a veneer of sophistication. But someone like Chiara could still fluster her. Or maybe it was just Chiara. She chose to think it was the latter, and her chest felt lighter.

The sound of the clock somewhere in the apartment reminded Chiara of the time and of how exhausted she was. "I'm sorry. It's late, and it's been a long, somewhat eventful day."

On Vi's face, an answering grin bloomed, a corner of that sensuous mouth lifting with self-deprecation. Unsurprisingly, it made Chiara happy to have coaxed that smile out of this sad, tormented woman.

Thinking that she needed to have her head examined for being glad about such things, and about how Renate and Aoife would have a field day with what she had just done and said, Chiara picked up her purse where it had fallen by the front door.

"What now?" Vi watched her warily now, but there was something like hope lurking in those ashen depths.

She actually lifted her eyes to the heavens. *Misericordia*, the hope, anguish, desperation in that voice... All the things that had been there five years ago and had undone Chiara again and again every time she'd rescued Vi from her torment, still had the same effect on her.

So weak. So damn weak.

Some things really never did change. Maybe she should just get with the program.

"There's a gala for New York's fashion magazines tomorrow."

Vi's brows lifted comically.

"Yeah, I declined, what with us going full steam ahead with the special edition. I didn't think we'd have time..."

"Reconsider, Ms. Courtenay. Pick me up after the shoot at 9."

Gray eyes narrowed and reddened lips thinned.

"Why are you doing this?"

She could have lied. Could have plucked out any of the thousands of thoughts in her head. Really, any single one would do. But when the truth seemed so much more expedient, Chiara closed her eyes and surrendered to it.

"Because I was wrong earlier. Some debts aren't so easily paid off, Vi. Yours or mine. And I think neither of us is done paying."

20

IN A FARAWAY LAND OF OLD
FAMILIAR FACES AND UNDERTOWS

Chiara Conti remembered that when you find yourself swept up in an undertow, they tell you to keep swimming parallel to the shore. Keep trying until you free yourself. Never stop. Standing in the middle of the Four Seasons Grand Plaza's immense ballroom, surrounded by hundreds of guests, Chiara felt herself being pulled underwater.

The lights, the movement, and the crowd battered her senses to the point where she felt numb, submerged. The mix of expensive perfumes, alcohol, and fragrant finger foods was jarring. The cameras, the flashes of white teeth, just as bright and just as predatory.

Amidst the noise and the sensory assault, her only raft was Vi's hand in hers. When had she even taken Chiara's ice-cold fingers in her own, warm ones?

They walked the red carpet separately, more so for Chiara's self-preservation than out of secrecy. She figured that, with Arabella and Benedict giving them rather suggestive thumbs up as they got out of the limo, the cat would be out of the bag in no time anyway.

But Arabella was also right. Chiara Conti and Chiaroscuro were unquestionably hot commodities in New York these days. The sharks were circling, all wanting something. The surrounding buzz—be it for the royal Savoy gown or Neve Blackthorne's wedding that, while officiated in private, still had massive reverberations in fashion media—felt like a category 5 storm, sweeping her up and throwing her around like a rag doll.

Perhaps that was when Vi, fresh out of walking her own gauntlet on the red carpet, as New York's photographer and lesbian-about-town du jour, caught up to her and slowly, gently, slid her fingers in between Chiara's. A careful gesture, so thoughtful, so grounding. Vi gave her a chance to shake her fingertips off, and she offered an anchor should Chiara wish for it.

And Chiara wished for it very much. *So very much.* The soft slide of skin against skin, the rough calluses on those slim hands, the tangle of fingers sliding into position as if they'd held Chiara's for ages, as if they actually had an established place that was theirs, a key for a lock to Chiara's sanity. They gave her a respite among the constant assault of fake smiles and inane questions and the very real avarice of the crowd around them.

"Thank you," she mouthed the words, barely an exhalation on her lips, but Vi's eyes still narrowed before darkening, surprise and pleasure evident in their depths. The answering squeeze of the fingertips was all the answer Chiara got before the hand in hers suddenly went limp and the languid, relaxed eyes went hollow.

A transformation unlike anything Chiara had ever seen. Or maybe she had? Except this was much more dramatic, and the sudden apprehension in Vi's features was so obvious even her lips had gone pale. Only the ashen color of the suddenly massive eyes continued to be in sharp relief on the now translucent skin.

Chiara's gaze followed the line of Vi's sight, bracing for impact. It was the gown that caught Chiara's attention first. And how could it not, when she knew it so very well? She'd been slated to model it herself once upon a time, before she took her stand and respectfully refused to deal with that particular fashion house.

It was another dress from the German Maestro's lost Silver Collection. Chiara had seen the showing. The only one for this particular line, despite the Maestro himself declaring it perfection.

The pieces had been considered lost or discarded for years now, and whispers about them still slithered around the fashion world. That he'd sold them. That the house burned them.

But Chiara knew better. He'd loved them. She had witnessed his love when she'd watched him work, how his fingers had run over every crease and tuck.

One gown from the lost Silver Collection surfacing was a surprise. Two? And in the same hands? A curious miracle.

With those observations running through her mind, Chiara was pulled back to the present by the hand in hers going cold as two figures started on a circuitous but clearly deliberate route towards them.

That sharp tug of premonition that had been plaguing her for days now jolted her again. Her stitches pulled tight, sang. She had seen that man before. She didn't know where, but she definitely knew him.

Chiara wanted to curse herself and her inability to, for once, remember faces. She'd gotten better with age and better with names, but faces remained nebulous, even in instances like these, instances that seemed important.

"Genevieve..."

Tall, silver-haired, and with an air of gentility manifesting itself in all that affected boredom, he didn't come closer or exchange the air kisses so customary at these sorts of events.

"Father..."

Chiara schooled her features to hide her surprise. Charles Courtenay looked nothing like his daughter. In fact, it was possible the two of them were the least similar looking father-daughter pair she had ever seen.

The woman on his arm clicked her tongue, reminding her companion about her presence, but Charles' eyes—the only feature reminiscent of his daughter, their gray light burning low—were focused on Vi's face. With the silence stretching, the tongue click turned into a head shake and an eye roll.

"Genevieve, where are your manners, chérie?" The rebuke grated on Chiara's nerves, even as Vi's hand in hers twitched as if startled.

"Apologies. Chiara, allow me to introduce the Earl and Countess of Rae. Father, Gwyneth, Chiara Conti."

The title wasn't a surprise. After all, Chiara had heard Aoife tease Vi numerous times with the proper address of Lady Rae. She even remembered looking it up and finding a now obscure but once-upon-a-time storied noble house. Yet, hearing it still unnerved her. Maybe it was the way Vi's hand felt clammy and even colder in hers. Or perhaps it was the tremor that ran through it?

"My Lord. My Lady." Chiara's past had exposed her to the blue-blooded patrons of fashion enough to know her address was correct even before Charles' regal nod of his head.

His eyes, so like Vi's, appraised her for a second before turning away and focusing again on his daughter, Chiara's presence dismissed with only a quirk of his lips. Another affectation he shared with Vi. Chiara watched, fascinated, as the two Courtenays simply took each other in, oblivious to the world.

"Ms. Conti, such a pleasure to meet you. I must say, I have

been quite desperate to do so ever since Genevieve made your acquaintance in Paris."

Gwyneth's smile dripped sugar, but Chiara felt every single granule of it abrade her skin. And what a way to describe Vi's work at Lilien Haus.

"The pleasure of having worked with Vi in Paris is all mine, I'm sure." She countered the fake sweetness with something approaching sincerity which seemed to placate Gwyneth, who obviously wasn't used to being ignored as both her husband and her stepdaughter were doing. Still, she didn't take Chiara's bait and—with an exaggerated turn towards her—continued to pursue her line of conversation, the nature of which Chiara recognized fairly quickly. Gwyneth Courtenay was a gossip and rumors were her currency.

"Is it true that you are to be featured in Poise? And with a brand new house? Finally set free from your shackles. How poetic." All teeth and molasses, Gwyneth fanned herself with a hand adorned with no less than five rings. The light playing off the gold distracted Chiara, making her think of Kitsch art installations. All bling and no soul.

"I am unsure whether divorce is all that poetic." Her own voice came out just a touch strained, and it was testament to Vi's awareness of her that she was immediately drawn closer, the gesture not escaping Charles or Gwyneth. The latter's smile grew toothier, and the former's brows furrowed.

Vi's voice was rough when she spoke. "It's too warm here, Chiara. Would you like me to bring you a glass of champagne? It's excellent."

Chiara was about to reply that she wasn't thirsty, but Charles' gruff interruption stopped her.

"You still haven't learned anything about your sparkling wines, Genevieve. The champagne was bland and lacking in the bouquet. Maybe if you'd apply yourself to something worth your time instead of whatever it is you do these days, you could dedicate yourself to more worthwhile pursuits. Matters worthy of your station."

Now bushy eyebrows lifted in a gesture of thorough disgust and suggestiveness, and Chiara felt Vi's fingers tremble again as she blanched, a blue vein fluttering manically under the pale skin on her long neck.

"I think some champagne would be splendid, darling." She deliberately half-turned away from the now gaping Courtenays and traced a finger over Vi's cheekbone.

Vi's throat worked, Chiara's eyes tracing the movement down and up before nodding towards the bar and letting go of the shaking hand. When Vi left without a word to her parents, Charles cursed under his breath.

"Goddamn it, I taught that girl better manners." The next moment, he had departed in the same direction as Vi, who had disappeared into the crushing crowd, leaving Chiara and Gwyneth in an uncomfortable silence.

"I swear, every time we see that girl, she grows more willful. Sadly, we don't see her much at all these days. With behavior like that, this may be for the best." Gwyneth looked at her nails, her entire air affecting boredom despite her earlier salacious interest in the details of Chiara's life. Well, this certainly seemed more like the apathetic stepmother Chiara had heard about years ago, even if Vi herself had talked about her very little.

"If by 'willful' you mean, independent, talented and successful, then certainly, Mrs. Courtenay." Done playing nice, Chiara thought she'd rather be dead than call this cold fish 'My Lady' again. Her mother, god rest her soul, had had many wonderful Italian appellations for just this type of person.

Too bad Chiara couldn't use any of them just now. There were many Page Seven reporters milling about, and the headline of "Newly triumphantly returned Chiara Conti calls the Countess of Rae various creative Italian insults, implying that she smells and might be in an inappropriate relationship with various blood relatives," wasn't something that appealed.

Although possibly funny, she assumed Vi would be mortified. Come to think about it, Vi seemed both apprehensive—if not completely overcome by dread—and also embarrassed to see her parents at the gala.

But, just because the last sentence uttered by Gwyneth grated, Chiara couldn't help herself. The proverbial knife in her hands needed just a little twisting. And she was never one to deny herself simple, petty pleasures.

"And while some things certainly may appear as though they're what's best for you, from where I'm standing, your husband is certainly hot in pursuit of his daughter, which is far from what you consider ideal, isn't it?"

Gwyneth turned to her then, opening her mouth to spew whatever invective had surely been on her tongue, only to be unceremoniously interrupted.

"Here I thought some establishments had better security..." The haughty tones of Arabella broke the standoff, and Chiara had the surprising pleasure of seeing Gwyneth's already razor thin lips disappear entirely from her now ruddy face.

Before Gwyneth was able to spit out whatever she was preparing to throw at Arabella, she, in turn, turned to Chiara and leaned towards her under the guise of air kissing her cheeks, murmuring, "I think our girl may need to be rescued."

A chin tilt towards the end of the bar where Vi's spine was so straight, it was surely about to snap as Charles spoke from between clenched teeth without taking his eyes off his daughter.

"If you would excuse me—" Chiara's departure, however, was delayed by a burning hot hand that landed on her forearm with slightly more force than was necessary to stop her. Nails dug in, paying Chiara back just a little for her earlier insult.

"This is a family matter, Ms. Conti. Given your humble

upbringing, I'm not sure you understand, but if I were you, I'd not intervene. Genevieve needs to assume her position in the society, although with the company she keeps, I'm not certain that is even possible. You've latched on to her before. Perhaps it's time to let her family take care of her?"

Chiara gave Gwyneth a pointed stare. "I've seen strangers treat her better than her family ever did, Mrs. Courtenay. Now, before I reconsider and give into the temptation to create a few potentially scandalous headlines for Page Seven, kindly unhand me." Leaning closer, Chiara lowered her voice. "You may not know this, but you can take a girl off the Italian streets, but you can't *quite* get the streets out of this particular girl."

She savored seeing fear in Gwyneth's eyes before she snatched her hand away. Chiara turned on her heel as Arabella chuckled, and Gwyneth slinked off into the crowd.

Given the fact that everyone seemed to know her and wanted to talk to her—from wishing Chiaroscuro well, to expressing the conviction that they'd always known it was her behind the meteoric rise of the brand—Chiara made her way through the throng of people fairly quickly. Several tried to coax her into divulging details or impress upon her their urgent need for a bespoke wedding gown, but Chiara was not able to really see them or register their words or comprehend what they were asking of her. Vi was still cornered by her father, so nothing else mattered.

Finally, nodding and smiling vaguely at a man she numbly thought was with a Poise competitor, she reached the bar. Once there, the sound of the ballroom seemed to recede, allowing her to overhear the last of the words being thrown in Vi's face by that gruff voice, wiping the last traces of blood from those features.

"...never could do anything right. Just like your mother—"

"Enough!"

Her own voice felt foreign to her. Both the word itself and

the low intonation, the command in it like a whip lashing at Charles and steadying Vi.

A memory intruded, breaking the reddening at the corners of her vision. A Parisian rooftop and Vi whispering so earnestly, *"Hold on to me. I'm here."*

Her own words, uttered from Vi's threshold just last night, rang in her ears. *Debts incurred. Debts paid.* It was Chiara's turn to prop up Vi, as the world whirled around them with cruelty and fury.

Before either Charles or Vi could say anything, Chiara took Vi's hand and, without another glance, walked away. She didn't care how rude or inappropriate her behavior was. Nothing mattered, except the absolutely empty look in those usually sparkling eyes.

The ride to Vi's apartment was silent, and only the hand, still cold and motionless in hers, kept Chiara anchored to the present, just as it had when they'd entered the cursed ballroom.

As THE KEYS trembled in Vi's fingers, missing the lock several times, Chiara took charge. The instinct that always seemed to overwhelm her where Vi was concerned, to protect, to care, to shield, had her gently take them from the listless hand.

As the metal latch turned several times, she pushed the door open, and the scent of verbena wrapped itself around her, bringing solace. The apartment filled her senses, and Vi sighed quietly next to her, leaning heavily on the wall, seemingly unable to move.

"C'mon, one foot in front of the other..." Chiara took both of Vi's hands in her own, carefully pulling her along as one does a skittish animal.

Despite having been here just once the night before, the

apartment felt familiar and comfortable. Chiara found the bedroom without really trying, another door, this one painted bright yellow, leading her to a queen-sized bed, pristinely made with the comforter pulled over it tightly. Even as she guided Vi in, slowly lowering her onto the mattress, Chiara peripherally imagined bouncing a coin off it and wondered who had taught Vi such precision, until her mind screeched to a halt in the understanding that this must have been Vi's life. Either the vestiges of the myriad of boarding schools, or her father...

She knelt in front of Vi, who sat on the very edge of the bed, unmoving, as if afraid to mess it up, and Chiara's heart squeezed as she reached for the laces on the polished Oxfords. One foot, then the other, just as she'd instructed earlier, and Vi still sat like a doll, following her movements with those haunted eyes, silent.

"Vi..." She trailed off, completely unsure about what she could say. Her mother had been disappointed in her. Lived that way and had died that way, leaving Chiara with enormous guilt and a lifetime of therapy bills.

Still, Chiara had been loved. No matter how much pain was in those eyes, they'd never looked at her daughter with anger. Sadness, yes, but never this much hatred. Chiara's mother bore her disappointment like a weight that ultimately sunk her, like the waters of Lake Como, but she had never been cruel. This specific, very targeted viciousness that rendered one paralyzed in humiliation and despair.

So while Chiara understood what had happened between Vi and her parents for what it was, she could not comprehend the scars it left. And so she didn't know what to say, how to alleviate whatever was eating at Vi and had left her nearly catatonic.

"Vi... I'm so sorry." Useless words were falling from her mouth, even as her hands rose to caress the still-so-pale face, thumbs tracing the gaunt cheeks in an attempt to bring some color to them, even as her own desperation at seeing Vi like this clawed at her.

She thought perhaps she should be stronger. More indifferent, apathetic even. After all, this woman had betrayed her before. But Chiara had no such strength and no such skill as to turn away and leave.

They watched each other, amber on ash, and then a tear trembled on Vi's lashes as she finally blinked and it was set free, rolling slowly down the tender cheek. Before it had a chance to reach Chiara's fingers, she rose up and kissed it away, her lips lingering on the cold skin.

The gesture set something off in Vi, because suddenly more tears sprang from eyes that no longer looked empty, but instead so full of longing, it took Chiara's breath away.

"Stay with me." Barely a whisper among the wretched sobs. Still, Chiara understood and Vi seemed to be completely unaware she'd even uttered the words as she rolled into a ball on the edge of the bed and buried her face in a pillow, weeping in earnest now.

Goddess... How could she refuse? How could she leave her in such despair? Chiara took off her shoes and climbed in bed from the opposite side, this once becoming the big spoon. She held the shuddering body against her chest, absorbing all the grief and all the pain, murmuring nonsensical words of consolation as the ragged sobs tapered off into whimpers that slowly subsided as Vi's breathing leveled.

Chiara stayed the night, her eyes unfocused, staring at the dark ceiling reflecting the shadows from the busy Greenwich Village street below, and wondered why she had never quite shaken off this emotion that lived in her chest. Why, despite all her attempts to stop, she had always been in love with Vi Courtenay, although she'd only truly trusted her for a single night and paid dearly for it.

She should probably be surprised by the revelation. Sigh or cry or laugh. Do something to mark this momentous occasion.

But Chiara was tired. And spent. Vi's breakdown somehow seeping under her skin and taking everything out of her, stripping everything bare and leaving only the realization that, despite the years and the pain, Chiara loved Vi.

And what would it mean to allow herself to quit those, at best, feeble attempts to exorcize herself from this feeling, and simply let it be? As she had once before on that rooftop.

Could you walk into the same river twice? And if you did, would the waters be the same? Would they carry you to the same end?

THE NEXT MORNING, she chose to walk towards the townhouse on Mercer Street.

Her thoughts were buzzing inside her head, angry bees that had been disturbed in their routine, and so she'd asked the cab driver to drop her off several blocks away, to try to sort through everything that was on her mind and through the emotions rolling in her chest.

As she approached, she noticed a figure sitting on the stoop. Chiara realized that whoever said you should always expect more trouble so as to never be caught unawares, had been right. And she herself had been quite mistaken. Because this particular trouble, she had not expected.

Frankie Lilienfeld unfolded her long, leather-clad frame from the steps and leaned in, her face inches away from Chiara's, smoke still playing on those smirking lips as she threw away an unfinished cigarette. Her voice, the lightly accented roughness of it, was harsher than Chiara remembered it when Frankie finally spoke.

"Hello, wife."

21

IN A FARAWAY LAND OF UNWANTED CONVERSATIONS

Chiara Conti was exhausted. The previous night had left her emotionally battered, with Vi asleep in her arms, tears still drying on those haunted cheeks and Chiara's heart responding with a painful contraction to each twitch and soft whimper Vi let out.

She'd looked forward to the morning; to an hour alone in her workshop, an hour to draw, to drink her cappuccino, to collect her thoughts, and to tuck away the scattered emotions that kept pulling her in all directions.

She was looking forward to making peace with her newly acquired knowledge that she was in love with Vi, and this was now something she would need to address, at least for herself.

Ideally, she would have liked to get all those things done before Vi and her team descended on Chiaroscuro for the long day of shooting and interviews.

Except the visitor at her front door pretty much ensured that, not only did Chiara not have anything to look forward to where the morning was concerned, she also had to rapidly raise all her defenses. The ones she'd mostly forgotten how to erect after years of not having to deal with her ex-wife.

As it was, she sidestepped Frankie and jiggled her keys as she stood in front of the townhouse. She had never regretted having an apartment in the same building as her studio and shop, the flat nestled under the roof, with a beautiful view and a convenient lack of a commute. But with Frankie here, Chiara resented that convenience just a little. Because it made her vulnerable to exactly these kinds of visits.

She couldn't even take any consolation in looking good. She knew she had no such armor to hide behind. In yesterday's finery—now severely tainted by a long night of twisting, turning, staring at the ceiling and holding Vi—she looked like she was making the infamous walk of shame. And perhaps she'd flaunt that in Frankie's smug face, if only it were true. As it was, Chiara was clutching her shawl around herself in a desperate attempt to cover up the marks Vi had left two nights ago.

Perhaps reading her thoughts, the smirk on her ex-wife's mouth grew lewder.

"Long night?"

"You came all this way from wherever you've been the past however many years to inquire about my night? What a waste of time, if you ask me."

To her surprise, her words—which were rather tame by anyone's standard, but certainly by her own, considering they had said so many, much more hurtful things to each other over the years—wiped the grin off Frankie's face.

"Apologies."

Chiara almost gasped, but stopped herself at the last second, her sense of self-preservation kicking in.

"That easy? Are you okay, Frankie? No fever? And you should probably quit whatever charade this is. I am really not ready for it to snow in September."

Frankie gave her a long look, one Chiara couldn't decipher, then lowered her eyes.

"I'm sincere, babe."

She pulled a pack of Marlboros from her leather jacket and Chiara watched with something akin to a déjà vu as the oh-so-familiar fingers performed the ubiquitous dance of tearing the filter off and flicking the Zippo to life.

As she searched for something to say, anything to end this dreadful silence that could only stretch between two people who were nothing to each other and no longer had anything to talk about, the door behind her was flung open, and Chiara could swear Aoife actually growled.

"What is it with all these bad pennies just effin' turning up around here these days? Are you lost then, Lilienfeld?"

Despite the reference that lumped Vi and Frankie into the same category, that was where the similarities ended. There was no warmth in Aoife's features, no begrudging welcome like the one she had bestowed on Vi after the initial ribbing. Here, it was open hostility, and Chiara winced, her frayed emotions abraded further as Frankie took a long drag and blew out the acrid smoke, enveloping Chiara whole.

"Wasn't aware I needed your permission to be on this side-walk, Sully. This being the land of the free, or whatever bullshit they claim…"

Chiara tuned out the rest of the sermon. Now this was the Frankie she knew. This was the Frankie who had hounded her in Paris for an entire year after she'd filed for the divorce. This was the Frankie that was painfully familiar. The one with the moralizing speeches and logical fallacies, sprinkled with a wounded expression that was fooling no one, least of all Chiara.

Still, one thing was certain: the sidewalk was no place for this argument. Someone was bound to recognize them, and Frankie and Aoife's bickering—something about rotten fish—was already turning heads.

Chiara rubbed the bridge of her nose, yesterday's contact lenses irritating her eyes. She was beginning to regret ever getting up from Vi's bed. Surely, an awkward conversation with her would not have been this painful.

As the voices around her rose in volume and in insults, Chiara had enough.

"Children, how about we take this inside?"

"How about Frankie leaves? She's not welcome here!" Aoife shot back immediately, and Frankie smiled victoriously.

"I love you too, Sully."

Chiara rolled her eyes at the two of them as she held the door open. Once inside, she laid a calming hand on Aoife's arm, squeezing gently.

"I'll handle this. You should get the showroom ready. The crew will be here in about an hour, and once they arrive, it'll be nonstop *go, go, go* for the day. Help me out here, Sully."

Her eyes must have been particularly pleading, because for once, Aoife didn't argue and simply shook her head and disappeared into the beautiful fall tones of the silks and satins strewn all over the showroom.

"Well, now—" As they walked towards the staircase, whatever Frankie had been about to say was interrupted by a stern voice that made even Chiara wince.

"Never would I have thought, Franziska Marie Lilienfeld. You had better be dying or something equally irrevocable to show your face after everything you pulled in Paris. What the hell are you doing here?"

Renate's bark was merciless. Unlike with Aoife though, Frankie just laughed at her sister.

"Missed you too, sis. And how are you?"

Before Renate could blow a gasket and do anything drastic, such as throw something heavy and sharp at Frankie, Chiara started to take the steps to the studio two at a time and motioned for her ex-wife to follow her.

"Renate, please, I will handle this. Go see if Aoife needs any help—"

"I will do no such thing. I will be right here in case you need assistance or if *she* gets up to no good."

Chiara closed her eyes, counted to ten and kept walking up towards the studio. She didn't want to let Frankie into her apartment, so her work area with its large, open floor plan would have to do. Plenty of space there to avoid whatever it was her ex-wife was trying to achieve with this early morning, five-years-too-late visit.

"I love what you've done with the place, Chiara. Though I have to say that this is like running a gauntlet before reaching Sleeping Beauty. All those dragons downstairs..." Frankie laughed again, the low, raspy tones of the familiar sound doing nothing to calm Chiara's thundering heart.

A second later, Frankie yelped and clutched at her ankle as Binoche stubbornly swiped at her. The sound of the angry cat, the curses of Frankie trying to protect herself, along with the shouts emanating from downstairs as Renate and Aoife sparred over something in the showroom, started to overwhelm Chiara.

Yesterday's clothes chafed, seeming too small and suddenly uncomfortable. The level of the sounds coming at her from everywhere made her want to put her hands over her ears. But she couldn't do that, no matter how much she wanted to. Instead, she scooped up Binoche and glared at Frankie.

"I'm exhausted, I didn't get any sleep last night, and I have a very long day ahead of me. So before I sic the cat on you again, why are you here, Frankie?"

Binoche squirmed in her hold, but she figured it was premature to let her go just yet. Not that she pitied Frankie's ankles, which, by the looks of them, had taken considerable abuse from the cat's attack. But another round of screeching and yelping would simply be too much, regardless of the sadistic pleasure she might deride from allowing the protective feline to have one more go.

Frankie straightened and looked Chiara dead in the eye, hands finding her trousers' pockets.

"I'm here for *you*."

Well, maybe she should give Binoche one more shot after all. Especially when Frankie was talking nonsense like this.

"Here for me?" She repeated, trying to process her ex-wife's point even as the meaning of the sentence was all too clear to her tired mind.

"I want you back, and I am prepared to do whatever it takes." Mindful of the cat, Frankie approached Chiara carefully, laying a hand on her cheek. A sudden movement in the doorway interrupted Binoche's loud meow.

"You forgot your phone at my place, Chiara. And I'm sorry I was still too out of it to see you on your way this morn..."

Vi trailed off, seeing Frankie standing much too close, her hand still on Chiara's face, and the devastation in those beautiful features, still pale and bearing the signs of yesterday's disastrous encounter, was painful to observe.

Frankie gave Vi a long once-over and raised an insouciant eyebrow at Chiara, who wanted to bang her head against the wall. Frustration, exhaustion, and guilt over Vi seeing her with Frankie were bubbling inside her.

On cue, sensing Chiara's mood, Binoche made a valiant leap onto the floor, and with one last swipe at Frankie, stalked towards Vi, who scooped her up gently, and in whose arms the cat started to purr loudly.

The same cat who had completely ignored Vi when she'd been there before, the one who hated absolutely everyone, was taking sides? *Well, wasn't this swell?*

"Courtenay." Frankie's tone was measured, but Chiara could hear the territorial inflection in it.

"Frankie." Vi's own voice landed somewhere between Chiara's exhaustion and pure rawness. Somewhere very close to pain.

"I see you've done very well for yourself..." Frankie had been so restrained, so careful with how she spoke to Renate, and even to Aoife, despite the anger that Chiara sensed boiling under that sheen of carelessness. But now Chiara knew the veneer was cracking and that Frankie's restraint had reached its tether's end.

She could tell what was coming next, and she was all too aware that Frankie would not care about the collateral damage she was making of Vi as she aimed her guns at her. "Photographer extraordinaire about town. Major publications. Too bad not a lot of people know you started your career in the yellow, paparazzi-fueled rags."

Frankie stared at Vi with raised eyebrows. Yes, she still gave no thought or quarter to any bystanders when she was vengeful. Vi scratched Binoche one last time before carefully setting her behind her and standing back up, just a touch taller, shoulders tense and hands in her pockets. Her thoughts racing, Chiara desperately tried to say something, even as Frankie continued.

"You had this sick obsession with my wife five years ago, and I see you finally took your shot—"

"Frankie!" Chiara's own voice sounded hoarse, her throat scraped raw.

God, was it only eight am? Would this day ever end?

"I'm sorry, Chiara." It was a very close call on what offended Chiara more, the insults to Vi or the meekness of Frankie's insincere apology given with down-turned eyes and hard-set mouth.

"Vi... Thank you for the..." She tried to remember what she was thanking Vi for. She hadn't had her meds yet, and everything was so jumbled, she wanted to curl up and sleep for a week.

When Vi lifted her hand with the phone in response, Chiara just nodded. "We still have some time before the shoot starts downstairs, and Renate and Aoife are there. Would you wait for me while I speak with Frankie, and then we can proceed?"

In her peripheral vision, she could see Frankie crow and throw Vi a triumphant look. Chiara approached Vi and reached to take the phone from her hands that were still so cold, infusing her own gaze with as much encouragement as she could.

She didn't know if it worked, because Vi turned on her heel and left the studio, the space vacated by her suddenly chilly and empty. For the hundredth time this past week, Chiara thought herself such a fool for all these emotions and all this need she could no longer not acknowledge.

As she turned, the concern and tenderness in Frankie's eyes seemed honest for once, and she felt foolish again. Years had gone by, and she still held on to all the guilt where Frankie was concerned, squeezing her heart.

"Frankie—"

"Please don't say anything. I really am sorry." With her booted foot scraping the floor, like a little girl who'd been caught stealing cookies, Frankie resembled the woman Chiara had fallen for all those years ago so much. Mischievous and funny. Tender and loving. Time had done a number on all of them. They'd done a number on themselves.

"This isn't how I wanted to bring any of this to you. Myself, my reason for being here, my anger, any of this. I can't even say I didn't expect all the dragons. I figured this would be how I'd be received by them. Even by the damn cat. You always inspire so much loyalty from those who love you, after all..." Frankie's eyes widened after that Freudian slip and Chiara let out a tired chuckle.

"And you always got in your own way, Frankie. Deeds, words."

Frankie had the decency to look at her with guilt written all over her face for a second before smiling from under her bangs.

"You know what I'm saying, Sleeping Beauty."

Chiara waved at her dismissively.

"Too many fairytale metaphors per square foot in this house."

"Are you all still calling Courtenay 'Cinderella'? She looks like she landed on her feet, poor little lamb."

"Would you stop that, Frankie? Honestly, why are you here? I can't imagine it's what you claimed earlier. So, what is it? Business not going well? Creditors on your tail? What?"

It was Frankie's turn to chuckle.

"So cynical, my love. None of that. Lilien Haus was taken by the bank three days ago. It will hit the press next week. I don't have anything anymore. No home, no atelier, no fashion house."

Chiara started as the words reached her, and Frankie laid a hand on her shoulder, thumb moving up and down her skin that was exposed by the flimsy sleeve, silky smooth, so unlike Vi's calloused hands. Chiara shook her off, more upset with herself for the immediate comparison than with Frankie for daring to touch her.

"So, what now?"

Frankie shrugged, and Chiara felt the gesture in her bones. Her ex-wife's nonchalance really hadn't been for show. She'd meant it. Years of her life, her entire life in fact, all up in smoke, and yet here she was, smiling serenely.

"Now I'm free. Of the ego, of the mistakes of the past, of those marble floors that continued to echo with your steps. That entire building still held the scent of you, Chiara. Years passed, and despite it being mine, every brick and tile infused with you. You brought so much more to that place than your talent."

The backs of Chiara's eyes stung with unshed tears. Why

did she feel like crying? She had made her peace with never being acknowledged, never once being given her due... Why did it hurt her so much now, to have Frankie speak these words she'd have killed to hear years ago?

She hadn't been her wife for four years. She hadn't been *anyone's* wife since Frankie had cheated on her. So why did it suddenly matter that she was acknowledging what Chiara had known all along?

Lilien Haus was Chiara Conti, and without her, it lay in ruins.

It should have soothed Chiara's ego. It should have given her that vindication she had been craving for so long. Instead, it rang hollow. It rang cheap. It rang way too late to give her any kind of satisfaction.

So was she crying because it was all so useless? Because they'd broken each other twice over and still ended up here?

For the hundredth time in the last hour, Chiara thought about how tired she was. And how much she wanted to not be here, in this situation, with these emotions running rampant in her chest, twisting that little sliver of glass that had been lodged there.

"Frankie..."

"No, don't say anything. I understand you are otherwise occupied and the special edition of Poise is a huge deal, babe. The first time I saw you was on the cover of that magazine all those years ago, after all. I lost my copy. I regret that so much. There is so much I regret, period. But you better believe it, I will treasure this one. And you also better believe that I won't make the same mistakes I made back in Paris."

With a soft kiss to her cheek, Frankie was gone, and Chiara's tears spilled then, washing the trace of those lips off her skin.

22

IN A FARAWAY LAND OF FINGERTIPS AND ATONEMENT

Chiara Conti thought that when it rained, it just kept pouring. And then pouring some more. The nagging headache at her temples slithered down to the nape of her neck, where it settled for the day, making itself very comfortable all the while making *Chiara* want to just keep on weeping.

She'd cried when she woke up beside Vi—at her own inability to stop loving this woman whom she did not trust. Then she cried when Frankie waltzed right back into her life as if she'd never really left, and once again tried to establish the rules by which the entire game was to be played. Talk about eerily familiar events.

And now, as the camera flashed in front of her eyes over and over again, Chiara simply wanted to cry in pain, the headache leaving her listless and numb, while her bones felt so fragile that a feathered touch might shatter them.

The smile she gave Morag as she applied yet another layer of concealer under her throbbing eyes must have looked weak at best, because the older woman just shook her head and reached for something else to goop on top of the heaps of makeup already failing to hide her rough day.

The interviewer was back as well, and both she and Renate were running through a series of questions, venturing from the profound and serious to the shallow and funny, and Chiara was grateful that she didn't have to speak. To her, the words were all a mixture of incomprehensible sounds.

And through it all, Vi was watching her with a look Chiara knew very well. It was the concerned Vi Courtenay stare. The one Chiara was familiar with from all those years ago, when the younger, less tortured version of Vi would be touchingly worried about Chiara forgetting to eat, or about her working way too late, or whatever else Chiara had found herself getting lost in.

"Perhaps we should take a break?" Vi's voice broke Chiara's reverie with the force of a hammer. She must have winced visibly, because a moment later, all eyes were on her, and Vi was suddenly so much closer, her gentle hands on Chiara's shoulders, propping her up.

"Yeah, okay, I think we are finished for the day, people. Morag, we will start early tomorrow. I will text you the details. Chiara needs rest."

The déjà vu—and why exactly was she having so many of them—was so strong, it made Chiara snort, which in turn made Vi's eyes grow even more concerned as she simply pulled on Chiara's arms and gently guided her up the stairs and all the way to her small apartment under the roof.

Perhaps under different circumstances, on a different day, Chiara would have been ashamed of the disarray, consisting of all her post-its and notebooks strewn across every available surface in her space. But as the saying went, today was not that day—and not those circumstances.

And what did it matter? Vi had been accepted into her sanctum sanctorum, where Chiara lived amongst constant alarms and reminders. One more glimpse inside wasn't going to change Vi's opinion of her.

Chiara smiled at her own thoughts chasing each other, even as Vi carefully deposited her on the cluttered sofa among several wedding magazines and swatches of paint that, months later, Chiara still hadn't decided on, and hence her kitchen remained unpainted. She'd get to them. She didn't cook all that much these days.

Before she could venture down that road of asking herself why and make her temples explode with more pain at straining to think, Vi was back with a fistful of pills and a warm cup of something that turned out to be chamomile tea.

There was chamomile tea in her cabinets? Another thought for another day. Chiara didn't bother voicing it as she gently put the pills on her tongue one by one, sipping on the water Vi had seemed to produce out of nowhere and placed in her hand, cursing softly after each tablet made sure to get stuck in her throat. Chewing them was out of the question. Even the thought of them powdering under her teeth made her shudder, and she downed the rest of the bottle in one big chug before reaching for the tea mug.

"Thank you."

Vi rolled her eyes, and Chiara couldn't suppress a frown.

"It's the polite thing to say, Vi. You are being nice to me. I'm appropriately grateful."

"You were very nice to me yesterday, when you made sure I got home in one piece and slept through the night." Vi gingerly sat down on the coffee table in front of her. The desire to rub her pained temples was strong, but she willed herself to finish whatever this conversation was going to lead them to.

"So this is a quid pro quo?"

Vi rolled her eyes again.

"Didn't your mother teach you that if you do that too often, they'll get stuck up there forever?"

As soon as she'd uttered the words, Chiara's hand flew to her mouth, mortified by her lack of sensitivity and tact. "God, Vi, I'm so—"

Vi reached out, and shaking her head, tugged Chiara's hand away from her face.

"No, neither my father nor my stepmother ever had to tell me that, because I've rarely allowed myself the gesture in their presence. That would have meant being grounded and losing whatever privileges I had left at the time. So I'm free to roll my eyes at you being silly. Now, tell me, how are you feeling?"

Chiara's frown turned into a pout at Vi not even allowing her to apologize when she was being thoughtless.

"You're so bossy."

She sounded petulant and didn't care that Vi was sitting there grinning at her lower lip sticking out. Chiara sighed and lifted a hand to the nape of her neck, kneading the taut muscles corded like ropes under her fingertips.

"I've been called worse, Chiara." There was a smile in the corners of Vi's mouth, but it didn't quite reach her eyes, and Chiara felt compelled to tug on this thread of the conversation, even if she knew it wasn't wise. Not after what she'd witnessed yesterday.

"Well, with a family like yours..."

The light in those wondrous eyes dimmed with such starkness and speed, Chiara gasped.

"Well, here's me putting my foot into it twice in one day." She tapped two fingers on her lip, thinking how to proceed. Except the truth was always more expedient. And she had fewer difficulties wielding it than any lies she ever could.

"Last night was a revelation, Vi. In more ways than one, and not just that you mumble rather endearingly in your sleep."

Predictably, that made Vi's smile appear again, and Chiara soldiered on, regretting now that she'd even waded into these accursed waters of Vi's familial trauma.

"They were awful to you. Well, he was, since I don't imagine you exist for her on this planet. I'm so sorry."

Vi's shoulders sagged before she drew a long breath and bit her lip. She looked like she was weighing the words, or even the decision of saying them at all. Chiara sat silently, counting in her head, feeling her heartbeat match the ticking of the grand-father clock in the corner.

Finally, after another measured breath that seemed to come from a place deeper than Vi's chest, she spoke haltingly.

"I've cut them off." The teeth bit harder into that plump lower lip, and Chiara felt her own throb in sympathy. "After Paris." A gulp and another sigh. "I've not seen them since. And I don't interact with them at all. I've been very careful to avoid them at all costs, no matter how…" She trailed off, and Chiara had a distinct notion that the Courtenays had been making life unbearable for Vi, in spite of being away from her.

"So it was just a shock to see him." The change to the singular pronoun wasn't lost on Chiara. No, she herself didn't know her father, but she understood love for one's parent. Knew how deep it went. How unfair it was in most cases.

Something in Vi's words pulled at her, tempting her to pry, to ask more.

After Paris… After what?

But with the continued overwhelming pain behind her eyes and at the base of her skull, everything felt murky. And one look at Vi told Chiara that, although she may be the one strug-gling with a migraine, she wasn't the only one in pain.

And so she chose not to prod any further. Vi would either tell her more, or she wouldn't.

As it was, Chiara had seen and heard enough to understand a few things. Others she did not, as the elusive thread of premo-nition once again simultaneously seemed close and far.

She chose to change the subject.

"By the way, in answer to your earlier question, I feel fine."

Vi looked up, a speculative eyebrow in such contrast with the relaxing shoulders, Chiara wanted to laugh. She almost did.

"I have seen dead people who looked finer, Chiara."

"My, no wonder all these Manhattan women are dying for you to get into their knickers, Vi, I mean the sweet talking alone..." Chiara waved her hand dismissively, but Vi simply caught it between hers and intertwined their fingers, stilling the motion entirely.

"This is the second time you've brought up my romantic exploits, and I sense perhaps you have some hangups about me not living like a nun for the past five years—"

Chiara swallowed hard.

"I don't care how many women you've slept with, Vi—"

"Good, because it's no one's business but my own and that of the women everyone keeps throwing in my face." The steady rhythm of Vi's voice was doing something to Chiara's stomach. Surely it must be anger. She was making Chiara really mad. By flaunting it all in Chiara's face... Yes, anger. It was only anger she was feeling. Either that or the pills were making her nauseous. And no, her vision was definitely not turning green at the edges. She had no right, just because she had suddenly realized that she had feelings for Vi.

"Surely, you've lived as you please." Another reasonable argument from Vi, one to which Chiara would sooner drop dead than reveal she had not taken anyone else to her bed—or her wall, or her desk or whatever other surface may have been available—since Vi.

No, better dead than to confess to something like that to the one woman who'd had her last, and who, in all honesty, had her in the one and truest form that mattered. Five years ago and now.

"It's none of your business how I've lived, Vi." Her voice

could really rival the muscles in her neck, taut and full of knots.

"Well then, we are in agreement."

Again that reasonable, calm tone. Chiara was getting tired of being lectured. Yes, she knew she was being petulant, but she didn't care how it looked.

She tugged at her hand, still held loosely by those long, once again warm fingers, ready to get up and seek refuge in her bedroom. Except Vi didn't let her go. Instead, she tightened the hold, making Chiara's eyes fly up to meet hers.

"What we seem to be in disagreement about, however, is our current arrangement."

Well now. Vi had her full attention. Or whatever was left of it in her current state.

"You may think that me having had a series of consensual relationships with a number of women might suggest I'd be satisfied with being one of many for you. But that is not the case, Chiara. If you want to jerk my chain and exact revenge on me for my sins from five years ago, so be it." Vi's thumb rubbed Chiara's skin and the dissonance between the gesture and the words was somewhat disconcerting. "I hurt you and I betrayed you, no matter what actually happened. I will accept the punishment, do your worst... But I won't be part of some game between you and Frankie."

The quiet, almost gentle cadence of Vi's voice, submitting herself as a lamb to Chiara's knife and slaughter, snapped her out of her childish petulance. This was far more than Vi setting boundaries when it came to Frankie.

This time, when Chiara tugged on her hand, Vi let go. Her eyes, downcast and dull, showed the loss clearly, only to widen, then close as Chiara gently splayed her fingers on Vi's cheek, thumb caressing the cutting cheekbone.

"No games, darling. We will deal with it. And with the fact

that you seem to know the entire New York queerdom. Was sticking to only one borough too much to ask for?"

She deliberately lowered her tone to teasing, turning everything into a harmless joke, allowing the old endearment to slip from her tongue, letting Vi know that she wasn't serious, and Vi brought Chiara's hand to her mouth, biting gently on the fingertips.

It felt good, even as her head became fuzzier under the effect of the pills finally dulling the edges of pain. She sighed. "Not right now, because I think I'm turning into a pumpkin here..."

"I thought I was Cinderella?" Vi's grin was infectious.

"Shhh, just be glad I'm in the right fairytale, the way I'm feeling... Anyway, if there is one thing I can assure you of, it's that. And no Frankie." Chiara smiled as Vi blinked rapidly. She could feel the lashes flutter on her thumb. A moment later, she leaned over and laid a kiss on Vi's forehead before moving lower and kissing first one eyelid, then the other, followed by the bridge of the nose and the cheekbones beneath her fingertips. Vi exhaled under the touch, and Chiara simply laid her lips on hers. For a moment, they were suspended, skin on skin, breathing each other's air.

"I allowed you to fuck me because I wanted to, Vi." The profanity jarred, even as it passed her lips, hoarse and ragged, but she was not yet prepared to call it anything else. 'Making love' would mean acknowledging out loud what she was not yet ready to even think about for any amount of time.

And so she didn't go where her heart was telling her to, nor did she bother moving even an inch from Vi's mouth, her words scattering on those full lips. "Furthermore, I did not fuck you because I wanted to prove something. Debts aside, I did that because I wanted to. I want you. I don't seem to know how not to. And while I'm working through the 'why', can you believe me when I say there are no games between us? That there is nobody else here but you and me?"

Vi's eyelids trembled, and Chiara saw a single tear slip and roll down her cheek. This time, she did not catch it, allowing it to fall to the floor, then simply moved her lips, caressing Vi's, not deepening the kiss, not demanding, simply giving, comforting as much as she could with the pain still splitting her skull.

Just before Vi could pull away, a frail, tenuous thought Chiara had been chasing and missing suddenly was within her reach. She slid her hand under Vi's chin, lifting her face, the midday sun playing on the planes of those cutting features, focusing Chiara on the torment that still lived within Vi, among that light, all those lingering shadows.

"Since I don't play games and haven't, in fact, since those months in Paris—which is a separate conversation—I will say only this, Vi. Atonement is overrated. So is martyrdom. So there is no revenge of any kind."

She felt more than saw Vi's lips tremble at her words and pressed harder, her kiss a little violent in its intent to impress the true meaning of those words on this ravaged person in front of her, who was ready to endure abuse to pay for what she'd done all those years ago.

"I either forgive you. Or I do not. And we either move forward together, or we move on separately. It's as simple as that, Vi." She said it matter-of-factly, words spilling out of her, and Chiara desperately wanted Vi to believe them, even as she tried her damnedest to make them be true. To speak them into reality and pray her heart had that forgiveness in it, as much as it had the love.

23

IN A FARAWAY LAND OF TUXEDOS AND REALIZATIONS

C hiara Conti went through the rest of September in a fever dream of photography, interviews and Vi. Which meant sex. Or at least it should have meant that.

But somehow, just as five years earlier, Vi managed to sneak under all of Chiara's already crumbling defenses, and something that they had agreed to be a 'no strings, all fun' entanglement, ended up becoming something much... Chiara stopped in front of the bathroom mirror as she slid on an earring and tried to think of an appropriate word.

Softer? More careful? Both of those worked, even if the sex was such that, in actuality, neither description could be ascribed to it.

She felt that every time they actually had a moment to spare for bedroom activities, they fell on each other like starving creatures, leaving bruises and greedy bites. Not that they *had* a moment. In fact, they almost never did, the last few weeks proving taxing and anxiety-inducing.

And yet Vi held the ship steady, professionally steering the photoshoots and the entirety of the project towards a successful climax. And amidst all of that, she also managed to do the same for Chiara.

Many times, actually. As Chiara slid on the second earring, her fingers gingerly touched the bags under her eyes that not even her considerable makeup skills could cover.

They'd gotten a bit eager last night. An adventure that actually ended in the early morning hours, with Vi rushing home to shower and get some last-minute details ready for tonight, and Chiara basking in the glory of the sunny New York morning with an immense mug of cappuccino and a stack of designs she thought she would choke on if she didn't finish.

Her creativity had taken a turn once again, from parched and barren to overflowing, and she'd been hunched over her work station for most of the day, coffee, food and the entire world forgotten.

She chose to not dwell on the fact that this was happening again. It had taken Vi one comment and one lost shoe five years ago to inspire her and perhaps change her professional destiny, and here she was again, providing inspiration in Chiara's hour of artistic need.

It was only when she'd automatically reached for the mug, taking a sip and grimacing at how cold and unpalatable it had become, that she realized it was almost 5 p.m. and it was time to get ready. Arabella and Benedict had planned a lavish reception in her honor to celebrate the upcoming release of the first ever Poise Wedding Issue, dedicated in its entirety to Chiara Conti and Chiaroscuro.

Vi Courtenay's name was emblazoned on the cover along with Chiara's, and for some reason it gave her a small thrill, seeing those letters arranged so close together. It seemed like a good omen for things to come...

Chiara smiled at her own pun and spritzed perfume on her pulse points. And here was another good harbinger, she hoped, as the scent of verbena reached her senses. She had not used this particular bespoke perfume in years. And then, on a whim, a few weeks ago, she'd reached out to her good friend for a resupply. There was a warm kind of solace in the familiar scent.

"You look happy."

Aoife's mischievous tone from the doorway didn't startle her, and Chiara took this as another checkmark in the positive column. Despite being tired, she was not feeling wired and jumpy. Perhaps the orgasms from last night and this morning had something to do with this languidness.

"I feel happy, Sully."

The word just slid off her tongue, so strangely truthful, so easily spoken, unlike the struggle she'd experienced with it a few weeks ago, when Renate had asked, and she'd been forced to pretend, to dissemble, and eventually sidestep the question.

"It suits you." Aoife stepped into the bathroom and fiddled with Chiara's bodice, lips pursed as she adjusted some imaginary imperfection. Which could really mean only one thing. Chiara watched her friend in the mirror and braced herself.

"You know I felt guilty for everything that happened five years ago. And not just overall sorry about how the papers got the pictures and how you had to be humiliated in that awful way. No, it was more than that, because I considered myself personally responsible."

Well, of all the times to rehash the past, Chiara thought tonight was the absolutely wrong moment. They were celebrating the culmination of all these years of hard work, and yes, humiliation had been part of that.

Still, the tense set of her friend's shoulders told her that this was important, that this was something that weighed heavily on Aoife. Chiara turned around and smoothed her hands over Aoife's suit jacket lapels and tilted her head to the side, listening silently.

"I knew..." Aoife faltered, took a long deep breath, and started over. "You see, I always hated Frankie's—"

Chiara let out a bark of laughter, sincerely delighted at Aoife's halting attempts to state the obvious.

"No, my dear, I was not at all aware. Not for years, not even a little." She smiled to soothe the sarcasm she couldn't hide from her voice. "Considering you never actually shut up about how you thought Frankie wasn't respectful enough or loving enough. It's okay, Aoife. It really is in the past. No matter what Frankie wants everyone to believe."

"I was right about it, too." Aoife stuck out her bottom lip, petulant, and Chiara ruffled her hair. "Hey, hey, easy on the mohawk. Took me an hour to get it right."

"You look wonderful." Chiara gave her a one-armed hug and laid her cheek on Aoife's temple. "It's okay. It really is."

"Well, maybe it is now." When Aoife pulled back, her eyes were serious and sad. "But you still haven't allowed me to tell you how I feel. I believe I owe you that much, you know? Because I've let this guilt slowly eat at me for years. I was aware Vi was in love with you." Chiara shivered and Aoife barreled on. "I knew she was. I mean, she was so obvious. A total puppy. And I didn't discourage her. Especially when I saw that you were also quite taken with her—maybe not equally, but still— and how much good all that adoration did you."

Chiara swallowed around the lump in her throat and lowered her eyes, not yet ready to look at her friend, smoothing the lapels of the jacket, allowing the material to sooth her angst away.

"Frankie was becoming unbearable." Aoife's voice sounded a bit choked. "The constant insults about your condition. Taking you for granted. I suspected she was up to something, but I didn't know she was cheating. Not for certain. Still, I think her humiliating you in front of people about your medication was the last straw for me. I hated her then. And so I didn't do anything to stop Vi. Not really. And when she sold the pictures... Let's just say, I should've seen that coming. Her going for the jugular and making sure you and Frankie broke up unequivocally and irrevocably."

Chiara absorbed the blow to her solar plexus with all the strength three hours of sleep, two mugs of coffee and a pair of Manolos could grant her. Which was both a lot and nothing at all. She knew her eyes were red when she finally faced Aoife.

"I have no idea why she did it, Aoife. And I appreciate everything you've done for me since... well, since forever. But there's no guilt for you to take on here, my friend. Whatever her reasons were, whatever everyone's reasons were, I have moved on."

The lump in her throat grew larger, and she almost choked on the lie. No, she had not moved on, not entirely. Some ramifications of what had happened still rendered her numb. Except she wanted so much to believe herself.

She gave Aoife a forehead kiss before she stepped back, looking herself over in the mirror one last time. Red-rimmed and hollow, her eyes would need to be hidden under shades for a bit, because being seen like this at her own celebration simply wouldn't do.

Chiara again wished Aoife had better timing. She didn't want to think about the fact that Vi was still the girl who'd betrayed her, and that she was still the woman giving Vi a second chance despite not trusting her. Because if she allowed herself to look too closely, to remember too much, it would mean they were doomed. And Chiara desperately did not want them to be.

She grimaced and rubbed her temple, confused and perplexed at herself. Suddenly, she had a lot of sympathy for her poor mother, who'd never quite understood her. How was that practical, unpretentious woman to grasp her idiosyncrasies when Chiara herself couldn't?

She shook her head, then mustered a smile at Aoife. It was

time to change the subject before she ruined her mascara. Fortunately, her friend changed it for her.

"Anyway, I just wanted to say, unlike Renate, I really am on board with Vi being back. She puts that expression on your face. It becomes you."

"The happy look?"

"The freshly fucked within an inch of your life look." When Chiara gaped at her, horrified, Aoife laughed and smacked her arm. "Well, don't look this blissed out then, and I won't be standing here all envious of your orgasmic glow, woman!"

Chiara chose to ignore the teasing. That way lay trouble.

"Renate doesn't approve?" She had to confess, she hadn't spent any considerable amount of time with either Aoife or Renate in the past few weeks, with the magazine, sex, and creativity bursts occupying her days and her nights.

"Renate hasn't been around much, for what that's worth. But mostly she just sneers every time she gets a whiff of Cinderella. And Vi jokes and laughs it off in that offhanded, self-deprecating way of hers. You know, where you want to be mad at her, but mostly you're just charmed?"

"Oh, I'm very familiar." Chiara laughed again and tension loosened from her chest a bit.

"I bet you are." Aoife wagged her eyebrows suggestively, then tugged at Chiara's hand when a knock sounded on the door. "Oh, speak of the devil. And a handsome one."

Vi stood at the entrance to the apartment, clad in a tuxedo. Frilly lace covered her hands to the knuckle, but there was no sign of a blouse under the jacket. In fact, there was just a wide expanse of completely naked skin under all that gorgeous velvet carelessly being held together by only one button.

Chiara felt her mouth water as Vi took a few strides into the room in four-inch, red-soled heels. After one look at Chiara's face, Vi tilted her head.

"You've been crying?"

Trust Vi to notice things she wasn't supposed to.

"No!"

"Yes!"

Aoife and Chiara replied at the same time.

"The two of you need to get your stories straight." Vi raised an eyebrow, and now Chiara wanted to lap at her like a cat would at a bowl of milk.

Binoche chose that very moment to stroll in, slinking her small body against Vi's leg, who didn't even blink at the fur being generously transferred onto the expensive-looking tuxedo.

Chiara opened her mouth to say something, but Vi just smiled at the cat's antics.

"Nice to see you too, Brioche."

The cat meowed in obvious protest but didn't move away, rubbing more diligently at the velvet-clad legs.

And when Vi bent down and gave the already purring Binoche an ear scratch, that old yarn holding together Chiara's chest slowly tore. A stitch, then another, and the protective shell around her heart gave in some more.

If she'd had the notion she could still stop this, still control this after that night in Vi's bed, listening to her breathe and whimper in her sleep, then the simple gesture of kindness shown to a finicky feline—who immediately proceeded to bite Vi's fingers—did irreparable damage to that conviction. And now Chiara wasn't at all certain she'd ever be able to mend what Vi had been steadfastly rending without even realizing it.

To SAY that Arabella knew how to throw a party was an understatement. A larger-than-life version of the cover, with Chiara's naked shoulders, lace, and eyes that screamed 'enigma' even when displayed at this size, surprised her.

She thought she'd had an idea of the direction Vi was heading for with the photoshoot, yet here she was, charmed and disarmed by the woman holding her hand and her breath, waiting for Chiara's verdict.

"You've got such talent, darling."

The tangled lashes flickered once and the eyes that had held such anguish closed, a smile that looked both unpracticed and sincere playing on the full mouth.

"She's fantastic, isn't she?" Arabella's voice sounded simultaneously bombastic and intimate, as if she was loudly sharing a secret—one meant only for Chiara, even though she was pretty certain half the venue heard them, since several glasses rose in salute.

"That is why I plucked her out of the obscurity she was languishing in years ago, and made her a Poise house photographer, before unleashing her on the world at large. And now Poise and I have to stand in line like simple peasants for a day of her time."

Vi actually laughed, the sound even rustier than the smile.

"Right. The 'peasants' who booked me with a simple phone call a few nights before, for several weeks of a full-on emergency issue that involved me sleeping maybe two hours a night, working on the images?"

"A few nights before?" With her head clear, Chiara latched on to some of the more nuanced details of this conversation.

Arabella had the decency to look sheepish.

"Chiara, would you fault me for believing in myself? In your ambition? For simply realizing you would not be able to say no to me? So very few ever could, after all." Her eyes flitted to the middle of the ballroom, where Renate was holding court with some people who looked suspiciously like bankers and investors. Arabella's smile blossomed with such honesty and affection, Chiara blinked.

Well, she would deal with that later, as she would deal with her friend keeping personal secrets from her, because while she hadn't spent any considerable amount of time with her, she still couldn't remember the last time Renate had cussed Arabella out and cursed the day she'd darkened their doorstep. Something had clearly given, and it looked like that *something* was Renate.

With that non-apology apology, the matriarch sailed away in a cloud of perfume and small talk, moving on to some familiar faces, leaving Chiara and Vi alone again.

"I'm glad you like it." Vi's voice tickled her ear, and Chiara wanted to shiver, wanted to fan herself, because surely the temperature in the room had jumped by a hundred degrees.

"I do. Very much so." Chiara leaned into Vi, just slightly, feeling her body heat, and it was enough to make her knees go weak. "But you knew I would. I could feel your eyes on me with every click of the shutter. I felt beautiful. You always make me beautiful."

She hadn't realized she had changed the subject. She wasn't even sure where the words had come from, but it seemed imperative that she said them. Because even five years ago these words were the one truth that had kept her sane. That she was not imagining it. That, under the light of Vi's eyes, she felt beautiful, special, unique. She felt like she was Chiara Conti, the one and only, the conqueror of many a catwalk and pretty much all the fashion magazine covers. The one whose collections were universally acclaimed and whose talent was celebrated, even incognito. She felt... invincible.

"You are beautiful. And unique. To me. To everyone." Vi's smile was once again shy, and Chiara had an overwhelming need to touch it, to feel it and so she did, not caring who saw them. She traced her fingertips gently over the corner of Vi's mouth before allowing her thumb to linger on the lower lip. Just for a second, to satisfy this indulgence, to have Vi's breath on her own skin. And when she spoke, she simply told the truth.

"I don't care what I look like to anyone else."

The gray in Vi's eyes darkened to black, possessive and hot, and Chiara could sense her heart speed up. The things Vi could do to her, with just one look, the power this woman had over her... But this wasn't the time, nor the place, and now that the shoot and the editing work were done, they had all the time to do as they pleased. And Chiara wanted to *please*, very much.

Her breathing grew shallow, and she knew she was getting ahead of herself, realizing that if she let the reins go, she'd be a runaway train within seconds. Chiara inhaled deeply and willed herself to be professional.

"I think I'd like something cold now, darling. Because this is getting out of hand."

"Oh, but this is where you're wrong..." The shyness was gone, scorching heat taking its place. "It is very much in hand, or will be. Hand, fingers, mouth, whatever you want."

"Vi!" Scandalized, Chiara pushed at the velvet shoulder, and Vi lifted her hands in surrender. Her face didn't look repentant for one second though.

"All right, all right, I'll go get us some champagne, and then we can continue this conversation."

Even as Vi turned to leave, Chiara couldn't resist having the last word.

"There won't be a lot of talking once we get out of here." With Vi's eyes hot and hungry on her once again, Chiara turned and started in the direction of Renate.

The ballroom was well-ventilated, and she didn't feel warm, but as she made her way towards her former sister-in-law, a flash of something, both familiar and unwanted, especially here and now, instantly made her turn around, her cheeks flaming.

Frankie Lilienfeld could wear the hell out of a suit, yet this one didn't fit. Too tight, too revealing. The cocky grin did nothing for Chiara either, except maybe make her want to roll her eyes.

"I can't believe you were invited to my party." She tried to keep her voice down, but in the noisy room it was difficult and only spurred Frankie to lean too closely into her personal space. Tobacco and whiskey.

Great.

"My companion was." Frankie waved at some buxom blonde ambling towards them and wiggled her eyebrows.

"Seriously? After all that talk of wanting me back, you are here, flaunting a woman in my face at my own event?" Chiara wanted to laugh.

"Say the word, and I will never see her again. But you won't, because you just can't let me up off my knees, Chiara." Frankie's face contorted into ugliness, all veneer of sophistication gone. "I see you've let Courtenay get back up easily enough. Or should I say, allowed her to work her way towards atonement on those very knees?"

"God, you never quite knew when to stop and not lead the conversation straight into the gutter."

Frankie laughed and tipped the fedora at her as she disappeared into the crowd with the blonde on her arm. Chiara stood still for a second, collecting her thoughts, trying not to focus on the one thing Frankie said that hit her square in' the chest and slithered into her psyche.

Let me up from my knees...

Was this what she was doing to Vi? But before she could embark on that train of thought straight to hell, her peripheral vision caught another unwelcome sight.

In yet another silver gown, Gwyneth Courtenay appeared resplendent, even if Chiara hated seeing her. Charles, at her side in a burgundy tuxedo, looked dignified and distracted, giving the ballroom a thorough appraisal. Suddenly Chiara knew without a doubt who he was looking for. And she would not have it. She would *not* have these people who treated their daughter like dirt—worse than that—ruin this evening for Vi.

"Gwyneth, Charles." She made her way towards them, all pretense at protocol abandoned. After what she'd witnessed the other night, she despised these people. They would not have her respect. And if she hated them just a bit too much than strictly appropriate for people she'd met only once and barely exchanged more than a dozen words with, this was not the time or place to analyze why.

"Ms. Conti." Charles wrinkled his nose, his displeasure oozing from every pore.

"It's a surprise seeing you here." She spoke nothing but the truth. And what exactly was it that they wanted to go to such lengths to be here? She had seen the guest list the night before, and they certainly hadn't been on it. Granted, several people had large groups indicated alongside their names with no details as to who would join those parties. Cue the reason why Frankie was here.

"Vi invited us to attend this particular personal triumph of hers."

Charles' attempt at smoothness did not land and skittered on the edges of Chiara's memories with the effect of sandpaper, rustling a particularly recent one.

"I cut them off. After Paris."

So Charles was lying. And not even in a skillful or particularly inventive way. Maybe he didn't realize that Vi and Chiara were together—the 'together' part being something she'd have to ponder at a later date—or perhaps he simply didn't care what Chiara thought, knowing full well that she wouldn't risk a scandal at her own party.

The fact that Gwyneth was totally unperturbed and supremely bored with this conversation, paying very little mind to what was happening around her, said as much.

"Well, then I hope you en,
her tongue, and Charles's gaze,*tions* | 335
craning his neck to look past ti
still surrounded Renate. Chiara right off
found what he was looking for, *wh*-rowd,
who was slowly making her way thi that
their direction—she knew she had to he

There was no way she was allowir,
the Courtenays' torment again. One i
enough.

She pushed through the crowd ana
Charles to her. Fury and glory warred inside .
Vi first, smoothly turning her around, ensurii
not see her approaching father. Then she simpl)
words in her ear. Simple words that would guara.
leaving the party in a flash, her own personal n.
professional triumph be damned. Just five syllables that .
ensure Vi was spared another vicious encounter with h.
family. Five words that would guarantee a long night.

"I want you, right now."

24

FARAWAY LAND OF SACRIFICES AND DESIRE

hiara Conti had always been attuned to her lovers. More so to Vi than anyone else. And whether it was due to her own feelings, or because of all the small and big gestures that Vi had shown her—from that affection for the grumpy cat, to the magnificent Poise issue that contained all that love she clearly held for Chiara—when they had reached for each other, hands and lips and mouth, Chiara gentled her touch.

For the first time since she'd seen Vi on Chiaroscuro's doorstep, their coming together and coming undone was neither fraught with uncertainty or anguish, nor fast, or rough or hectic.

It started with passionate words, breathed into Vi's ear in the room full of people—people who neither cared, nor saw them. Not really. Since Chiara knew for a fact that nobody in the entire world looked at Vi the way she did. And when those wondrous eyes had widened before darkening, Chiara knew she had her.

Then, when they had gotten into the waiting limo and Vi's shoulders relaxed, away from the prying eyes and meddling people, away from the potential heartbreak, Chiara was sure she had done the right thing.

But Vi's words, cushioned by the intimacy of the darkness of the backseat with Manhattan flying by them, confirmed as much.

"He was there, wasn't he? Just now, with you. I didn't imagine it."

Chiara felt more than heard Vi gulping back emotions, because the words were coming out strained, tortured. And so she simply took the cold and clammy hand in hers, intertwining their fingers, and stared unseeingly as the lights of The City that Never Sleeps accompanied them on their journey.

"You always seem to save me. I've never told you how many times in Paris..."

The backs of Chiara's eyes stung, and she wondered why she was trying to hold back the tears. She was safe here. Despite everything, she felt safe. And what a realization to have after all these years?

"I always knew."

Vi's hand tensed in hers, and Chiara lifted it and placed a kiss on the prominent knuckles, enjoying the catch in Vi's breath.

"I knew. I may not have said. And I may not have shown, because the times you came to me, hurting and confused, it was more expedient to simply comfort you rather than telling you how much I hurt with you."

"Thank you." The hand in Chiara's relaxed a bit, even if the roughness did not leave the trembling voice, and Vi's breath was coming out raggedly now, despite Chiara's best efforts to calm her down.

"And yet, you realized he was with me just now. Still, you were walking in my direction anyway. Talk about saving, darling. Or talk about a complete lack of self-preservation."

In the darkness, the swatches of street light gave Vi's face an eerie glow, making her look ethereal. Why had Chiara never thought that about her before? Five years ago, she'd been all angelic innocence, and now she was a fallen one, tormented by her own descent.

"It seems my self-preservation isn't worth much when it comes to you, Chiara."

There was self-deprecation in the words, but the tone had evened out, and Chiara could sense the raggedness leave Vi's breath.

"Yes, it does seem that way. Even five years ago, you should have stayed away from me. Though I have to say, I was perhaps the perfect temptation for someone like you. Unhappy, lonely, lost as I was. And that knight in shining armor in you, that guardian angel... Well, you were doomed from the start, weren't you?"

Chiara wasn't sure where the words were coming from. They were certainly insulting Vi's intelligence and the power of whatever feelings she fancied she'd had five years ago. But even as Chiara recoiled, Vi chuckled.

"We should have talked about it years ago. I loved you for your brilliant mind, for the generosity and kindness you showed me, for your beauty and for the gentleness of your heart. For the post-its and marinara sauce. For the careful way you made me love myself. I loved you for so many instances of wonder and magic that you brought to my days back then. And for all the dreams of possibilities and hope you filled my nights with." Chiara trembled at the words and Vi lifted their joined hands for a gentle kiss on her knuckles before continuing.

"I loved you despite the circumstance and against every-thing that was right. I crossed so many lines drawn by god and man—well, woman—for you. I think the only thing I regret about Paris is not crossing all of them..."

Chiara watched Vi's eyes get misty as she looked into the night that was speeding by them and felt her own chest fill with both regret and affection. Her heart was so full of both and her tears spilled hot on her cheeks, for all the time they'd lost.

And yet, there was something else there, that thread, that thin, barely-there silky filament that kept tugging at Chiara's memories and at her consciousness. At times, it seemed within her reach, and today she was certain she would grasp it.

The car stopped abruptly, and the driver exited to open their door, pulling her out of her musings. As they climbed the steps towards her apartment, the townhouse seemed to settle around them, the empty showroom glimmering in the dark, the cozy offices and their deep green, soft tones soothing with their presence.

Her own atelier, allaying her regrets and her anguish with the splendor of the night seeping into the space through the massive skylights.

Chiara was reluctant to turn on the lights and just allowed the house to do what it always did best. She let the space that had become home more than any other, comfort her, as she felt the silk of that weightiness, the significance of the moment, wrap itself around her thoughts, offering both hope and solace, while Vi's hands steered her into the dim living room.

Binoche welcomed them with a meow and a hiss, as though she resented her own demands for attention.

"This is such a cliché. Me bringing you this cat. Such a romcom thing." Vi's voice held a smile, even if Chiara couldn't see it in the dark.

"Except ours was never a romcom, darling."

"A tragedy?" The cat was purring now, and Chiara realized that, while she was lost in her own thoughts, Vi must've picked Binoche up.

"One of our own making. I never apologized. And neither did you..."

"I've been trying to—"

"No, Vi, what you've been *trying* to do is atone. To let me,

Aoife, Renate, life, your parents—you name it—hurt you for something you did five years ago. You've been attempting to pay penance. The lost weight, the unhealthy, no-sleep lifestyle you..." Chiara struggled to find the right word, and instead waved her hand at Vi, hoping that she could see the gesture in the shadows.

And Vi must have managed, because her answer was a low laugh, which made Chiara roll her eyes.

"Nuh uh, don't you dare brush this off. You don't sleep, you don't eat. You work 'till you drop and you make love like you owe me."

Vi set the cat down and her voice suddenly sounded much closer, a dangerous note emanating from it. "No one ever complained, Chiara. You certainly haven't."

The low tone shrouded Chiara's ability to reason with fog, a haze of sudden lust. A feeling that had taken a back seat on their drive, in spite of a deep desire that had been slowly winding her up like a spring ever since she had seen that tuxedo. Or maybe ever since she'd first laid eyes on Vi in New York again.

Events, places, Vi's face all formed a kaleidoscope in her mind, and Chiara knew their time for words was over. She had said plenty, yet not enough, and she hadn't convinced Vi of anything, but perhaps during this past hour, she had persuaded herself. And allowed herself that first careful step. Towards trust. Towards Vi.

And so she took another one, and then another, closer, until she could see the narrowed eyes, filled with that same lust. And love.

Vi had spoken of her feelings in past tense, but Chiara knew enough of the world, of people, and most importantly of Vi, to recognize this one thing. To know it for certain. After all, it had been undisputable even five years ago. Vi loved her.

When their lips touched, Chiara realized it would be different. It would be sweet. And it would be gentle. And as she slowly tasted Vi's mouth, those full lips gentled too, slowing down, taking their time.

With the one exception, they'd never had the luxury of time with each other, and so they did now, Chiara slanting her mouth over Vi's, taking and giving in equal measure, even as their breaths mingled and their lips danced.

Her hands dove into the auburn silk of Vi's hair, tugging and scattering the pins, feeling scalded when the fiery strands fell over her fingertips, yet holding on tighter, gratified and electrified by Vi's whimper, licking deeper into her open mouth, feeling powerful, feeling free for the first time in years.

The gifts this woman bestowed on her, giving her strength and courage, and yes, freedom. Freedom to be herself, freedom to stand on a ledge and watch the city slip by underneath her and to know that, should she fall, she would be caught.

The warm hands on her face told her as much. Told her that she should have made the leap sooner, that no matter the past, she should have let go, let it all be.

Who needed proof when these fingers caressed and tended to her while tears were tumbling from underneath Vi's closed eyelids?

Even falling apart, Vi was gentle and careful and self-sacrificing. It was time for Chiara to let her. And to trust her.

"I love you. And I forgive you. For everything you think you need forgiveness for, darling. I should have taken your word. I should have listened. I'm so sorry."

Vi's tears fell in earnest now.

"Chiara... No... You can't. I lied. I lied so many times. You don't understand... I couldn't—"

"No, *cuore mio*. My heart. We will figure it out. I promise you. Let go now. With me."

Her mouth and her hands acted in tandem with her words, making quick work of the tuxedo jacket that was indeed hinging on a single button. As she slowly pushed the lapels to the sides, her breath caught in her lungs.

"God, if I'd known you were naked under this with just the one brass closure..."

Vi's laughter was strangled, a mix of want and tears.

"You'd have done what?"

Chiara licked her lips, then realized she had nothing to hide here and trailed her tongue from Vi's sternum to the collarbones, where she sucked on the skin, eliciting a moan, then sucked all the harder, because the sound opened a floodgate within her, and her desire to mark was not to be denied.

And so she left another mark where the shoulder curved into the neck, where the neck sloped into the jaw, biting and soothing the aches with her tongue, her lips, swearing she might die if she stopped, if Vi asked her to stop.

But Vi didn't. Her hands clung to Chiara's back, surely ruining the priceless Armani, bunching it up to the point where Chiara could hear it tearing under the onslaught of long fingers. She didn't care. Giorgio would simply have to send her a new one.

They stumbled into the bedroom, almost losing themselves halfway there, when Chiara pushed Vi into the closest wall and proceeded to unzip her trousers and followed the tight velvet down those endless legs with her lips, licking and biting at every new inch of exposed skin, all pale and shivering.

By the time she rose from her knees, Vi's breath was coming out in whimpers and short incoherent words that Chiara simply kissed off her mouth. There was no need for any of them.

They stood face to face, lips a hairbreadth away from each other, and watching those tortured eyes open and gaze into hers, Chiara wished the years away, wished they'd been together all this time, her own pain be damned. At least she would have spared Vi all the anguish of atonement.

But she couldn't do a thing about it, and so her hands were feather soft as they rose to Vi's face yet again, unable to keep away from those angular planes, surely sharpened by Vi's torment of herself.

"Let me, Vi... Let me do what I always did..."

Help you. Take care of you. Save you.

Vi's quiet sigh and the way her lips reached for hers were all the permission Chiara needed.

When she laid Vi on the unmade bed, naked while she was still in her torn dress, it was Chiara who felt vulnerable and split open by the onslaught of emotion, by the last few stitches around her heart tearing, leaving the jagged edges of the threads split and loose. And when she bent her head to taste, to savor and love, it was Chiara who felt pleasured, who felt touched and taken.

As she knelt in front of the bed, her lover opened her eyes, and there was still so much pain in them, so much incredulous awe, it broke Chiara all over again. That look of being lost in her own hell..., Chiara had done this, had caused this. It was her time to atone, her time to serve, to worship and please.

When her hands spread Vi's legs further apart, giving herself more access, when her fingers caressed the silky skin of the inner thighs, and finally, when her mouth descended on trembling flesh, Vi cried out, the loudest sound she had made during the entire night. A cry of longing and want, a cry of desperation and torment. And when minutes later, Chiara lifted her head, leaving Vi wrecked by a climax, the eyes did not close, even as the tears spilled again.

LYING in Vi's embrace hours later, Chiara noticed the bed dip slightly and Binoche pad towards them. The cat sniffed, sneezed, turned a few times on the blanket, then started making biscuits before finally settling down after a long stretch.

Chiara could certainly understand the inclination to do pretty much all of the above. She also wanted to stretch happily. She wanted to run her hands up and down the lanky body cushioning hers, to curl up in these arms and sleep the weekend away. Chiara was warm and cozy, she was loved, even if they hadn't spoken at all since she'd begged Vi to let her love her.

And Vi did let her. Many times over.

Chiara felt invincible and sexy and desired after ravishing Vi within an inch of her life, then doing it again because she could. Well, if the limp arm barely capable of lifting to pull her closer was any indication, despite being worse for wear, Vi didn't mind all that much.

"I always wondered if you'd kept the cat."

The lazy drawl proved Chiara's earlier point.

"Why on earth..." Chiara cut herself off before thinking better of what she'd been about to say. Some things she did need to tread around carefully, still. There were so many things they had to talk about more than the damn cat, even if that's what Vi chose to focus on in her blissed-out state.

"She's my cat. I wasn't going to leave her behind. It's as simple as that."

"Maybe, but I gave you Binoche."

It seemed like she'd have to say at least some things out loud now, blissed out or not.

"I never hated you, Vi. I was hurt, and I was broken. But I never hated you. And again, it's as simple as that."

There was silence then, until Vi sighed, the chest under Chiara's cheek moving up and down quicker.

"You make it sound simple. It's not though, Chiara. Not by a long shot, and if you only knew..." Another sigh and more silence. "If you knew the truth—"

"I'd what? Leave? I did that once already. I'm here now. I have an entire life planned here. It's laid out in detail in Renate's accounting books and all over my post-its."

That drew a smile, as she had hoped it would.

"Well, if your sticky notes are involved, it's serious."

"You are lucky I know you mean it the way you do, otherwise we'd be having words, Courtenay."

Vi ran her hand down Chiara's cooling back in a long caress, the mood shifting.

"Still, with everything that's going on, I owe you the truth. I should have told you years ago. But I couldn't. The gala was the last straw, I think. I hadn't seen him in years. And I've kept his secrets for far too long—"

The buzzing of her phone interrupted, and Chiara tsked but didn't get up. She hugged Vi tighter, signaling her to go on, both dreading and wishing for a resolution. But Vi remained quiet, the phone buzzing insistently again and again.

"I think you should probably get that. Whatever it is that demands your attention enough to bother you at 3 a.m. on a Saturday morning."

Chiara had to smile at the words. At the contrast to what Frankie would have said. Her ex-wife would have wanted to know who it was. Her ex-wife would have demanded answers.

Vi did not ask who, nor did she seem particularly anxious about the call, lying back on the pillows, arms behind her head, small breasts distracting Chiara from her phone's flashing screen. She had to smile at the role reversal from five years ago.

When she tore herself away from the view and answered, her brain was miles ahead of her heart. On the other end of the line, she heard the familiar sound of Arabella's voice choosing her words with care, informing her that Renate had a heart attack and would Chiara please come to the hospital immediately since she had power-of-attorney and was needed to make some medical decisions.

As the phone fell out of her numb hand, Vi reached out to catch it and got up from the disarrayed bed.

A moment later, Chiara heard her speaking in low tones, but she could not for the life of her understand a word Vi was saying. Her heart was finally catching up with the news her brain had already processed, and now her lungs were so tight, she thought she would choke. Renate couldn't be in a hospital. Renate, who was her family. Renate, who was her rock.

Suddenly, Vi appeared in her line of vision, sitting down on the floor in front of her—how had she ended up naked on the soft carpet herself?—and slowly, gently lifted her chin to meet her eyes.

"The driver will be here in twenty minutes, Chiara. We need to get dressed."

THE CITY that Never Sleeps looked disheveled and unkempt, tired and worried, and Chiara realized that, perhaps for the first time in her life, she had found her place, with the woman who held her hand in the car that she herself had arranged without a need for Chiara to even say a word. All she needed now was for her family to be okay, and then she could finally breathe again with a full chest.

25

IN A FARAWAY LAND OF BEDSIDE CONFESSIONS

Chiara Conti blinked at the lights speeding by, her eyes dry, lids scraping the irises like sandpaper. How different this ride was except for Vi's hand holding hers, the one tether to this world, to this present, stayed steady and warm.

"How long? How long do you think?"

She wondered why she was asking this question when time had never meant anything to her. She herself hated being asked about this. Chiara knew she could never master it. Timeframes constricted her unlike anything else. It would take as long as it would take.

One street after another, one red light, one green light, they would eventually get there. Perhaps even quicker than she'd imagined. And that imagination of hers, tired and unmedicated, stretched and compressed time into weird, unknowable shapes.

She felt like a child.

Are we there yet? How about now?

Vi didn't seem to hear her, and the steady beat of her pulse in her wrist under Chiara's fingertips did what she needed it to do most—measure that unfathomable time for her.

Silence stretched again. Vi gently squeezed her fingers, and Chiara burrowed into her neck.

"Arabella called. I don't know why it was her."

She heard her own voice like a spectator in a theater observing from the wings. She didn't bother wondering why she'd said it. She didn't even care to hear the answer. Just something to say. How silly, how surreptitiously useless and yet such a crutch.

"I caught the phone when you dropped it, baby, and spoke to her." Vi's voice was matter of fact, and she again squeezed the hand she was holding reassuringly, as if Chiara completely missing everything that was going on around her was par for the course. Maybe it was. "As for why, well, they've been together for weeks now, Chiara."

She raised her head off Vi's collarbone so fast, her cheekbone connected sharply with the chiseled jaw. Pain radiated across Chiara's face, and Vi lifted her hand to cradle her own chin. Chiara did not even yelp but wanted to reach out to touch the bruise that would surely form on the beloved features. Still, she had to know.

"What do you mean?" Her voice rose a few octaves, the higher pitch somehow sounding even more awful than she felt.

"They've been sneaking around pretty much since the day Arabella hired me to do the shoot. I caught them in the Poise offices when I stopped by to sign my contract."

Vi's matter-of-fact tone still did nothing to soothe Chiara's frayed nerves.

"But why didn't she tell me?"

"Renate." The name did not sound like a question, but a statement of fact. "I always thought she didn't share easily. I'm not entirely certain that it has anything to do with you. And Arabella is so smitten, it's rather endearing. I think it's serious between them, so it's possible Renate was taking her time with it?"

"*Serious between them...*" Among the anxiety of what was awaiting them at the hospital, Chiara felt a sudden touch of elation. Her lips stretched, a strange sensation, like her body was moving without her express command. But she was smiling, and Vi's own smile answered her tentatively. Chiara leaned closer and kissed it, that sweet, sweet corner of the full mouth lifting with shyness and hope. And then she kissed the reddening spot on the sharp pale jaw.

"And Arabella is smitten? How do you know?"

"She really is. It's very sweet. Such a tough old dame—"

"Hey, hey easy on the mature people there, baby!"

Vi's smile grew wider, a flash of white teeth gleaming at Chiara with mischief, as the hold on her hand changed, turning more intimate, fingers linking.

"She was the second person to save me. Arabella took one look at Benedict's dilemma about what to do with me, and proclaimed me her personal project. I always suspected she knew exactly who my parents were and what they did, their reputation preceding them, as always."

"Vi—"

"Hey, it's okay. Renate did hire a private investigator to keep Lilien Haus safe from my name alone. And all things considered, Zizou did not step one foot wrong. After all, what happened was something nobody could have predicted. Nobody but me, if only I was smarter." She gulped and soldiered on. "When this is over, you and I have things to talk about. I lied to you that morning in Paris. I don't deserve anything, but you do deserve to know—"

"Shhh..." Chiara murmured and then decided that it was by far not enough of a gesture to stop this barrage of words that seemed absolutely superfluous right now. And not only because the hospital was coming into view, but also in light of all the revelations tonight. Trust either worked or it didn't, and Chiara's simply did. And that was enough.

So, for the second time within the last few minutes, she pressed her lips onto Vi's. She chose to ignore that the sensuous mouth tasted of pain this time.

They both ignored that metallic taste, and the car stopped right before Chiara could deepen the kiss. So she closed her eyes, forehead to forehead with Vi, and took a deep breath, feeling Vi do the same. *Just one more second.*

Once again, the driver opened the door for them and then they were running.

~

ARABELLA'S CONNECTIONS at Presbyterian proved to be legendary. They didn't even need to introduce themselves. One word, and a tall, stooping man in his sixties with a dignified, if tired, expression gestured for them to accompany him. Someone addressed him as they passed the nurses' station and he simply waved them away, Chiara barely catching the nurse's awed, "...someone important since the Administrator is ferrying people around."

"Arabella is a huge donor." Vi didn't bother to keep her voice as quiet as the nurse's, since the man stopped in front of the bank of elevators and dipped his head.

"We are very grateful for Ms. Archibald Avant's generosity. This way, please. I'm afraid I will not be able to go into the ICU with you, as we are limiting the number of people permitted... Nosocomial infections... You understand."

Chiara nodded numbly. Her breath became shallow and threaded at the mention of the ICU. The Administrator escorted them up to the fifth floor. Within seconds, a nurse in a full ICU garb handed them gowns before taking them through a blindingly bright hallway. Soon, they stood in front of a glass wall, and behind it, hooked up to monitors and endless IVs, lay Renate.

Arabella sat by the bed, her head bent and face hidden in shadows. Chiara hiccuped and suddenly her cheeks were wet, tears falling freely, so fast she wasn't able to catch them.

They must have made a sound, because behind the glass, Arabella lifted her head, and the exhausted eyes closed with, dare Chiara say *relief*? And why relief? Surely not because Renate was dying and Arabella was afraid that Chiara would not make it in time?

Ti prego, Dio...

She so rarely asked anything of the almighty anymore.

A hand that used to be bejeweled, extended and beckoned them in. For some reason, the bony fingers, unadorned with the customary gold and gems, made Chiara's throat tighten.

Please, please...

But as the door opened to allow them passage, Renate's eyes opened, and Chiara felt the air whoosh out of her lungs. The pale blue gaze was clear, sharp as always, and when her former sister-in-law spoke, the voice was quiet, yet firm.

"Told her not to call you before dawn. She thinks I'll die. No chance. I've waited for forty years to pay her back. I'm not kicking the bucket before I have my fill."

Arabella sniffed, trying to hide the obvious sob behind an arrogant sneer, but she couldn't pull it off. The tears that had been filling those eyes earlier spilled, and soon everyone in the room was crying. As she tried to dry her eyes, Chiara thought there had been too many tears in the past five weeks. More than in the past five years.

"Bella, can you..." Renate's limp fingers gestured to Vi and to the door, and Arabella was in motion instantly. "Nothing personal, Courtenay. And thank you for being here with Chiara. Or should I say, being with her, period?" Renate tried to sit up and Chiara rushed to her side to help her, only to be waved away as her former sister-in-law settled back on the pillow and rasped, still addressing Vi. "I'm sorry, you know, for before. And for five years ago. We will talk. Later? Please go keep Frankie company, before Aoife maims her for annoying the hell out of the staff here."

Vi's wet eyes twinkled.

"And you assume she won't irritate *me*? Of all people?"

Renate's smile was tired. "I have an inkling you can take her. *Out of all people.* And all things considered, perhaps you should? Don't you think?"

Vi lowered her head, and Chiara felt like they were speaking in a language she didn't understand. But Vi was already giving her hand another squeeze before allowing Arabella to accompany her back to the other side of the glass and down the long corridor, where Chiara could clearly see a pacing figure. How had she missed Frankie on their way in?

"Chiara..." Renate's voice drew her out of her thoughts, as always, gentle yet firm. Chiara swallowed around the lump in her throat.

"I'm here."

"I can see just fine, *Liebling*. I'm not dying, no matter what those hacks told Arabella. They figure if they sell this as them saving me, she will pour even more money down the black hole of this place. Plus, she lost one of her four husbands in this very ICU. I'm not doing this to her, even if she deserves that and more..."

Renate cackled, then closed her eyes, taking deep breaths. Chiara reached for her fingers and held them carefully.

"No, no, stop with the maudlin nonsense. I don't mean any of that. I realized something in these few weeks with Arabella." Chiara raised her eyes in surprise and Renate's were serious, looking at her with so much intensity she wanted to flinch. "Forgiveness, Chiara. You either give it, or you don't. Love, lust, trust... They are all good and fine. But forgiveness? If you don't give that? Wholeheartedly? All of it? It will sit inside your chest like a stone. And one day, you'll reach for it and throw it and break everything you have been building."

Renate took a shaky breath, and Chiara knew only her formidable will was keeping her talking. And so she didn't interrupt.

"Vi... You deserve the truth. So be honest with yourself. With her too. Either forgive. Or forget."

"I already did—"

"Did you?"

"I love her, Renate. I feel the same way I always have, even in Paris."

"So you're the prince..." Renate smiled, and Chiara raised an uncomprehending eyebrow. "Prince to her Cinderella." The chuckle, exhausted and pained, still sounded self-satisfied. "How the mighty have fallen. A Converse-wearing Cinderella and a Blahnik-adorned Prince. Only you, Chiara..."

Chiara scoffed, but Renate's face was serious again.

"You love her. Super." The German accent deepened on the last word. "Now forgive her. Or let her go. And forgive yourself. Both of you atoning for your imaginary sins." A disdainful tsk followed and Chiara thought this was a good moment to interrupt, but Renate kept going, barreling over her in a gesture so familiar, Chiara had to smile.

"You think you were wrong in Paris. To allow her to love you. I know. You've been making up for it ever since. And she will never stop atoning for everything that happened after. Peas in a pod, the two of you. You love her and she loves you. Amazing. Now, for fuck's sake, forgive each other."

Another deep breath, and now the somber eyes were wet as well. "And forgive me, too. With any luck, you already have. Because you have this absolutely dumbass capacity to just up and move on from everything that happens to you, then internalize them 'til they choke you—'"

"Are you psychoanalyzing me from an ICU bed? Was there a light at the end of the tunnel? Did you get to talk to some supernatural being?"

She tried for levity and saw the bluish lips twitch.

"No deity. No light. Must not be the end yet. But I am sorry. And I ask you to forgive me. *Business.* That was my line. The one I crossed when I sacrificed your happiness. It was even more stupid than Aoife's. At least hers was love." Renate stopped and motioned for a glass on her bedside that held water. Her hand was remarkably steady when Chiara helped her drink.

"Mine was family and business. I knew she was cheating, yet I said nothing. In the end, I lost neither, because, first and foremost, you are family. And you built something that's bigger than Lilien Haus. If not in size, then certainly with how special it is. Iconic. Forgive me."

Chiara lifted the limp hand she'd been holding and kissed the knuckles.

"Always. Anything. Everything. I love you."

Renate tugged on her hand. "Say it." When she let go, Renate splayed her fingers on Chiara's cheek. The dry skin was now trembling slightly, whether with exhaustion or emotion, Chiara didn't know.

"I forgive you."

Renate sighed. "Good, now I can—"

Chiara thought the room tilted.

"No!"

"Sheesh. Sleep! Now I can get some sleep. Get Bella back in here. She can sit in that uncomfortable chair and sigh over me for a few more hours before I send her home to rest. She's not spry enough to pull the entire day by my bedside anymore, especially after I wore her out the night before in another bedside—"

"TMI! And you did not!" Chiara waved her hands. "No, no,

wait. I don't want to know." She laid her head on the chemical-smelling sheets, next to Renate.

"You scared me. So much. Don't die. I need you."

She knew she sounded childish. She didn't care. Renate obviously didn't either, as the trembling fingers stroked her hair, and Chiara closed her eyes.

"I don't intend to. And yes, I realize plans usually don't factor into all of this. But I don't imagine I will. If that makes sense? I'm happy for you, though. Even if Frankie is back."

"Are you going to ask me to be kind to her, too? To forgive her as well?"

"Screw her." Chiara's head spun at the uncharacteristic profanity. "No, I'm not even sure she's truly sorry. Maybe for cheating. But I believe you forgave that a long time ago."

Renate sighed before making one last effort to speak.

"Chiara, you need to stop thinking it was your fault..."

The fingers moved slowly in her tresses, and Chiara waited with bated breath for what came next. But Renate was silent, and after another minute, the fingers stilled, the breathing evening out, and when Chiara lifted her head, Renate was asleep, her face peaceful.

26

IN A FARAWAY LAND OF LONG OVERDUE REVELATIONS

Chiara Conti hated hospitals. Yet when she exited Renate's room, she felt almost peaceful. She peered in the hallway, where she could hear Vi and Aoife speak in quiet tones, before she turned towards her intended marks.

In an almost empty waiting room, Arabella sat gracefully, reclining in a chair that did not, in any way, look comfortable. Maybe some of that discomfort was responsible for the stink eye she was aiming at Frankie, who had her head between her hands, seemingly oblivious to the matriarch.

"She asked for you to come back, but she's asleep." Two pairs of eyes shot her way, and Chiara gave Arabella a sheepish smile. "She said, 'Bella can sit in this ghastly chair for a few hours and watch me, before she goes home to get rest,' or words to that effect."

The smile that lit up Arabella's face was so sweet, Chiara's heart soared, and then she had to laugh when it turned triumphant as she passed by a slumped over Frankie who watched her walk away with envy.

"Overlooked yet again."

The bitterness in Frankie's voice held an undercurrent of something akin to loneliness, and Renate's words about forgiveness rang in Chiara's ears. No, she didn't owe Frankie forgiveness, but Chiara's heart was light where Frankie was concerned, and wasn't that a kick in the teeth?

She sat down next to her ex-wife, who was still and dejected, eyes unseeing, fixed on the black-and-white tiles under their feet.

"She asked me to forgive." That got her the attention she wanted as Frankie's head shot up.

"Me? Is she dying then? I can't see her asking something like that if she's convinced she'll make it."

"I don't think she's dying. She certainly has big plans." Outside, car horns blared, reminding her of the waking city. "No, you know how she is. Silent for years, then every once in a while, she slaps you across the face with some universal truth that has been eluding you for what seems like forever. Yet it's simple and she is, as always, correct—"

"In what? You needing to forgive me?" Frankie lifted her eyebrows in surprise.

Chiara proceeded as though she hadn't been interrupted. "—and this time, despite the sickbed, she's right once again."

Frankie's mouth dropped open and she lowered her eyes. Chiara reached for her hand and went on. "I don't need to forgive you. I need to stop blaming myself for what happened."

The plastic clock on the wall counted the seconds.

Chiara was surprised by how hot the hand in hers was and how this particular silence was soothing—something she could never say about Frankie before. Her ex-wife wasn't someone who could be comfortable in the quiet of the unspoken. So she saw the need to continue talking, to keep the silence at bay, even if she herself was completely fine giving Frankie nothing.

Still, Renate had been so right, maybe Chiara should just lay it all on the table?

"I had so much anger in me when I caught you, Frankie. So much disappointment."

"Chiara, I'm sorry—"

"Yes, you are, and I believe you and that's fine. But I wasn't disappointed in you. I was angry and disillusioned with myself. Because I thought I did everything right. And yet you cheated anyway. Moreover, you'd been doing it for years. Once again, I wasn't enough."

Chiara felt her hands go numb, the old, familiar anxiety filling her to the brim. But she had to voice this, had to form the words and let them out of her chest. No more snakes at her breast.

"And this time, it was me, the real me, not someone who was pretending so hard to please her mother, or to satisfy her manager. It was just me, doing my best every day to be worthy of you, and yet... Not good enough again." She shook her head, feeling Frankie tense up next to her. "And maybe I need to let go of that and forgive myself. It does take two, after all."

"That's not what happened, Chiara. And if Renate told you that—" All the tension in her ex-wife spilled, but Chiara was no longer prone to appeasement for appeasement's sake.

"She didn't. She said that I should move on and forgive myself for everything. For you, for Vi."

"Well, whatever your sins against Vi were, let me absolve you of the ones you think you've committed against me." Frankie drew a shaky breath and closed her eyes. "I was the one who wasn't good enough, Chiara. I never was. It was so painfully obvious from the very beginning. You have so much shine. The beauty, the talent, the kindness. I never measured up to you. You were not just out of my league, you might as well have been playing another sport altogether."

Chiara stared, her brain on fire, trying to process what was happening. She was catching the words like they were base-balls volleyed at her, very much afraid that, if she dropped one of them, the rest would just pummel her into a stupor and nothing would make sense.

"I am not a good person, Chiara. And my ego was bruised. With one idea, you created a collection in that very first year of ours that was miles ahead of anything I've ever put out. Everyone knew it, too. Renate, Aoife, the seamstresses. And since that day, nothing was ever the same. One smile and every room you entered was yours. Every new piece you designed was just better, more. So much more than mine." A sudden sob left Frankie's mouth, and she covered her face with her hands while Chiara sat paralyzed by her words.

Frankie groaned, angrily wiping her eyes, and continued.

"So I started seeking that high of being something, someone better, someone needed, wanted, lusted after—like you were by all those adoring faces no matter where you went."

"I wanted you and I needed you..." Her own voice sounded foreign to her, choked and ragged at the edges.

"I... I don't know why you ever did. I loved you more than I ever loved anyone. And I hated myself for what I was doing. Eventually, I despised myself so much, I *wanted* you to catch me. To punish you for making me do it. To punish myself, because I knew you'd throw me out that very second. You have no idea how many times you came close to walking in on me. Fuck, even Vi caught me that time in Como at the very end."

Frankie gulped loudly, but Chiara didn't care anymore. So Vi had known. And had kept it secret for weeks. If Aoife was right, and Vi's reason for selling the pictures had been to break them up, all she had to do at the time was to tell Chiara...

Was this the last piece of the puzzle? That Vi might have lied to her, but she'd never betrayed her? Never sold the pictures? Because what would have been the point?

Chiara blinked once, twice, then realized she hadn't been hanging by this thread for a while. That, after her admitting her love to Vi and letting go of the past, this confirmation that her lover was innocent, was—while sweet—thoroughly unnecessary.

Frankie's hoarse voice brought her back to the present.

"Vi knew, Renate knew, and I felt like I was walking a high wire. I felt it was time. But then it happened in the worst possible way. And I dragged all those people into my mess. Not just Véronique, but Vi and Renate and Zizou and everyone."

Chiara was stunned. All the threads, fragile lines of thought, were suddenly forming a pattern. She looked around the room with unseeing eyes, the light shockingly, impossibly brighter, hurting her eyes. Well, that pain would pair perfectly with her aching heart then.

"I don't know how you can forgive me, Chiara. I don't know how you can think you were not good enough. The harder you tried, the more I hated myself, because I could never ever touch you. Could never, ever reach you."

"Frankie..." Words felt like razors. "God..."

"No, now you stop. I should've told you all those years ago. I ruined us. *I* did. Nothing you could have done to fix it. And Renate knew from the start that I was sinking. She kept trying to pull me up, for years, to build me up. But then she found out about the cheating, and she dropped me faster than a hot potato. She was done with me. And I walked into that room today when they brought her in, because Arabella called me. Reluctantly, I might add. She couldn't find you, I guess, so she called *me*. And Renate refused to see me. Flat out. So I am begging you, if you can't forgive me, then at least don't hate me."

The ticking of the clock on the wall played a tune in Chiara's mind, saving her from this mental overload, which surely would have overwhelmed her by now otherwise. She clung to her earlier realizations and to the monotone sound.

Tick Tock...

She had been good enough...

Tick Tock...

She had always been good enough...

Tick Tock...

And Vi never needed to sell the pictures to break her up with Frankie...

"I don't want you to hate me like Renate does. At death's door and she's refusing to see me, Chiara."

Tick Tock. Time was running like sand through her fingers, the sensation so real she lowered her face to her hands that lay limp in her lap.

"*I* am not at death's door." Her own voice was muffled, but Chiara heard the note of steel in them, nonetheless.

"No, but you and I are. I saw Vi earlier. I saw her face. It was the face of a someone who'd been exonerated, someone who won—"

Chiara's head shot up, her eyes on Frankie. "Maybe if you'd stop talking about me like I am some kind of damn prize to win, to hold, to conquer! Maybe then none of this would have ever happened!"

Her own outburst took her by surprise, her mood careening from heartbroken to angry—and no longer at herself. For once, that made her feel good. It made her feel strong. Vindication tasted sweet, and so Chiara allowed it to flow.

"Don't drag Vi into this. She has nothing to do with you and I or this goddamn notion of winning. She did not *win* me. I almost ruined her, and she never asked for anything. Instead, she paid for those damn pictures for years, and I have continued to punish her ever since she came back into my life."

At Frankie's utterly blank stare, Chiara barreled on.

"I used her five years ago, and I thought she used me, and we never forgave ourselves for any of that. All that guilt, choking us both. So don't tell me she was in here gloating, because there is absolutely no way she'd ever do that, despite having every right to. And also, why can't you see how all of this is just so wrong?"

Frankie blinked at her a few times before shaking her head like she was trying to clear it. Chiara tsked, impatient. Frankie's eyes widened.

"My god, you still believe she sold the pictures, don't you?"

"No!" Her own response was so quick, too quick, and she saw the realization in Frankie's eyes. "Not anymore."

"But you did?" Frankie shook her head and turned away. "Of course you did. I mean, I was nasty enough to insinuate it just weeks ago when I saw her at your atelier."

"Yes, you were. Nasty. And for the longest time, I was sure she'd done it. For years." Chiara closed her eyes, the bright lights too much for her.

"Ah, well, that would make sense. She had a massive crush on you that summer, though. Maybe not even a crush, because it sure looked like love. When she caught me with that model in Como, she was so broken... Only a person in love can be that devastated when the object of their affection is about to be hurt. I wish you'd known." Chiara opened her eyes to find Frankie staring at her intently. "That kind of love? I didn't even wonder why she never came to you to warn you, to tell on me. But now I get it. She would have never been able to. She loved you. Hurting you? That wasn't an option for her. She would have taken my secret to the grave, Chiara."

Chiara lowered her face again, and now her hands were no longer limp, fingers balled so tightly, knuckles white, and the short-filed nails about to break the skin of her palms. But she didn't relax them, something needed to tether her to this moment, and pain was certainly appropriate.

"I guess this is another check in the column of my sins—you believing for five years that she's at fault." Chiara looked at Frankie then, who was running her hands through her hair. "I think I can at least strike this one off the ledger. If you'll let me." Unable to sit motionless anymore, Chiara stood up and walked towards the large window overlooking the East River and Roosevelt Island in the distance over the water. Frankie cleared her throat, waiting, and Chiara simply nodded for her to go ahead, unable to find her voice.

"The Courtenays' lawyer reached out to me late that night. I was drunk. I don't even remember where I was. I had a ton of missed calls. From Renate, from Aoife, and all sorts of unknown numbers. And you weren't among them, you weren't calling me. So I finally picked up, and this man said they had pictures. Of me and of you. And they would publish them, unless I paid."

The first rays of sun were making their way onto the horizon, and beneath Chiara's eyes, the FDR Drive was getting busier with the early morning traffic. Her mind refused to allow the magnitude of the coming revelations to penetrate, not just yet, so she listened as a detached observer, as if nothing Frankie was saying could touch her.

"The damn magazine was offering them sums that I simply couldn't get my hands on, not without Renate co-signing, and I knew she'd never agree. So we made a deal. The magazine would get the pictures, but only ones that would be less damaging to me. And in return, the Courtenay name would be kept out of the press."

Behind her, Chiara could hear Frankie taking a deep breath, but she still refused to turn around. Not yet.

"I have no idea how they got the photos, but they were very careful in trying to make sure nobody knew the source of them. I was raging and told them I would sue every single one of them, and the lawyer was so exacting, trying to make sure Vi's name was never part of the conversation, to make sure I never reached out to her. It dawned on me very early on that whatever they did, they'd simply used her. She might have taken the pictures, but she had no idea what they were doing. She was never in on this, Chiara."

And now her mind finally allowed Chiara to fully immerse herself in the narrative and damn, if it wasn't painful. Because what Frankie just revealed wasn't quite true. Vi had known who was responsible and kept that secret. She'd also known Frankie cheated and didn't reveal that either. All the while taking all the blame and allowing Chiara to walk away. Vi had accepted the punishment, as if earned, as if deserved. And Chiara? What had she done? Believed the worst. About herself. About Vi.

God, this jumping to conclusions really needed to stop. Now that so many things made sense. Now that Renate had imparted her wisdom on forgiveness.

Isn't that what was supposed to propel the main character into changing her ways? Into realizing that she had been wrong? Into fixing all the wrongs she herself had committed? An honorable and beloved supporting character pushing the protagonist to do right just as things are about to come to a head? Such a literary cliché.

Well, it was time to fall back on some of those.

"I don't hate you, Frankie." Well, cliché one down. "I hate what you've done. I despise that you allowed me to loathe myself for years. But then look at what I've done? Absolutely the same thing. I let Vi believe she was to blame. I didn't believe her, and I let her burn for someone else's sins." The second cliché off her list.

She laughed, a broken, awful sound that further scraped raw her nerve endings. "We seem to have this whole theme of sins and damnation going here, Frankie. How very morbid of us."

"Chiara—" She turned around to see Frankie looking at her with trepidation and not a little fear.

"Oh please, no, I don't hate you. But I don't ever want to see you again. It is so fucking awful what you did. Allowing me to blame myself for years. So yeah, I wish you..." She couldn't even say 'all the best,' and rather laughed again, dry and painful. "I wish you *whatever*, Frankie. Do well, but don't look for me again, god... And if you think that you giving me this piece of truth fixes something for you? No, Frankie, you sold them the pictures with my face and kept the ones that would have embarrassed you most out of the press. So you doing the right thing now?"

Frankie was on her feet too now, pacing, trying to come closer and perhaps seeing clearly what was in Chiara's eyes and not daring.

"Doesn't it count for something?"

Chiara smiled at her bitterly.

"I thought it was all on me. Everything. For years. And it wasn't. And I assumed Vi betrayed me. And she never did. Her keeping her family's secret, in retrospect, is something someone like her, starved for love, loyal to a fault, would have done. Taken on all the blame and trapped it in her chest and allowed it to choke her. Maybe we are peas in a pod, or whatever Renate called us. Be well, Frankie, but do it far away from me."

As she crossed the room to the door, one hand already on the handle, Frankie's voice stopped her.

"What are you going to do?"

"Beg her to forgive me, Frankie. Something I should've done years ago. And hope beyond hope that she does. Hope she will be much more merciful to me than I am to you. Pray my sins will be wiped off that proverbial ledger. Maybe some balance in that book is finally due. All that bleeding red is too much, and Vi has bled enough all over its pages."

27

IN A FARAWAY LAND OF HEROES
AND VILLAINS

C hiara Conti never really believed in magic, but as she made her dramatic exit from the waiting room, as if by the flick of a wand, the subject of all the preceding drama was leaning against the wall opposite the door, watching her with tired, concerned eyes.

The image of all that disheveled hair, the rumpled clothes, the linen shirt she'd hastily pulled on, the slightly too big trousers held up by the stupidly attractive suspenders, and the naked ankles peeking out from under the material... It did something to Chiara on a visceral level. *Stupidly.* That was the correct descriptor of how this woman affected Chiara.

But next to the unvarnished lust, there was also intricate adoration, tenderness, and above all else, limitless love. And guilt. So much guilt, Chiara felt she might suffocate on it.

And the wondrous eyes kept looking at her, despite Aoife saying something to Vi, despite people milling back and forth in the now crowded corridor, and the distance between them. Vi was seeing only her, and the hope in Chiara's heart bloomed.

Maybe they would make it to the other end of this clusterfuck they'd created. All these things that should have been so simple. All of this, which was supposed to have been a quiet divorce, a quiet courtship, and a quiet, happy five years of love.

Except while happiness was always straightforward, misery had no such requirements. And you always had to pay the toll.

Had Renate been her wake-up call? Was Frankie's confession the first strip of her heart she had to pay for knowing the truth? And would whatever happened with Vi next, force her to surrender the rest of it?

Perhaps seeing her indecisiveness, Vi strode over, took her hand, and in a matter of minutes, they were making their way through the hospital's labyrinth of hallways and passageways. Before long, Vi had them outside and was hailing a cab with one of those attractively self-assured gestures that Chiara knew would never go unanswered, because a car was at the curb next to them in an instant.

The trip to the Village was a blur of a cigarette-smoke-filled backseat and the dimming lights of the awakening city. Vi's hand in hers, warm and sure, was an anchor amidst the stench and the sensory overload.

Even as Vi's building appeared in front of them, that thin thread that had been tormenting Chiara for days tugged at her until she turned around.

She knew they were there even before her eyes caught sight of them, because that wonderful warmth was gone from Vi's hand in an instant.

And as Charles faced them under the dying light of the lamp, Chiara remembered exactly where she had seen him. No, the dawn of Manhattan wasn't the dusk of Paris, but she knew. And suddenly, so many things made sense. Only one question remained.

"We've been ringing the doorbell for ten minutes, Genevieve. You certainly keep inappropriate hours."

Charles' voice sounded haughty and a little rough, maybe

due to the early hour or the fact that both he and Gwyneth were decked out to the nines, clearly coming from some fancy reception. Possibly even her own, since the Poise party surely continued until dawn, despite the guests of honor leaving early.

He looked tired. His wife looked as bored as always.

"I'm an adult, father."

"Being an adult doesn't permit you to be rude, Genevieve. Invite us up. If your date can stand an interruption."

His eyes swept over Chiara with the same indifference as always, and the last pieces of the Courtenay puzzle slid into place for her. Some things really were that simple. She had no more questions. Only answers. And now was the right time to share them. Vi had suffered enough.

"This is actually fortuitous, Charles. I would have sought you out within the next few hours myself." Chiara straightened to her full height, looking Charles directly in the eye. Clearly, this wasn't something he was accustomed to, because his gaze narrowed, and he lifted his aristocratic chin, the shadow of gray stubble making him look so much older.

"Chiara..." Vi's voice trembled, and it was all she could do not to give in and gather her in her arms, as she should have done countless times five years ago.

Still, better late than never.

"Darling, I will explain, even if I would have preferred to speak to you first. Alas, there is only one way to untangle the Gordian knot. So please bear with me."

The fear in Vi's eyes almost stopped her, but instead, Chiara squeezed her hand before sweeping into the building, impassive as to whether she was followed. She knew she would be. At least one of the Courtenays would be curious. And Chiara counted on that curiosity. It had killed the cat, after all.

By the time they all found themselves inside Vi's apartment, Charles was even more disgruntled, perched uncomfortably on the sofa, Gwyneth was apathetic, lounging in the armchair farthest from Chiara, while Vi stood in the middle of the living room looking at the entire gathering with somewhat bewildered eyes.

Chiara affected a smile and felt it stretch her lips unpleasantly. "Well, I don't know about all of you, but I've had quite a night, and with as much bullshit and aggravation as you have caused me over the past several years, I have a lot to say, so I will make this, if not painless, then at least succinct—"

Charles' jaw clenched before he seemed to will it to relax. "I have no idea who you think you are and what you are doing here, Ms. Conti, but I won't allow you to speak to us like this. To order us around, to threaten us like common criminals—"

"There's nothing common about you, Charles. Nothing whatsoever. And while law enforcement might be fascinated with this *uncommonness*, I must tell you, I simply don't give a damn."

She could see he was taken aback by her words as he looked around himself and invariably at the one person who was keeping her silence—the same as always.

Chiara took a step towards the windowsill and leaned on it —another window, another view, and the same city now almost fully awake and alive at her fingertips. She felt the anger she'd been trying to hold back roar to life, for herself, for Vi, for the time that they had lost.

"Five years ago, I was on top of the world. Yes, my wife had just been caught cheating on me, but I was the happiest I had ever been. I was in love, and I was loved back. Until I wasn't... Or so I thought."

"Chiara..." The sorrow in Vi's voice made it sound hollow, her eyes alight with so much pain, so much self-recrimination. It had to end. Chiara knew she had to end it.

"For years, I believed Vi had betrayed me. That she had her reasons for lying to me when I asked if she had sold the pictures of me catching Frankie in the act. To this day, every time I remember that night, I remember her eyes. Just like now, they were full of self-loathing, because just like now, she was torn between her love and loyalty to you—the only family she has, Charles—and her sense of honor and doing what was right."

"Chiara, please, I did lie that night." The tremor in Vi's voice was breaking Chiara's heart. And when she finally looked from Charles' astonished face to Vi's beloved features, she smiled at her with as much love as she was able to convey.

"No, darling. You didn't. Or, at least, not entirely. You shook your head when I asked you if you knew who did it and I chose not to believe you, because how could you not know? After all, it had to be you, right? Nobody else had access."

"I did lie, because I did know. My father—"

"How dare you!" Charles was on his feet in a second, but before he could approach Vi or even say anything else, Chiara simply stared him down and lowered her voice.

"If I were you, I'd call a lawyer, Charles."

Vi gasped, and Charles' already red face turned a peaked, ruddy shade.

"I will ruin you, Conti. Defamation—"

"But I didn't defame you, Charles. Not yet anyway." Chiara shrugged, infusing it with as much nonchalance as she could muster. "It took me a long time to remember where I'd seen you before. Too long. And perhaps, had I remembered, I'd have figured things out sooner. Alas, faces are not my strong suit. Gowns are, though."

She looked beyond Charles, but in her periphery, she saw him take a step back. "In fact, I gave you excellent advice just now. Because you *will* need that lawyer. Make it a very good one. I hear family law attorneys are hard to come by on the cheap. Your finances being what they are."

In the silence of the room, Chiara actually wished for

Binoche. That cat knew how to cut through tension in the most irreverent of ways. The strange detour her brain had taken made her smile. She'd never appreciated her thought processes more than in this moment. When her emotions were running her ragged, her mind had conjured up the perfect distraction to give itself a small, much-needed breather.

"I don't understand." Vi's voice brought her back to the moment. It no longer trembled, and she wasn't focused on Chiara anymore. Her burning eyes were now aimed at the one person who still hadn't uttered a single word.

Gwyneth stood up, her lip curling in a move to rival any fairytale villain worth her salt. She tilted her head, a smirk now distorting her face. "What is there to understand, Cinderella? It's like you've not read the fairytale. It was always the step-mother." She turned and took a few steps towards Chiara, completely ignoring the other people in the room. "Was it the *Silver* gown?" Her words were flat, emotionless, as if she were discussing the weather and not years of theft, commercial espionage, and just plain old treachery.

"I was in London when that dress was shown, just before it was stolen, Gwyneth. And it *was* stolen. The Maestro would have never given it away."

Gwyneth waved her hand. "Eh, the man is dead, and nobody else can say different."

Chiara raised an eyebrow at the brazenness. "Be that as it may, I am alive, and I know it was you stealing designs and blackmailing Lucci and D&B throughout that summer. What, couldn't quite get a foot in the door at Lilien Haus? Did Renate and Zizou actually outsmart you?"

"Neither Lucci nor D&B will say a word. They both paid one way or another—"

"I couldn't quite figure it out, you know. Lucci and D&B perhaps were careless in screening their employees, but Vi didn't get full access, because Lilien had nothing to show, and

Zizou kept a close eye on her all summer. So it was the one piece that didn't fit. And then I finally realized who it was I'd seen leaving her building with a camera. At that point, I thought I knew. I thought I had it all figured out."

Charles gaped, his mouth opening and closing, and Vi watched, her face turning paler.

"But I was wrong, wasn't I, Gwyneth? Look at him. This man? A co-conspirator in commercial espionage? I bet he never even suspected a thing."

Gwyneth rolled her eyes and sucked on her teeth with disdain.

"Yes, he is rather pathetic for anything, really."

"Gwen?" For a moment, the silence could have fooled Chiara into thinking that they were alone. Not even breathing could be heard from either of the other two people in the room. But now things were suddenly very loud. Charles' voice booming with sheer shock and his ragged breathing like thunder in the distance.

"What, my dear?" Gwyneth spat the word, then turned away from him, her shoulders completely relaxed, her countenance clear, as if the actual weather was the subject of their conversation, rather than the storm brewing inside the room.

"You like to dress well, and you like to be the center of attention, and you like to be seen for the Earl that you are. Except you squandered everything you had when I married you! And you're well aware of it, yet you've never once asked how it is that there is money in our bank accounts."

"Gwen—" He was no longer screaming, he was pleading with her, and Chiara looked on in astonishment at how little Gwyneth actually cared. Vi stood completely still, her face impassive, pale as a sheet.

"The camera was connected to the cloud. I had every photo she ever took. And I would have gotten the pictures of the collection from Como, too, except this klutz damaged my

Nikon, and I couldn't get access to them. So no Charles, don't worry. I didn't ever need your help. It was already a done deal when you brought back the camera. I had everything I needed the moment Genevieve clicked the shutter. All her sappy infatuation with Chiara, all four months of it. It seems pathetic runs in the family."

Vi's eyes that had been hollow now filled with so much rage, Chiara thought she'd be forced to restrain her. But Gwyneth just waved her hand and continued, ignoring the two Courtenays and the hearts that seemed to be breaking all over the threadbare carpet, betrayal and anger evident on both their faces.

"I was the only one who knew what was going on. Her puppy-dog adoration, his obliviousness, and the complete stupor every time he as much as glanced at her—"

"Stop!" And now there was indeed something of an Earl in Charles' bearing, in the authority with which he stepped between Vi and Gwyneth.

"Father?"

Charles rubbed his face with his thin, bony hands, and when he finally spoke after what seemed like forever, his voice was full of sorrow.

"I could never look at you and not see your mother. You are such a strange child, Genevieve. It's like genetics were punishing me from the start. I loved her. Her death broke me, and I couldn't reason that it really wasn't your fault. That she died to give life to you, but you did nothing wrong. I blamed you for years. I couldn't stop missing her and then you... You are her! Down to the tips of your ears, to the way you tilt your head, how you sometimes bite your lower lip..."

Gwyneth tsked before speaking up, disgust permeating her voice. "And you couldn't look away either, my dear. I could have slit my veins in front of you, but if Cinderella was in the room, I didn't exist, my daughters didn't exist. And all throughout you wallowed in your grief and in your pathetic ambitions of royalty. Well, someone had to do something. Someone had to take charge. How do you think I single-handedly ensured this family would still be received all over the world?

"Not for long." The words took so much out of her that Chiara wanted to sag, wanted to curl up on the windowsill like Binoche and just sleep. Twice in one day she'd thought of the finicky cat. She might just buy her a new toy. Although Binoche would probably ignore the toy and play with a pipe cleaner instead. Maybe Chiara should just resign herself to buying packs of them from now on. It would be much cheaper that way.

She was rambling inside her own head, while Charles and Gwyneth were arguing in high-pitched voices, accusations and insults hurled angrily back and forth.

In the meantime, Vi looked so sad and so lost that Chiara went to her.

"How about we take a cab to Mercer Street, darling? I could sleep for a week." The fingers that she laced hers with were shaking, and Chiara lifted that pale hand to her cheek, cradling it there, warming it up, feeling like Vi was slowly coming back to life, her eyes getting some of their fire back even as her parents were still screaming obscenities at each other.

"I think just for once in my life, I would like to stand my ground, Chiara. You have been doing so much of it. Maybe it's my turn?" She bared her teeth in something not even closely resembling a smile and tugged her hand free of Chiara's. Then she strode over to Gwyneth, grabbed her by the forearm and marched her towards the door, Charles being forced to scramble behind the two of them.

The front door slammed, and when Vi came back, she was alone, although the screams were now audible from outside the apartment. But Chiara didn't care.

"That was... well, hot? It's the only word that comes to mind."

And now the smile on Vi's face was shy and achingly familiar, the girl from five years ago back and here in the room with Chiara, so sweet, so kind, so beloved. Chiara's chest seemed to crack, and she touched her sternum, trying to hold whatever was escaping in, except there was no more containing it.

"I love you, Vi Courtenay."

She closed her eyes, letting the words wash over her, feeling that thread gain strength and finding roots of it in Vi's chest, tying them together, making them whole again after so much wandering and so much fractured misery.

"You weren't the only one who was wrong that morning in Paris five years ago, darling."

Vi's graceful eyebrow lifted, and the smile playing shyly on her lips wobbled. But Chiara would have none of it, so she leaned in and kissed the corner of that mouth, desperately trying to make the joy last. And if not that, then at least taste it, feel it, keep its memory in her own heart.

When she pulled back, she traced the tense jaw with her fingers and looked into Vi's eyes, trying to convey with every word, with every caress, the truth she'd kept hidden for years.

"I loved you then. I've loved you since you fell at my feet and lost your shoe, Cenerella. Some stories are that simple and we are the ones complicating them. Ours should have been easy, straightforward. And then we started crossing all these thin lines, one by one, until they turned into a tangled mess." She sighed and placed her hands on Vi's cheeks, thumbs tracing the beloved sharp cheekbones.

"I should have believed you. I should have had faith in you. In your heart. Because I'd known it for months, and it had been the one thing that was true the entire time."

Vi lifted her face and kissed Chiara's forehead, then simply allowed her own to rest against it.

"I don't know how you survived that blow. I know I wouldn't have been able to."

Chiara held Vi tighter. "You thought it was him."

Vi's quiet sob was heart-wrenching in the silence of the room, despite the continued screams outside the door.

"I did. I was so sure. He'd left my place just minutes before you knocked and he took the camera with him—"

Chiara tucked a lock of auburn behind Vi's ear, and on pure instinct and muscle memory from five years ago, gently tilted Vi's chin up, holding her face in her hands.

"I thought it was him too, for just one tiny moment, before it all slid into place for me. Then I realized it could have never been him. He is your father and you love him, despite him being totally worthless, but he never had the balls, Vi. He never did."

"Did you really recognize the gown?"

"The rest of the little things just never added up. The stolen gowns, and then the fact that he did not give a damn about me."

Now it was Vi's turn to lean back to take a better look at Chiara's face.

"Excuse me?"

"Well, yes, I am rather magnificent in my own right—"

"You are magnificent in every right!" Vi laughed, and Chiara smiled along with her, the expression remaining and warming her voice despite what she had to say.

"I would like to think that, if I'd have ruined someone's life, the next time I see them, I would at least spare them a passing glance. And Charles had eyes only for you that night at the event and again at my party. He could not have cared less about Lilien Haus, some wretched gala or Poise's Chiaroscuro launch. He was there to see *you*."

"Ha, only because I wounded his pride by refusing him access to myself. I took away his heir. And I honestly don't know how to deal with him blaming me for my mother's death. Has he really hated me that much all my life? And if he has, why seek me out again? My therapist will have her work cut out for her for years." Vi shook her head, and the laughter was now mirthless.

Chiara wanted to tell Vi that she suspected there was more to Charles' reaction to seeing her again after years of not being allowed, after years of being deprived. Hell, she herself had the exact same look in her own eyes when she had first seen Vi again at Mercer Street that September day. Longing. Love. And a rending of the heart that could only come with that emotion.

But she kept her thoughts to herself, allowing Vi to gather her closer and nuzzle her cheek.

"I don't want to talk about them anymore, not tonight..."

Outside, police sirens were sounding very close to them, and now someone was shouting out of the opposite building's window, a cacophony of voices mingling into the unintelligible.

"You might be called in to post bail. Unless your stepsisters do it."

"I am no longer certain about anything where my family is concerned. Only that they ruined me five years ago, and I was so close to losing you forever."

"You wouldn't have. I would have come to my senses."

Vi peered at her from beneath her bangs, and Chiara grinned.

"What? I would have. I did! In fact, I knelt in front of you right by that wall over there."

"Oral sex is coming to your senses?"

"Darling, you are confusing all the metaphors and we once agreed that is entirely my prerogative."

"I didn't agree to any of that, Chiara. And since you're allowing me to change the subject, let me do it again by telling you that what was truly hot was you, standing there, casually leaning against the windowsill, single-handedly saving me from my horrible family, slaying the dragon, breaking the curse, climbing up that tower and rescuing the princess."

"Vi, now you're not just mixing up metaphors, but your fairytales as well. All I ever did was help you with your shoe."

Vi placed her hand on Chiara's chest, under the collarbones, and she could feel her own heart beating steadily against the now warm-again skin of Vi's palm.

"You did so much more than that. You saved me. Back in Paris and again in New York."

Chiara lifted the tender fingertips to her lips, kissing them one by one.

"Oh darling, you have it all wrong. You saved me, on the rooftops and so many, many times with the big and small things you did. From giving me inspiration to giving me the courage to live—"

"If Aoife was here, she'd roll her eyes, throw a piece of remnant fabric at us, and say we are being absolute bloody fools. Lovely, but fools."

She said the last bit of it with such a bad imitation of Aoife's Irish accent that Chiara had to laugh.

"Now you've gone and ruined the mood, darling. My god, good thing you're a talented photographer, because this right here was terrible. If not for how awful your Aoife impersonation was, all this talk about 'hot' would make me want to actually do something about it."

Vi gave her an exaggerated pout before sighing and bringing their foreheads together again.

"I think you wanted to say if you weren't so tired, what with saving the day and all that."

And she was very, very tired. So exhausted, in fact, that from up close, Vi's eyes were converging into one, a big gray orb watching her with tenderness and humor.

Chiara shook her head, smiling at her own train of thought.

"How about sleep then, Cyclops?"

Vi tugged at her hands as they made their way to the bedroom, losing clothes in their meandering walk, and then cushioned Chiara's fall as they stretched in the cozy bed under a dark green ceiling.

"Cyclops? You really do need that rest, Chiara. But you'll have to explain your thought process to me here. Plus, if it's Cyclops from X-Men, I could be game. Marsden is handsome. But if you're talking about the Cyclops from Odysseus, I'm out, because he was damn ugly and met an even uglier end."

Chiara kissed her, stopping the stream of consciousness and tasting Vi's blooming smile, this new memory made replacing the ones from half an hour ago.

"I love you. Comic book references mixed with classic literature talk. I love you so much."

As Vi argued that X-Men were, in fact, part of world art heritage due to their cultural importance and impact, Chiara closed her eyes and allowed the sound of her beloved's voice to carry her to sleep, safe and warm in the knowledge that this nerd was hers, now and forever.

28

IN A FARAWAY LAND OF HAPPILY EVER AFTER

The steady beat of the heart under her cheek mirrored her own so perfectly, Chiara wanted to burrow under this skin, warm, silky smooth, so beloved.

Vi's breathing was even, unlike the ragged state it had been just half an hour ago when Chiara had done her best to beat their record of climaxes per round. She did manage, too. Five. She smiled, feeling smug and powerful and so happy, her heart might have skipped a beat, if only that weren't a sign of arrhythmia rather than just romance novel drivel.

"I can hear you thinking. Smug is not a good look on you."

Chiara actually shivered, the things this voice did to her. How did she ever get this lucky?

"I think it looks amazing on me, darling. You're just upset that it's 5:4 in my favor."

Vi rolled her eyes loudly. Yes, loudly. Chiara could swear she actually heard her do so.

"It's only because you are so stressed. And tense. Otherwise, there's no way I'd have lost."

"Oh please, I have nothing to be stressed about."

But Vi hit a bit too close to home, and Chiara chose not to

dwell on it for too long. Instead, she planted a kiss on the collarbone closest to her mouth and got out of bed.

She stretched languidly, enjoying the way Vi's eyes, despite all those many, many orgasms, devoured her naked form, and was quite sad to cover herself with the black satin of her robe. But needs must, since she didn't want half of Mercer Street getting an eyeful.

With a wink and another kiss blown in Vi's direction, she made her way through the debris of the active construction site that was currently the top level of Chiaroscuro. Expanding her apartment just made sense. Running between Vi's place and the townhouse was becoming too onerous, and why should they?

Chiara smirked to herself, remembering how she didn't even have to ask. They had been arguing, their first actual argument, both of them irritable over some work-related issues, grumbling into the phone, pissy, and desperately trying not to take it out on each other.

"I don't think I'm fit for company." She'd said back then, only to have Vi get even more upset.

"Yes, because it's healthy to not want to talk about things."

"Nobody ever accused me of having those kinds of aspirations. *Healthy* is not my thing, Vi. But I also know that, if you'd been here, you would have caught me in a very bad mood. Why would you wish for that?"

A heavy sigh on the other end of the line was initially her only answer before she heard the honking of cars on Vi's end and understood that her lover was hailing a cab.

"Because I wish everything with you, you exasperating woman." Vi's voice, muffled as it was, sent warmth spreading through Chiara's chest.

There were more words in the background, away from the phone, and then Vi was back. "Mitch here figures I should just move in, since I'm foolish enough to hail a cab during rush hour, in the rain, by jumping in front of it." There was laughter and another exchange between Vi and the driver. Chiara felt that warmth expand and push out the dregs of the anxiety and aggravation of her day.

"He is right, you know. I mean, a man named Mitch who picks up a person who bodily stops his cab like that cannot be wrong. Tell him I appreciate his input, and that he has helped two useless lesbians U-Haul."

Vi was silent for the longest time before Chiara finally heard a loud, relieved exhalation.

"I will leave a very large tip. I'll see you at home."

~

A WEEK after that phone call, a U-Haul was parked in front of Mercer Street, delivering Vi's plants and other possessions.

The plants, in fact, were what actually impressed the foolishness of their speedy move upon them. In Chiara's tiny attic, there was no space for anything.

Hence, the current chaos of construction.

Chiara touched the plastic spread over the new balustrade and strolled down the equally new stairs towards her recently completed spacious kitchen. The design plans Vi and she had poured over, included a terraced roof that ensured Chiara's workshop one floor below still allowed her access so she could continue to meander and sneak rooftop cigarettes.

And the apartment gained a level, making it spacious enough for all the potted greenery. Vi as a plant mom would never not be endearing to Chiara.

Binoche, after initially pretending to completely ignore the newly acquired forest—which Vi had taken painstaking care to make sure was completely safe for her—now refused to leave the green space, lounging on the windowsill either in their bedroom or the kitchen. She lifted her head as Chiara walked in and emitted a prissy meow. Her food bowl was almost full.

Chiara topped it up. Exactly four more pieces of kibble fit in it, but Binoche pounced as if she'd been starving for days. A haughty look in Chiara's direction told her as much.

She wandered around the kitchen, trying to resurrect the last thought she'd had before leaving the bedroom. A bright pink post-it on her state-of-the-art coffee machine seemed to wink at her. Yes, she'd come here to make coffee. Or at least to use the brew as a pretense for not talking to Vi about why she was as tense as she was.

A few presses of a button later, and she stood in the silence of the kitchen, illuminated by the light of the dawn.

When hands gently touched her shoulders, she jumped nearly a foot in the air.

"If you deserting the bed at 5 a.m. wasn't a clear indication already, this climbing out of your skin is a dead giveaway, Chiara."

Vi turned her around and, when Chiara refused to look at her, lifted her chin with a tender finger, ash meeting amber.

"Hey."

Oh god, her knees went weak. The tenderness, the love, the outpouring of support. They'd been together for a year now. When would Chiara allow herself to simply get used to this? To this love? To this woman?

Never, she thought as she wrapped her arms around the lanky torso, burrowing her nose into the silky auburn hair.

"I don't think I've ever been this nervous prior to New York Fashion Week."

Vi ran her hands up and down Chiara's arms, making her shiver.

"Understandable. The collections were never fully yours before. And this one is. All yours. Only yours. And it is absolutely astoundingly unbelievable in how utterly gorgeous it is."

"Oh no, it's the gigantic Thesaurus Rex!" Chiara bit Vi's earlobe and made them both giggle just before she grabbed the angular face with both hands, holding Vi still. "I love you, you nerd. So much. I don't believe I tell you enough. For your adorable geekiness, for the support you give me when I act the fool, for the steady presence when I need a foundation. For being you. For being with me."

Vi smiled at her and freed herself from Chiara's hands before turning her around again, and now they stood front to back, slotted together like puzzle pieces in front of the floor to ceiling windows with Manhattan at their feet. Vi slowly rocked them back and forth and quietly hummed a song that eluded Chiara at the moment. Yet she felt like she knew it, the rhythm of their movement soothing in its familiarity.

"Slow dancing in the kitchen. And we have checked all the wishes off my list." Chiara turned her face to the side until she could see Vi's eyes that were surprisingly wet. "I never wanted to complete the list with anyone but you, Chiara."

Chiara swallowed around the lump in her throat and allowed her head to rest against Vi's.

"Well, then I guess we need a new list, darling. How about we start with a quickie backstage during the biggest showing at Fashion Week?"

Vi laughed and kissed Chiara's temple.

"Arabella may blow a gasket. It's her party, after all."

"Ha, if you think she and Renate didn't christen the place last year when Poise officially took over the sponsorship, you are mistaken."

"Oh please, I really don't want to know." Vi's voice sounded pained, but her chest shook with suppressed laughter.

"Aoife told me all about it since she walked in on them. You're my girlfriend. For better or worse, Vi. I know, so you have to as well. I don't make the rules."

"I see how it is." She felt Vi's smile on her throat as Vi

dipped her head, and she shivered. Vi held her tighter, and Chiara could sense her getting ready to say something she was certain would be big.

But Vi was silent, simply holding her, slow-dancing with her in their kitchen, now only interrupted by the sleepy, rather disgruntled-sounding purring of the sated cat. The cozy moment stretched, Chiara content and safe in those lanky arms. Vi nuzzled her temple before tensing up as she spoke tentatively.

"For better or worse?"

Ah, Chiara closed her eyes and turned in the embrace. Their lips met with the now habitual precision, the kiss deepening instantly, hunger that had been suppressed by nerves and the mundane, sparking to life instantly.

But Chiara couldn't surrender to it just yet.

"In sickness and in health, Genevieve Courtenay. I did fit the shoe on you after all, Cinderella."

Eternal, Chiara thought, reminded of a distant conversation that had made her sad years ago and brought happiness now. Vi held her closer, sharing her warmth, with Manhattan waking up around them.

AFTERWORD

Once upon a time in a faraway land, there was an A student with an eidetic memory. And because the kid excelled, her parents had very strong ideas about what their child would become. They wanted a doctor in the family. No other profession would suffice nor make them as proud as a surgeon or a cardiologist would.

Fast forward a few years, and a child who aced every subject—with the small exception of having to cheat in geography when longitude and latitude were involved—failed math. Then failed it again. And again. Then failed chemistry, because... math. Goodbye, medical school.

Teachers were puzzled. "How is it that you don't understand math? You do so well in everything else? Are you just being willful? Stubborn? Do you need tutoring?"

Three tutors later—a deeper financial hole for the already struggling family—and more failed math, the kid became a lawyer, medical school remaining a dream brought up occasionally at Christmas and Thanksgiving tables.

The mystery of the no-longer-a-kid's "willfulness" about math was recently put to rest with the diagnosis of dyscalculia, or math dyslexia. An estimated 3 to 6% of people in the world have it. It's much better understood now.

Like Chiara's, the kid's mother worked three jobs to make ends meet, and like Chiara, this kid has lived with the guilt of crushing her mom's biggest and only dream for twenty years. They've both come so far, worked through so much, and are now at peace with the realities of their lives.

Our brains and our hearts work in wonderful, mysterious ways.

The End

ACKNOWLEDGMENTS

In May 2022, I put on paper 20,000 words of another story. It didn't quite flow, but I was working through it when a character popped into my head and refused to leave.

I mentioned her in a second epilogue to A Whisper Of Solace, and the more I thought about her, the more Chiara Conti crystallized in my mind in all her mischievous, tormented, beautiful and gentle glory. *I had to write her.*

I am surrounded by the best people, who, for once, did not roll their eyes—maybe they did so quietly, and hence I don't know about it—at my excited 'I have an idea!' proclamation and told me to just go with it. With *her.*

And to those people I have to say many, many thank yous.

To Em.
   Not just for Chiara, not just for the Lines, not just for the cover, or the editing. For basically everything. For the shoulder, for the hand, for the ear. For the airport *hellos.* For the subway stares and escalator cuddles. For the Starbucks and Rewe sushi. For *you.*

To Caulfield.

Not just for the hours on my walks. Not just for the constancy and the ocean of calm. But for sunrise pictures and for the kittens. For believing in me before many others did. For finding a newbie and for not being afraid. For your eyes and for your brain and for your heart. And for your accents and offended sensibilities.

To Laura.

Not just for allowing me to feel confident in writing an Italian. Not just for telling me that Lago di Como isn't "all that clear". But for seeing and understanding things and for pointing them out and making me change them, because it's time we stop using certain terms. For telling me "a week" and then coming through in three days. For the guesses.

To my readers.

For your support, for your steadfastness, for your encouragement and your kind words, be it in reviews or emails or tweets and posts. I have so much gratitude for each and every single one of you.

Thank you!

ABOUT THE AUTHOR

Milena McKay is a Lambda Literary and Golden Crown Literary Society award-winning author.

Milena is a romance fanatic, currently splitting her time between trying to write a novel and succumbing to the temptation of reading another fanfic story. When not engrossed in either writing or reading, she runs and practices international human rights law.

She is a cat whisperer who wears four-inch heels for work while secretly dreaming of her extensive Converse collection. Would live on blueberries and lattes if she could.

Milena can recite certain episodes of The West Wing by heart and quote Telanu's "Truth and Measure" in her sleep.

Her love for Cate Blanchett knows no bounds.

www.milenamckay.com

ALSO BY MILENA MCKAY

The Delicate Things We Make

The Perfect Match: A Valentine's Day Novella

The Headmistress

A Whisper of Solace

Printed in Great Britain
by Amazon

17829221R00228